Potions & Proposals

Potions & Proposals

KATE CALLAGHAN

Edited By: Emma O' Connell
Cover By: Pru Schulyer

ISBN: 978-1-916684-35-5
ISBN: 978-1-916684-36-2

www.callaghanwriter.com

Readers! Please note: this is an adult paranormal romance with mature content and not suitable for those under 18. This novel contains themes of and not limited to violence, death and discrimination of magical creatures.

Never forget to love and believe in yourself as much as you love and believe in others.

Other Books By The Author

Young Adult Dark Fantasy | A Hellish Fairytale Series
Crowned A Traitor I
Where Traitors Fall II
When Traitors Rise III

Towerwood | Novella
Stepmother | Novella

Village of Yule | Interconnected Stand-Alones
The Naughty Or Nice Clause
Tis The Season For Secrets

Village of FoxFord | Interconnected Stand-Alones
Potions & Proposals

Romantic Suspense | Stand-Alone
Ms Perfectly Fine

In the mystical town of Foxford, tenacious translator Lucinda Hawthorne is on the brink of assuming the prestigious role of High Priestess. However, fate has a mischievous twist in store for her: an unexpected coven gathering reveals that her lifelong nemesis, Benedict Matherson, is also nominated for the esteemed position. They are presented with a grave ultimatum: either become magically bound to one another on All Hallows' Eve... or risk a fateful vote that could strip them of everything.

Both fiercely independent and driven by their unwavering desires to lead, Lucinda and Benedict reluctantly agree to the binding ritual. Unfortunately, the spell Lucinda's family casts to thwart the coven's plot misfires with surprising consequences, and the pair find themselves magically intertwined in ways they never could have foreseen.

With the shadow of All Hallows' Eve looming over them, the veil between love and hate blurs. Could it be that amidst their rivalry, they will unearth a hidden longing to remain united? Together, they must confront their demons and discover whether they truly desire to be parted after all.

🦇 Lucinda & Benedict's Playlist

Season Of The Witch | Lana Del Rey
About You | Jessie Murph
Devil I Know | Allie X
So It Goes | Taylor Swift
I put A Spell On You | Nina Simone
Fetish | Selena Gomez
Double Take | Dhruv
Collide | Justine Skye
You Really Got Me | The Kinks
Like That | Bea Miller
Shut Up And Listen | Nicholas Bonnin
W.I.T.C.H | Devon Cole
The Great War | Taylor Swift
Always been You | Jessie Murph

Scan Me

Potions & Proposals

A VILLAGE OF FOXFORD NOVEL

KATE CALLAGHAN

Benedict

"There can be no community between you and me; We are enemies."

Shrill shouts stopped Benedict Matherson mid-sentence while he handed out the morning assign-ments in the lobby of Matherson Manor. He frowned. Guests should be enjoying a peaceful morning breakfast on the terrace, taking in the morning sun – not running down the grand staircase, shrieking and crying out for help.

Benedict dismissed his staff and started for the break-fast room to find the source of the terror. Today's morning check-in was only ramping up, so now was not the time for a crowd of complaining and frightened guests to flood the lobby.

"What happened to the breakfast group?" he asked Suzy, the day manager, who was trying to calm down an elderly guest sat in an armchair. She rose from her crouched position, smoothing her hands over her navy pencil skirt.

"Davis, the new waiter, said someone jinxed the teacups," Suzy whispered, so the guest wouldn't hear. "When the guests took a sip, they transformed into butterflies."

Benedict ran his hands through his hair. The residue of product reminded him it needed a cut. The top was getting a little heavy, and he prided himself on always being put together and in control.

"No one was harmed?" he asked, knowing exactly who would have pulled such a harmless yet startling prank.

"No." Suzy shook her head. "But I can't go too close to the terrace with the sun beating in." A vampiric day manager might not be very practical, but she was the best he had on staff.

"It's fine – they could use you in the lobby. Dealing with this mess and check-in will swamp them," Benedict said, looking towards the breakfast room to see the waiters sweeping up some broken dishware. Hopefully no one had been injured in the rush to flee.

"Check the gardens. A few guests reported seeing piranhas in the fountain. No one has been bitten. They're just frightened, and probably embarrassed," Suzy explained.

Benedict let out a long exhale as she escorted the older guest to the lobby and began to soothe the frightened crowd. Of course Lucinda had jinxed the fountain; water was her familial element.

Before he'd even reached the terrace, a middle-aged woman had blocked his path, wagging a finger in his face.

"This is an outrage," the guest barked, dragging her child behind her. "Our six-year-old son was playing by the fountain, and he would've had his hand bitten off if I hadn't noticed the fish. You're asking for a lawsuit!"

Benedict dismissed her legal threat; people said all types of things when angry or scared. It also helped that the High Priestess of their coven dealt out the law in Foxford: a simple spell, and the disgruntled magless family would forget about their visit to their small town of Foxford. However, he wouldn't let it get that far. Using spells on magless, those without magic, was frowned upon. Though the coven and their leader did only what they had to, they didn't need a member of the Order sent to inspect Foxford and its magical inhabitants for any odd uses of magic this close to the Autumn Festival.

"This is a terrible prank that will be dealt with immediately." Benedict glanced around, feeling the stare of some new guests. "Please consider the rest of your stay complimentary, Mrs—?"

"Ladbrooke! Don't try and buy me off," Mrs Ladbrooke grumbled. "And to think we were to return for the Autumn Festival. Today is the last time I'll step foot in Foxford, and I'll make sure anyone else who reads Travel Digest feels the same."

Benedict clenched his teeth, trying to contain his frustration. Of course; she must be Mrs Ladbrooke, the travel writer he'd been expecting. The small town of Foxford relied on tourism, and its Autumn Festival was the biggest celebration of the year. The town had previously only had small inns, but as tourism increased every year, Benedict had decided to convert the Matherson family manor into a hotel after graduating university about four years ago.

"Is there any way I can help rectify the situation?" he asked, willing to do anything – within reason – to prevent any guest from leaving the Manor with a sour taste in their mouth because of some adolescent prank. He hated the thought of something connected to the Manor tainting Foxford's reputation.

"Yes, send someone to come and collect our bags," she said, turning her nose up. "My family and I won't stay another minute in a place that doesn't put the safety of its guests first."

"Again, I'm sorry for this experience." Benedict motioned for Reid, the porter, who was passing with other guests' bags.

Reid stopped. "Sir?"

"Reid is the best we have," Benedict announced, trusting his staff to handle the guest. There was no point in giving the woman a platform, since she had refused to accept his apology.

"That's not saying much," Mrs Ladbrooke snapped.

Reid smiled despite the snub. He was wonderful with disgruntled customers, probably because he could control them with the mere sound of his voice. Not for the first time, Benedict was very glad to have hired a siren.

"I promise that you and your family will be smiling from ear to ear by the time you leave," Reid said charmingly in his velvety voice. Mrs Ladbrooke's scowl eased. "Lead the way."

Without any hesitation, Mrs Ladbrooke obeyed, and Benedict reminded himself to give Reid a raise. He was sure he'd find a glowing review in next month's Travel Digest.

The smell of pastries and bacon filled the breakfast room, and despite some broken glasses and spilt drinks on the white tablecloths, the mess was minimal. Benedict sighed with relief; the clatter of rushing guests had made the event sound far worse than it was. Most of the butterflies had left through the open doors to the terrace, where he found two toppled tables.

Benedict breathed in the fresh air as he followed the gravel path through the gardens and past a discarded game of croquet, appreciating the peaceful morning sun far more than the crowded lobby. Hidden amongst a square of hedgerows sat the ornate fountain that predated the Manor. People loved to get married by the embracing granite couple, and the hedges provided a natural division between the gardens and the rest of the manor.

Putting his cufflinks in his pockets and rolling up his sleeves, Benedict peered into the waters and let out a long exhale. Snapping piranhas swam in the rippling depths. He hesitated, his fingertips lingering on the edge of the fountain. Lucinda would never pull a prank that could harm anyone. Hawthornes were sickeningly good-natured, and though he enjoyed bringing out her dark side more than he cared to admit, she'd never crossed the line.

Swishing his hand in the water, he stifled a laugh as the fish transformed from jaw-snapping piranhas into beautiful silver and orange koi fish. When he removed his hand from the water, Lucinda's spell reasserted itself and the koi disappeared.

"Lucinda, of all the days you might've chosen to get back at me," he muttered, fidgeting with his M cufflinks as he lowered his sleeves. He still remembered the smell of burning rubber when he'd melted her bike tyres the previous week. He felt justified in his vandalism, considering she'd parked it behind his car while he was getting groceries in Duncan's Market. Tit for tat — this was how they'd worked for as long as he could remember. He wasn't sure they could stop trying to get under each other's skin.

Back at the reception desk, Suzy nudged him as he finished checking in a new family. Benedict looked up from the computer to find his mum staring at him. *Just when I thought this morning couldn't get any more exhausting.*

"Benedict, what the hell is going on?" Gwendoline – his mum and right hand to their High Priestess – stood by the revolving doors as visibly upset guests left with their bags. Benedict's jaw nearly dropped when he realised she was bare-faced, and her usually slick bob was a wavy mess. She never left the house without her lipstick or hair out of place. Someone must've called and woken her. Benedict was well able to handle whatever the Manor could throw at him, but whenever there was a crisis, Gwendoline sprang into action; she spent her life putting out the fires of others. Ironic, since the Matherson bloodline was gifted with fire as their element.

Her scowl reminded him how similar they were: the same piercing blue eyes, dark eyebrows and angular features, on which was stamped the Matherson scowl. People used to slander his family, though it was now considered magically incorrect, by saying that a Matherson's hair exposed the darkness of the magic they conjured. There was nothing darker than raven black. Generations of his family had indeed used all types of magic, never believing one type was darker than another, because magic always came with a cost. During the war between the Order and magical folk, his ancestors had fled to Foxford, where some older practices of magic were restricted so Foxford could keep its neutrality. Then again, he'd never particularly wanted to sacrifice an animal or resurrect the dead.

"Nothing – a misunderstanding," he said, trying to reassure her. Unfortunately, the lobby told another story. Trying to look casual, he turned to gather his morning messages from the front desk, his black tie threatening to strangle him. It had been his mother who taught him that those with tainted pasts must always look after their appearance, because they will always be judged more harshly.

"Piranhas in the fountain, butterfly teacups," Suzy told Gwendoline. Benedict glared at her, but she merely shrugged. She'd seen him go through his awkward teenage years, so his moods hardly phased her now. She'd worked for them for years – ever since she'd turned up in Foxford as a newly changed vampire with little to no memory of how she'd got there.

"Ben, please tell me this isn't another damn prank! I thought you and Lucinda had left this nonsense behind you. You aren't schoolchildren anymore. You're both pillars of this town, and need I remind you that she is to inherit her mother's position? You don't want to be at odds with the leader of our town in the coming months."

Coming months? He hadn't heard anything to suggest Wilhelmina Hawthorne was thinking of retiring. Then again, since his mum and Wilhelmina had been best friends for years, it made sense the High Priestess would confide in her.

Benedict opened his mouth to speak, but she arched her dark brows, daring him to come up with excuses. She was right; Lucinda and Benedict had spent most of their lives making each other miserable. Despite being in his late twenties, when it came to Lucinda, Benedict knew he became irrational and irresponsible. She was the bane of his existence, and today not only had she embarrassed him and disrupted his morning, but she'd diminished the hotel's reputation and startled the guests. That wouldn't just harm him, as she'd probably intended, but the town she was set to lead. He clenched his jaw to stop a smug smile tugging at the corner of his mouth. Lucinda was in trouble, and for once, she had no one to blame but herself. Thankfully, it seemed that his own part in their latest antics was still unknown to his mother.

"Whatever is going on between the two of you, I want you to fix it now." Gwendoline's hiss snapped him out of his thoughts. "We've had to work too hard to claw our way back into the good graces of this town, and I won't have meaningless, petty pranks damage our reputation."

Benedict started to back away to the revolving door before his mum learnt that the breakfast china she'd only just imported was ruined.

"I'll talk to Lucinda," he promised, glancing around the lobby filled with complaining guests. He didn't want to even guesstimate the cost of the complimentary stays. Hopefully they'd recoup the cost in the coming weeks, since they were booked solid between now and the Autumn Festival.

"Go now, or I'll call a meeting with the coven and get to the bottom of this," Gwendoline warned, narrowing her eyes. "I'm beginning to wonder what caused Lucinda to do such a thing. Perhaps she was provoked?"

"I'll get right on that, and I can assure you that Lucinda and I will be on our best behaviour from now on," he promised, crossing his fingers behind his back.

He clicked his fingers and found himself outside the town's library, which had been converted to look something like a grand gothic cathedral. The very woman he was looking for, wearing enough colours to stop traffic, was tending to the flowerpots lining the stone steps. Completely unaware of the chaos ensuing across town, she watered flower after flower.

Benedict rubbed his jaw, astonished by how innocent she appeared. Just a good-natured, doe-eyed librarian watering the daisies – but there was a vengeful streak behind those gold-rimmed glasses, and his petrified guests testified to it.

Lucinda glanced in his direction as though she sensed he was close.

"You were probably waiting for me to appear, right?" he asked her, though she was too far away to hear him, and the trees surrounding the town square shielded him from sight.

Dried leaves crunched under his feet; he watched her tuck a strand of chocolate brown hair behind an elaborately pierced ear while she searched through her bag. The jewellery glittered in the sunlight, and she wore her bright personality on the long sleeve of her yellow dress. Lucinda couldn't help but stand out; even in a crowd of people, he always seemed to focus on her. It irritated him beyond belief, because he did everything in his power to blend in, to be accepted. The darling of Foxford never had to worry about acceptance; *she* didn't carry any shameful family past.

Benedict stepped off the curb across the street, readying himself to confront her about the piranha and butterfly incident. He'd almost crossed the road when an idea hit him.

If he confronted her, they'd undoubtedly argue, and the cycle would continue. But if he didn't... He smirked to himself as he watched her open the library door. Ignoring her prank would probably drive her crazy. She'd obsess over why he hadn't confronted her, why he hadn't retaliated and why he was ignoring her actions.

Benedict tucked his hands in his pockets, deciding to fix her mess before the coven of founding families heard about the chaos. As overseers of the town, they made sure that nothing offset the delicate balance between the magless and the magical folk. If word got back to them and the High Priestess, neither he nor Lucinda would escape the next coven meeting unscathed.

Besides, the idea of her spending each day wondering what he might be up to put a spring in his step.

Lucinda

Deep within the library, hidden away in the archival vault, Lucinda Hawthorne – or Lucy, as she was known to her friends – ran her fingers over the aged pages of a grimoire, trying to figure out if a potion ingredient translated to 'dragon's blood' or 'dragon scales'.

The text could mean essence of dragon, and the caster could use either to complete the banishing potion, she thought, tapping her pen against the glass desk. Even with her Master's in potions, some concoctions listed on the worn pages were far more complicated than she had ever studied – probably due to her ancestors having access to far more ingredients and the ability to use them in ways that would be frowned upon now.

She wrote 'dragon's essence' into a new red leather-bound grimoire with crisp cream pages. *This is the best I can do. It's not like those in the Vatican archives will brew such a potion anyway... and its overall purpose or effect should remain the same.* She stretched her arms over her head and let out a yawn. The only thing keeping her awake was her multiple cups of tea and the awful fluorescent lighting in the ceiling of the temperature-controlled glass vault.

"Are you still translating that musty book? I thought you went home to get ready for the coven meeting," Rosie said, appearing in the doorway to the vault with her amber eyes narrowed.

"Bark or something – you scared me to death!" Now she was no longer distracted by her work, the room felt darker and colder, telling her the day was long over. The autumn was truly here, and though she missed her summer dresses and sunny days, she loved crunchy leaves and Halloween candy.

"I'll ignore that comment," Rosie said amusedly, stepping into the room filled with grimoires and artefacts too dangerous to be kept on the walls of the catacombs. Everything in the vault was glass—the shelves, the desk—so nothing could be taken or concealed.

"I'm still down here with this musty book because I'm three months late in getting it back to the Order," Lucy said, waving the letter she'd picked up from among the scattered papers and reference texts on the desk.

"I told you to give yourself more time with it! You've taken twice as long as you said you would," Rosie pointed out. The Order's Occult Research Department at the Vatican weren't patient people. "I'm beginning to think you don't want to give it back."

"They wouldn't have sent me a confiscated Hawthorne grimoire if they thought I was going to try and keep it." Lucy didn't want to risk shattering the trust she'd built with the Order. Of course she wished the grimoire could stay in her family, but relations between magical folk and those who'd prosecuted them had come a long way. One grimoire, no matter how sentimental, wasn't worth the cost.

"What if they're testing you, just looking for a reason to pick a fight with us magical folk after all these years of peace?"

"The Order have no reason to doubt me, and if anything, the previous grimoires they've sent me have been far more ancient and powerful," Lucy argued, not liking the idea of being tested. "It's a show of their trust."

"Do you even wonder if they use the spells you translate for them? Just because they haven't so far doesn't mean they won't." Rosie had never liked the arrangement between the library and the Order, which Lucy had agreed to continue after her grandfather's death. But even if the work was challenging, Lucy couldn't bring herself to complain about working in her favourite place on earth.

"Studying magic is all that interests them. Even if they wanted to, they can't read grimoires or cast spells. Magic isn't in their blood, like a car without an engine. They can study it, but they can't drive it. If they could, they wouldn't have started sending the grimoires to us." Despite their knowledge, without her help, all these potions and incantations appeared as utter nonsense to the magless. They could touch the letters, smell the aged pages, and collect the ingredients, but they were powerless.

"I'm surprised they didn't just coerce a witch during the war to translate them," Rosie said, flicking through the illustrated pages.

"I'm sure they tried hundreds of years ago, but if a witch was coerced I doubt she'd give them the real translations," Lucy mused. She didn't like dwelling in the past. The hurt her ancestors had suffered was too overwhelming, and Grams had always taught her that hate was the body's natural poison.

"'Essence of dragon'?" Rosie shivered. "What's that supposed to mean – blood, nails, scales? Heart was very popular in the fifteenth century, but rare." She was one of the top researchers of magic in the country, and full of useful knowledge.

"I don't know which; it's my best guess. It's ambiguous wording like this which is making all of this take so long." Lucy released her long, dark hair from its messy bun and rubbed her scalp, trying to relieve the dull headache caused by staring at dull cursive lettering for over eight hours.

"I didn't think a Hawthorne text would contain blood magic," Rosie said, putting down the note as if it would hurt her. Not being a witch herself, she understood the evolution of their magic and the history of it, but not so much how it worked.

"Back then, there was little difference between light and dark magic. Though Hawthornes moved away from sacrifice and rituals and towards healing magic, it's still part of our past. Many potions that are banned today are scattered throughout every family's history."

"Some still might use them." Rosie smirked, clicking her long nails – always polished to perfection – against the desk. She might lose her clothing when she transformed into a grey wolf, but she'd never be seen without painted claws.

"Those are just rumours."

"C'mon. The Mathersons might appear squeaky clean, but look at what happened with the dad, and the younger brother!" Rosie said, fidgeting with her rings.

"They might not have a perfect record, but they've

helped the town a lot in the last few years with the Manor. Everyone benefits from the increased tourism," Lucy reasoned, trying to be diplomatic. Since Benedict hadn't retaliated after the teacups-and-koi-fish prank, she was hoping he might've turned over a new and more mature leaf.

"I never thought I'd hear the day when you defended the Mathersons," Rosie quipped, sitting on the edge of the desk.

Lucy closed the grimoire before her friend could see anything else that might frighten her, putting it back in its protective case. "Even if Benedict's brother and father made mistakes, the rest of the family shouldn't be judged." The Matherson family had seen more tragedy than most – though her sympathy for them didn't mean Benedict, the eldest son, didn't drive her crazy. "Would you like it if you were blamed for what the wolves in the woods got up to?"

Rosie chewed her pale pink lips. "Fair point. So long as they don't bring the Order's hunters to our door again, I promise to think better of them."

Lucy heard the concern in her best friend's voice and had to admit there was a valid reason to worry. Though the magical village of Foxford was well defended, the Vatican's hunters were still a threat. It was for that very reason she hadn't even thought about keeping the grimoire that rightfully belonged to her family.

"Good, and I promise to show my face above ground once I've finished the final three spells." She sighed, pushing her glasses up the bridge of her nose. After another long day, even the wired rims felt heavy.

"I'll hold you to it. If you don't show yourself upstairs every once in a while, the town will think I'm keeping you trapped down here – which you'd probably enjoy. However, the more you're down here, the more I have to be." Rosie peered through the glass walls to the enchanted artefacts lining the stone shelves beyond and shivered. "This place still gives me the creeps. I always feel like the armoured knights along the tunnels are going to wake up and skewer me."

"They'd only skewer those who try to steal," Lucy chuckled, knowing Rosie would never do such a thing. "You wouldn't hate it so much down here if you spent more time here!"

Rosie backed away towards the glass door. "No thanks! My speciality is researching mystical creatures and artefacts. I don't do spells or potions."

Rosie had never fully trusted magic, and Lucy understood why. Over the centuries, there had often been discourse between witches and wolves. Their transformative ability was said to have come about by the curse of a jilted witch and a human; distrust was in their DNA.

"Then why darken my vault this evening? Because I know it wasn't just to check in," Lucy said, cleaning up the scattered papers and piling up the reference texts.

Rosie began to pace, her running shoes squeaking on the glass floor. "There was something I needed to tell you..."

Lucy groaned. "Please tell me it isn't Order related!"

Her worries were confirmed when Rosie started twisting a strand of auburn hair between her fingers, avoiding eye contact. "They called today. You didn't respond to their last letter. I wanted to wait to tell you tomorrow so we could enjoy the Equinox tonight, but since you were still here..."

"Serves me right for taking so long," Lucy muttered, "but I wanted to wait until I was finished." She glanced down at the book. Only three more spells before she could finally be rid of it.

Rosie was finding the cement floor fascinating.

"What else did they tell you?" Lucy folded her arms.

"They're sending someone to collect the grimoire, and to ensure the work is getting done."

Lucy gritted her teeth to stop herself from taking out her frustration on the messenger, but she could feel her diplomacy starting to slip. A babysitter was the last thing she needed. She was already stressed about being behind schedule, Mum had been acting weird about the coven meeting tonight, and Benedict had been oddly quiet lately. Every day on the way to work, she'd been paranoid about what he might've planned for her as payback. Maybe that was why she'd fallen so far behind on schedule, busy looking over her shoulder instead of focusing on what was right in front of her.

She shook away all thoughts of her nemesis, not wanting Rosie to suspect that anything other than the book was bothering her. "They know the grimoire can't leave the vault. If they wanted their babysitter to come down here, they'd need the coven's permission, and God knows how long it'd take to convince them. Some of the older families in Foxford didn't like me working with the Order in the first place."

"I don't like the idea of anyone other than coven members or us having access to the vault. The Vatican would love to get their hands on some of these texts and enchanted objects, and we don't have the time to babysit the babysitter," Rosie agreed. "How about we say to hell with the Order and keep the grimoire locked up? We can bury the damn thing far away somewhere where no one can find it, not you or them."

She'd never been one for diplomacy. Lucy wished it were that simple.

"You know we can't do that. The High Priestess has spoken; challenging the Vatican isn't an option." She held open the glass door for Rosie to go through. "Translating the texts is for everyone's benefit. Between the dark spells and questionable potions, some of the natural remedies could advance medical discoveries. I don't want the people of today to suffer because of the past."

Silence fell between them. They'd run the library together since they'd left college, and the thought of someone disrupting their sanctuary made them both uneasy.

"Hopefully, whoever comes has an open mind. The village won't like it if whoever arrives has a negative attitude," Lucy said at last, locking the vault door behind them. The fluorescent lights went out, leaving only the torches lit on the walls.

"Then it might not be the grimoire who goes missing. We could send them down a tunnel. They might get lost." Rosie winked, though she'd never hurt a fly – not even a spider. "But let's not worry about that today! Tonight will help you relax. Nothing like a good barefoot frolic in the woods and a skinny dip in the lake to celebrate the end of summer."

"I'm afraid you'll have to frolic for the both of us." Lucy grimaced at her beaming friend, who loved a good time. She was the extrovert in their dynamic duo. Lucy wanted nothing more than a soak in her tub and too many candles to rid her mind of all the ancient spells.

"Don't bail again." Rosie's face fell. "Harriet and Luisa returned from their dig to celebrate with us. It won't be the same without you."

"Mandatory coven meeting. If I don't go, I'll get an earful. I can't exactly skip out when my mother is the High Priestess."

"You could come after!" Rosie took her arm pleadingly.

The grandfather clock chimed for seven o'clock, echoing through the tunnels. Lucy was already pushing it if she planned to get to the temple by eight. "By the time the meeting ends, it'll be late. I need to gather my strength if an Order member is on the way to inspect my work."

Rosie gave up. "Next time, no excuses! I love this library just as much as you, but there *is* more to life than these dusty books."

Lucy stuck her tongue out at her, but she felt guilty for missing the equinox tonight. She wished she *could* spend the night relishing in the beauty of nature. Not that she didn't love her job, but between the whispers of her becoming the next head of Foxford coven and her translation work, she was beginning to forget how to relax.

"Now, can we please get out of here? It's freezing down here," Rosie complained, though she was wearing a sweater vest over another jumper, and wolves ran a temperature that would kill a human.

"That's a lot of layers for someone with—"

Rosie shoved her playfully. "Don't you dare make a fur joke!"

"I'd never," Lucy said innocently, giving Rosie a cheeky grin. "And I know how much you hate the cold, but we have to keep the vault climate controlled."

"Don't remind me. I'm the one who had to beg the coven for it to be installed," Rosie said. Her face looked a little paler than usual as they approached the gilded knights, making her freckles stand out.

"And have I told you how much I appreciate it?" Lucy

batted her eyelids, trying to distract her. She didn't like asking the coven for anything herself, even if she had good reason to. She never wanted the village to think that her requests were granted because her mother was their High Priestess, or because the Hawthorne family had helped build and maintain Foxford during the war on witches.

"With every morning coffee you bring me." Rosie stayed close as they made it through the dark tunnel lined with sword-bearing knights. Their gilded heads turned ever so slightly as they passed. "I really hate that your grandfather installed these. We could have got a dog."

"Already have one." Lucy smirked when they reached the gargoyles by the secret entrance.

"At least this dog doesn't have to go to a coven meeting," Rosie reminded her.

"*Veritas se revelet*," Lucy incanted: *let the truth be revealed*. What had been a dead-end stone wall transformed into a row of bookshelves. With a loud crack and hiss, one of the bookshelves slid open to the second floor.

Rosie disappeared to turn off the lights, and Lucy hoped she wasn't too disappointed about tonight. Lucinda brushed her hands on her tights. The reminder of the meeting had made her palms sweaty; she could only hope it was to talk about the upcoming Autumn Festival and not her pre-destined future.

Walking through the stacks and down the stairs, she couldn't help but wonder if she was ready to follow in her mother's footsteps. Surrounded by books in this converted cathedral filled with vast knowledge and a thousand stories, she knew there was a difference between studying leaders and becoming one.

At the centre of the library's first floor, she lifted the reception desk's divider and took off her pastel pink unicorn slippers. Without the lights, moonlight broke through the stained-glass windows and cast their colours over the desks and antique study lamps. She couldn't believe it had grown so late.

"Not keeping your fluffy slippers on?"

"I doubt the founding families would appreciate them," Lucy said, placing them on their very own shelf. They were a necessity in the chilly vault.

"The back door is locked, and everything is off. I'll be in at twelve tomorrow, and I've put up a sign out front to say as much so you can tidy up the vault for our guest while I'm recovering," Rosie said, leaning over the counter as Lucy pulled her knee-high black boots over her purple woolly tights.

"I'll be surprised if you make it in at all," Lucy said, jealous of her freedom.

She wrapped her multicoloured scarf around her neck. "Go ahead, I'll lock up."

"Are you sure? You don't have much time to get to the temple," Rosie pointed out, tucking her hair behind her ear.

"It's fine, I'll go straight from here. If I'm late again, the Crawfords and the Mathersons will hold it against me. I don't want Mum to have to defend me again." Lucy pulled her long maroon coat over her knitted cream sweater and black skirt, which was a little higher on her thighs this autumn than last. Funny how when you gained a few inches, clothes seemed to lose them... Not that she cared; every woman in her family was blessed with fuller curves, and she had never been taught anything other than to embrace them.

After a quick hug, Rosie disappeared out the towering front doors, the back of which were inscribed with protection spells. If the village ever came under threat, the library would be their fortress. Though the markings had long since faded, their design was a reminder of how far Foxford had come since its beginnings, and Lucy promised herself she'd do her best to be civil when the Order member visited them.

She had thirty minutes to get across town to the woods where the temple was concealed within the foot of the mountain. Her hand on the brass door handle, she realised she had forgotten about cleaning up.

At a click of her fingers, a broom flew towards her and awaited her command. The enchanted broom was two generations old. The magic usually faded from enchanted objects when the caster died, but somehow the broom remained the library's keeper and cleaner.

"Broomhilda, you neglected the portraits this week. Tomorrow they'd better be dusted to perfection. Please make sure you remember to sweep the tunnels and the second floor."

The broom tipped slightly, expressing its shame.

Lucy tutted. "Don't sulk! If you do a good job tonight, I'll enchant the mop tomorrow and you can work together."

Broomhilda wiggled gratefully before moving to sweep between the shelves far more eagerly than usual.

Lucy removed the brass key from its hook and locked up the library behind her. She'd only made it halfway down the steps before she noticed the old defender parked obnoxiously across three spaces and groaned. What the hell was Benedict doing here?

Lucinda

Benedict Matherson walked around the car. "Not like you to cut it so close, pumpkin."

He was the only person who called her by the infuriating nickname. Clenching the library key in her fist, Lucy tried not to react. His satisfied smirk did nothing to soothe her annoyance.

"Come here to ruin my day?" she asked, putting the key in her bag. Eyeing his black suit, she wondered why he even bothered wearing a black tie with a black shirt. She suspected he was allergic to bright colours, whereas she liked to wear as many as possible.

"I didn't know I had the power to ruin your day," he quipped, threading his hand through his raven-black hair.

"Don't flatter yourself. I thought you'd already be at the temple, trying to convince the other families I don't deserve to be the next High Priestess." She huffed, making her way down the library steps.

"Why must you always think the worst of me? Wasn't it you who put a certain vicious fish in my fountain and disturbed my guests' breakfast only a month ago?" He was blocking the path to her bike. The steps erased their height difference, so she at least didn't have to stare up at him.

"I don't know what you're talking about," she said, thinking of her earlier conversation with Rosie, how she'd defended him. Now she just knew he'd been biding his time.

She didn't like the way his eyes lingered on her. He'd been able to see through her since their childhood, when they'd been forced to spend so much time together thanks to their mothers' odd friendship. However, past or present, whenever they were around each other, disaster struck sooner rather than later.

"I can't remember the last time I saw you with your hair down." His eyes settled on its loose ends, curled from being trapped in her signature bun all day.

Lucy brushed them over her shoulder, wondering what he was up to. "Probably because we're better *not* seeing each other at all."

His ocean-blue eyes narrowed at her rejection. It probably spurred him on that she was the one woman in town he couldn't have. She wasn't going to be another woman who fell for his long stares and solemn attitude. They were seduced by his darkness, at the thought of being with a Matherson – getting a taste of the darker side of magic.

"I was only trying to pay you a compliment. Since I've failed at that, I will continue with the task at hand. I was leaving the hotel and ran into Wilhelmina, your mother." Benedict rocked on his heels, hands in his pockets.

He was plotting something. When they were seven he'd lost his favourite stuffed toy and cried until she gave him hers. It would've been a kind gesture, but when their mothers found them, he'd told them she had stolen his in the first place. Twenty years might've passed, but they were still getting each other into trouble.

"I know who my mother is," Lucy grumbled.

"She asked me to make sure you didn't forget about the meeting," he explained, ignoring her quip.

"As you can see, I'm headed that way now. You can leave." She wished her mother hadn't sent her nemesis to remind her of her responsibilities.

"You'll need a ride up the hill if you want to make it in time. You can't use your bike; it's been raining all day and your tyres won't make it through the mud." He opened the passenger door and motioned her inside. "Please get in. I'd hate to disappoint our High Priestess."

"You're up to something. Your help usually results in my punishment and your amusement." She was used to taking the fall. If a Matherson, a descendant of dark magic, did something bad, it was excused as their nature. If a Hawthorne miss-stepped, it brought shame to the light.

"Let me guess. You'll drive me into the middle of the woods and leave me there so I don't make it to the meeting at all." It was only one in a million scenarios she could think of.

"Why would I do that? I'd make myself late in the process."

"To get back at me for the breakfast incident?" she snapped.

"So you admit it!" He grinned.

She gritted her teeth, refusing to respond.

Benedict let out a long exhale. "If I wanted to get back at you, don't you think I would've done it by now?"

"Maybe you're biding your time, and this is the perfect

excuse to drive me off a cliff," Lucy countered, shoving her hands in her pockets to keep them warm.

"I'm afraid such a scheme would cost us both our lives. Can we please put the paranoia aside for tonight? I don't want you to be late for another meeting." He tapped his foot, still waiting for her to get in.

Lucy narrowed her eyes, sensing his impatience as he pulled at his tie. Something was off. She didn't like that he could still surprise her, and never in a way that brought her any joy.

"Need I remind you that I was only late to the last meeting because of *you*? You melted my bike tyres into the ground."

He smirked, exposing his dimples. "You've no proof."

"Only Mathersons harness fire magic. I doubt your mum sabotaged my bike." She preferred him scowling, so she could tell she'd got under his skin.

Benedict sighed again. "Whether or not I melted the tyres has nothing to do with my desire to bring you to this meeting. Nor am I trying to trick you because of what you did at the manor."

Thinking of the piranhas in the hotel fountain, Lucy chewed her lip to stop herself from smiling. They'd been harmless but frightening; she'd only wanted to plague him with complaints. She'd never harm an innocent with their petty quarrels.

"I only did what I did because you volunteered me to work on the fireworks display for the summer solstice, when you know how afraid I am of fireworks!" she barked, only to grimace when a passing elderly couple looked upon them with concern.

"Lovely evening," Benedict said to them, and they passed with soft smiles.

"Great. I'm sure everyone in the village will hear I was giving out to you in public by morning," Lucy groaned.

He closed the gap between them, limiting the risk of them being overheard. However, it forced her to stare up at him – impressive, considering she'd worn her tallest boots in anticipation of seeing him at the coven meeting.

"How far do you want to go back?" he asked, scrubbing his jaw. "I did this, and you did that? Going over twenty-odd years of history would mean neither of us will make it to the meeting." He stared at her, dark eyebrows pulled together.

He was right, they could keep going for hours, so she moved around him and continued down the steps. "Please, feel free to stay here and reminisce. I've a meeting to attend."

Going down memory lane never led anywhere good. She could go right back to their first day of school, when he had set her backpack on fire. In retaliation, she had suspended him in a bubble of water. The teachers had accused her of trying to drown him, but she'd just wanted to teach him a lesson. Remembering the face he'd pulled behind the teachers' backs sent a spike of fury through her all over again. She'd far rather use her magic to travel to the temple than be subjected to a fifteen-minute drive with *him*.

"*Evanescere*," she whispered, blowing him a kiss as she disappeared.

Lucinda

L ucy appeared in front of the temple entrance a few seconds later. Teleporting wasn't one of her natural talents, and she would've preferred to use her bike. Placing a hand over her queasy tummy, she waited for it to settle, assuring herself the nausea was worth it. *I don't feel like replacing another set of tyres if he decided to melt them again to ensure I went with him. He'd probably do anything to follow my mother's orders.*

Her thoughts were interrupted by the sound of crunching leaves.

"You shouldn't be so careless with your use of magic. The magless in the village tolerate us for history's sake, but we're supposed to use magic discreetly in public," Benedict said, lifting his fancy shoes out of the muck.

Lucy heard him cursing under his breath as she bowed before the towering statues guarding the entrance: the Goddess of War carrying her sword, and the Goddess of Peace, a dove cradled in her hands. The entrance, stone engraved with protective symbols and shrouded in overgrown branches and woven ivy, opened for her.

"Pot, kettle," she muttered, heading into the temple hidden in the mountain with *him* following close behind.

"Will you wait for a minute? I want to talk to you," Benedict whispered as they walked the tunnel.

The smell of incense and clay comforted Lucy, but if the torches were already lit, she dreaded to think how long the coven had waited for them.

"Lucy!"

She stopped at the archway to the meeting hall, nearly causing a collision between them. He never called her Lucy. She hated his nickname for her – pumpkin, the food she hated more than any other – but her name on his lips was jarring.

"What?" she started, but an echoing clap interrupted her. The fires lining the temple shone brighter, highlighting the gods and goddesses, each the embodiment of the element and season they harnessed.

Lucy frowned when she saw all twenty-four families sat around the table: the Sundurns, Crawfords, Rodriguezes, Emerys and Larks, to name only those in higher standing positions. It was rare that everyone would attend, unless something serious was to be discussed. Lucy's mum was at the head of the table, her robes shimmering in the moonlight cast in from above. Within the temple, her mum was their leader, and Lucy was just another witch subject to their laws.

"What is going on?" she whispered, nervous under the coven's gaze. She offered them a faint smile as Benedict moved a hairsbreadth away from her.

"What makes you think *I* know?" he stressed as they took the remaining seats at the table.

She didn't trust him. *I should've known he was leading me into a trap.* The thought did nothing to ease her fidgeting beneath the table. They were the only descendants in attendance, which meant they were here to discuss something far more important than the upcoming Autumn Festival.

"How good of you both to join us," said Gwendoline, the head of the Matherson family, sitting at the right hand of the High Priestess.

"Sorry, Benedict had trouble with his car," Lucy lied, happy to dump him in it. Benedict's gaze bore into the side of her head, but she was too busy analysing the half-empty silver goblets on the table. It looked like the rest of the coven had arrived much earlier than both she and Benedict had been informed to attend.

"It's not like the two of you to travel together," Gwendoline commented, tucking a strand of her severely cropped silver bob behind her ear.

"I commissioned Benedict to collect her," High Priestess Wilhelmina said, addressing the table. "Since they're the topic of tonight's meeting."

"Sorry to keep you waiting. I had to portal us here," Benedict conceded, leaving out Lucy's refusal to go with him. At least she knew he'd been telling the truth about her mum requesting him to attend with her.

"It seems you're both getting a little too comfortable using your magic in front of the magless," Gwendoline said, her angular nose in the air.

Lucy's surprise stopped her from fidgeting. The Mathersons believed magic shouldn't be hidden; it wasn't like her to scold them for its use.

She's probably trying to show the rest of the coven that they have changed their ways, she thought, noticing how the coven watched Benedict favourably. Since he'd converted

Matherson Manor into a hotel, bringing both magical beings and magless to the town from all over, he'd become the golden child. Lucy couldn't resent his success entirely; he had increased the small town's revenue, and she wanted Foxford to flourish.

"We didn't wish to keep you all waiting," Benedict apologised.

"You're both here now. Let's get down to it." Gwendoline rose from her chair, her statuesque figure towering over the rest. Lucinda eyed her mum with a frown, wondering why Gwendoline was addressing them.

"Before your arrival, Lucinda, Wilhelmina informed us of your progress with the Order. We're all impressed by how much you have improved our relations with our ancient enemies," Gwendoline said. Lucy followed her piercing blue gaze cutting through the members around the table, gauging their reaction to her working with the Order. The Crawfords, ever stoic, both offered Lucy what she perceived to be an attempt at a smile. Lucy wanted to tell them not to hurt themselves.

"You could call *our* families ancient enemies, but like my work with the Order, we overcame our differences for the greater good," she replied to Gwendoline, hearing everyone hold their breath. She needed to remind the coven that she wasn't a supporter of those who had hunted them. "We called a truce for the sake of the formation of Foxford, and this coven, my work with the Order, ensures that a mutual understanding and respect continues to grow between us. We can and have learned a lot from each other. I do my best to ensure that relationship continues to develop and doesn't sour, for all our sakes."

"A Hawthorne through and through." Gwendoline

beamed. "Your power for forgiveness has no limit. Everyone here can attest to it. We all know you'll do great things, for both this coven and Foxford." Gwendoline rested a hand on Lucy's shoulder. "As your mother's right hand, I'm happy to inform you that our dearest High Priestess has expressed her intention to retire her position this coming All Hallow's Eve."

There was a round of applause, but Lucy froze. All she could do was stare wide-eyed at her mum. She barely noticed Benedict tense beside her. At breakfast this morning, her mum hadn't uttered a single word.

She swallowed her surprise, forcing her expression to remain neutral. She knew how much her parents wanted to travel, and didn't blame the High Priestess for wanting to retire. The women in her family had sacrificed themselves for five generations, and Lucy had accepted long ago that she'd be next.

Taking a steadying breath, she addressed the coven. "I'll do my best to fill the position to the utmost of my ability. I hope you'll put as much faith in me as you have in those who have come before me. I can only hope for your support and guidance during this time," she said, playing up to the egos of those nodding in agreement.

"How can we be sure you're ready to handle such a responsibility?" Mrs Crawford chimed in, resting her elbows on the table.

"I don't speak as her mother, but as a member of this coven who wishes the best for each citizen of Foxford." Lucy's mum finally spoke, offering the table some assurance. "I wouldn't consider stepping down if I were not sure of my daughter's ability. In Lucinda's work with the Order, I've witnessed her ability to navigate relationships with those who seek any excuse to harm our kind with grace and patience."

The words helped ease the tension in the temple. At home, Mum was light-hearted and playful, and never did anything without music to dance along to. In this temple, however, she was downright fierce. Lucy was proud to be her daughter.

"There is no arguing about Lucinda's love nor dedication to our town, but we have to take into account her recent actions," Gwendoline said. The rest of the table nodded.

The other shoe finally dropped. Lucy pressed her lips together; Gwendoline's earlier comments must have been merely a show of politics, and this was her true intention.

"My actions?" Lucy asked, resisting the urge to look at Benedict.

"Did you not put piranhas in the manor fountain?" Gwendoline purred sweetly. "Or jinx our teacups to turn into butterflies?"

"I admit that." Lucy blushed at her childish behaviour being outed. "I may have taken the prank too far, but they were only koi fish. Even if they didn't present that way at first. And who doesn't love butterflies?"

"Our guests, who stampeded out of the breakfast room in fright!" Gwendoline produced a magazine from the pocket of her silver robe. "And then there is this." She cleared her throat, and the rest of the families leaned forward in their chairs, eager to listen.

"'Last month, my family and I visited the luxurious and classically designed Matherson Manor in the quaint town of Foxford. The isolated town is known for its mystical shops and yearly Autumn Festival. Previously when assigned to review a hotel, I have always attended alone.

However, after reading so many glowing reviews from others enchanted by the town, I thought it would be the perfect place to bring my family. Upon arrival, the woods surrounding the town created the landscape for the perfect escape into nature, and the boat ride on the lake was utterly breathtaking. I understood immediately why this town was winning over the hearts of so many, and I was sure that by the end of the stay, myself and my family would be vowing to return.

"'I couldn't have been more wrong.

"'Let me preface this by saying that I cannot fault the town, nor the locals. It was during our stay in the Manor itself that our nightmare began. Two days before we were due to leave, I came upon my child playing by the fountain in the gardens – a fountain whose rippling waters, I was horrified to realise, contained flesh-eating piranhas! When I went to confront the owner of the establishment, Mr Benedict Matherson, I was almost caught in a stampede of guests fleeing the breakfast room as it suddenly filled with butterflies. Taken entirely by surprise during their peaceful breakfast, the guests were clearly unnerved and alarmed, and more than one bruise must have been sustained in the process. I've never stayed in any establishment that would pull such elaborate pranks on their guests, and if they continue to show such utter disregard for the safety and comfort of their clientele, then it won't be long before their doors are closed for good.

"'2/10 stars. Wouldn't recommend it to anyone with a pulse.'"

"At least that doesn't rule out all your clientele," Lucy said weakly, sinking into her chair. Vampires didn't have a pulse, nor did ghouls or ghosts... She decided it was more important to focus on Gwendoline glowering at her than trying to think of all the magical folk without a heartbeat.

"I'm glad you find this so amusing." Gwendoline slapped the magazine down on the table. Lucy wished there was a fountain in the temple filled with piranhas to gobble her up.

"No one was harmed during either incident, and the guests received every attempt to rectify the situation," Benedict interjected. He might not be defending her, but she was somewhat relieved he didn't make it worse.

"I had hoped that you'd both put these petty tricks and schemes behind you," Mrs Crawford sighed, tucking a strand of tangerine-coloured hair behind her ear.

"We have," Lucy and Benedict said in unison. They stared at each other.

"How are we to believe an event like this won't happen again? Last year, Benedict nearly set the library on fire—" Mrs Crawford began.

"That damn broom was chasing me!"

Lucy rolled her eyes. She couldn't blame Broomhilda for being protective of her.

"—and Lucinda flooded the community pool at the start of the summer—"

"Only because Benedict put hot sauce in my tea while I was on lifeguard duty!"

"Enough. You are both to blame for these events," announced the High Priestess.

"At least those prior events weren't shared with the world. This time, your actions have gone too far," Gwendoline said, reclaiming her seat. "I don't want to hear what Benedict did to justify your actions; this review could seriously affect our tourism. With the Autumn Festival in the coming weeks, this is the worst time for such a stunt, and that's not even taking into account what might happen if word got to the Order that you were using magic that could have harmed a magless. We might've woken up to Hunters on our doorstep! We must consider if these are the actions of someone who can lead us."

Lucy looked at Benedict, who avoided her gaze. The attention of the room had shifted not only to her, but to him by her side. She couldn't help but think this was how he was getting back at her – by using what had happened at the manor to make her unsuitable to lead them. It was a bold move... one she'd have respected him for, if she hadn't been the target.

"You wish for another to claim my mother's seat?" she asked, trying to sound neutral. The thought of losing the position her family had maintained for generations caused a cold sweat to break out on the back of her neck. To have the balance of their sanctuary threatened by a struggle for power would do nothing for the magical *and* magless who called their village home.

"The Hawthornes have guided this coven since its establishment. If we're no longer fit to lead, then I trust this coven will decide on someone worthy of the position," Wilhelmina said.

Lucy gripped her thighs under the table to stop herself from rising, telling her mum they shouldn't concede so easily.

"I believe Lucy should remain a candidate for the position. However, I'd like to nominate another for the seat," Gwendoline said.

"Who?" Mr. Emery asked.

The Emery family had sided with the Mathersons for generations. They were also descents of darker magic with a questionable past. It made sense they'd pick whoever

Gwendoline nominated. And there was only one obvious choice. Lucy noted that the only descendant amongst them, other than herself, was Benedict. She noticed him clutch the armrest and wondered if he was readying himself to accept, or if he was as blindsided as she was.

Gwendoline strode past Lucy and stood behind her son. "My son, Benedict Matherson."

Lucinda

L ucy's throat tightened. Her gaze snapped to Benedict, but his stoic expression revealed nothing about how he felt. He rose slowly and tipped his head to the High Priestess, waiting for her to accept his nomination. The table looked on in a tense silence. The moment lasted a lifetime. Lucy didn't think she'd ever seen Benedict speechless before.

"Accepted," Wilhelmina ruled.

The words distracted Lucinda from her adversary. Her eyes froze on her mother's lips, making sure it was she who'd spoken. The High Priestess didn't even appear at all startled by the nomination.

Lucy wanted to protest, but the last thing she wanted to do was play into Gwendoline's hands. The Crawfords and the Emerys would be waiting for her to slip up, too.

The table broke out in an argument, giving her an opportunity to confront Benedict, but he spoke first, tilting his head towards hers.

"I didn't think you'd give in so easily. If it were my birthright, I'd have spoken out."

Lucy stared at the stars overhead, folding her arms over her chest. "I should've known you were up to something, that you'd find some way to retaliate, but I never thought you'd go this far."

"I didn't arrange for this. My mother arrived in the middle of the chaos you caused. Don't blame me for putting us in this position," he said.

She rolled her eyes.

"I've more experience in dealing with town issues. Why shouldn't I be nominated?"

"Your experience in what? Running the hotel, the manor you inherited? I'm sure making all that money is *very* challenging. I'd like for you to try and deal with the Order and other magless who think they've got a right to our magic," she said, trying to remain calm.

"Those relationships you can negotiate in the safety of your precious vault?" Benedict smirked. "Try rooming werewolves on a full moon next to a banshee. The noise complaints would test the patience of Lucifer himself."

"Speaking of Lucifer, you didn't by any chance sell your soul for my position, did you?" she muttered, only half-joking.

Benedict sighed. "I'm not after your position. However, if the coven believes I'd be a better fit, then who am I to decline?"

"How nice it must be to be so arrogant," she mused. "Need I remind you that we are both to blame for our current predicament? If I'm not fit to lead, then neither are you!"

Ms. Sundurns's voice brought them back to the room and broke up the arguing families around them.

"With all due respect, High Priestess, by our laws, no descendant of those who've practised dark magic may lead this coven. No descendant of darkness has governed a coven since before the war on witches. If those who hunt us think we might turn to the old ways, it could ruin the relations it's taken generations to build." Sarah Sundurn might be the youngest leader of any family at only fifteen, but she had a strong voice. She'd inherited her seat when her parents died last year. Her words were followed by a murmur of agreement.

Lucy kept quiet. Sarah was right; the law played in her favour. And for Benedict to take her place, it would have to be rewritten.

Mrs Crawford scoffed. "Those laws are outdated. There is no evidence Benedict has ever used such magic. Why should we be ruled by fear or judged for our ancestors' past? Converting Matherson Manor into a hotel has brought many to our village. Visitors who've helped increase the economy of our town. He has proved in the management of the hotel that he can manage relationships between magless and other magical folks exceptionally well."

"I agree that Benedict has been of great service to Foxford, but the issue raised was that of suitability, and the Matherson family has transgressed in the past. Even that issue of the late younger son—"

Mr Rodriguez was cut off by Benedict's sudden outburst.

"You'll not speak of Peter! He was only sixteen and acted out in his grief over our father." His knuckles rested on the table as the coven went silent; Lucy seethed beside him.

"Let's leave family members out of this discussion, and focus on what's best for the coven," she snapped. She'd grown up around Peter. She'd never want his loss to be used for politics.

"I'm sorry to upset you. I'd never wish to cause you or your family any hurt, but we must be careful about how this election will be presented to those who might misunderstand," Mr Rodriguez stated, affirming that the actions of the younger Matherson would work against Benedict whether they liked it or not.

"Benedict lacks knowledge of the intricacies of magical histories and artefacts that are essential to the role. Lucy works in the vault, and with the Order. She has a depth of knowledge that can also benefit us greatly," Sarah added. Lucy was grateful for her support, especially as she represented the younger generation.

"I don't negate the work Lucinda has done to improve our relations with the Order, and her work has helped us understand magic in a new light. But this is about the town as a whole. My son spends his days with the people of Foxford, while Lucinda spends hers in the vault," Gwendoline countered. The table broke out in a cluster of whispers.

I should have listened to Rosie's earlier warning and come up for air more often. Lucy was far more introverted than her mother, and she had to admit that Benedict had the personality to charm anyone when he needed or wanted something.

"Benedict does have a greater understanding of the village and its everyday needs. However, Lucy's connections to the magical community and other occult arts are vital," Mrs Crawford argued, surprising Lucy. She'd never have thought a Crawford would speak out on her behalf. Perhaps they didn't want to disturb the balance when their business was already gaining from the way things were.

She sneaked a glance at Benedict, who looked as uneasy as she felt. She guessed it had to do with the mention of his brother. She remembered how close they'd been; to have his life viewed as a negative must hurt.

The families argued over each other, getting nowhere in a hurry.

Mr Lark rose, addressing the table. "I believe we've already discussed these matters sufficiently before their arrival. We agreed that both are suitable for the position, but that both are guilty of letting their issues endanger this town."

"Thank you, Mr Lark, for reminding us. We brought you here to propose a solution. It's up to you both to accept or decline," Wilhelmina said. Her mum's gaze troubled Lucy. "If one or both of you decline our proposal, then we will go to a vote."

"I'm sure we'll accept whatever the coven decides is best," Benedict said, bowing his head. Lucy resisted the urge to fake gag.

Gwendoline sighed. "Unfortunately, this is not something we can decide."

There was a long pause. If someone didn't speak soon, Lucy thought she'd scream.

"A vote on what? Who would lead in my mother's place?" she asked, trying her best to sound calm.

"On which of you will lead this coven, and which will leave town," Wilhelmina said, looking at her daughter. Sadness clouded her eyes. Leave town? Clearly the coven had grown tired of their endless shenanigans.

"What's the proposal?" Lucinda's stomach dropped; she didn't want to leave her home. Her family, her friends, her books... "What do we have to do to stay?"

"Before we continue, we want you both to know we

didn't come to this decision lightly, but we believe it's what's best for you and the town," Mr Lark told them, exchanging a troubled look with Mrs Lark by his side.

Lucinda felt her mouth dry. "I don't understand."

"We've come to see that one of you might not be the best option for Foxford," Sarah Sundurn said, looking anywhere but at them.

"Get to the point," Benedict snapped.

"We wish for you to be bound together. To unite the two strongest families of our coven," Gwendoline said suddenly, clapping her hands excitedly.

Lucy wondered if *this* had been her plan all along. First the compliments, and then placing doubt in the coven's mind by bringing up the prank. Maybe she doubted Benedict being elected on his own right, when a union between two of the strongest families would be far more agreeable.

Benedict shook his head. Lucy thought he almost appeared amused by the wild suggestion.

"This is a terrible idea," he muttered, low enough for only her to hear.

"Bound? A binding ritual as in *married?*" Lucy couldn't help the nervous laughter that escaped her. *They can't be serious. They're worried about us destroying the town, and their solution is marriage?!*

"Marriage is for the magless," Mrs Crawford corrected with a sneer, even though it was pretty much the same concept; Binding was just a lot more permanent. "Binding is far more special. It'll bond your souls together so that your magic will be unified. The water and fire elements you both harness will be united, and we hope that your having to work together might settle the rifts between you. As you said, Lucy, sometimes we have to come together for the greater good."

"I wasn't talking about till death do us part!" Lucy gripped her seat. She had always thought she would bind herself to someone one day, but Benedict certainly hadn't made the list. As in a marriage, would they be expected to live together, to be intimate? A binding was intimate enough; to share your magic, your soul, with someone was as personal as a connection could get. How could she accept a proposal to a man she didn't even trust?

"I don't see how such a binding would be possible. Our magic repels each other. Fire and water elements have never been unified," Benedict argued.

"We thought about that, but Gwendoline has informed us that during next month's All Hallows' Eve, there'll be a blood moon. If the ceremony is performed under the moonlight, and with the permission of the ancestral magic, it should work," Mrs Crawford explained.

Gwendoline must have been the one to propose it to the coven. This had been her plan all along. She knew she couldn't get the coven to elect Benedict outright, but as a pair, two sides of the same coin, it would be much easier to get everyone on board than to get rid of her entirely by ordering a coven meeting after her latest indiscretion.

"What if our souls don't bond? Even with your blessings, elemental magic is temperamental, and could backfire," Lucinda said desperately. "Without any love between us, there would be no reason for our magic to accept the binding."

Mrs Crawford leant forward. "We believe that it's up to both of you. Should you desire to be bound for the good of the coven, that match will be what you need to complete the ritual."

"And if it fails, one of us will be banished from town?" Benedict asked coldly. "This seems rather extreme."

Lucy tried to assess his body language. Was he acting, or had he known this was coming? It would trap him just as much as it would her.

"Not as extreme as endangering our town with your refusal to get along with each other. Teacups turning into butterflies? What if hunters heard about this flagrant use of magic? We've had enough. Should you decline our proposal, we can go straight to the vote," Wilhelmina said, leaning her elbows on the table as she looked at both candidates.

Lucy tried to stop tears from escaping her eyes. She couldn't believe her mum was willing to see her cast out and replaced. There had to be something she was missing – or her mum had faith that the coven would pick her in the vote.

"Both of you have merits we wish to see in our next leader. We think your union would be quintessential for the furthering of our town, and getting over your petty hatred for one another will be the first test in becoming the leaders I hope you'll be. That being said, we won't force you into this decision." Wilhelmina sat back in her chair, looking at her daughter with troubled eyes. "A binding ritual is a lifelong commitment and not something to be trifled with. If the ritual fails, then we'll vote."

Lucy weighed her options, chewing her lip. *If they hold an election now, there's no guarantee I'll win. I could spend the next month trying to prove I'm worthy of the position. There's no way our souls will join during the ritual, and that gives me a month to prove I deserve to stay in Foxford. Even my acceptance of this proposal should prove my desire to lead this coven.* It was the only way she could see to buy herself some time.

"Lucinda, this must be hard for you. You've spent your whole life preparing for the position," Gwendoline said sweetly. "If you feel wronged and wish to decline, we can vote now and let fate decide."

This had to be a test. A test to see how far they'd go to protect and lead their town. She wouldn't disappoint them again, even if a fire in her belly smouldered with resentment over being backed into a corner. And she didn't want Benedict to have the upper hand.

"I accept the proposal," Lucy blurted out.

Benedict touched her hand, shaking his head. Lucy snatched it away, not wanting to be comforted by the person trying to take what was rightfully hers. *If he doesn't want to accept, then he can put an end to this and decline.*

"If this is what the coven has decided, I'll do what's asked of me. But I can't force Benedict to agree," she added. Surely he would decline. There was no way he'd want to spend his life with her for the sake of the Manor. She had far more to lose than he did.

"I accept." Benedict spoke clearly, with no doubt or hesitation.

Wide-eyed, Lucy stared at him, expecting to find him smirking as though he had called her bluff. Instead, he looked as startled by his answer as she was to hear it.

A round of applause buried their silent exchange of confusion. The coven offered their congratulations, but Lucy only heard her heart beating in her ears. As goblets were raised in cheers, all she could do was stare at Benedict, who was accepting their congratulations with poise. He'd been faster to shake off the shock.

She forced a smile and accepted a glass of wine, wondering what the hell they'd got themselves into. They might be celebrating the prospect of binding two families, but by All Hallows' Eve, she'd be surprised if either one of them made it to the altar.

Lucinda

"Grams? You home?" Lucy called out, in desperate need of her grandmother's famous healing hugs. Benedict had tried to catch up with her after the meeting, but she needed time to think, and she hadn't wanted to argue in front of the coven.

Her call echoed through the corridor and went unanswered. Grams was probably at the tarot shop or in the brewing room on the third floor.

Hanging her coat on the golden hook by the front door, Lucy noted that the forest-green wallpaper was beginning to peel again. She'd hoped the masking spell would hold it in place for longer than a week. Slipping off her muddy boots, she sighed as the floorboards creaked beneath her feet, reminding her of another much-needed repair. Hawthorne House had been in their family for generations. It needed constant repairs because Grams refused to move out, to modernise the dark floral wallpaper, wood, and pointed doorways. Lucy preferred something a bit brighter – a little less Gothic – but the house had been left unaltered for so long it had a spirit all its own, and changing it felt wrong.

"Grams?" she called again, turning on the antique lamps in the hall. It was already past ten. Despite being in her eighties, Grams never worried about breaking a hip in the dark. She insisted on maintaining the lamps, though, for when Gramps visited from the afterlife; they were one of his favourite features.

"Lucy? Is that you? I'm in the brewing room. Come up – I can't leave the pot, or the lizard skin will burn!" Grams yelled. Her voice was still clear and strong from years of giving orders. Since Lucy's dad worked at the university in the city and was away from home during the academic year, it was just Lucy, her mum and Grams at home.

"Please tell me you didn't use the dried skins again. They stink out the house..." Lucy got a whiff of something rancid. "I just got the smell out of the room from last week's brew!" she huffed. The spiral staircase always winded her.

"Bring me the bat's blood when you pass the pantry," Grams requested.

"What are you working on?" Lucy shouted back, stopping on the second floor. Trying to figure out what Grams was up to was a welcome distraction from the night's earlier events. Mum still wasn't home, and she couldn't wait to have *that* discussion. She could only hope her mum had a plan.

"Stop shouting through the house. You'll wake your uncle." Grams had forgotten, again, that Uncle Gregory had passed away years ago. Not that it mattered; Gregory popped into Foxford from time to time when he had a soul to collect, though his job as a Grim Reaper kept him from making regular visits.

At the pantry, Lucy found the spare brewing ingredients kept in the coldest cupboard, thanks to the floor being the most visited by those who had passed on. Only Grams slept on the second floor, because she wanted to stay in the same room when Gramps visited. Lucy hoped to one day love someone as much as her grandparents loved each other. Her stomach sank as she passed their bedroom, reminded that she was to bind herself to Benedict on All Hallows' Eve. The thought of never having such a love made her heart heavy, so she decided to focus on the task at hand.

She brushed aside the cobwebs in the top corner of the doorframe of the cupboard. "The spiders must have got out again. This is why I say not to buy live ones when the dried ones are just as good," she muttered, finding the vial of bat's blood between the rattlesnake venom and the dried cockroach. She didn't want to know why Grams needed it, but after the day she'd had, it was probably better not to ask.

Grams spent her well-earned retirement concocting spells and potions for those willing to pay for the unrivalled talent of their former High Priestess. From falling in love to curing your cystic acne, she was the one everyone went to for help, and since Gramps had passed away, she liked to keep busy. To be honest, the more she helped others, the less she meddled in Lucy's life. She always joked about setting her up, so Lucy figured Grams would get a great laugh out of her arranged marriage.

Reaching the third floor, she was almost out of breath. *Those stairs never get any shorter.*

"Hi, Gramps," she said, pausing at his portrait. "Making sure she doesn't blow up the house again?" She smiled, hearing Grams chatting to herself through the slightly open door. "One vial of bat's blood. Please tell me you aren't helping the vampires with the blood substitute again. The last one gave them awful hives."

The brewing room's black and white chequered floor tiles were littered with scraps of paper. Grams was working at the other end of the room, surrounded by bookshelves and cases of vials, both filled and empty.

"No, they've given up on a substitute blood, and this" – she popped another ingredient into the cauldron – "has nothing to do with vampires." Thankfully, whatever she was brewing smelt sweet, like honey or maple syrup. Her white curls were frizzy from hours of standing over the bubbling cauldron.

Lucy started to clean up, finding the scribbles of what looked like an original spell, with a list of characteristics and potion ingredients.

"'Kind, capable, passionate'? What is this? Please tell me it's not another love spell. They never end well!"

"How was the meeting?" Grams dodged her question. "Your mum couldn't settle before she left. Gwendoline might be her friend, but I think she is asking too much." Lucy listened intently. "Suggesting her son take your place was rather left field, even if I do like the boy."

Hearing Benedict referred to as a boy almost made Lucy laugh, but to Grams, she supposed they would always be young ones causing trouble.

"You knew Gwendoline was going to nominate Benedict? Why didn't you warn me?" she asked, sitting up on the counter lined with labelled brown bags for orders.

"I don't like to meddle in coven business. Anyway, your

mum and I discussed it this morning, and she didn't have a choice but to let the coven decide your punishment. I can't believe you jinxed the teacups – *and* you took my koi fish! I'd really hoped you and Benedict had put all that behind you."

"Did Mum know about the binding ritual? The coven gave us a choice: risk banishment from Foxford, or agree to lead together," Lucy said, pulling at the ends of her sleeves.

Grams hesitated, confirming her worst fear.

"Your mum wanted to tell you, but she's still the High Priestess, and there are some things she just can't share with you." Gram's glasses fogged up as she added black pepper, causing the potion to steam.

"I understand she had a duty to the coven, but I'm still her daughter, and this is about my life. If I'd known I was going to be confronted, I could've prepared something to say other than standing there like a blindsided idiot! It was only by the grace of the goddess that I didn't flood the temple." Lucy slumped forward. She didn't have the energy to argue about what had already passed.

"I'm sure Benedict felt the same way. Maybe working together won't be so terrible. If there is one thing you have in common, it's your love of this town," Grams said, removing her glasses and letting them hang on the crystal chain around her neck.

"He knew. You should've seen him accepting their congratulations, as though we really were a newly engaged couple. I could barely string a sentence together before I left," Lucy admitted. "How can you be okay with this? You want us to be bound, or to see me banished?"

Grams calmly shrugged. "You'd never be banished. The coven is overreacting because they don't want others to think they can pull such tricks without consequences. If you both decided against the binding and you'd lost the vote, you'd only have to leave for a year or two at most."

That was clearly supposed to be comforting, but even a year or two away from home felt like an unreasonable punishment for some silly pranks. Lucy couldn't believe she might lose everything all because she'd lost her temper over some damn bike tyres.

"Don't look so surprised; you should've been more careful." Grams sighed, stirring her potion. "The Mathersons have had their eye on the coven since Foxford became a sanctuary. With that handsome son of hers charming the town and the hotel lining everyone's pockets, Gwendoline was going to make her move for power sooner rather than later. Your mum deciding to retire with your father was the perfect opportunity for them to strike." Grams clearly wasn't too pleased with Lucy's parents' decision to relive their youth, but given how much they had sacrificed, Lucy wouldn't pout too much.

"But Mum and Gwendoline have been friends for years. It doesn't make sense that Gwendoline is risking a divide between our families. What if Benedict *is* the right choice?" Lucy didn't know if she was being logical or if the weight of the day had exhausted her will to fight. "He's more involved with the town and enjoys politics. What if I abdicated? Do you think we'd both get to stay?" She might lose her right to lead, but she'd still be able to stay in town and keep the library. "Our family has watched over Foxford for generations. Maybe it *is* someone else's turn to lead?"

Grams side-eyed her. "Is this your way of telling us you don't want to inherit the seat? I had my doubts when I saw how composed you remained when the proposal was made."

"My reaction? You sent a dove to spy, didn't you? If you'd been there, you'd have seen it was shock, not composure. I'm already on tense terms with the Order. I don't need to add a political rivalry with Benedict to my plate."

"I don't spy; this matter involved my family. And you're able to handle far more than you give yourself credit for. The work you've done for the Order speaks to that," Grams said, wiping her hands on her polka-dot apron. "If you're so ready to hand the position to Benedict, why did you agree to the binding?"

Lucy hesitated, eyeing the spy doves in their gilded cage.

"To buy myself some time. I never expected Benedict to agree... I thought he'd object, and I wanted to appear willing to go along with their wishes. I figured my acceptance would earn me some points if there was a vote." She'd also hoped her mum had some plan to get her out of this, and that the coven would cool down once they saw the attendance at the Autumn Festival wasn't depleted due to that damning review.

"There *is* fight in you yet, otherwise you wouldn't worry so much." Grams winked. "And though we may have lost this battle, I might have just the thing to help you win the war."

Lucy felt the hairs on her arm stand on edge. "Please tell me whatever you're brewing doesn't have anything to do with Benedict? As much as I detest him and his family's ambition, poisoning him is not the way to go."

"How little you think of me." Grams tutted. "Benedict's a good man; I'm not going to poison him. I'm old, not crazy."

"You've always had a soft spot for him."

"If you weren't so determined to hate each other, he might've conceded the nomination. If you'd chosen honey over vinegar, neither of you would be in this position."

"What's your plan?" Lucy stepped closer to the table, feeling the temptation of some kind of magical solution. She stirred the potion for Grams, who added some apple seeds.

"We need to make sure that neither of you is forced into a binding neither of you wants. That can lead nowhere good."

Lucy examined the ingredients on the cutting board. *Rose water, apple seeds, cardamom...*

"This isn't exactly a traditional love spell," she muttered, glancing at the diced chickweed and chilli.

Before she could ask, her mum came through the door. Her usual pale complexion was now red and blotchy; gone were her stoic expression and priestess robes. She was Mum again, with her wooden clogs and flowing patchwork skirts. She was a big fan of upcycling; nothing ever went to waste in their house.

"Found the damiana root. Thankfully, Myrtle had some left," she panted, then stopped dead as she saw her daughter by the cauldron.

"You're in on this?" Lucy looked between the two matriarchs.

"Don't worry about a thing. We've a plan to get you out of the bonding," Mum said.

Lucy tried to understand what hairbrained scheme these two had concocted. "But... you agreed with Gwendoline at the temple. I thought you wanted us to be bound?"

"Yes, I agreed, because I'm supposed to be impartial. However, as your mum, I'm not going to let you bind yourself to someone you don't love," Mum explained, removing a small, muddy root from a paper bag.

"How about you stop whatever spell you've concocted, and we go back to the coven? We can tell them that I've changed my mind, and to proceed with the vote at the end of the month so that Benedict and I have an equal chance to prove ourselves," Lucy said, trying to find a neutral solution. "Using magic to manipulate a situation never ends well."

Both women stared up at her, as if they weren't the ones who'd taught her that very lesson.

"Are you mad? You can't go back on your word. Not when Benedict has agreed. They'll stand against you." Mum took a deep breath. "I promise, your grandmother and I aren't going to hurt or manipulate anyone."

"We discovered there's a flaw in Gwendoline's ritual. If you find your true love before All Hallows' Eve, your soul won't bond with Benedict's because you'll already be connected to another," Grams explained, while Mum grated the foul-smelling root over the cauldron.

Lucy hesitated, then laughed, thinking it had to be a joke. When Grams and Mum didn't falter, her nervous laughter disappeared.

"You can't be serious. You want to use a love spell on me?"

They stopped her from putting the lid on the cauldron.

"By ensuring you find your true love, your magic will never let you bond to another. Love is stronger than any magic, so the coven won't be able to force your hand," Grams insisted.

Lucy waved the makeshift spell in the air. "I hoped you'd have a plan to help, but love potions never work the way we want. Love magic usually ends up with some crazed obsession, or worse, even dying of a broken heart. Love can be lethal in certain doses. I've seen the horror stories in the archives to prove it."

"There's no need to worry. We've taken every precaution, and mixed two spells," Grams started.

"Combining incantations with potions will only make the spell more potent!" Lucy groaned.

"It's not an incantation – just a list of all the qualities we thought would make your perfect match. Technically, we aren't making someone fall in love with you, nor you with them. We're only setting you on a path to find each other, but not dictating it," Grams said.

It sounded reasonable, but also insane. Was there such a thing as reasonably insane?

"What about the potion?"

"Just a simple mixture. It'll draw the two of you together. We only have until the 31st October for you to find each other." Mum seemed as convinced as Grams that their scheme would work.

"This is too risky! You can't just *design* a man for me," Lucy argued, pacing. "How did you even have time to come up with all this?"

"Risky is binding yourself to a man you can't stand," Grams muttered, but Mum interjected.

"When Gwendoline called the coven to gather, I knew something was up. This wouldn't be the first time she has hinted at another successor, and when she showed me the review I knew she had the ammo she needed to put doubt about you in the other's minds." She took her daughter's hand. "With the whole town seeing the review, my hands were tied. I do agree that Benedict is a worthy candidate, but a loveless binding is out of the question."

"I wish you'd just spoken up at the meeting if you were

so against it." Lucy sighed, removing her hand. "It would've been far easier than casting whatever Frankenstein love spell you've got simmering away."

"I would've been accused of nepotism."

Unfortunately, Mum was right.

"We thought you'd be happy to hear our plan," Grams chimed in, arching her eyebrow. "Maybe you don't despise the man as much as you claim?"

Both women stared at her, as though she was harbouring some secret love.

"Just let me think! What if I find the person I love, but the coven finds out we cast a spell intending to disrupt the binding? They'll view it as a betrayal."

Mum gripped her hand and, before Lucy could stop her, pricked her finger.

"Ow," Lucy hissed as her mum squeezed a droplet of blood from the wound over the sizzling pot. The potion shimmered, and the bubbling settled.

"Sorry, we needed it to strengthen the spell," Mum said, releasing her hand. "Your concerns are valid, but we know how hard it is to be in power, and to do it with someone you don't care for at your side would be a life sentence. We only wish to see you happy. If the coven finds out, then we'll worry about that when the time comes."

Lucy pressed her finger to her lips, feeling guilty for questioning the two people who'd only ever wanted the best for her. Still, she couldn't shake the feeling that a spell was too drastic, and she couldn't believe they were willing to go so far to protect her heart. It was something the Mathersons would do, not the Hawthornes.

Gram took the list of qualities from the table and held it over the cauldron.

"Don't even think about it! If those who wish to see us ousted find out—"

Grams dropped the list into the potion. Mum followed up with the final rose petals.

"I should've skipped the meeting and gone to the lake with Rosie," Lucy grumbled, wishing she wasn't witnessing this madness. If she were at the lake, she'd have had plausible deniability.

A sharp bang caused the trio to jump, and Mum swished her hand through the rising smoke. Glancing inside the cauldron, they found a piece of paper burnt to ash and the potion gone.

"I hope for all our sakes that didn't work," Lucy prayed.

"We'll have to wait and see. It shouldn't take long," Mum said, tidying up the mess Grams had made. Lucy felt like they were hiding the evidence.

"How can you know how long it'll take to work?" Lucy wasn't sure if she even wanted to know the answer.

"We added a clause to the spell that if the person you are meant to be with is of magical descent, your elements will call to one other. Elemental power has an incredibly strong call," Grams informed her.

"Great! Not only did we mess with a love potion, but also elemental magic! What makes you think he'll be of magical descent?" Lucy asked, wanting to learn as much as she could about the spell. "Dad is a magless."

"We don't, but it was worth adding just in case," Grams said.

That brought up a new worry. "What if the coven doesn't like the idea of another coven leader marrying a magless? Dad was only approved by the coven because he'd been attacked by a vampire when he was younger, and then spent the rest of his youth researching myths and legends until he stumbled upon Foxford and fell in love with mum."

"You should've seen his face when he learnt the true nature of this town. Nearly scared him to death when he saw Broomhilda at the library, sweeping away," Grams chuckled.

Mum continued. "And yes, such unions were quite the scandal back in our day, but only because many people thought marrying a magless would lessen the magic passed down to the next generation. Pure elitist nonsense. It was also said that marrying a werewolf or vampire would create hybrids, but they are either born vamp, wolf or magless. There is no lessening of power. You might be lucky to marry a magless. He would be of no threat to your position, and the families are far more accepting now."

Lucy didn't need a history lesson, but she had been raised not to interrupt her elders.

"If Benedict discovers we've been conspiring..." She fidgeted, wishing she'd discovered their plans earlier. She wanted to inherit her mother's position fair and square, not because she'd interfered with magic.

Grams and her mum exchanged puzzled glances.

"Maybe the line between love and loathing is rather thin between you?" Grams suggested. Lucy rolled her eyes.

"Gwendoline always suspected there might be something between them," Mum agreed. "I can't count how many times the school called us because you were both too busy making mischief to focus on your schoolwork."

"I don't mean that it would hurt the chance of us being together. I meant he could use it against me," Lucy clarified. "I only agreed to the binding because I didn't think he'd agree. And need I remind you he nearly got me expelled? I wouldn't call that mischief."

"You can hardly blame him entirely for the threat of expulsion. You did cause the lake to burst," Grams countered.

There's that soft spot rearing its ugly head. Lucy grimaced.

"Only because he set the trees along the riverbank on fire. My *flood* saved the woods and spared the coven having to answer to the werewolves who dwell in them!"

"The lad had lost his father," Grams reminded her softly, putting the ingredients back on the shelves. "You shouldn't judge him for what he did during that time. Both of you broke the rules by using your elements while under eighteen. Using that much power could have flooded the entire town." She raised a hand before Lucy could argue back. "Yes, just as he could have burnt it down."

Lucy rubbed her temples, wishing she'd never got up this morning. "To be clear, there is nothing, nor has there *ever* been anything, between me and Benedict. Please no more spells for my benefit." She headed for the door. "Let's wait and see how this month plays out. We can only trust that the right person will be watching over Foxford when the time comes."

Grams started to argue, but Lucy interrupted. "If fate says that's Benedict, and I have to leave, I'll accept it."

"It could be both," she heard her mum mutter as the door closed behind her. She wished they loved her a little less; their good intentions could ruin them all.

On the carpet by her feet, she noticed a scrap of paper with a barely legible list of ingredients. She scanned the words, trying to figure out the spell they'd used to make her element call out to another, only to notice there was no black pepper on the list. The cursive read *Bat's Blood*, not black pepper. She realised Grams hadn't uncorked the blood she'd brought from the pantry. *Grams must have got confused while we were talking and put in the wrong ingredient.*

Lucy smiled from ear to ear. Hopefully, the mistake would stop the spell from working. She scrunched up the list of ingredients and put it in her skirt pocket before Grams realised her mistake.

Benedict

Benedict ran through the woods, failing to avoid the puddles. After being blindsided at the coven meeting, he desperately needed to clear his head, and running through the tall trees listening to the rain pattering against the leaves was his favourite way to escape. He didn't care about the rain or filth – only about trying to escape the confines of town. His agreement to the proposed binding still rang in his ears. On the winding trails, it was just him and the lawless woods, and no one needed him to be or do anything.

What is Mum thinking, trying to pair Lucinda and me together? Stumbling to a halt, he rested his hands on his knees to catch his breath. He'd thought the proposal was a joke, but Gwendoline had ambushed him outside the temple before he could catch up with Lucinda. With the other coven members hovering close by, he couldn't argue with his mother. He wished he'd taken more care to hide the magazine review; he'd only managed to calm her down about Lucinda's prank because he'd promised it would amount to nothing. Banishment, a binding ritual, both, either – all far too extreme. However, if the coven wanted to make a point to the rest of the town, they'd certainly warned off any future incident that put Foxford at risk of outside criticism.

I could've refused to accept the nomination, but I said yes. Maybe I wanted to see Lucinda's reaction. I've spent so long trying to get her to see me as more than a Matherson, someone without a tainted ancestry.

He had to admit it had felt good to have the High Priestess accept his nomination, even if he'd spent most of his life trying not to care what anyone thought of him. To know he was worthy of even a nomination was a recognition of all he'd done for Foxford. Still, he didn't know how the vote would land. He didn't want to leave Foxford, especially not everything he'd built, and he didn't want his mum to be the last Matherson in town. She'd lost his brother and dad; he didn't want her to have to lose anything else.

After all these years, he'd never expected his and Lucinda's rivalry to come to this. To spend the rest of their lives together... he didn't know if he'd survive her goody-two-shoes act, even if it delighted a twisted part of him to consider it. They'd both worked hard throughout school, maybe a bit too hard, in their attempts to get the other expelled. He enjoyed bringing out her recklessness more than he cared to admit, even if it was at his expense.

The battle lines had been drawn when he'd turned the Manor into a hotel, the only thing left to the Matherson name, and Lucinda had traded the school library for the vault. They'd kept to their territories, and incidents had grown few and far between. Tasting blood on his tongue, Benedict wished they'd called a truce before the coven had

had to take such drastic action. Maybe they deserved to face the consequences.

When he stood straight, sparkles formed in his vision. He scolded himself for running on an empty stomach. He reached into his pocket to check for the bar he usually brought, but found nothing. As he started to walk back the way he'd come, the smell of burning plastic drifted around him. He sniffed the air to see what direction it was coming from. It was usual for people to light bonfires during the autumn equinox, but it was so wet tonight one wouldn't be easy to light, and the smell was far too strong for a flame he couldn't see.

Feeling something crispy in his hand, Benedict glanced down to find he'd burnt a hole in his pocket. *He* was the burning smell.

What the—? He patted down the singed edges, startled by the sudden loss of control over his element. His fire magic always acted up whenever his emotions were heightened.

He decided to return home before he set anything else on fire. Thankfully, Lucinda wasn't here to see the mishap; she'd have loved to see him lose control.

He'd started back down the trail when, as if his thoughts had brought her to life, Lucinda appeared on the trail. *Now I'm imagining things. Great.*

"Lucinda?" he called, narrowing his eyes. She seemed to be swaying.

Benedict walked towards her, needing to make sure it wasn't his mind playing tricks on him. A branch cracked under his foot, and the startled figure darted into the shadows of the trees and disappeared.

I've lost my mind. I should've known it would be her to send me over the edge. She wasn't his to worry about; anyway, he wasn't even sure it had been her. It was the last moon of summer: many would be in the woods, doing gods knew what. Most activities were kept to the lake at the other end of the woods, where the gap between woods and town was smallest and safest.

Still, he couldn't shake the feeling he was being watched as he walked down the trail. If it was Lucinda, he couldn't blame her for wanting to blow off steam after the evening they'd had.

He only made it a few feet when she jumped out from behind a tree with a mocking roar.

"I could've hurt you!" he snapped. He'd already lost control of his fire once this evening.

She dropped her hands to her sides, giggling as she circled him.

"What are you doing out here so late? Are you alright?" he asked, as she stopped to hug a tree.

"Why wouldn't I be fine? Nature will always protect me!" She sounded far more relaxed than normal. It wasn't that she was uptight, but she certainly wasn't going around hugging trees most days. Benedict's concern amplified when he realised she was in her underwear.

"Where the hell are your clothes?" He turned away, fearing she'd disappear. The idea of others seeing her in her underwear troubled him more than he cared to admit.

"I was swimming! And I didn't want anything to separate me from all the glorious nature," she told him. "There is no shame in my natural state." She spun him around; her skin, glistening with droplets, and soaking wet hair confirmed her story.

"It's not safe to be out here alone, especially half-naked!" he grumbled, shrugging off his raincoat. Even with twigs in her hair and her fringe a damp mess at the sides of her face, her natural beauty remained.

"Don't be such a downer, Benny. I'm not alone. You should join me. It's such a beautiful night!" Her smile brightened her eyes, and he realised she wasn't wearing her glasses. He hoped she was wearing contacts, because he wasn't going searching for them.

"Benny?" he muttered, running his hands over his face. There was no way she was in her right mind. She couldn't get away from him fast enough after the coven meeting, and now she was calling him Benny? "You think that now, but when you wake up tomorrow you might not be too happy with me having seen your... natural state." He turned her around so she'd stop looking up at him with those big green eyes.

"I think we have far more important things to worry about than you seeing me like this," she grumbled, with her back to him.

He was too distracted by the tattoo between her shoulder blades, a crescent moon, to register her words. *She's always had a thing for piercings, but the tattoo was a surprise.* It suited her – delicate in detail, yet a force of nature.

"Have you taken anything?" he asked, trying not to spook her as he slowly approached with the raincoat to protect her modesty. She didn't seem to notice, too busy petting the tree bark. He wondered how many splinters she was going to wake up with tomorrow. It wasn't odd for those frolicking to forgo their clothes, but she wasn't the type to throw caution to the wind.

"Just some tea that Luisa got from a witch overseas. Tastes awful, but very soothing. Even Rosie said it was all right if you held your breath while you drank it." Her eyes were watery, and the whites seemed brighter.

"I should've known Luisa would be involved," he muttered. Lucinda's old school friend had been suspended for selling all types of *relaxing* goodies in their senior year. "You do seem very... relaxed, but I think that tea must have had mushrooms or something else in it to help loosen your inhibitions." She'd never call him Benny, or ask him to join anything if she wasn't under something's influence.

She beamed at him. "Trees have so many stories to tell. I can almost hear them."

"Yes, trees are wonderful. How about you just put this on?" He held the jacket out to her, averting his gaze.

She took the raincoat, only to hug the fabric to her skin. "Smells so good," she breathed.

Benedict tried and failed to suppress a chuckle. He hoped she'd remember this in the morning.

"That would be my sweat," he said, trying to keep a straight face. *She might not remember this, but I will. I'll cherish this forever.* "Where are Rosie and Luisa? I doubt they're happy about you running off."

"They're still at the lake!" Thankfully, she didn't protest as he helped her into the raincoat and zipped it up. The tea must be keeping her warm; it was cold tonight, and though her lips were paler than usual, she gave no sign of feeling chilly.

"Why did you leave them?" He wanted to make sure the others were okay and nothing had scared Lucinda into running off. She didn't seem frightened, but on Luisa's tea, anything could happen. He'd fallen victim to her tea himself after his college graduation. He'd woken up on a beach miles from home. Unlike Lucinda, he'd thankfully kept his clothes on, although he had been wearing someone else's shoes.

"Fireflies," she said, like it was the most rational explanation in the world.

He couldn't exactly ask for her phone, considering her current state, and he doubted the others would even answer if they were in a similar state. "How about you come with me? We can look for fireflies together."

He didn't want to leave her alone so far from her friends. If she had wandered away from them once, he didn't trust her not to do it again, and he didn't fancy returning her to the lake in her current state either. The coven had already questioned their actions; if they were seen like this, it would only work against them.

Running a hand through his damp hair, he waited while she pulled the long sleeves over her hands. The raincoat only covered the tops of her thighs, so perhaps it was a good thing the tea was keeping her warm. He wished she'd left her shoes on. He didn't like to think of the rough ground cutting up her feet.

"Do you know where we can find some?" Lucinda asked, wide-eyed. "I thought I saw them, but they were just the street lights." He had to scrub the smile from his face at the genuine disappointment in her tone.

"I even know where we can see a *giant* firefly." Benedict tried to sound convincing. Her eyes widened, revealing her dilated pupils. *I can't believe Rosie let her wander off! She should've tracked her down before she got this far from the group.* He didn't have time to be angry now; he needed to get her somewhere warm and safe.

"Lead the way." Lucinda smiled, offering him her hand. He stared at it, but she rolled her eyes. "We don't want to lose each other." She threaded her fingers through his, swinging their arms back and forth.

Please let her remember this in the morning. He took her hand, and she wrapped herself around his arm.

"Stay close and you won't be disappointed," he promised, leading her away from the woods to Matherson Manor. He couldn't bring her back to Hawthorne House like this, but there were plenty of spare rooms in the Manor.

"Wait a second! This is the way to the Manor! You don't have fireflies!" Lucinda huffed, tugging on his hand as Benedict opened the tall back gate shrouded in green vines.

"Trust me," he said, gently giving her hand a reassuring squeeze. The hedgerows separating his property from the woods meant no one used this entrance, sparing them both from being the topic of tomorrow's gossip.

"Promise?" Her eyes narrowed, taking in the gardens as though they might swallow her up. She'd never follow him sober, but he hoped this version of her would trust him.

She studied him for a few seconds before letting him lead. Once inside, he sealed the gate to make sure she couldn't run back to the woods. He didn't want to spend the rest of his night tracking her down. The only small mercy was the drizzle had dried up and the clouds had cleared overhead, giving him some hope that his plan would work.

"Promise." Benedict pressed a finger to his lips, and she

mimicked the gesture. "We have to be quiet – we don't want to wake the guests," he whispered, even though there was no chance of them being heard this far from the guest quarters. Whether their binding was a political matter or not, if they were caught spending the night together and sneaking around it would be like confirming they were in a relationship.

"Shh," Lucinda agreed, and giggled.

Walking through the wine cellar, Benedict opened one of the older doors so they could sneak through the old servants' passageways without being seen by the night staff. Unfortunately, he'd never thought to put lighting in the old passageway.

"I can't see anything," Lucinda whispered, crushing his hand in hers.

"Are you afraid of the dark?" he asked, not wanting her to freak out.

"Always."

He didn't want to read any more into that. "Let there be light," he said, clicking his fingers to try and start a fire in his palm. Much to his dismay, it took more than a few tries to spark a flame.

"There are so many cobwebs. I don't like spiders," Lucinda whispered, gripping his hand tighter. Panic edged her voice.

A ball of fire finally shone from his palm. "I'm sure the spiders are sleeping," he lied, not being a fan of them himself.

"This doesn't seem safe." Lucinda eyed the elevator,

which was older than both of them combined. She took a tentative step back, but he didn't release her hand.

"Because running naked through the woods, where there are all manner of creatures, is far safer," he muttered. "Don't worry, it's been well serviced. This is the old escape route if the manor was ever invaded. This is the last step, and you did make me promise. Don't make me break it."

Lucinda swallowed, but stepped inside. The iron shaft creaked under their combined weight as it rose, and the rusty smell revealed just how old it was.

"I can't give you fireflies, but I hope you'll accept the stars," Benedict said, opening the grate to the rooftop pool area. The loungers would be a little damp from the rain. Hopefully she wouldn't notice.

"This is everything! How've I never been up here?" She hurried out, dragging him behind her. It took all his will not to smile at how easily pleased she was, all thought of the creepy elevator gone in an instant as he carefully directed her around the pool. It was covered, but that could be even more dangerous, and he didn't fancy going in after her.

Thankfully, she didn't notice the water. She let go of his hand and hurried to the edge of the roof. With the old battlements, there was no worry of her going over.

"Your desire to stay as far away from me as possible probably had something to do with it," he said, nervously watching her leaning over the wall. His jacket rose higher on her pale thighs and he diverted his gaze, only to see how dirty her feet were. All thoughts of her bare skin disappeared, replaced with the worry that she might have cut herself during the run in the woods.

From behind the closed bar beside the sun loungers, he filled a jug with warm water and carried it over to a sun lounger. While she was distracted by the stars and the views of the woods, he grabbed some towels and the first aid kit for her feet. He didn't want the binding to fall through because she died of sepsis. If one of them had to leave Foxford, he didn't want it to be in a coffin.

"Such a pity that Matherson Manor comes with Mathersons." Lucinda covered a shallow yawn before plonking herself down on the lounger beside the towels.

"I'm afraid it can't be helped." Benedict covered her legs with a towel, trying to keep her warm, as she kept her gaze tipped towards the stars. So far from the city and high above their village, there was nothing to hinder the starlight. Her mood seemed to have mellowed out, so he could relax about her trying to run off.

Suddenly, she reclaimed his hand and brought it to her chest. "We aren't fighting," she mused, tracing her fingers over the exposed part of his ivy tattoo that travelled from his hand and over his shoulders. It was the same ivy that coated the walls of the manor he'd known all his life.

"Don't worry. I'm sure normal service will resume once you've sobered up," he said, pouring warm water on a clean towel.

"How exhausting," she groaned, collapsing back on the lounger. He knelt by her feet, and she sat up on her elbows, frowning. "Are you proposing?" She laughed.

"No, I need to clean the muck off your feet to make sure you haven't cut yourself," he explained, trying to keep her legs still as he balanced them on his lap.

"Pity."

He stared at her.

"It would've been nice to be proposed to properly, now I'm stuck with you."

The sadness in her voice tightened his heart. She was

right. They'd both missed out on a special moment because of the coven's proposal. She probably wanted to be proposed to with some grand gesture by someone she loved and who loved her in return. He'd never really given it much thought; he'd hoped one day he would have someone who'd accept him and his family name without shame. Someone who would be proud to stand by his side.

"I'm flattered by your sacrifice," he said, trying not to sound irritated. She was high; he couldn't hold her accountable for what she said under the influence of Luisa's tea.

"You should be, but we're in the same boat – you're stuck with me," she chuckled. "It could be worse, though."

"How?"

She shrugged. "We know each other. What if we'd been bound to strangers?" How like a Hawthorne to find the silver lining in her punishment. "I know everything about you."

She yawned and stopped squirming for a second while he cleaned her foot. By some miracle he found no cuts or abrasions.

"That tickles." Lucinda wriggled her toes. He moved to the other foot before she could take it away.

"You don't know everything," he said, trying to distract her.

"You love pumpkins, hate snakes, love lizards." She counted the facts on her fingers. "You're terrible at geography and can't swim, which is crazy, since you've got a freaking pool."

He wanted to explain that fire and water didn't mix, but he didn't want to ruin the longest conversation they'd ever had without arguing.

"You've got a birthmark on your calf that kind of looks

like a skull. You're afraid of needles and cried when we got our injections at school for werewolf flu, which makes no sense, since you have tattoos."

"Okay, I get the picture, you know me." Benedict held up his hands defensively before she got to anything embarrassing. Then he glanced at his birthmark. He'd never considered that it looked like a skull, but now that she'd said it, he couldn't unsee it. He wondered what else she had noticed about him.

"You probably don't know half as much about me," she said, reaching for the sky.

"Just focus on the stars," he said, carefully checking her second foot.

"Far better than fireflies," she mused.

"The stars appear brightest here because this is the highest point in Foxford, except for the bell tower in the town hall," he explained. Incredibly, it seemed both her feet were uninjured in spite of the evening's escapades.

"I'd be up here every night if I could. I'm surprised there are no guests up here," she said, tucking her feet under herself. Benedict sat on the lounger beside her, exhausted. He stared up at the stars she was attempting to trace with her fingers.

"They aren't allowed up here after midnight. I come up when I can, to enjoy the peace," he admitted, wondering again if she'd remember any of this tomorrow.

"I'm jealous," she sighed. He glanced at her to see her eyelids growing heavy. "You escape to the sky and I to the underground. Grams was right when she called us opposites."

Benedict arched his brows, wondering what else had been said about him. He had a soft spot for Lucinda's grandmother. She'd been there for him when his father was tried for assisted death by magic, and never judged him for the actions of those related to him.

"Come here whenever you like. Just come through the way I showed you. The guests or the staff won't even notice," he said, resting an arm under his head. "It's nice not arguing with you; maybe we can make it a regular thing, now that we're to be bound. If we'd made peace earlier, we'd have saved ourselves all this hassle. We could tell them we've changed our minds?"

He held his breath, waiting for her to defend herself or accuse him of trying to trick her into backing out. However, his words went unanswered. Turning to see if she was considering it, Benedict found her sleeping peacefully, one of the fluffy white towels tucked under her head. With a sigh of relief, exhaustion overcame him, and he laid his head beside hers.

Up close, he admired her freckles, her long lashes, and wondered how the hell they were going to navigate the next month. He brushed a strand of hair from her forehead, and her eyes fluttered open.

He stilled, but she reached out to him. Her fingers gently traced his ear, his cheekbone, his jaw while he watched the stars, afraid to move an inch in case she stopped her exploration.

"How can you be so beautiful?" she said, sitting up on her elbow. He turned his head slightly to watch her.

"I really need to get the recipe for that tea," he said, wondering what she was up to.

"You know you're handsome, don't be modest. Every woman in town wants to fuck you," Lucinda informed him, settling against his chest.

"Christ, pumpkin." He did not want to think about

fucking with her so close. He swallowed, trying not to think about how her body fitted against his.

She smiled and kissed his shoulder, and he clenched his jaw, not understanding how such a small gesture could stir a hunger in him he hadn't known existed. Her lips grazed his cheek, inching closer to his lips. This wasn't why he'd brought her here. He'd wanted to protect her and he would, even if that meant from herself and the desire coiling inside him.

Benedict turned away. Lucy sat up, her frown making it clear she was startled by his rejection. She clung to his back, stopping him from standing up.

"I'm sorry, it's the tea," she pleaded. "Don't go."

He looked over his shoulder, hating how embarrassed she looked.

"You wouldn't be saying or acting this way, if you weren't under the influence," he said, pointing out the obvious.

"I'm hardly under the influence. I know who I am and who I'm with." She placed her hand on his chest. "You're Benedict, I'm Lucy we are sitting on the top of the Manor. I wanted to kiss you." She stared up at him, her eyes drifting to his lips.

He shook his head, resting his hand over hers. "You don't know what you're saying. It's the tea speaking."

"Do you not want to kiss me? Am I not good enough for you? Oh God, you're forced to marry me and now I've forced myself on you!" She buried her face in her hands.

Benedict turned to face her. "There isn't a man alive who wouldn't want to kiss you," he said, tilting her chin up to face him. He never wanted to hear her say that she wasn't good enough ever again.

"Then kiss me."

"You hate me."

"What does that have to do anything?" she asked softly, inching closer to him. Her hand drifted from his arm to his shoulder. He knew he should get up and walk away, but as she cupped his cheek he couldn't.

"You'll hate me."

"I thought we already established that I do," she said, resting her forehead against his.

"I should take you home."

"You should shut up and kiss me."

The desire in her words was his undoing. A low groan slipped through his lips; her eyes shifted to meet his. That was all it took.

Benedict's lips crashed against hers, hand gripping the back of her neck. No kiss had ever tasted as good as hers. Her soft lips were now his favourite drug. A moan escaped her as she parted them, letting him explore. He took everything she was willing to give as her hands travelled from his chest and slipped into his hair, pulling him closer; he smiled against her lips.

As if she couldn't get enough, Lucinda moved onto his lap, wrapping her legs around him. Their bodies pressed together. They'd barely started, and he was already painfully hard beneath her. He couldn't believe how desperately he wanted more, like he'd been starving his whole life and she was his favourite meal. Part of him hated himself for not stopping her as she slipped her hands under his T-shirt, exploring the planes of his back – she wasn't in her right mind. And he would stop her, but right now, he was going to kiss her, hold her, like this kiss would be their last.

His hand began to slide up her thigh. A whimper slipped up her throat, and she began to rock against him.

He wanted to please her, to be the one to make her feel an ecstasy she'd never forget, but when he opened his eyes, he was reminded of how they'd got there. He refused to get carried away. Easing her off and away from him was easily one of the most painful things he'd ever had to do.

Lucinda wrapped her arms around him, tucking her legs beneath her. "I'm sorry, I got carried away."

"You've nothing to be sorry about." He grabbed handfuls of his hair, trying to distract himself from the way his body ached at the loss of her touch. "But we need to stop," he pleaded with his conscience.

"Why? It's not like this is real." She smiled teasingly.

Benedict bolted upright to find Lucinda sleeping peacefully, curled into him for warmth. He sank back on the lounger, resting a hand on his forehead, trying to push out the memories of the all-too-real dream.

Lucinda snuggled closer, distracting him. He had to get her inside before she froze; he'd forgotten she didn't have his element to keep her warm out here.

Careful not to wake her, Benedict carried her to his private wing so she wouldn't be disturbed by housekeeping. She needed to sleep off Luisa's tea, and he didn't want her disturbed by those who rose early for breakfast. He told himself it was her closeness, the smell of her strawberry shampoo, that had caused the dream.

Laying her down on his poster bed, he pulled the midnight-blue velvet comforter over her to keep her warm. She curled into it, tucking it under her chin.

If someone had told him hours ago that he'd have a Hawthorne in his bed, he would've accused *them* of drinking Luisa's tea. At least here she'd be safe. He didn't want the coven to penalise her for her night of freedom, and since she lived with the High Priestess, there was no way she'd have been able to hide it.

Benedict lit the fire in the corner of the room to ensure she was cosy after being out in the cold rain, then sat in the armchair and watched the flames. He needed her well rested. Tomorrow, they'd have plenty to talk about.

Lucinda

Startled awake, Lucy found herself in a room styled as though it was still the 1800s. Had she somehow gone back in time? Then she saw the engraved M at the centre of the mantlepiece across the room.

How the hell did I end up in Matherson Manor? The room spun as she attempted to recall the previous evening. With her mouth furry and head foggy, it started to come back to her in pieces. *The lake... Rosie... Luisa's tea? Stars?* The last thing she remembered was being surrounded by countless stars. *And the smell of chlorine?*

Her stomach grumbled loudly; she was starving. She went to move, only to realise an arm rested across her lap. Bringing a hand to her mouth to silence her cry, Lucy gently eased it off, resting it on the pillow wall between herself and—

Her heart stopped as she saw Benedict Matherson, her nemesis, fast asleep.

Her only relief was that he was fully clothed. Slowly, she eased herself off the bed and made it into the bathroom on the other side of the room. Only then did she take note of her bare legs and a raincoat that was certainly not part of her wardrobe. She didn't need to check to know there was only her underwear beneath it. She hung her head in her hands, mortified. She guessed she had him to thank for the jacket.

Did he see me half-naked? Oh God, not just half-naked but on that damn mushroom tea! I should have just gone to bed as I planned. Why did I let Rosie talk me into going? She wanted the black bathroom tiles to open up and swallow her whole.

"What was he even doing in the woods?" she asked herself, leaning on the gold-coated sink. In her desperation, she even considered waking him, needing to know what the hell had happened and how they had ended up in the same bed. Which one of them had built the pillow wall? Either way, she was grateful for its presence.

As much as she wanted to jump into his oversized shower – filled with more products than she'd ever thought a man could want – and wash away her humiliation, she wanted to get out of the Manor before he woke up and lorded her crazy night over her. The shame of him witnessing it was too much to bear. Quickly, she replaced the raincoat with a navy robe, only to see his initials over her breast. She rolled her eyes as she let her fingers graze the gold embroidery.

Staring at herself in the mirror, she was instantly thankful to find she hadn't lost any of her several earrings. Some were handed down through the family, and to lose one would have been devastating. However, her eyes were bloodshot and sore from leaving her contacts in for far too long. She removed them, still able to see up close, to give her eyes a break. She only wished she hadn't lost her clothes... she let out a groan, reminded of the fact that Benedict had seen her semi-nude. She would've preferred it if Hades himself had found her and dragged her back to the underworld.

She was getting off track. *What if he uses this against me with the coven? I suppose I could argue that if I was out, he was too?*

She tried to use her element to fill the sink with water, afraid the sound of running water through the old pipes would wake Benedict, but nothing happened. She steadied her breathing and tried again. "The tea must have weakened me," she muttered, but she'd tried Luisa's tea before when they were doing a seance, and she didn't recall it having any effect on her element.

Putting it down to the stress of the last twenty-four hours, she told herself she'd be fine in a bit. Thankfully, the clock on the bathroom wall showed that she had some time before dawn, but someone was bound to notice if she walked through the hotel in Benedict's robe. She sat on the edge of the tub, contemplating what to do. She'd left her phone at home before she'd gone to meet the others at the lake.

I could try teleporting, but it might not work. If my element isn't working, my teleporting skills might also be weakened. She considered putting on a brave face and waking Benedict, demanding he take her home, but when she opened the door a crack, he stirred and she quickly closed it again. There was no way she could face him.

Praying her magic would still work, even if her element was off, she squeezed her eyes shut and pictured home.

The warmth of the heated tile was replaced with the damp feel of the porch beneath her feet. Lucy couldn't help but jump for joy as she found herself at her front door. If she hadn't been afraid of the neighbours seeing her in a Matherson robe she would have kissed every inch of the porch, damn the splinters.

"Strange... the tea allowed me to portal, but not to use my water magic. How does that make sense?" she murmured to herself.

She didn't have a chance to think about it before she spotted her neighbour coming out across the street with their dogs. Lucy darted inside before she could be seen. Avoiding the creaky floorboards, having mastered them as a teen, she made it to the attic without incident. Taking her first calm, deep breath of the morning, she turned on the ornate lamp by her desk, careful not to knock off the pile of annotated books. She didn't have time to tidy up, and she desperately needed to wash up before her mum or Grams saw her in Benedict's robe first thing in the morning only hours after agreeing to his proposal.

An image of him on his knee, with her foot on his lap, sprang to mind. It couldn't be real, but his smirk in her memory seemed all too real.

Chaos, her grey cat, climbed out from the many pastel cushions on the unmade bed and stretched out her claws.

"Morning, girl," Lucy cooed, reaching for her furry friend, in desperate need of a cuddle.

To her surprise, Chaos jumped out of her reach, arching her back as though Lucy were the enemy.

"What's wrong with you?" She followed the cat, who quickly hopped on top of her antique wardrobe and out of her reach. "Fine, stay up there!" Chaos had never run from her before; this morning was getting stranger by the minute.

Her old alarm clock told her she had an hour to open the library. She didn't have time to worry about her element being off or her cat ignoring her. Grabbing a pair of sheer spotty black tights and a dark green sweater dress which hugged her curves, she shoved them under her arm in a bundle, picking black ankle boots to keep her warm. Her feet were a little sore after going barefoot through the forest. Taking her phone from the nightstand, she grimaced when she saw she had twenty missed calls. Hopefully Rosie had her clothes and wasn't too mad at her for running off.

Why did I have to take off my clothes? I'm never drinking anything Luisa gives me again. She made her way down the attic stairs, listening to Rosie's panicked voice note once she reached the bathroom.

"LUCY! Call me when you get this! How could you run off like that? You scared us to death. I tracked you to Matherson Manor, but the gate was locked. How did you end up there? I've got your clothes – please, please let me know you're okay. I'm never letting you drink Luisa's tea ever again."

Thank goodness Rosie hadn't tracked her inside the manor and caused a scene in the middle of the night. Not wanting to wake her friend, Lucy decided a text would be best.

> I'm fine, please don't worry. I'm home safe and sound. Thank you for keeping my clothes and no I will never drink any of L's tea again! Sorry for scaring you all. I'll see you later and we can talk. X

In the shower, she untangled a cobweb from her mess of dark hair. The night came back to her in vague flashes.

Staring up at the stars by a pool, the manor rooftop. As she washed dirt from the random parts of her body, she could have sworn she remembered Benedict washing her feet. She groaned in humiliation, letting the hot water burn away the memories.

She didn't remember how she'd got to the room. Only the warmth of resting her head against Benedict's chest, the sound of his heartbeat. How she fitted perfectly in the crook of his arm.

No, no, no. I didn't fit perfectly anywhere. It was the tea. He was just being a decent human being. Oh God, did I ask him to stay with me? He has to know it was the tea. There's no way he thought I was in my right mind last night.

Steam billowed around her, and she darted out of the path of suddenly scorching water. *What the hell is up with the water?* She stared up at the nozzle. The dial was on her usual setting; she hadn't bumped it or anything. *Did I somehow heat the water? No way! It might be the boiler acting up again.* She got out, afraid more memories of the previous night would surface if she stayed in any longer.

Dressed, she swept her hair up into a loose ponytail. At least her fringe helped conceal her tired eyes, still red from having worn her contacts too long. Her glasses would also cover the less-than-perfect job she'd done on her eyeliner – something she wouldn't attempt again while hungover.

Leaning against the kitchen counter, Lucy stared at the toaster, waiting for it to pop. Her fringe had dried quickly, though the ends were a little damp. She pulled her sleeves over her hands; the house was always a little chilly in the mornings, thanks to all the old windows and stone walls. She hoped she wasn't getting a cold after running half-naked through the woods last night.

Without warning, the toaster burst into flames, filling the kitchen with black smoke.

"Holy hell!" she cried, yanking the plug from the wall before summoning her water magic to extinguish it. To her amazement, the flames only grew as she tried to use her element. She froze. The flames licked at the counter, threatening to spread.

"What in the goddess is going on?" Grams hurried up behind her in her floral robe. Her pink curlers were still in her white hair.

"I don't know! I tried to stop it, but I couldn't—" Lucinda stammered.

Grams clapped her hands. The fire disappeared, leaving only smoke behind. Lucy opened the windows above the sink, letting it escape, and wiped her steamed-up glasses, stopping when she realised her hands were shaking.

Grams took hold of her hands, trying to soothe her, only to snatch her hand away as though she'd been scalded. "You're burning up!" she exclaimed.

"What do you mean?" Lucy touched her hand to her cheek; it felt cool. "Feels normal to me."

"How did the fire start?" Grams asked, tightening her robe around her waist.

"I don't know. I was thinking about the binding with Benedict," she lied, unable to explain that she'd been remembering how her sort-of-fiancé had found her wandering in the woods in her underwear. "I can't explain it."

"How did you feel in the moment before the flames burst?"

"Overwhelmed? Then the toaster was on fire!"

"Could you have *set* it on fire?" Grams asked carefully, raising her fair eyebrows.

Lucy shook her head. "That's not possible. It was an old toaster. I probably put the setting up too high. I was preparing Chaos's breakfast; I could have hit the dial." It must have been a mistake. Why did her grandmother's questioning gaze make her so anxious? "Don't look at me like that! I can't be channelling fire! No one in our family has ever done that. Also, it's far too late for another element to show itself." Once the brain was fully developed at twenty-five, so did the possibility of developing another element.

"There's a first for everything. I think we should talk to your mum about this," Grams said, rocking back and forth on her slippered heels.

If it was just the fuse, why did Grams think my skin was burning? Lucy remembered the boiling water in the shower this morning. Had she caused that too? She needed to escape the conversation. She forced herself to smile, to conceal her concern so that Grams would let her leave.

"Later. I'm sure it's nothing to worry about. It was an old toaster – we're probably overthinking this." The last thing she wanted was her mum asking what she had been up to in the last twenty-four hours. There still the chance it was the tea, and she didn't want her mother to think she wasn't coping with the Benedict and coven situation.

"Okay. If you think it's nothing," Grams said, still looking as uneasy as Lucy felt. The smoke might've cleared, but the smell of burnt toast lingered.

On the counter, Chaos distracted them by kicking her breakfast bowl off the counter.

"I want you to call me at the tarot shop if anything else happens. I'm doing readings in the afternoon," Grams said, stroking the cat, who hissed at Lucy as she grabbed her bag from the counter.

"What's up with you?" Grams asked, picking Chaos up with ease. She snuggled into her shoulder. Grams frowned. "Odd. She never usually cuddles in like this."

Lucy rolled her eyes. "I don't know, she's been like that all morning." She kissed Gram's cheek, careful not to touch her, just in case. "I'm going to work. I'll see you tonight."

Closing the door behind her, she stared at her hands for a minute, but she didn't have time to think of who she'd woken up with this morning or last night's coven meeting if she was going to open the library on time. She grabbed a smoothie and a bagel on the way to the library, careful not to accidentally use her magic.

Gram's words played on her mind. What if she *had* set the fire?

Suddenly it hit her. Grams had mixed up the last ingredient of last night's makeshift love spell. *What if the mistake altered the meaning of the spell?* She figured the only place she would find answers was the very place she was headed.

Lucinda

Outside the library, flowers wilted on the windowsills. Lucy's gut told her not to try and use her element after what she had done to the toaster, but she needed to know if there was any trace of her water element left. She ran her fingers over the petals, expecting droplets to appear.

Her breath caught in her throat as the petals withered and crumbled to ash.

This can't be happening. She opened the library door quickly, wanting to hide before anyone saw what she'd done. The smell of old books and melted candles hit her, and she hesitated on the threshold. How could she open the library and have a normal day when something was wrong with her element?

If there was one person who would know if fire emanated from her, it would be Benedict. Finding her phone, she tried to call him, but it went straight to voicemail. Quickly, she left a note on the door of the library stating she'd be back soon.

"Answer your damn phone!" Lucy tried again, hurrying

across the quiet street. She kept her head low to avoid any small talk, but as she rounded the corner at the butchers, she nearly crashed into Mrs Crawford opening the awning of her flower shop. Muttering a half-arsed apology, she failed to stop. She was far more worried about what was wrong with her element than offending Mrs Crawford.

When she reached the Manor gate, she decided Benedict was either ignoring her calls or had turned off his phone. There was no way he wasn't awake at this hour, which didn't make her feel any better, since she had left him without a word and apparently somehow taken his element with her.

Benedict will be able to sense if there is any fire within me, she thought, making her way down the gravel path to the ivy-covered manor she'd fled only hours ago. *What if he sabotaged my element on purpose? The same way Grams and Mum cast a spell to stop the binding ritual?* She wanted to believe he wouldn't go that far. Such a move went way beyond any pranks they had pulled in the past, and elemental magic was dangerous if messed with, because it was tied to a person as much as their soul. It took years to master. Fire was the most volatile of the elements, and she didn't want to believe he would put her in danger like that.

"I believe congratulations are in order, Ms Hawthorne." Rodney, the doorman, tipped his top hat as she reached the revolving door.

"Thank you. How's the gout?" Lucy asked, trying to divert the conversation away from her engagement. She should've known word would travel fast. Rodney had worked at the Manor for as long as she could remember – longer than most could remember.

"All cleared up, thanks to your Grams," he said, his broad smile enhancing the lines around his eyes.

"I'm delighted to hear it, but I thought you were supposed to be taking some time off?" Lucy knew Grams had advised some time off his feet. She tried to recall whether he had a family or not, but all she knew about him was that he lived and worked in the manor. His whole world revolved around the Mathersons.

"Mr Matherson, the young master, gave me some time off while they were fitting the new chandeliers in the lobby a while ago and that was plenty. Like his father, he has a kind heart, even if he doesn't like to let others see it," Rodney said, straightening his tie.

In this case, Benedict's kindness wasn't a surprise. Sadly, Rodney had been in his life longer than his father.

To Lucy's relief, Rodney was distracted from further questions by the arrival of some guests checking out. As he took their bags, she stepped into the expansive lobby with its new low-hanging chandeliers and high-beamed ceilings. A rich navy carpet led from the entrance and up the grand staircase to the guest rooms. The back entrance she'd escaped through this morning wasn't nearly as pretty or grand.

Behind the reception desk, she was surprised to see Suzy, a vampire, was working the morning shift. Then again, the ceiling let in no sunlight, and the revolving door was the only entrance. As all the promotional material boasted, the Manor was inclusively designed to suit the needs of all magical folk. Benedict had even updated the interior and gone to bat with the historical society so he could put ramps and elevators in. She wondered if a bribe had helped sway their decision; they very rarely allowed changes to the oldest buildings in town.

"Hi, Suzy, I need to see Benedict... Mr Matherson, please," she told the day manager.

"I'm afraid Mr Matherson is dealing with a crisis," Suzy said, with a forced smile that exposed her vampiric canines.

Lucy wondered if the crisis was code for wanting to be left alone. However, she wasn't taking no for an answer, even if they were busy with morning checkout.

"Please, if you could call up to his room?" Afraid she'd set the hotel on fire, she couldn't help pulling her sleeves over her hands. She doubted she'd be appointed High Priestess if she destroyed one of the greatest sources of income in their small town. With the interior riddled with wooden beams and long tapestries, she didn't doubt the place would light like a match.

Suzy shook her head. "It's out of the question." Her pale skin was highlighted by the dark navy uniform, white shirt and flawlessly tied black tie, matching the Manor's interior.

"I'll forgive your late returns for the last few books you borrowed," Lucy bargained.

"It's not my fault you aren't open at night. Otherwise, I would've returned them on time," Suzy argued quietly, so the guests checking out beside them wouldn't notice.

The library had a night return box, but Lucy didn't have time to be petty.

"Okay, forget about the late fees. Please can you try to call up to his room? I wouldn't bother you, or him, if it wasn't urgent," she pleaded. If Suzy was telling the truth, what emergency was he dealing with? She hoped it had nothing to do with his element. The thought caused her hands to simmer. She desperately needed to get out of the lobby.

Suzy smiled at the guests behind her. "I'm sorry, but

there is nothing I can do. Please move aside so I can check in the next guests."

Lucy glanced at the family. They looked like magless, but she couldn't be sure, and she didn't want the coven to hear she was causing a scene at the Manor, again.

"Sorry to keep you waiting," she told them. "I've just got one more thing."

Suzy sighed.

Lucy leaned in close. "The new monster romance came in yesterday. There's a waiting list, but I could let you have it first."

"I can't call him. I like my job, and Benedict lets me sleep in the basement so I save on rent while I'm saving for daylight protection on my cottage. I'm not risking it," Suzy said, tapping her nails on the counter.

"I don't want to cause any trouble. How about you tell me where he is? In his wing? Has he gone out?"

The family behind started to huff about the wait. Suzy smiled politely at them, but Lucy could see she was weakening. She put her hands together in prayer and pouted.

"Fine! You didn't hear it from me. Mr Matherson was by the fountain, and since he hasn't checked the guest count for the day, he's probably still there."

"Thank you, thank you!" Lucy patted the counter, delighted. "I'll make sure you get your hands on the book first."

Suzy beamed, letting her professional mask slip. "You'd better! I need to know if the princess rescues the count from the demon king."

"You and me both. I'll leave it in the pickup box tonight," Lucy promised, before thanking the family for their patience and heading out.

"Benedict?" She found him pacing by the old fountain, his back to her. She wondered if he'd kept Gram's koi fish; it had been a rather expensive prank. Damp grass squished under her feet as she approached him. She couldn't believe he still hadn't noticed her.

She paused, watching as Benedict placed his hand on the old fountain. Instantly, the water stopped flowing. When he pulled his hand away, clear water flowed from the statue of lovers again.

Water. He has my element! Her heart pounded, and heat throbbed in her hands. Benedict looked as startled as she felt. She opened her mouth to call to him, but then she saw the dark clouds forming above them.

"Lucinda?" he asked, finally seeing her. "What's happening to me?" She'd never heard him sound so frightened.

"I don't know," she stammered, clasping her hands tightly, trying to calm down. The more her mind raced, the harder they throbbed. *Could the spell have done this?* Words flooded out before she could stop them. "No, they said my element would only call to another. There's no way the spell could have switched them. Why would the spell even affect you?"

But Grams used the wrong ingredient. Black pepper instead of bat's blood... Lucy's skin burned as if flames were trying to crawl out of her to get back to Benedict. Squeezing her eyes shut so she wouldn't have to see his panicked expression, she tried to focus on slowing her heart rate.

"What the hell are you talking about? What spell? Did you do something to us?"

The smell of burning wood made Lucy open her eyes again. Bright red flames ate up the lush green hedgerows surrounding them despite the rain suddenly cascading from the stormy sky. Benedict stared at the flames, his hands on his head. Heavy droplets landed on her scorching skin and sizzled.

Transfixed with horror by what she had done, Lucy barely felt it when he grabbed her shoulders.

"Stop the storm, I'll put out the fire," he pleaded, tightening his grip on her. "What the hell are you thinking?"

Lucy glanced up at the emptying dark clouds. Her element had caused the storm, but it was emanating from his emotions. The cool water against her skin snapped her back to reality, and the flames began to reduce before finally extinguishing.

"You can't put it out!" she yelled over the rain, which was growing heavier by the second. "It's *your* storm, I'm not doing this!"

"That's not possible!"

Lucy stepped into his space, forcing him to listen to her. The burning within her subsided, but the storm continued to rage, confirming her worst fear.

"I set the hedgerows on fire, but *you* started the storm to put it out," she explained, but her words only caused the rain to pelt harder. It was probably his desire to protect the manor and the grounds from the flames that had started the storm, whether he had meant to summon it or not. Elements tended to react impulsively.

She placed her hands on his chest, feeling his heart race. "I can explain, but you need to calm down or you're going to flood the whole town." She kept her voice level and calm, trying to put aside her own confusion and fear before the storm turned nasty.

"I don't understand. How could I be doing this?" He was staring at the sky like it would answer.

"Just breathe, and close your eyes," she ordered, hoping he would listen to her for once.

Benedict's jaw clenched, but he hesitantly obeyed. With each breath, the rain lessened until the dark clouds cleared and the blue sky returned. Lucy loosened her grasp on him as she felt his heart rate settle beneath his soaking black shirt.

"What the fuck is going on with my element?" he demanded, looking down at her for answers. "*Our* elements."

"Can you let go of me first?" she pleaded, staring at his hands.

His expression softened. Muttering an apology, he released her.

"We need to remain calm. Getting worked up will make you lose control again," Lucy told him. He grimaced defensively. "Make *us* lose control again."

His shoulders dropped a little as she split the blame, though preventing a fight was more for her benefit. Getting upset risked starting another fire and harming the guests, who now felt far too close for safety's sake.

"Calm? I've got your element, and you started a fire. Why would our elements trade places? What spell were you babbling about? Did you do this to us? Is this payback for what Gwendoline did at the meeting? I had no idea she was going to suggest a binding ritual." He kept his voice low, but the weight of his words chilled her.

"This isn't my fault. I didn't cast any spell," she said, telling a half-truth.

His eyes narrowed. "Why are you so calm about this? If you didn't do anything, then why are you here?"

His panic told her he hadn't done anything to their elements. Lucy's stomach flipped. That only left one possibility.

There's no way Benedict is the man Grams's spell called to! It must have gone wrong. Between the wrong ingredient and our agreement with the coven, we're technically destined to be together, but by choice. Perhaps both clauses caused the spell to divert from its course. This is why you don't mess with love magic!

She couldn't explain her thoughts to him, but she was afraid that if she left him in the dark it would only put them in more danger. She needed to get the Hawthorne grimoire and see what ingredients were in an element swap spell to compare it with what her family had cast.

"Our elements have switched," she admitted.

"Switched? How? I've never even heard of such a thing!" Benedict ran his hands through the damp hair sticking to his temples.

"I don't know." Unable to meet his accusing gaze, she pulled at her sleeves. She was terrified that if she revealed the truth, he'd drag her before the coven and reveal what her family had done. If he did, she wouldn't be the only one banished from Foxford.

His eyes narrowed, scrutinising her guilty expression. "You're lying."

"I'm not." She was, but she wasn't ready to tell him about the spell. Not when his reaction could get not only her kicked out of the coven, but her mother and Grams as well. She wasn't going to let their mistake ruin the Hawthorne legacy. They had done it to protect her, and she was going to protect them.

"We've known each other since we were born. I know when you're lying, pumpkin." He drew closer, and her heart began to pound.

"Don't come too close! I don't want to start another fire," she begged, thinking of the toaster. Even if setting him on fire would solve a few of her problems, she didn't want to be stuck with his element for the rest of her life.

"You're not leaving these gardens until you confess." Benedict folded his arms.

Lucy backed away to the burnt hedgerows to make her escape. "Just give me some time, and I'll fix this!"

He blocked her path. "You can't leave me like this without any explanation! Start explaining, or I'll go to the coven right now! Regardless of whatever the hell caused this, we're a danger to not only ourselves but the town."

Lucy knew she couldn't outrun him, and even if she did it'd make her look guilty. Taking a deep breath, she prayed he wouldn't use what she was about to say against her. "Grams cast a spell." She left her mum out of it. If he went to the coven, she didn't want to see her mum stripped of her position for trying to spare her daughter a loveless life.

Benedict's gaze darkened. "What type of spell?"

Lucy stumbled through the explanation. "Grams meant well. It wasn't supposed to swap our elements... You shouldn't have been affected at all. If anything, it was meant to keep us apart—"

"Pumpkin, stop stalling!"

"I'm trying to explain! I'm only making sense of it myself, so stop yelling at me!" she snapped, trying to ignore the hateful nickname. "Grams heard about the binding ritual. She thought casting a harmless little spell would spare us both from a loveless marriage. The spell was meant to call out to my soulmate so neither of us would have to go through the binding. She figured that if we couldn't be bound, and with so much time having passed for us to make up for past indiscretions, they'd forget about voting one of us out and we could get back to our lives."

Benedict stood frightfully still. She'd expected him to yell, pace, or storm out of the garden. Hell, he hadn't even blinked.

"In other words, our souls wouldn't bond during the ritual because you'd have already found your soulmate. Essentially, forcing an election." He sounded far calmer than he should.

She nodded at the unveiled truth.

"Are you crazy? Love magic can be lethal, unpredictable —" He paused and turned sharply. "When was the spell cast?"

"After the coven meeting. Why does that matter?"

"Last night, I burnt my running shorts... it doesn't matter. In the woods, I was dizzy just before I came across you..." His disjointed thoughts made it difficult for her to keep up. "I could barely create a flame when we went through the wine cellar. The spell must have been starting to take effect. The timing fits, and it explains my lack of control."

She considered that. "When I woke up at the manor, I couldn't summon my element," she admitted. She should have known the tea could never have had such a profound effect.

"I can't believe you would be daring enough to get mixed up with love magic! Love is one of the most powerful forces – you can't trick or entice it. Now we're stuck like this, our elements trapped in the wrong body!"

"But it wasn't meant to swap our elements. Grams used the wrong ingredient, which must've altered the spell. I'm going to go through the love spells in the library and see how the ingredient altered the potion's chemistry. There were some mentions of elemental spells in the grimoire I recently received from the Order. I can double-check and see if I can fix this before anyone finds out," Lucy told him, hoping that all would be sorted before the day was out.

Benedict's glower told her he was unconvinced. "The spell worked. It called to your intended."

"When I agreed to the binding ritual, *I* became your intended. Even if there was a mix-up in the ingredients, the spell did what it was meant to do, bring you closer to your intended. What's a better way to do that than to swap our elements!" He paced back and forth, his hands on his hips. She had never seen him so flustered.

"But our agreeing to be together can't hold the same weight as those who are fated to be together, surely? Like you said, love is a powerful force. I don't think an agreement could alter our fate, just like that."

He stopped pacing. "If anything, it could hold more weight. We decided against what our fate might be, and chose for ourselves."

"But we chose out of necessity, not out of any true desire to be together!"

"We're going round in circles," he huffed.

"Let's simplify this. How about we focus on the wrong ingredient for now? I'll do some research and see if I can find a reversal spell," Lucy said. She couldn't take any more of his ands, ifs, or buts.

He arched a brow. "And if it wasn't the wrong ingredient?"

"Then maybe our elements have a sense of humour and decided to pull a prank on us," she quipped, trying to ease the tension.

His scowl erased her smile. "There is nothing funny

about this. We're both ill-equipped to handle each other's element. This is dangerous."

She'd have been entertained by his discomfort if she weren't so terrified about setting the town on fire. "I'm only trying to lighten the mood! Yelling at each other isn't going to make getting through this any easier. Our other magic doesn't seem to be affected by the swap. We just need to try and refrain from using elemental magic."

"That's not going to be easy, but I suppose we have no other choice," he sighed.

The ensuing silence could have lasted five minutes or fifteen, both getting used to the idea of being stuck with each other's element until further notice.

"If you were willing to go this far to stop our binding, why did you agree in the first place?" he asked eventually.

"I didn't cast the spell! I'd never have gone so far." Lucy squished a soggy leaf under her foot, avoiding his gaze. "I hate the idea of the coven thinking I was trying to deceive them."

"Doesn't explain why you agreed to the ritual." He tilted his head so she'd look at him.

Lucy wanted to ask him the same thing, but she *had* agreed first. She didn't want him to suspect what her family had – that she had some love for him buried deep, deep, *deep* down somewhere.

"I thought we could buy ourselves some time. Push out the vote so that the coven would've time to see that the town needs *both* of us, and to see who'd make the best leader," she reasoned.

He nodded, but stayed silent. She would have given anything to know what he was thinking.

"If anything, my agreeing helped both of us. There's no way of knowing which of us they'd have picked if there was a rash vote that night. Now we've time to prove ourselves," she added, needing him on her side.

His sudden low laughter unnerved her. It wasn't the reaction she had expected.

"Only a Hawthorne could look on the bright side right now. We might have time to prove we deserve to stay, but that's only if you don't set the town on fire, and I don't flood it."

Benedict sat on the edge of the fountain with his elbows on his knees; the weight of her admissions had drained the colour from his cheeks. Defeat wasn't a good look on him. Lucy blamed herself.

"Could we try and undo the spell?" he asked, looking up at her. His hope only added to the weight on her shoulders.

"It depends. There are only two ways to look at this," she began, standing in front of him. They'd both calmed down enough to talk rationally. "If what you said is true, and the spell worked and swapped our elements because we agreed to be together, then it should wear off once the ritual is over."

"And the other way?" he asked, staring at the grass.

"If the wrong ingredient altered the spell from its natural course, then I might be able to reverse it. Theoretically, performing the correct spell might switch our elements back." It was a gamble, but she didn't want him to freak out even further by admitting that.

"Our options are: to be bound to get our elements back. Or to perform the corrected spell, which will reverse our elements, but it might stop you from being bound to me?" he summarised, finally meeting her eye.

"We might not have to complete the binding ritual to get our elements back. The spell was set to last *until* All

Hallows' Eve; we should switch back anyway. If the corrected spell works, and I find my soulmate, then we'd be spared from spending an eternity together." She hoped her logic was sound; she couldn't imagine his fire coursing through her veins for the rest of her life. It felt far too... intimate.

"Either way, our elements might be stuck like this until All Hallows' Eve?" He didn't sound as pleased as she thought he'd be about their not being bound. She'd thought he'd be jumping for joy.

Lucy nodded.

"In that case, let's assume we've got to wait out the spell effects until then. If casting the correct spell doesn't work, we can reassess. In the meantime, we need rules to protect ourselves."

She had to respect him for thinking ahead. If the Mathersons were good at anything, it was a cover-up.

"We can't tell anyone about our elements switching. If the coven learns of this, neither of us will be appointed." It seemed obvious, but she wanted his word.

"Goes without saying. I won't tell a soul," he promised. "The last thing I need is another blot in the Matherson ledger."

Lucy's phone rang, making her jump. Rosie's name lit up the screen. She answered, not wanting her friend to sniff her out.

"Why am I getting calls about the library being closed? Caffeinated students worried about their potion exams are not the best people to talk to first thing in the morning," Rosie grumbled, clearly suffering from her late night.

"Sorry. I'm running behind. Don't worry about it," Lucy said quickly before hanging up, not wanting her friend to hear Benedict in the background.

"I was thinking... we were both so worried about being cast out that we agreed to the binding. And now, if the coven finds out about our elements, we'd be cast out. Together."

"Your point?" She folded her arms.

"Maybe we are destined to be together," he said, his voice edged with uncertainty rather than humour.

"I've got to go. If I don't open the library, Rosie is going to know something is up," she said, putting her phone in her bag. Now was not the time to unpack whatever he was trying to get at.

"I can come with you, help look for a spell," he suggested, clearly forgetting he looked like a drowned rat. A strikingly handsome drowned rat.

"It's probably best if we avoid each other as usual, so we don't make our elements worse." She didn't want him breathing over her shoulder as she tried to fix the mess her family had created. "Rosie will be suspicious if we're suddenly hanging out, and it would give the town the wrong impression of our relationship."

"Didn't you say the spell was meant to bring us closer together? Our elements might act out if we stay away from each other." Benedict followed her to the breakfast terrace. Luckily, the rain had sent the guests inside.

"It was intended to find my soulmate, not the person I agreed to be in a political marriage with. I still think it's the wrong ingredient that did this, and not our agreement," she said as they reached the doors. She didn't want to entertain the idea that they might be soulmates.

"Fine. Call me if anything goes wrong, and try not to set the library on fire. We should refrain for using our – your – my element as much as we can."

His calm demeanour troubled her. "I can control your

element, don't worry about that," she scoffed, wondering if he was willing to let her leave because any loss of control would reveal their secret to the coven. She didn't like feeling paranoid, but it was easier to think the worst of him than imagine he might trust her. Even the thought made her shiver.

He smiled at her retort.

"Get into some dry clothes – you look like a drowned rat," she snipped as she headed down the grand staircase, feeling him close behind. At least in all this chaos, the topic of last night hadn't come up.

"Pumpkin?" Benedict said as she reached the last step. His soft tone made her uneasy.

"Yes," Lucy hissed, wondering why he had to ruin such a civil conversation.

Glancing over her shoulder, his eyes lingered on her back like he knew something. "I never knew you got a tattoo."

Lucy flushed. He must have seen the crescent moon between her shoulder blades last night. Well, he'd seen pretty much all of her.

"Looks good." He winked, standing at the end of the staircase.

"Hope you enjoyed the view," Lucy said, trying not to let him see that he'd caught her off guard, "because you'll never see it again."

As embarrassed as she was about his discovery, she was relieved he didn't say anything else about last night's events. They had enough to worry about, and their night beneath the stars wasn't one of them.

Benedict

"Except in my dreams!" Benedict called, and Lucinda flipped him off across the lobby. He hadn't planned to tell her about the tattoo, but he couldn't resist an opportunity to see her flustered.

Droplets fell from his hair down the back of his shirt, reminding him of his current state. He didn't want his guests to see him, as she had put it, looking like a drowned rat.

The private elevator took him to the fifth floor – his private quarters. Shrouded in the darkness of his wing, far from any guests, he waved his hand to light the torches... only to be greeted by darkness.

"Damn spell." Benedict dropped his head. The torches helped keep away the draughts the stone walls attracted, no matter how frequently he had the gaps filled. "I should've known better than to agree to the binding. The Hawthornes are meant to be Good," he muttered to himself.

His wet shoes squelched against the carpet as he took the silver key from his pocket and unlocked the tall double doors. No one else had a key; his quarters were strictly off-limits. Shivering, he tossed his damp shirt onto the black velvet couch in the sitting area, regretting his decision not to install lighting instead of keeping the old candelabras on the walls. There was only one large window by his desk to let in some light. It looked out on the whole town; these rooms used to be a watch tower, dating back to when there had been a threat of invasion during the war on witches.

"They wouldn't have pulled such a stunt if Mum hadn't put forward my name. Without that, we wouldn't have had to agree to the binding ritual." He wasn't used to the cold – usually his fire kept him warm, no matter the weather. At least Lucinda's coat had protected her from the worst of the storm he'd created. He'd had no idea how much power she held in that small, curvy frame. She was a force to be reckoned with.

I could go to the coven and tell them I changed my mind about the binding... but since the town knew of their engagement, he feared damaging the Matherson name. *People need to see us as steady and reliable. Once the spell runs its course, we can figure out what to do.*

He considered stopping by the Hawthornes. In two days they'd have dinner together, so he could be sure to see and talk to Lucinda. Maybe even clear the air between him and her family; given the spell they'd cast, he got the impression he wasn't in their good books. It wasn't like the visit would be unusual. Ever since his father passed, he'd been dragged along to Hawthorne House on a regular basis. Not that he minded all that much: Grams Hawthorne was a sweet old lady, and Wilhelmina was one hell of a cook.

Benedict's mum had always left the cooking to Dad, and when he'd died, the kitchen, filled of his untouched pots and pans, had sent her into a deep depression. They didn't have to worry about such memories now, since their old kitchen was full of chefs and built to feed their guests. He'd made sure she never had to stand over a stove again, unless she desired it.

He was dripping everywhere – he needed to get changed. He moved around his desk, but in the dim light he caught his shin on a side table. "Son of a—" he exclaimed, rubbing his shin. "Pumpkin is going to pay for this."

He glanced at the desk drawers, but he wouldn't have any matches to light the candelabras; he'd never needed them before. He sighed, exhausted by the day that had barely begun.

In his bedroom, he quickly pulled on a white T-shirt and grey sweats. He loved his neutral shades just as much as he loved order and structure. Unlike Lucinda in her many colours – the definition of chaos. Usually, he'd never leave his quarters dressed like this, but all he cared about right now was finding some matches and lighting the fireplace.

He thought of the spell again as he stormed out of his room. There was no way he and Lucinda were soulmates. The spell had made a mistake, either because of the ingredient she had mentioned or their agreement. But he couldn't help but shake the feeling there was more to it.

Maybe the solution is for one of us to leave town – but as he marched down the stairs to the third floor (the fourth four was strictly for vampires and nocturnal guests; it would be a waste of time to search there), did he get struck by a sinking feeling at the thought? The rush of unease stopped him in his tracks. He wasn't sure what disturbed him more

– being bound to Lucinda forever, or never seeing her again.

Thankfully, he didn't have time to linger on the revelation. A cleaner's cart sat outside the first guest room he passed. Benedict's sudden appearance startled the cleaner coming out of the room.

"Sir? Can I help you with something?" Marty asked, his arms bundled with dirty towels. Glancing at Benedict's sweats, bare feet and dripping hair, Marty added, "Were you looking for a towel?"

Benedict groaned internally. He prided himself on professionalism, and he certainly didn't want the coven to hear he'd walked around his hotel barefoot.

"I'm fine, but there was a problem with my shower. I was on my way to look for someone to help when a guest asked me for some matches," he lied, trying to stop the gossip before it started.

Marty nodded. "I'm sorry a guest disturbed you, sir. If you give me the room number, I can bring them over," he offered, dropping the dirty towels into his cart.

"No need to trouble yourself – their room is on my way back." Benedict grabbed a packet of matches from the cart. "Let's keep this between us."

Marty nodded, closing the door to the room he'd finished cleaning. Benedict knew he could be trusted; he'd worked for their family since before the manor had become a hotel.

"Can I assist with anything else? Perhaps some slippers?"

"No, no, you carry on." Benedict hurried away. It was hard to sound like the boss while barefoot.

Back in the safety of his quarters, he lit the torches and hoped the rest of his day would be less eventful.

He'd spoken too soon. His younger brother was sitting cross-legged on his desk. Benedict jumped.

"What are you wearing?" Peter asked with a grin.

His ash-blond hair had grown out since he'd last made an appearance, and he was wearing a green hoodie and black jeans. Usually, Grim Reapers were meant to keep their hair short and always wear their black robes, but his brother had a way of charming people into letting him bend the rules. All Mathersons did.

"Clothes. What are you doing here?" Benedict asked, waving Peter away from his desk.

"Nice to see you too." Peter raised his eyebrow, moving around him. His long, black coat signified that he was on the job, even if it wasn't strictly Reaper uniform.

Benedict had forgotten how much he'd grown. The brothers were nearly the same height now, whereas in Benedict's mind Peter was still the sixteen-year-old who barely reached his shoulders.

"Peter, I don't have time for whatever you're up to." His work would be building up thanks to all the morning's disturbances, and he didn't want his brother delaying him further with his mischief.

"I'm up to nothing," Peter protested.

That would be a first, Benedict thought.

"You missed the anniversary of my death last week. Thought I'd pop in and make sure you were okay."

Peter had aged since his death to look like he was in his early twenties, but on the day of his anniversary he appeared as his sixteen-year-old self, who'd died in his favourite football jersey. Benedict found it too painful to see him that way; even if he wanted to honour the day of Peter's passing, it wasn't as if he was gone. Thanks to his job as a Grim, Peter maintained his physical form despite not being part of this world or the next.

"I was busy. I didn't have time to stop by the grave," Benedict lied, hating the pathetic excuse as it left his lips. "And you don't leave me alone long enough for me to miss you."

Peter placed a hand mockingly over his heart. "Ouch. Way to make your baby brother feel loved."

"Which poor soul are you haunting this time?" Benedict asked, giving him a quick hug.

"No one in particular – and technically Grim Reapers aren't ghosts, so we can't haunt anyone," Peter reminded him, picking up the guest ledger from the desk and flicking through the names.

Benedict's chest tightened. He didn't have time to deal with an in-house death right now. "Stay away from the guests! You frightened that elderly couple of magless to death last time." He wished the Grims wouldn't take souls at the Manor. People tended not to think about dying in hotels, but it happened more than many assumed. "The clean-up and paperwork always add to my never-ending to-do list."

"It was their time! It's not like I enjoy the job. I did give them an extra week to enjoy their last vacation. The least I could do was let them have some fun here before I collected. A promise is a promise, though; I won't work on the premises again." Peter crossed his heart.

"If you aren't here to collect a soul, then to what do I owe the pleasure?" Benedict asked, ducking through the archway that divided the living space from his bedroom and taking a new suit from his wardrobe. Another black shirt, too, but this time he decided to forget the tie.

Peter leant against the archway, peeling a banana. He

also liked to steal food. "Other than to enjoy your company, I heard from Lucinda's dearly departed uncle Gregory that you and she are to be bound. I swear, if I had a heart to stop, hearing those words would've done it. I had to come and hear it for myself."

He studied his brother's reaction as he tossed the peel over his shoulder. The dead don't tend to care about the mess they leave behind.

Benedict pulled at his collar, which suddenly felt too tight. "Word travels fast in the spiritual realm," he mused, not wishing to discuss it.

"He's my mentor in all things Grim. Gregory was so shocked by what Grams had told him, I don't blame him for not being able to keep it to himself," Peter said, his mouth full.

"So you came to me to confirm it?"

"You caught me. He wanted to make sure Grams wasn't winding him up. I couldn't say no; I'd still be stuck in the soul-sorting department if he hadn't helped me get promoted early."

Benedict was grateful to Gregory Hawthorne for helping his brother return to them and being there for Peter after his early passing, but he'd still have preferred for his brother not to have become a Grim at all. Even if it would have meant never seeing him again. It was a hard life, taking souls, and there was no leaving the job once accepted.

"It seems we can't escape Hawthornes even in the afterlife," he muttered.

Peter chuckled and plonked himself on the couch. "Since when have you ever wanted to escape a Hawthorne? My whole life – well, former life – you always found a way to torment poor Lucy. She was so nice to us when Dad passed. She held my hand at the funeral, and Grams stopped Mum from going after the killers. We would've been orphans if they hadn't interceded."

"It's Lucinda," Benedict corrected him. Peter was right about the Hawthornes' help during one of the worst stages of his life. It hadn't been improved by his brother's death only months later.

"Everyone calls her Lucy except you. What did you call her? Sunflower?" Peter narrowed his hazel eyes. He looked nothing like a Matherson, with their usual striking blue eyes and black hair. He'd always been the light to their dark. However, his dabbling in dark magic had cost him his life. "It was a type of seed..."

Benedict finished styling his hair, ignoring him.

"Pumpkin! That's it!" Peter snapped his fingers, beaming in triumph. "You've always had an odd fascination with her. I mean, who didn't? Beautiful and smart. If only I were five years older, and not forbidden from having relations with the living. Any man who gets to go home to her every night..." Peter whistled.

"Watch it! You're not too dead to have your mouth washed out with soap," Benedict warned, suspecting that Peter was only trying to get a rise out of him.

"Why did you decide to name her after something she hates?"

Peter didn't need to know the reason he called Lucinda pumpkin, his favourite type of pie. Her hatred of the fruit only played in his favour. He loved how her irritation caused her to blush, highlighting the cluster of freckles across her nose.

"I take back what I said," Benedict said, fixing his silver M cufflinks to his wrists. "Please feel free to take as many souls as you like from the manor."

Peter raised his hands, decorated with an assortment of rings, in defence. "Trying to get rid of me? I understand it must be hard to admit your feelings for the one person who despises you almost as much as you pretend to despise her." He sighed, getting up from the couch. "Love is wasted on the living. Tell Mum I'll stop by soon."

"Still avoiding her?" Benedict slipped on a new pair of socks, avoiding Peter's opinion on his non-existent relationship with Lucinda.

"Only for this month. When she sees me around the anniversary, she won't stop crying about my wasted potential. At least I got to come back; collecting souls isn't a bad gig. You could say I get the best of both worlds." Peter winked. Even in death he looked on the bright side. Benedict wondered if he was truly happy, never finding peace, always stuck in the in-between. They'd never discussed it, and he doubted if they ever would.

"Have you seen Dad?" he couldn't help asking, even if he already knew the answer.

His brother shook his head. "I think he's at peace. Otherwise, our paths would've crossed in the past few years." Peter rested a reassuring hand on his shoulder, putting an end to the sore subject. It was Peter's desire to see their father which had cost him his life, so Benedict could only imagine how hard it was to accept this.

One of the candles on the wall went out. He used the opposing candle to reignite it, then caught himself as he realised what he had done. Hopefully Peter had missed the small detail, but—

"Why didn't you use your fire?" Peter tilted his head in concern.

"I'm tired." Benedict shrugged his jacket over his broad shoulders, not wanting to reveal his and Lucinda's elemental switch. The less his brother knew about the spell, the better.

"You've always been a terrible liar." Peter blew out the candles on the candelabra closest to him. "Light it."

Gritting his teeth, Benedict focused on the candelabra, but nothing happened. He was afraid that if he forced it, Lucinda's element would flood the place.

"I don't have to prove anything to you." He turned his back on Peter and the extinguished candles.

"Holy shit, you *can't* light it."

Benedict glared at him. "You want all the damn guests to hear you?"

"Sorry." Peter covered his mouth. "What's up with your element? Don't tell me you were messing with the dark side. I'm meant to be the black sheep of the family, and Mum needs one of us to live to a ripe old age or she'll start resurrecting us!"

Benedict ran his hands through his damp hair. There was no way he was getting to work without explaining. "Lucinda's family cast a spell in an attempt to stop the binding ritual. It backfired," he admitted.

Peter drew back as though struck by some invisible force. "They stripped you of your magic? That's a punishable crime."

"No, nothing so extreme. I still have my magic," Benedict said hastily, afraid Peter would disappear to confront them.

Peter frowned, glancing at the damp clothes dripping over the chair in the corner. Benedict watched him put two and two together.

"*You* have the Hawthorne element?" Peter laughed, placing a hand over his grin. "Wow! My big bro crossed over to the Good side."

"If only you had done the same."

Peter faked a wince. "That cut deep."

"What doesn't kill you..." Benedict muttered. "And there is no Good or Bad side anymore. That's all in the past. We're one community now."

"Yeah, yeah, peace and unity. It's easy for those who've always been on the Good side to believe. They haven't had to suffer with the prejudice of *our* legacy – same with dozens of other families."

"It doesn't help when we break the rules and use dark magic," Benedict pointed out.

Peter ignored the reference to his own mistakes; he'd already paid for them with his life. "It's easy to break the rules when people expect little of you. Anyway, it doesn't matter now. Lucy must be losing her mind without her water. It must feel like losing a limb!"

Of course he laughs at me and pities her. He's only my flesh and blood. Benedict remained silent.

Peter recoiled, as though reading his mind. Benedict hated how well his brother could read his expressions. "Wait. Does his mean she has our fire?"

"Keep this to yourself. We don't need this getting out – the swap wasn't intentional," Benedict warned, hoping his brother wouldn't tell his mentor or his superiors. He didn't want the Hawthornes to get in trouble with higher forces. It would be bad enough if the coven found out.

"This is crazy. I didn't think it was possible to exchange elements. What are you going to do?"

"Hope we switch back. The spell was meant to keep us from being bound, so once All Hallows' Eve passes, we should swap back." There was no point rambling about the wrong ingredient and potion troubleshoots. Lucinda's element stirred within him, testing its shell, knowing it was in the wrong vessel.

"The town would be up in arms if they knew this happened. She spends all her time amongst those dusty relics; she might find a way to swap you back sooner rather than later," Peter reasoned. His serious expression was replaced with a cheeky grin. "This might even bring you two closer together."

Benedict didn't want him interfering. "I think we're close enough."

He made a mental note to stop by the library after work. In the meantime, he'd try to keep his stress levels down and hope no water-based drama happened. He didn't want to accidentally flood the hotel when it would be at capacity coming up to the Autumn Festival in a couple of weeks.

"When you see Lucy, try a smile. You'll get farther with her that way than with your usual grimace." Peter headed for the door as Benedict found himself wishing the dead would stay dead.

"I don't need to get anywhere with her," he said, opening the door. "We just need to swap our elements back."

"I don't know why the two of you can't get along. She was always so nice to me."

"She's nice to *everyone*," Benedict huffed, pushing his brother out of the door and into the corridor.

"Except you." Peter smirked. "Maybe that's why you look at her with those moony eyes – because she's the one thing you can't have."

"Be gone. I'm sure the underworld misses you."

Peter rolled his eyes. "Careful, brother, don't get too worked up. I wouldn't want you to flood the place."

He disappeared before Benedict could react.

It killed him to admit his brother was right. Lucinda was kind, polite and Good through and through. It only made Benedict want to corrupt her even more; making her act out made him feel like they were on the same level. And maybe then he would feel worthy of her.

He slammed the door behind him, silencing the demons his brother had awakened. They would never be anything, and he'd accepted that long ago. No spell or coven proposal was going to change that.

Lucinda

Having spent two days scouring through the library shelves and reading enough love and elemental spells to make her head spin, Lucy finally found what she was looking for – in the aged pages of a Matherson grimoire, of all things.

She ran her fingers over the ingredients, comparing them to the list Grams had used. Mum and Grams had altered a Matherson protection potion. The potion pre-dated the war on witches. Its purpose was to call out to lost loved ones to help them find their way home. The ingredients made no reference to black pepper, confirming Grams's mistake.

She wanted to let out a shriek of relief at finally having got somewhere, but thought the better of it, considering the library was crowded with people studying. Taking her phone out of her back pocket, she texted him what she'd found and explained her theory that the black pepper/bat's blood swap had changed the potion's effect from calling elements to exchanging them.

Waiting for Benedict's reply, she delved deeper into the grimoire for more answers.

Her phone pinged with a text as she discovered there were no concoctions or incantations listed to stop the effects of the potion.

> Is there any way to reverse it?

She had been hoping for a little more enthusiasm.

> Not that I can find, but the potion's effects, using the correct ingredients, should wear off when our elements decide it's safe – whatever the hell that means. However, given the ingredient mix-up, we can't know for sure. Maybe if we make the potion again with the right ingredients, our elements might switch back. The only problem is that from what I've read so far, the further we are from each other, the more intensely our elements will try to bring us together.

Waiting for his reply, she copied down the correct ingredients from the grimoire and prayed a redo would work. She wanted Benedict to read the ingredients himself in case there was something she was missing. She'd never thought she'd see the day when she'd be seeking a second opinion from him.

> What if brewing the potion again only strengthens the effects?

I can't know for sure. If it doesn't work, I also found something in my notes from the Hawthorne grimoire the order sent me, but it's a curse-stripping potion and it's old magic. We could end up losing our elements altogether. I haven't been able to get down to the vault to double-check, but it's a back-up option.

It's been two days, why haven't you checked the vault?

I have my translations to work off. Rosie is only coming in for the evening study hall so I can't leave the desk.

Why didn't you call her in? I think this is an emergency.

Stop snapping at me! I couldn't. She would've smelt something was up.

There was a pause before he responded.

I'm not snapping. When you know, text me.

I'm working as hard as I can. A little patience would be nice.

Three dots told her Benedict was typing, but she shoved her phone in her bag when she saw Rosie putting her umbrella in the holder by the door.

"I'm sorry I'm late, I got stuck in traffic dropping Harriet and Luisa to the train station." Rosie hurried around the desk and wrapped her arms around Lucy. Her coat transferred droplets of rain to Lucy's jumper; the autumn showers were coming more frequently.

"Don't worry about it, I didn't even feel the day go. I've been lost in some research on the final spells in the grimoire," she answered, hating to lie.

"I feel like we haven't really had a chance to talk since the other night," Rosie said, eyeing her suspiciously. Lucy didn't want to admit she'd been avoiding her, but she couldn't risk her finding out about her element. "You've been a little off since you disappeared from the lake."

"I'm fine. Probably a little burnt out and anxious about the Order member set to appear. As for the lake, I don't think I'll be drinking Luisa's tea again anytime soon. I'll be back to normal once All Hallows' Eve passes and we can get back to our usual routine." Lucy removed the tote bag containing the grimoire from Rosie's desk chair. She didn't want her to see she was bringing it home. They were dancing around the topic of her engagement, but since Rosie had been working the evenings, there hadn't been time to talk.

"I forgot how lethal her tea was. At least you went home. I shifted form and ended up drinking out of my neighbour's dog bowl." Rosie grimaced, shrugging off her jacket and collapsing in the seat beside her.

"Not your cute neighbour?" Lucy was relieved she wasn't the only one who'd suffered a night of humiliation.

"Yes, and he saw me! I don't think my ego will ever recover." Rosie turned on the old computer on her side of the desk that was in desperate need of replacement. She had a laptop for her own work, but the computers were mandatory for checking books in and out.

"I'm sure he found it funny," Lucy said, trying to ease her mind.

"Speaking of funny events, you never told me how you cut through the Matherson estate the other night. I tried to track you, but the gate was locked." Rosie took a sip of her coffee while she waited for the old computer to load.

Lucy's eyes widened in panic; she couldn't tell her she'd been with Benedict. "Maybe the tea affected your sense of smell? I must've found some other way to cut through their estate." She avoided Rosie's gaze in case the werewolf sensed she was lying.

"We were just glad to hear you got home okay. I tried barking at them to get out of the water, but they were too wrapped up in the stars."

"I hope they fared better than we did in the aftermath." Lucy tried to conceal her relief when Rosie didn't pry any further about the manor.

"They were sad you couldn't come to say goodbye. They wanted to stay longer, but Harriet wanted to get the afternoon train to meet her girlfriend, and Luisa had to get back to work," Rosie explained, tucking a strand of cropped hair behind her ear.

"I couldn't get away," Lucy said guiltily. She stacked the other volumes she'd been going through, keeping their titles out of sight. "Next time they come into town, let's stick to a lake swim and forego anything to do with tea."

"Agreed." They shook on it.

"Good morning, girls," a patron said, hooking her walking stick onto the desk.

"Morning, Mrs Khan! I see you're loving the Immortal Lovers series," Rosie said, taking the books she wanted to borrow.

"I can't get enough of that Mr. Trenton character – so dashing on that white horse of his. And how he slayed the Vampire King," she cooed with an exaggerated shiver. Lucy stamped her to-be-returned date inside each book.

"No spoilers!" Rosie covered her ears. "I'm only on the second book."

Mrs Khan mimed sealing her lips. "I shall say no more, but I was hoping the new book had come in."

"I thought I'd seen it here. I promise, you're first on the list when it comes in." Rosie frowned, looking at the cart of newly delivered books.

Lucy froze as she put the books into Mrs Khan's tote bag. She'd given the new book to Suzy, but thankfully she hadn't entered its arrival into the system yet. She made a mental note to put it in once Suzy gave it back.

"You're all stamped and ready to go," she said, handing her the full bag.

Mrs Khan turned to leave, but then turned back with a wide grin. "How could I forget? I believe congratulations are in order! My wife told me this morning about your binding to Benedict."

Wincing, Lucy felt Rosie staring at her. So far she'd avoided talking about it with her friend, but she certainly couldn't escape it now.

"I can't believe two of my brightest students are going to be bound." Mrs Khan had taught them botany. The older woman leant in close. "So you know, you have the support of the Khan family no matter what you decide." She winked.

"It's all rather sudden, but Benedict and I thank you for your support." Her words remained steady and certain, but she was sweating. She couldn't believe the news was spreading so fast. Mrs Khan's wife worked at the flower market, which was run by Mrs Crawford. The news had probably been spread before she set the toaster on fire.

"Be sure to pass on our congratulations to Benedict. You do make a gorgeous couple; I think you'll both do an excellent job heading the coven together." Mrs Khan left with her bag secured on her arm.

"So, are we going to talk about it? Or are we going to keep dancing around the topic?" Rosie side-eyed Lucy once Mrs Khan was out of earshot.

"We can talk about it," Lucy sighed. With heat swelling in her hands, she put down the book Mrs Khan had returned before it burnt to ash like the flowers out front.

"Only if you're ready. When you didn't bring it up, I thought it wasn't true or that you needed time to tell me – but how the hell are you engaged to Benedict Matherson?"

Lucy appreciated Rosie for never pushing. It was probably because there was plenty in her own past she never discussed; Lucy had never asked her about her life in the woods with the wolves before she came to Foxford.

"Technically, I'm not engaged." She picked up her iced tea, trying to calm down. The ice was a lame attempt at keeping her hands cool. The last thing she wanted was for the library, which she loved above all else, to go up in flames. She hoped Benedict wasn't struggling as much as she was. "I wanted to be the one to tell you, but I was in shock about the whole thing. The coven wishes for me and Benedict to lead the coven together, so the town can benefit from our joint leadership and to stop us both from destroying the town with our petty squabbles." She sounded far more rational than she felt, evidenced by the ice turning to water in her drink. She put down the cup, afraid of melting the plastic.

"They think forcing you together will magically make you get along? Sounds more like mutually assured destruction." Rosie's words echoed around the library. A few readers in the fantasy section stared at them, alerted by the sudden outburst. Lucy muttered an apology, and the readers went back to their books.

"Either we agree to the binding, or one of us will be voted out of town. And since it was my actions that led to that God-awful review in the magless magazine, I wasn't risking rejecting their offer."

"But how could Benedict even be nominated for your position? He's as much to blame as you for the stunt," Rosie pointed out.

"Technically, anyone can be nominated. It was never seen as necessary before."

"But you won't really accept an arranged marriage, right? You must have some plan?"

Lucy stared at her bag. She was currently trying everything to undo her family's plan to stop the binding; she didn't have time to plan her own.

"I have to. If there had been a vote then and there, I'd have lost. We both know I've neglected the town since I took over the library, and with the last prank threatening to expose the magical nature of our town to the outside world, saying yes was my best option to buy myself some time."

Rosie let out a sigh. "Stuck between a rock and a hard place. When I found out, I thought you might've wanted to be bound to Benedict – not that he isn't a tall drink of water."

"A tall drink of water?" Lucy smirked, though wished people would stop thinking she harboured feelings for him.

"What?" Rosie frowned. "I heard your Grams say it."

"You really were raised with wolves."

"No diverting the topic. There is no way Benedict isn't

scheming to get out of this. What about your opposing elements?" Rosie asked.

Lucy looked away. "Gwendoline says there's a ritual that'll make it possible."

"At least you've plenty of time to reconsider your options. Engagements can last years nowadays."

Lucy picked up a bunch of books from the returned pile to avoid answering.

"Wait. How long did they give you?" Rosie asked, following her so she couldn't escape the conversation.

"All Hallows' Eve," Lucy admitted, stopping on the staircase. "The ritual will only work when the connection between us and those who came before is the strongest."

"Gwendoline could be bluffing. What are the chances that we've never come across such a ritual in all our research?" Rosie was the best occult researcher in the town, if not the country. She could find a needle in a pile of needles.

"I wish she was, but she's spent decades rebuilding the Matherson reputation. I doubt she would lie to the coven."

"Decades or not, a Matherson is a Matherson. Being deceitful is in their blood," Rosie grumbled.

"No one picks their family or the magic they inherit," Lucy reminded her. She appreciated her friend's support, but she didn't like judging anybody for their past. "Benedict and Gwendoline can't help being Mathersons, like I can't help being a Hawthorne."

Rosie sighed. "And I can't help being raised in a pack."

Silence sank between them, along with a sense that everything was about to change.

"I should get you a wedding present," Rosie teased.

"Don't you dare! No magless traditions. This is a binding, not a wedding," Lucy snapped.

There was a second of tension, and then they both erupted into laughter at the ridiculousness of the situation.

Rosie suddenly stopped, grabbing Lucy's arm. "What about the Order? Are you going to tell them about your engagement?" she asked, worry creasing her brows. "Two of the most powerful families in Foxford are binding their descendants; such events would pique their interest."

"They've no say in coven matters," Lucy shrugged. They were the last of her concerns.

"What if they find out on their own? They're sending someone for the grimoire; they might find it strange you didn't mention it in your correspondence."

"We don't discuss personal matters. Once whoever collects the grimoire arrives, they'll be on their way." If Lucy let the stress of another thing get to her, she might combust into one giant flame. "Can we talk about anything else? My head is starting to throb, and everything'll be fine." She was reassuring herself as much as her friend. She wished she could tell Rosie everything about the element swap, but it was the coven who'd granted Rosie refuge when she'd left her pack; it would be unfair to make her keep a secret from them.

"Not another word on the subject." Rosie zipped her lips. "I've got to start ordering the Christmas books. We can't put it off any longer."

Stopping by the portraits hung between the shelves, Lucy noticed they were dusted to perfection. *A promise is a promise.* She whistled, hoping it was safe to use her magic to summon their cleaner. Thankfully, nothing burst into flames, and Broomhilda came clattering from the cleaning closet at the end of the hall.

So far so good; no flames yet. She tried not to get too cocky.

"You did a great job, and I did promise you could have some company," she told the broom. With a click of her fingers, another clatter echoed from the cleaning closet. The mop fell out of the door before picking itself up and swishing over to them. The broom and mop stood before her, awaiting instruction.

"You two can clean together today, but no repeats of last time. I don't want to have to move another shelf to hide another ink stain not even magic could get out of the carpet," Lucy warned.

The enchanted objects dipped forward as if ashamed of themselves.

"Off you go. Have fun," she ordered, and they hurried away to their chores on the various floors. She hoped they wouldn't be too much of a nuisance to visitors.

Sliding along the laddered shelves, she put the grimoires back in their rightful places. Rosie had been too distracted by the binding revelation to notice her potion research. Now she needed to get to the vault and find the curse-stripping potion before the Order member arrived.

Lucinda

L ucy woke up with a terrible crick in her neck after spending the night in the vault. She suspected she'd have ended up with a cold if Rosie hadn't put a blanket over her. Not that she felt it – Benedict's element kept her at a temperature she could only compare to the fires of Mordor.

A soft, deep voice caught her off guard as she put a book back on the shelf.

"Sorry to disturb you. I'm looking for Lucinda Hawthorne?"

Lucy whipped round and then rubbed her sore neck. She hadn't expected anyone to stop by the library first thing. The book she'd been holding landed on the creaky wooden floors with an almighty thump.

"You found and nearly killed her," she said, stepping down from the ladder and noting the new scorch marks on the wood. *The fright must have triggered the fire's desire to protect me.* She slid the ladder away before the visitor could notice. With the study area littered with books, she'd decided to do a quick tidy up.

"Sorry. I didn't mean to startle you. Rosie, the woman downstairs, told me you were up here," the stranger said, clutching his satchel to his side. Lucy wasn't sure if he was afraid of her or just awkward.

Her eyes went to the pin on his jacket: the Vatican seal.

"I called to let you know I was on my way." He followed her gaze to the pin and awkwardly adjusted his glasses. Handsome, in a nerdy way. "Emerson Hughes," he added, extending his hand.

Lucy picked up the dropped book instead. She didn't want her magic to sense her discomfort and burn him.

He drew his hand back. "I'm a professor at Darworth University with your father." With his tweed jacket, and brown shoes, he looked every bit the scholar.

Lucy cursed silently. She needed more time to study the curse-stripping potion before she handed the Hawthorne grimoire over. She still had to double-check her translations and make sure she wouldn't rid them of their elements entirely.

"The Order of Occult Research sent me, and since I've heard so much about you and Foxford, I thought I'd kill two birds with one stone," Emerson concluded.

"If you're here for the book, you'll have to wait a few more days. The final incantations are proving tricky," Lucy said firmly, wondering if she should warn him about referencing stones and killing while in town. His tight grip on his satchel revealed his nerves, so she let it slide.

If her dad had known Emerson was coming, she was surprised he hadn't called to warn her. Then again, he was off on a dig for a rare artefact, so they'd missed their last few weekly calls.

"There's no hurry! Any delay gives me more time to see the town. I'm merely here to collect and assist at your leisure. If I'm being honest, I volunteered for the job. I studied the Forgotten text you discovered and translated last year... Sorry, I'm babbling. I've been excited to meet you." He cut himself off, clearly embarrassed by his own outburst.

Lucy stared at him, taken aback. "I just translated it. Rosie tracked it down; she found the text in the desert in a forgotten tomb while searching for a different relic altogether. A happy accident. If it wasn't for her it would've remained Forgotten.

She guessed that Emerson was somewhere in his early thirties. There was something gentle about his eyes that put her at ease. Even if he belonged to the Order who'd once hunted her kind — and still did, in certain circumstances — it looked like he'd spent most of his days studying. He didn't seem like the *hunting* type. Then again, a witch could never be too careful.

"You can relax! You look like you're about to pass out," she said.

Emerson looked down at his white-knuckled grip and released the strap. "Rosie. Is she a witch?" he whispered, curiosity evidently getting the better of his manners.

"You don't have to whisper. Witch isn't a dirty word." His eyes widened, and Lucy grinned. "But she isn't."

He waited for her to continue.

"Think more... claws and teeth," Lucy explained.

Emerson swallowed. She got the feeling he hadn't suspected that the soft-spoken, quirky young woman one floor below them could rip his throat out in a matter of seconds.

"Claws and teeth? You wouldn't be talking about me, would you?" Rosie appeared, and Emerson flinched.

Clearly, this was his first time in a refuge town around such creatures. Lucy rolled her eyes. She didn't want to have to babysit him to keep him from becoming someone's snack; she had enough on her plate. To avoid embarrassing him, though, she said nothing.

"This is your first time in a town like Foxford?" Rosie, on the other hand, had never mastered the act of subtlety.

Emerson scratched the back of his neck. "I've always wanted to visit and learn about the different..." He hesitated. "Cultures."

Rosie circled him like a wolf stalking a lamb. "I was the same when I left my pack in the woods for the mysterious town beyond, but it was rather disappointing the first time I met a vampire."

Feeling a morsel of pity for Emerson, Lucy hoped her friend wouldn't get too much enjoyment from teasing him.

"My postman," Rosie explained. "A balding man named Ted – or Theodore, back in *his* day. He hadn't drunk blood in over a hundred years. The only time he ever appeared even slightly frightening was when he chased a warlock through the town after he'd found him in a compromising position with his youngest daughter. By youngest, I mean fifty-six in vamp years."

Lucy expected him to look frightened, but Emerson hung on to her every word. "And the...?" He pointed hesitantly to his teeth.

"The fangs? Nothing remarkable. They could be easily assumed to be magless canines, only a little sharper. Mine are far more impressive," Rosie told him, before offering to introduce him to a vampire to show him the difference. He quickly declined.

"I've just arrived – I need to get settled first before I

start meeting people." Emerson looked like he was chomping at the bit to ask Rosie exactly *what* she was, but it was terribly impolite to ask as a magless. It made magical folk feel as though they were nothing more than their species. To put him out of his misery, Lucy winked at her friend behind his back.

Rosie took the hint and extended her painted nails. Her eyes glowed a vibrant amber, telling him she was a werewolf.

"Wow, your eyes... I've heard how bright they can appear, but—" He struggled to finish, transfixed by the sight. Then his eyes dropped to her claws and he backed up slightly.

"Don't worry, I don't bite," Rosie said seductively, retracting her claws. Emerson smiled nervously, gripping his satchel once again.

"Let's not frighten him off," Lucy said. He seemed harmless, even if the people he worked for weren't. She didn't want him to get a bad impression of them – but at least he now knew how well-protected the library and what lay beneath it was. "What do you plan to do while I finish my work?" she asked, cutting right to the point.

"I can help you with research?" he offered, clearly eager to help.

"I've got the best researcher in the country," Lucy said, gesturing to Rosie. She couldn't have him looking over her shoulder as she studied up on curse-stripping potions.

"I could use an assistant, if you don't want him." Rosie batted her long eyelashes at Emerson, who stood a head taller.

If he's not careful, he really will become her prey. But Rosie was the perfect person to keep him distracted.

"I'm not sure if we can trust him. The last email the order sent was rather threatening." Lucy sharpened her tone to see how he would react. Maybe he'd reveal a harsher side when threatened.

"I'm only here to help; I'm sorry if our head office weren't as understanding about the complexity of work such as yours," he said, his tone assertive but apologetic. "I can explain to them that you require more time with the grimoire, but I will need to check that it's still in your possession – just a formality, really."

"The grimoire is sealed in our vault, and unfortunately magless aren't allowed in. They've been warded for generations," Lucy explained.

"Oh, I wasn't aware. Can we try? I've got a suspicion I'll be fine." He smiled sheepishly.

Lucy frowned, wondering what he wasn't saying, and Rosie looked suspicious.

"I should warn you, if you fail to pass the warding you'll get what feels a bit like an electric shock. It won't kill you, but it's said to hurt something awful." Lucy thought of the poor magless who'd tried to break in a few years back. She'd found the intruders passed out by the gargoyles within the secret entrance.

"I think I'll survive." He sounded far more confident than before.

"I love your optimism." She wasn't sure if he was arrogant, but least if he was knocked out for a few hours, it'd buy her some time with the grimoire uninterrupted. "Rosie, can you please grab me a blanket?"

"A blanket?" Emerson gave her a puzzled look, following her down the main staircase to the reception desk. The main entrance to the vault lay at their feet; the secret entrance on the second floor was for coven eyes only. In case of a raid, they'd be able to escape fast. The main entrance was a much longer and more winding path. Rosie pulled out a multicoloured blanket from beneath the desk and handed it to him.

"In case you pass out. I wouldn't want you to get cold lying on the stone floor." Lucy moved aside the chairs to expose the entrance concealed beneath the tiles.

"The tunnels are awfully draughty," Rosie added with a smile.

"Open it up." Lucy motioned for Emerson to stand on the tiled owl beside her.

Rosie twisted the neck of the brass owl on the desk. With a clunk and clash, they were lowered beneath the library until the stone ceiling replaced itself above them.

"Impressive," he muttered, admiring the domed roof.

"You've seen nothing yet," Lucy told him.

The platform hit the ground, and the tunnel before them lit as soon as her foot hit the stone. It was on instinct; she hadn't even tried to summon Benedict's fire. *Maybe my blood isn't rejecting the fire as much as I thought it would. Having his element might actually come in handy.* Usually, she would've hit the fire symbol at the start of the first tunnel to light them.

"It looks like..." Emerson started, noting the arched holes in the walls.

"A crypt?" she finished for him. "You'd be right. When witches were persecuted, we hid the burial grounds of our loved ones here to stop the church from getting to their bones, or anything they might have been buried with."

"And now?" he asked, stepping off the platform.

"The last of the coffins were moved above ground to

the cemetery behind the town hall. There's been no need to hide in Foxford for the last few hundred years."

He didn't respond to that. He already knew their history, of course, but Lucy understood first-hand what it was like to read about something and then actually witness the evidence.

At the entrance of the tunnel, eyeing the gargoyles on either side of the tunnel, she waited. Though she worried about showing him the entrance, it was the easiest and fastest way to test him.

"Even with the torches, it's freezing down here," he said, rubbing his hands together and walking past.

Lucy frowned as the gargoyles failed to act, but she followed, not wanting him to know he had passed the first test. She studied his hands and neck; he wore no anti-warding amulets that she could see.

"It's worse in the summer – like a sauna," she remarked. His passing the first test might be because he held no ill will or intent, since the gargoyles' main purpose was to protect against thievery first and foremost. She was already breaking the rules by not bringing him before the High Priestess once he'd made his presence known to her. If the coven got wind that she'd brought a member of the Order beneath the library without their approval, they might not need a vote after all – she could just hand her inheritance to Benedict – but the warding was the fastest way to figure out if he was a threat.

Emerson followed her through the tunnel with no concern about where he was being led. Lucy couldn't believe how trusting he was. Many in his position would have been as suspicious of her as she was of him.

"Where are you staying in town?" she asked, looking

over her shoulder at him. "You've no bags with you, so I take it I wasn't your first stop?" She wondered if one of the professors from the university had put him up. Hopefully there was at least one person in town to not only vouch for him, but to guide him.

"At the Manor – I checked in first thing. I've never stayed in such a well-maintained manor. They must've spent a fortune restoring it."

Lucy rolled her eyes. Benedict would just *love* being praised by a member of the Order. In fact, she wanted to make sure she was there if and when he discovered someone sent from the very Order that had sentenced his father to death was staying under his roof.

"They did, so it'll be expensive if you're staying indefinitely," she warned, wanting to stay off the topic of the Mathersons. Even the brief mention made her palms sweat, as though Benedict's element was trying to remind her of him.

"The order is covering the cost until my room is ready at the university."

Relief cooled Lucy's element – with any luck, he'd leave the manor sooner rather than later – as he continued. "Your work here is important, so they deem it a worthy expense, and it will only be for a short time."

Slowing her pace as they reached the armoured knights through the next archway, she tried to stifle a smile, sure he wouldn't pass the next phase.

"So excellently maintained," Emerson marvelled, stopping to examine the knights that could cut him in half.

Lucy walked ahead, not looking back, and waited for the thud of his body hitting the stone. The guardians wouldn't skewer him unless he was truly evil. She hoped.

"How will I know if I've passed?" He jogged up beside her.

"H-how?" Lucy stammered, mentally preparing herself for a fight. What if he wasn't who he said he was? There were plenty of magical folk on the fringe who'd do anything to gain access to these vaults, but she couldn't think of any mad enough to disguise themselves as an Order member.

"Technically, I'm not entirely a magless," he admitted, putting some distance between them. Apparently her silence was read as a threat, because he hurried to explain. "My great-great-grandmother was a healer, but she was never part of any coven. She had no magic herself, but she could work with nature. Understood plants and animals as though she could speak to them."

Lucy considered his last name. "Hughes? I don't recall any Healer name in our old ledgers." She could've overlooked it...

"She never made herself known. She worked with the sick, disguised as a nun, mostly; she wasn't one for rules when it came to helping people," Emerson said.

"If she worked for the church, that explains why we have no record."

"If you can't beat them, join them," he agreed, admitting to a crime the Order would have burnt his ancestor for.

"Is that your philosophy? To hide amongst them?"

"Yes and no, but she was my inspiration to join the Order."

"Do your employers know this?" She'd never heard of the Vatican letting those of magical descent into their ranks.

His smile became shaky. "Technically, there was nothing to disclose, as I've no magic myself."

"Then how did you know you'd pass the warding?" Lucy asked, trying to remain calm, so she didn't end up accidentally setting an Order member on fire. With everything going on with the coven and Benedict, it couldn't have been a worse time for him to arrive.

"I didn't. To be honest, I was testing myself just as you were testing me. To see if any trace of magic lingered in my blood." He smiled.

"I can't decide whether you're gutsy, clever, or dangerously naive. I appreciate your honesty, but if I were to report you, the Order would imprison you. You've put yourself at great risk coming here!"

In spite of her words, Emerson appeared relieved to share his history with someone.

"My only hope in sharing my past with you is that you don't have to be on guard. I read in one of your translations that warding might also fail if a person, magless or not, harbours no ill intent. I hope this will further confirm that my presence isn't a threat, and that I only wish to help," he said, his eyes wide with hope.

Lucy took a moment to consider. If he stepped out of line even an inch, she could report him. His own would do far worse to him than her kind would, and she could use her knowledge to keep the grimoire longer, should she need to. She didn't want to use blackmail, but – her palms burned – desperate times called for desperate measures.

"You're right about the warding. *Some* magless who wish no ill intent or self-gain from our magic will be allowed to pass unharmed," she told him, "though it's very rare." Together, they passed through the tunnels lined with ancient relics and cursed objects. "Please don't touch anything; not all magic down here has good intentions," she warned.

He nodded, his broad smile like that of a child in a sweet shop as he slowed to look over book spines and rare items. When Lucy stopped at the intersection of all the tunnels, he nearly walked into her, transfixed by the sight of the vault.

"Can we go in?" He walked around the glass room filled with dozens of shelves with books and artefacts that were far more sacred than those he'd already observed. Lucy let him look, waiting to see if his intent would switch now that he'd got this far. "It's a far larger collection than I anticipated. This is exceptional," he breathed, not daring to get too close or linger too long in one spot. Still, she wasn't going to let just anyone touch the ancestral texts; she had already taken him far enough.

"Not today. I'm sorry, but I need permission from the High Priestess. As you can see, the grimoire is safely within the vault; that should be enough to prove my co-operation," she said, guiding him back the way they'd come. His gaze lingered on the text only a few feet away, before backing up.

"Forgive me for assuming, but if I've made it this far... I wonder if I've passed your tests?" Emerson asked, clearly pleased with himself.

"I still need permission to bring you into the actual vault."

He sighed. "I won't press. I just wanted you to know you can trust me."

"I think this is enough for today. Let's not run before we can walk." Lucy was far more worried about touching the grimoire with her untrustworthy hands. If she burned, singed or even marked the book in front of him, the Order might believe she'd done it on purpose to stop them from getting their hands on it again. Or, worse, Emerson could report back that she couldn't control her element. Such a revelation would have consequences of epic proportions, even if she did have something on him as well.

On their return, the armoured knights remained frozen. She didn't know whether to be relieved or worried that their warding might've failed. She ignored his repeated success, not wanting to let him know where the tests were in case he reported back on the inner workings of their vault.

"Can I give you some advice?" she asked as the platform came down for them, wanting to reward him for his honesty. Many wouldn't put themselves in harm's way to prove their story.

"I'll take any help I can get," he said, clearly on a high from making it this far. His joy radiated off him in waves.

She eyed the pin on his tweed blazer. "Don't wear *that* in public. I'm surprised you were able to check in to the Manor with it on. Though we work together, there are still some in town who would prefer if we didn't." *The same few that would love to use his arrival as a great excuse to take my position from me. The wounds of the past may have healed, but the scars remained.*

"I was wearing a coat when I checked in," he admitted, touching his fingers to the pin as if to conceal it.

"I'd hate for you to run into anyone who'd take issue without knowing the full story. There's no way a Matherson would allow anyone from the Order to stay within their establishment unless the coven ordered it. Old vendettas die hard." And the matter between the Mathersons and the Order wasn't all that old.

"I suppose I'm so used to it opening doors. I never

thought it'd be the reason some closed." Emerson removed the pin without hesitation.

"Maybe in the magless world. Just be glad you weren't meeting with the wolves in the woods."

He frowned as the torches dimmed around them. "Why?"

"I believe the Order still has hunters..." She trailed off.

"Different department," he said quickly. She was surprised he didn't deny it. "I don't agree with all their practices. My role is to bridge the gap between us. There are many, especially as new generations move up in the ranks, who wish for us to move forward together."

The gargoyles confirmed his words. If he believed in harming magical folk, they wouldn't have let him get this far.

Curiosity won over subtlety. "If you feel this way, why join the Order in the first place? Where there are those who would wish we didn't exist at all?"

He hesitated. "Are there not some in your own communities who believe that magless are second to your kind?"

He had a point, even if she didn't want to admit it. "Touché." If he was going to be honest, so would she. "There are some of magical descent who believe magless are inferior, but I suspect such ideas come from the pain of the past. A desire to punish those in the present for crimes committed against their ancestors," she said, stepping up onto the platform. "Like you said, the more we work together, the more time can change things."

An air of understanding settled between them as the ceiling opened above them. "There's a safe in my room. I'll leave the pin there for the duration of my stay," Emerson said, putting it in his pocket.

"Now that the awkwardness is out of the way, you can

relax. I'll discuss your vault access with the High Priestess this evening."

He let out an exaggerated breath. "Thank you."

"You mentioned that you worked with my father?" Lucy asked.

"In passing. I've been to a few of Mr Hawthorne's lectures on lost relics. Due to my position with the Order, I bounce around a lot, but I hope to settle soon."

Lucy wondered what else he did for the Order. He'd done everything she asked and more, so there was no need to be hostile. It'd also be easier to learn more about him if she introduced him to her family, and a welcoming dinner was the perfect excuse.

"Dad would want me to invite you to dinner. You don't know anyone in town, and they don't know you. If you come to Hawthorne House, it'll let everyone know that you're here with good intentions, especially if you're going to work at the university. The town can be awfully suspicious of newcomers, particularly magless with Order connections." She reminded herself to ask later how he'd managed to get a position at the university. Perhaps her dad had given him a good if not great reference, and that was why he hadn't gone into more detail.

"I'd be delighted. The drive here was rather endless, and service station food leaves much to be desired," he said, clearly excited to meet the High Priestess of Foxford.

"We eat at seven – bring your appetite. Once I tell Grams we've company, she'll put on a feast. Are you okay to get around in the meantime? I've got some translations to finish." It didn't look great that she'd been organising old texts when he arrived. She didn't want him to report that she wasn't working on the grimoire.

"Don't let me keep you. I can get to know the town, and meet you back here when the library closes?"

They returned to the library floor. Rosie was in her usual spot, trying to fix the outdated computers. Lucy wasn't sure about letting Emerson wander freely before she had a chance to talk with her mum about his arrival.

"If you've got time to kill, you could help Rosie with her research? She's working on a cold case for the next village over." Rosie would get plenty of information out of him.

Emerson looked unsure as he gazed at the petite werewolf.

"You don't need to worry. She might've claws, but she also has one of the biggest hearts in town," Lucy whispered.

He swallowed at her mention of claws. *God, this town will eat him alive if he's allowed to wander at will.*

"I'll ask her," he decided, colour returning to his cheeks. "After all, I did come here to be of service."

"She can also fill you in on the town." Lucy didn't want him heading too far into the woods by accident. "Show you some of the no-go areas."

"I'd be happy to help," Rosie said, returning to the desk with a computer under her arm as though it weighed nothing.

"Eavesdropping again?" Lucy nudged her friend.

"I can't help it – that tea really messed with my senses." Rosie pouted, putting down the computer with a clunk.

"Tea?" Emerson looked between them, brows pulled together behind his glasses.

"Long story." Lucy grabbed her lunch and melted iced tea from the desk. "I'll meet you out front at closing."

"What about lunch?" he offered, pushing his glasses

higher on his perfectly straight nose. "You could update me on your progress, or if you've notes you'd like me to transcribe—"

She waved the sandwiches in her hand. "I've got to work through, and no materials relating to ancestorial magic, not even notes, are allowed to leave the vault," she informed him, heading back down. She didn't always follow that rule, but she didn't want him knowing that.

Before the ceiling sealed itself over her head, she heard Rosie eagerly accepting his help. Lucy swallowed her nerves as she lit the torches again, this time intentionally. She rolled her fingers over her palms. *Fire might not be so hard to control after all. I just need to make sure I don't use it in front of Emerson.*

Within the vault, she settled into her seat and pulled the grimoire from its secure case. She clenched her fists, afraid of touching its delicate pages, but she needed to conquer her fears if she was going to find the potion.

"Hopefully I'll still be able to read it. If it senses Benedict's element, it may refuse to open," she muttered to herself.

She ran her hand gently over the spine, testing the latch. The knots in her stomach unravelled when it popped open.

Turning the first page, she let out a sigh when she was able to read the first line. *Okay. This confirms that Benedict's element hasn't affected my ancestral connection. That should help us both get through the rest of the month.* Flipping through the pages, she found the curse-stripping potion, but she still had to translate the ingredients perfectly or risk doing more harm than good. She hoped they wouldn't have to use it.

She didn't want to keep Emerson waiting, so when the

clock struck six, she latched the grimoire and tucked it away. Her phone showed several texts and two missed calls from an impatient Benedict, but she didn't want to reply until she had a back-up plan. That way, if correcting the original spell Grams used didn't work, they'd have an alternative potion ready to go. She dropped her phone in her bag with a huff. She understood his frustration, but she was working as fast as she could.

Benedict

enedict paced in front of the white picket fence surrounding the Hawthorne property. Every breeze reminded him of his missing element; without the heat he felt overwhelmingly vulnerable. With all that had happened at the coven meeting, he wondered if he'd still be welcome here, but he hoped his sudden appearance would earn him an invitation. The last thing he wanted was to intrude on their evening. However, Lucinda hadn't replied to his last several texts, and he was beginning to feel like some jilted ex rather than her fiancé.

He'd stopped by the library, where Rosie had told him Lucy had gone home to have dinner with the handsome professor who'd just arrived in town this morning. Hearing how helpful and polite this professor was had made Benedict want to flood the library. He couldn't believe Lucinda would invite a stranger to Hawthorne House, yet ignore his calls.

Then again... Benedict paused with his hand on the gate, smiling to himself. Lucy had always loved strays. At school, he'd once discovered her trying to heal an injured fox in the seniors' brewing room. All she'd managed to do was turn the poor creature green. A Hawthorne inept at healing was like a vampire without fangs, and seeing the tears in her eyes had been more than he could stand. In fact, seeing any woman cry made him uneasy; he suspected it was something to do with his mother's grief for his father. But seeing Lucinda, who loved to smile and find the silver lining in every situation, in tears had caused an uncomfortable tightness in his chest. The only way to make her smile had been to help the fox, but he'd known she would never willingly accept his help. He'd tossed her a healer's guide for animals and goaded her into trying it.

As he'd hoped, she couldn't resist his challenge. At school the next morning, Benedict had spotted the fox picking at the school bins, healthy and restored to its normal self – as was Lucinda's smiley nature.

He clenched his jaw, suspecting the new professor wasn't going to be as easy to handle as the fox. Shaking away memories, he pulled off his suffocating tie, shoving it in his jacket pocket, and opened the gate. As he walked the cobble path dividing the overgrown garden, he couldn't help but admire the colours. Beautiful, bold and a bit chaotic, like all Hawthorne women.

Sitting on the front porch was who he was looking for.

"Benedict! What a lovely surprise; we weren't expecting you," Grams Hawthorne said, a thick blanket wrapped over her rounded shoulders. Her creased smile reached her eyes, the same as Lucinda's. He put on his most charming smile.

"Excuse my intrusion. I wanted to stop by and say I'm sorry for the other night at the coven meeting. How Gwendoline approached the situation..." Benedict fumbled through his excuse. "Anyway, I wanted to drop off some new herbal teas made from the Manor Gardens. Mum said she forgot to give them to Wilhelmina at the meeting." Hopefully the gesture would help mend some fences and ensure his invitation to dinner. Grams was the last person he wanted to upset.

"No need for you to be apologising. You had nothing to do with the scheme, and you're always welcome here." Grams winked, putting him at ease, rocking gently back and forth on the chair. "As much as you tease each other, I know there's a good heart beneath that shirt, and you'd never hurt Lucinda."

Her faith in him never failed to surprise him. He'd never forgotten her kindness when he'd lost his brother. Gwendoline had ordered him not to cry during the funeral. However, after the service, when everyone had left the cemetery, Grams had let him sob on her shoulder until there were no tears left. He realised that was probably the last day he'd cried.

Grams watched him peer in the window behind her. He wanted to meet the stranger lingering around his intended.

"Are you sure that's the only reason you stopped by?" She smiled knowingly, exposing the deep smile lines around her lips.

"I don't know what you mean," he said, handing her the tea before they were interrupted.

Her eyes narrowed. "You're a terrible liar, Benedict."

His smile flattened. He wondered if she could sense the Hawthorne element within him.

"Mum, what are you doing out here? I thought you were preparing the dessert?" Wilhelmina said, popping her head out of the mint-green shutter.

"The dessert is in the fridge, and it would've been

terribly rude not to welcome our guest," Grams said, winking at Benedict – who went unnoticed, due to the angle of the window.

"Our company is sitting at our dinner table, waiting for tiramisu. Come inside, and don't even think about smoking your pipe. Doctor's orders!" Wilhelmina added, wrapping her eye-searingly colourful shawl around her shoulders. Benedict had never understood the Hawthorne obsession with colour; a rainbow would find these women intimidating.

"I wasn't smoking my pipe, and I wasn't talking about the new professor," Grams said.

Wilhelmina opened the front door and was visibly taken aback when Benedict greeted her with a nervous smile.

Sorry for intruding. I wanted..." He didn't get a chance to finish his lame excuse.

"That was kind of you, but we've got company." Wilhelmina's welcome was far cooler than her mother's. Benedict didn't doubt she suspected him of scheming for her daughter's position. He didn't even know how the High Priestess would react if she knew her daughter's element ran through his veins because of the spell she'd cast. He wanted to be angry about the hypocrisy, but any spike in mood might cause another inexplicable storm.

"I know it's very late in the evening, but I felt I had to stop by and apologise for the other night. No matter what happens between me and Lucinda I only want the best for the coven," he said, stepping up onto the porch.

Wilhelmina, usually all light and warmth, studied him for a moment longer than was comfortable.

"I'd never do anything to intentionally hurt Lucinda or your family," Benedict added. He hated sounding so vulnerable, but he needed them to see he could still be trusted. If he and Lucinda were to solve their element situation, he couldn't have her family blocking his path to her.

Wilhelmina's expression softened. "There's no need to apologise. I only hope things work out – not only for the coven, but for my daughter and you."

"You don't need to worry," Grams jumped in. "Everything will work out as it should." She winked again.

Benedict swallowed. He knew exactly what they were up to to ensure it did. He only wished they truly believed in his good intentions. If they did, they never would have cast such a spell to keep him and Lucinda apart. *I suppose I can't blame them for wanting to protect their own.*

"He even brought the teas you were looking for from the manor." Grams handed the paper bag full of teas to Wilhelmina, who quickly accepted.

"Thank you, they work wonders for my digestion!" Wilhemia beamed, though she didn't follow up with an invitation to join them as Benedict had hoped. Instead she glanced inside, as though concerned about something, which only piqued his interest about the stranger at their table. "Have a good evening."

The High Priestess headed back inside, and Grams rose from her chair. Benedict set his jaw. The best way to get to Lucinda's heart and Wilhelmina's table was to get Grams on his side.

"On my way over, I popped into Myrtle's Herb Shop. The rare waterworm root you were looking for last month came in." He reached into his inner jacket pocket and pulled out a small glass jar, exposing the golden root within. "I thought I'd save you the trip."

"Are you trying to bribe your way into this house?" Grams whispered, accepting the jar.

"Is it working?" Benedict offered her his arm and cheekiest grin.

Tiny Grams slapped him on the back with the force of a woman who'd worked for the benefit of others for her whole life. "Come inside. There's plenty of dessert to go around."

She shoved him through to the dark purple dining room before disappearing into the kitchen. Benedict found Lucinda alone; the dinner table had already been cleared, and she was laying out dessert bowls. He noticed the fire in the corner of the room. He wondered if she had used his element to light it. He met Lucinda's gaze. She rolled her eyes as though reading his mind. The thought of her using his magic stirred something unexpected in him.

"What are you doing here?" she asked, eyes wide.

"Hi to you too. Grams kindly invited me for dessert."

Lucinda's eyes narrowed. "What did you bribe her with?"

"How well you know me," he quipped, but his smile faded when a man in a cream jumper entered the dining room, the sides of his floppy fringe hanging over the rims of his glasses. He didn't need to guess that this was the professor, though he was far younger than expected. Benedict had assumed Rosie was just trying to wind him up, and hoped to find a balding middle-aged man who lacked any form of social etiquette. This one was young, put-together, had an aura of aristocracy about him...

"And this is?" Benedict asked, staring down the man standing a little too close to Lucinda.

"Emerson Hughes." Emerson extended his hand, which Benedict would've accepted had the professor not continued. "The Order sent me to collect some work Lucinda has done for us."

Benedict's jaw clenched. Though he preferred to focus on the future, anyone with his lineage wouldn't want to look back either. However, Lucinda's pleading eyes forced him to take the man's hand.

"Benedict Matherson," he ground out, and shook the man's hand before taking the empty seat beside Lucinda. She glared at him, but there was no way he was letting an Order member get so close to her. *Wait. Why am I getting all protective of her? It must be her element.*

"It's a pleasure to meet you. I'm staying in your hotel, or manor, I should say," Emerson took the seat across from him. A few inches further away from Lucinda, but still not far enough for Benedict's liking.

"I hope you have a pleasant stay." He forced himself to be civil; the man was a paying guest after all. Also, upsetting Lucinda could result in the room burning down around them. He didn't like that she was letting a member of the Order who had hunted their kind for generations eat at her table, let alone see the vault, one of their most sacred places. She'd never extended *him* any such invitation. Lucinda would never let him assist her – unless under the influence of a mysterious tea.

He wasn't jealous, he told himself, and yet when Emerson smiled thankfully at his intended when she offered him a dessert spoon, Benedict felt the wash of her element threatening to spill out.

"I'm sure I will," Emerson answered him. "The place is exquisitely restored. The Victorian mouldings are so tastefully maintained. The porcelain statues, the teardrop chandeliers – I never thought I would get to see the inside of a Matherson Manor."

The flattery came with ease, but Benedict wasn't sure how genuine it was. A little temper test wouldn't hurt. "Probably because there aren't many Mathersons left, thanks to the Order that sent you."

Emerson's face fell, but to his credit, he recovered his polite smile quickly.

Lucinda silently scolded Benedict. He cleared his throat, wishing Grams and Wilhelmina would join them so he wouldn't have to suffer through more pleasantries.

"How do you two know each other?" Emerson asked, breaking the tension.

"Old family fri—" Lucinda started.

"She's my fiancée," Benedict announced.

Lucinda choked on her wine.

"You shouldn't be drinking. It might make the fire worse," he whispered in her ear, passing her an empty glass. When it touched her hand, it was filled with water. He gave himself a mental pat on the back for using her element without causing a mess.

"I won't survive this conversation without it, and I'm managing fine," she hissed, swapping the water for wine. "Stop using my element!"

Emerson glanced at Lucinda, as though waiting for her to confirm whether or not they were to be married.

Don't even think about it. She's mine. Always has been, and always will be. Benedict's possessive thoughts startled him.

"I didn't know you were engaged. Congratulations," Emerson said.

"It's c-complicated," Lucinda stuttered, her eyes darting between the two men as though she didn't know where to begin.

"What relationship isn't?" Benedict said cheerfully before she could keep going, though he doubted she'd explain the exact workings of their engagement to a stranger.

"Lucy, could you help me with the dessert for a moment?" Wilhelmina called from the kitchen down the hall.

"Don't antagonise him," Lucinda whispered, placing her napkin on the table. Benedict rubbed his jaw to conceal a smirk as he watched her leave.

"I hear you've accepted the vacant position at the university," he said. "I'm surprised your Order would allow you to settle in a sanctuary town." Even the mention of the Order made him wince, but he wasn't going to let Emerson see that. The university had been looking for someone to replace the Classical and Mythical Studies spot since the last professor had decided to study dragon remains in some undisclosed location. The head of the University often visited the Manor spa with his wife, and Benedict hadn't heard the dean had approved anyone until Rosie mentioned it.

"I've been working in Darworth University. Lucinda's father gave my CV to the university board. My work with the Order required moving quite often, but I want to settle somewhere, put down some roots," Emerson said. "When Lucinda's father told me about the opening, I didn't hesitate."

"I hope you don't mind me saying, but you look rather young for such a position." Benedict was surprised he'd worked with Mr Hawthorne, never mind having his approval. At least now it made sense how he'd got past the hiring committee.

Emerson sipped his wine, and Benedict wondered if his patience was beginning to thin. "I've done the work, and I'll be thirty-two this year. All those years in libraries and out of the sun kept me youthful. I'm sure you get the same assumed about you, considering you run such a successful business."

"I didn't have a choice after my father passed," Benedict said tightly.

Emerson stilled, realising his mistake. It was the Order that had taken his father's life as punishment for a spell gone wrong. Would Emerson report those at this very table for the same sin if he knew about the elemental mishap?

"I didn't mean..." the professor started.

"Foxford is a special place. I understand why you'd want to stay here. The people are trusting and kind, and we look out for each other," Benedict cut in, drinking from Lucinda's wine glass. "But if that trust is broken, and anyone tries to harm our sanctuary... I'm afraid little mercy is shown." His words were laced with threat.

"I understand you want to protect your town," Emerson began, but Benedict's laughter cut him off again.

"The town itself can burn." He leant forward, pointing to the door. "But the women in the next room mean a great deal to me. If *anything* happens to them, or anyone brings them any trouble, then no sanctuary in this world or the next can help them."

Emerson took another drink, no doubt considering his reply carefully. A veiled threat directed at an Order member could get Benedict in a lot of trouble, but he didn't care. Not when it came to protecting those he cared about. He couldn't protect his dad, his brother, but he would sure as hell protect the Hawthornes.

"They're lucky to have someone who cares for their safety more than their own," Emerson said at last, and

Benedict mentally shook hands with him – begrudgingly. "I can assure you that I mean them no harm."

"Sorry for keeping you waiting – the dessert was a little on the frozen side," Wilhelmina interrupted, carrying in a dish filled with perfectly layered tiramisu.

"Benedict was telling me about the town, and I was congratulating him on his engagement," Emerson said, watching Wilhelmina cut into the dessert at the head of the table.

"Yes, it's certainly a *special* occasion." Grams smiled, taking a seat beside Emerson.

"Are you going to be helping out at the library? I saw you earlier with Rosie," Benedict said.

"I didn't know you had so much time on your hands, to be watching others," Lucinda muttered, serving everyone.

Playing his role as doting son-in-law perfectly under Lucinda's glare, Benedict offered Wilhelmina more cream from the side dish. "I was leaving a meeting about the Autumn Festival – a meeting you failed to attend – when I saw Rosie, and I didn't know who she was with at the time."

"There was a meeting about the festival?" Lucinda frowned, her spoon stilling.

"Maybe if you'd answered your phone, you wouldn't have missed it." Clearly, from her guilty expression, she'd been ignoring his calls on purpose. "Don't worry, there'll be plenty more, assuming you wish to attend the next one." He hoped she would; dealing with Mrs Crawford and Mr Lark arguing about what bunting to use through the town was more than he could stomach alone.

"I'll be there, don't worry," she said, forcing a smile.

"Sorry, you were interrupted. You were telling us about your assisting at the library?" Benedict said to Emerson, taking a bite of the delicious dessert. It was so creamy, offset with dark chocolate and coffee, that it almost made sitting at a table across from an Order member bearable.

"I don't start at the university until the current exams end on the fourteenth, and with Lucinda finishing up her work on a grimoire the Order gifted Foxford for the summer. I figured I'd come early and settle in before returning the grimoire to Rome," Emerson explained.

Benedict saw red. "I wasn't aware you could 'gift' what was stolen in the first place," he snapped.

Lucinda placed a reassuring hand on his clenched fist, and he was so surprised by her kind touch that he released it.

"I apologise for my choice of words," Emerson said awkwardly. He hadn't touched his dessert. "History between the Order and your people has been rather unpleasant, but I think we've come a long way."

"Easy for you to say. You weren't the ones hunted down and slaughtered. It's *our* people that must appease yours even now!"

Benedict could feel Lucinda pleading with him to stop, but he couldn't. This man belonged to the very Order who'd hunted, maimed, and killed his ancestors, his *father,* because of a spell gone wrong. Now they were sharing a meal in the very house of those they'd stolen from. A lesser man would have leapt across the table and drowned him in his wine. Benedict's ancestors would have done far worse.

"There were lives lost on both sides," Emerson growled, adding to the chewable tension.

Both men stood. *I knew there was more to him than his scholarly act.*

"Gentlemen, please," Grams snapped. "This is not the

discussion to have over dinner. "Emerson is a guest and has a job to do. He isn't here to cause any harm."

Lucinda gripped Benedict's hand, and the waves of rage within him began to dissipate.

"Please, let's forget this conversation and calm down," she ground out.

He grimaced as his palm sizzled. Her fiery touch had its desired effect, distracting him from their guest.

Pretending to kiss her cheek, Benedict whispered, "Don't use my fire against me," against her skin.

"Then play nice," she hissed, releasing his hand.

"Lucinda is right. I shouldn't have let my emotions get the better of me. I apologise for my hostility," Benedict said, sitting down. He needed Lucinda to see that he was willing to work with her, even if his simmering rage bordered on boiling.

"I'm sorry for my outburst as well; this is not how I wished to start our friendship," Emerson said, taking his own seat. "I understand my being here is a shock to you, but I must tell you that I'm of healer descent myself. My lineage has also suffered at the hands of the Order, but I truly wish for both sides to work together for the greater good – as hard as it may be."

Taken aback by Emerson's confession, Benedict found himself unable to eat, too busy trying to digest the idea of an Order member with magical ancestry.

"And you joined the order?" He couldn't help laughing. "You're far bolder than I gave you credit." He might even be a worthy contact to have, so long as he wasn't using his supposed ancestry to manipulate their trust.

"If you can't beat the enemy, why not join them?" Emerson smiled, resting his elbows on the table. "There are many of us who wish to... not forget, but move on from the past and bring the Order into a new age. You need fear nothing from me. I'm no spy, and I hope I can gain your trust in time."

"I can't slight you for that," Benedict conceded. Emerson had to have some serious balls to walk into the vipers' nest for the sake of his ideals.

"You don't have to prove yourself to anyone," Lucinda said to Emerson. Benedict couldn't believe she was defending the professor. "Especially not to him."

"What's that supposed to mean?"

"The Mathersons can hardly claim superiority; they've had their equal taste in blood."

"That's enough, Lucy," Wilhelmina snapped, resting her hands on the table.

Grams ate another mouthful of tiramisu, eyes flicking from Benedict to Emerson with evident enjoyment. Lucinda ignored her mum, keeping her attention fixed on him.

"She's right. My family have many sins to repent for. Not all families can be as Good as the Hawthornes," Benedict said, not caring to let Lucinda see how much her words had cut him.

Wilhelmina turned her attention to Emerson, and Benedict leaned in close to Lucinda. "Though I think you're being a little hypocritical," he added, glancing pointedly at the fire roaring behind them.

"I warned you not to antagonise him! This is *my* work you're threatening with your dick-measuring contest!" she hissed back. For a moment he thought she might pick up her dessert and throw it at him.

"Are you sure you two are engaged?" Emerson half-joked.

"Yes."

"No."

Their replies came at the same time. Still glaring at each other, neither were willing to be the first to break away.

"You're so beautiful when you're angry," Benedict said suddenly, pulling Lucinda close and kissing her cheek for real this time. He didn't know what had come over him, but when he leaned back he could still feel the warmth of her skin against his lips.

To his delight, Lucinda blushed. "Benedict, why do you have to be such a—" she started, but Grams interrupted.

"Lucy, will you give me a hand clearing the dishes? I think we've all had enough for one evening."

Benedict sensed the old woman wasn't talking about the dessert.

"Happily," Lucinda bit out, nudging him away. He didn't even attempt to hide his smile. Even if she was angry at him, Emerson was no longer her main focus.

"Let me give you a hand cleaning up," the professor offered as Wilhelmina reached for his plate. "No, I won't hear of it. Benedict will help," Wilhelmina smiled, but it didn't quite reach her eyes. Benedict evidently wasn't the only one eager for him to leave the table.

"She's right. You're a guest – you shouldn't have to lift a finger," Benedict said, taking the plates from Wilhelmina. Clearly, the High Priestess wasn't going to let the two of them be alone in the same room together. If every inch of him hated the order Emerson belonged to, he hated the thought of him getting close to Lucinda and the Hawthornes even more.

Hearing hushed voices within, Benedict lingered by the kitchen door, plates piled in his hands. He didn't want to eavesdrop, but he couldn't resist once he heard his name.

"I think Benedict has feelings for you," Grams was teasing.

His chest tightened as he waited for Lucinda to respond.

"Don't be ridiculous. The only thing he feels for me is disdain."

Only when you bring strangers to your house! He heard what sounded like a cupboard opening.

"I wouldn't be so sure. He looked at Emerson like he was going to steal you away," Grams said. "He came here of his own volition. When has he ever simply dropped by?"

Lucinda sighed. "None of this would've happened if you hadn't cast that damn spell."

Benedict's ears perked up. He was eager to hear if she'd told him the truth, but the sound of running water quietened their voices and he was forced to move in closer.

"What if the spell did something to him that made him act like this? There's no way to know what's true. Anyway, he's just trying to make sure he doesn't lose his chance to take my seat as head of the coven. His heart has nothing to do with his motives for being here."

"A spell or potion can't fabricate love, nor force anyone to feel or act a certain way. We acted for your own good. Was it rash and in hindsight a terrible decision? Yes, but it's done now, and you need to keep your eyes and heart open," Grams said.

The tension in Benedict's shoulders eased at the knowledge that Lucinda truly hadn't had any part in causing their elemental switch.

"What about this new professor, then? He seems to have a kind spirit, loves books and history, and works at the university. You both have plenty in common – and he turns up the day after the spell is cast. That's a lot of coincidences!"

Grams's list did nothing to ease Benedict's irritation towards Emerson. It seemed she thought, and maybe Wilhelmina did too, that the spell had called Emerson here. *I can't believe they'd prefer to see Lucinda with a member of the order than with me.* He wanted to interrupt before Grams could convince her further, but he also wanted to hear Lucinda's reply.

"Love should be about more than common interests, and Emerson is here for *work*. The Order told Rosie they'd be sending someone days ago; he didn't come here on a whim. He volunteered to collect the grimoire and because he is going to be working at the university," Lucinda stated firmly.

"Even so, no harm in getting to know him. The spell *might* have brought Emerson to you. He made it past the gargoyles and the armoured knights, which tells us he has a true heart. And he's of magical descent – a healer at that!"

Grams! Whose side are you on?!

Lucinda made no instant reply. Waiting for her response, Benedict forgot to breathe. The previously empty jug in his hand started to overflow as he lost control of her element. He put it on one of the bowls to stop it soaking the wooden floors.

"I can't get to know him, Grams. I agreed to the binding. What would the town say if I'm with one man while about to be bound to another? I'm trying to win over the coven's confidence; a love triangle won't play in my favour."

Grams laughed. "A love triangle? Perhaps it's you who has feelings for Benedict. I suppose you've known each other since you were kids..."

"Benedict and I are a *political* match. Can we please not talk about this when both men are in the next room?"

"I won't push you to do anything you aren't comfortable with. I only ask that you don't close yourself off. Let your element guide you," Grams said, her words slightly muffled. Benedict guessed they were hugging.

She only has my fire to guide her, Benedict thought. He was grateful that Lucinda had kept their switch a secret, even when mentioning it could have stopped Grams's pestering. Such information would've sent her family into a tailspin. To discover their beloved pure water was in the corrupted veins of a Matherson – he couldn't imagine the uproar. Even if they'd treated him and his mum as family, magic ran thicker than friendship.

"The last of the dishes," he announced, pushing open the door, unable to take another second of Grams convincing Lucinda to give Emerson a chance. A member of the Order, bonded to a High Priestess? The heavens would burn, and hell would freeze over. Regardless of biblical consequences, there was no way he'd allow her heart to be won by another. Not before he had a chance to claim it for his own.

Pausing, he told himself to get a grip. Her heart was none of his concern. She might be his fiancée, but as she'd said herself, they were a political match, nothing more.

"Thank you for your help." Grams took the dishes.

Benedict wanted to talk to Lucinda, but she fled without a second look. He wished she'd stop avoiding him.

Grams rested a hand on his arm. "If you want her trust – her heart – I'm afraid you're going to have to earn it."

Peter had said something similar. "I don't know what

you're talking about," Benedict lied, helping her load the dishwasher.

Grams rolled her eyes. He decided to leave before he overstayed his welcome.

"I'll say my goodbyes," he said, kissing her cheek. "Thank Wilhelmina for dessert for me, and tell Lucinda there's another meeting for the festival tomorrow morning."

Grams shooed him from the kitchen.

Outside, he pulled at the collar on his long coat. His feet refused to move; he couldn't leave without talking to Lucinda. He knew how dangerous it was to sleep with fire magic when you were riled up – one bad dream might burn down the house. He didn't know why he cared all of a sudden. Then again, he didn't want to be accused if Hawthorne House went up in flames the same night he'd come for dinner.

Benedict rounded the house, spotting a tall oak tree which gave him access to her balcony. He looked down at his leather shoes and sighed. *Not exactly the best for climbing,* he thought, plucking up the nerve to reach for the first branch. *She'd better not set me on fire for trying to help her.*

Lucinda

"I'm sorry for how Benedict spoke to you. His family were prosecuted by the Order for generations. Don't take it personally," Lucy said to Emerson by the front door. If she were to be honest, she considered Benedict's reaction better than it could have been. She figured he'd shown restraint because her mother and Grams had been present.

"With the Mathersons' history, and all that has transpired between his family and the order, I wasn't expecting a warm embrace from him. I wouldn't have been surprised if he'd set me on fire – at least you'd have been able to put me out," Emerson quipped. Thankfully, he didn't hold a grudge. She didn't want him to report Benedict's hostile behaviour.

"Thank you for understanding. I'm sure once you get to know him you'll see he doesn't quite live up to their reputation," Lucy said, taking the topic as far away from elemental magic as possible. Even if they didn't get along, the thought of the Order coming for Benedict caused a lump in her throat. It made her uneasy that Emerson knew so much about them. She reminded herself he'd passed her earlier tests. *And if Grams had sensed anything off about him, she certainly wouldn't have been encouraging me to date him.*

"Leaving so soon? I've put on a pot of coffee," Wilhelmina offered, finding them in the hallway.

"It's been a long day, and I wouldn't want to overstay my welcome," Emerson said, putting on his jacket. He'd taken Lucy's advice and not reattached the pin. At least he was polite enough to say goodbye. Benedict had disappeared without a word, which did nothing to settle her nerves.

"I'll see you tomorrow; we open up at eight. Please don't feel you have to come first thing."

"I'm used to university hours, so early works for me," Emerson assured her.

"There's another meeting about the Autumn Festival tomorrow morning. Benedict told Grams before he left," Wilhelmina added, her strained expression telling her daughter she had no choice but to attend.

"I won't miss it. Rosie will still be there to open the library. I'm sure she would be grateful for your help again," Lucy said, hoping Emerson wouldn't mind.

"No rush. Rosie invited me for breakfast, so I can walk with her."

"She does make a great mimosa!" *Though it's more alcohol than orange juice.* She silently thanked Rosie for making him feel welcome. Rosie knew what it was like to be new in town.

"I'll see you tomorrow!" Emerson waved, heading down the path. Lucy waited until he'd secured the gate behind him before she closed the door.

"He is so handsome; that sandy hair reminds me of

your grandfather," Grams sighed, lingering at her back. "If I was forty years younger..."

"Ha. Don't let that stop you," Lucy teased.

"Don't encourage her," Wilhelmina said.

"I was just saying to Lucy, Wilhelmina, what a lovely young man he is. Exactly what we asked for, in fact."

"He also held up impeccably well under Benedict's scrutiny," Wilhelmina agreed.

"*You* can't think the spell brought him too," Lucy groaned. *There's no spark between us!* Then again, she and Benedict might have spark, but it was more like full-blown forest fires. Maybe her mum and Grams had a point. "Dad recommended him to the university weeks ago. He would have come whether or not the spell was cast."

"Still, the timing is interesting," Grams pointed out. "But even if it was the spell, the choice is yours."

"Don't you think he's... *too* perfect?" Lucy asked, replaying dinner and their earlier introduction. Benedict had managed to get a rise out of him, so she knew there was at least some anger beneath his passive demeanour.

"I'm sure he was nervous, but coming here shows courage. Nothing's stopping you from getting to know him. Forget about the spell and let your feelings guide you," Wilhelmina said, echoing what Grams had said in the kitchen.

"What about the binding and my responsibilities to the coven?" Lucy fretted, pulling at her sleeves. "If they even get a whiff that I'm getting close to someone, it could ruin my chances."

"The world won't end if you don't bind yourself to Benedict, or decide against leading the coven," Wilhelmina said, resting a hand on her shoulder.

Lucy was taken aback. They'd been talking about her

taking her mum's place since she was in nappies. Her palms began to sweat; she really couldn't handle any more ifs. She resolved to only focus on what she did know.

"I'll do as I promised the coven unless Benedict changes his mind. Emerson is only here to collect the grimoire and work at the university. That's all we know for certain. I already have to deal with—" Lucy stopped herself before she said too much. Thankfully, they didn't catch it.

"Everything seems overwhelming now, but a good night's rest can make everything better." Grams wrapped her arms around her granddaughter.

"Let's see where the next few weeks take you. I've no doubt things will work out as fate intended," Mum said, leading them towards the staircase.

"Do you always have to be so cryptic? I wish you'd tell me what to do," Lucy whined, hugging her mum goodnight.

"It's my job to let you find your path, as we chose ours." Mum looked at Grams with a soft smile.

"Are you speaking as a mum or High Priestess?" Lucy asked. They might understand what it was to be a High Priestess, but they'd inherited their seats, whereas she was meant to either marry Benedict or face an election. It was a totally different set of stressful circumstances.

"Both." Mum winked. "Get some rest."

Lucy nodded, before heading upstairs to her room.

"Please don't jump!" Benedict appeared from the shadows by the balcony as Lucy stood by the circular window seat.

Thankfully, her room was protected with a sound-proofing spell, so Lucy's squeal shouldn't disturb the rest of the house. However, Chaos – peacefully asleep on her cat tower – jumped as much as her owner with a hiss.

"How did you even get in?" Lucy snapped, before noticing the balcony door by the right of her bed was open. However, the smell of smoke distracted her. *What's burning?*

Benedict rushed past her. She gasped in horror as he ripped her smoking curtains from the window and stomped out the sparks.

"Damn it, Lucinda, you've to be more careful!" he barked, gathering up the singed material. "You could've set the house on fire."

"It's a pity it wasn't you," she grumbled, glad he hadn't used her magic to put them out and accidentally flooded her room.

He tossed the curtains under her desk to conceal them from sight and straightened his jacket. Seeing him rattled, cheeks flushed, was new and worth nearly setting her room on fire.

"I didn't do it on purpose, and I wouldn't have set them on fire if you hadn't surprised me!"

Chaos stretched before leaping down from her tower. Lucy tried to pick her up, but the cat only hissed.

"We need to fix this before one of us gets hurt." The worry in his voice arrested her. In the silence, she looked at her ruined curtains and hoped the fabric shop still had some of it left. She loved the silver-threaded florals.

"I can't believe you broke into my room," she said, frowning at Chaos and trying not to be upset about her furry friend's snub.

"I didn't break in. I climbed the tree and your balcony door was open," he explained.

Lucy usually left the door ajar so Chaos could get in and out, since her favourite spot was the tree outside. She tried to picture Benedict climbing the tree in his long coat and expensive shoes. *How could I have missed that?* The mental image made up for the jumpscare.

"Well, feel free to climb back down," she said, turning on her bedside lamps.

"I wouldn't have had to come at all if you'd answered your phone!"

To Lucy's intense irritation, Chaos weaved herself through Benedict's legs, purring.

Benedict bent to stroke her. "Strange. Didn't she use to hate me?"

Chaos climbed into his arms, purring happily. The only satisfaction Lucy got from the betrayal was that his immaculate suit would be covered in cat hair.

"I think she senses our elements switched. She won't let me near her, and that's the only thing that's different," she sulked.

"Speaking of our elements, why *didn't* you answer your phone?"

"I meant to get back to you! I ended up sleeping in the vault last night going through everything, and I found the curse-stripping potion in the Hawthorne grimoire, but I don't know if it'll remove our elements altogether or swap them back," Lucy said, crossing her arms. "Our best option is to try the original spell again and hope it'll cancel out the mistake in the first attempt. Now, if you wouldn't mind leaving, I'm tired."

"When can we try? The sooner we get back to normal

the better," Benedict insisted, following her around the room as she cleaned up. "Can you please stand still for a minute? We need to talk." He put Chaos back on her tower.

"We talked at dinner. And please don't refer to me as your fiancée to others. It gives people the wrong impression about us."

"Afraid your new friend will be scared off? We're to be bound by the end of the month," he reminded her.

She stopped cleaning. Two things she couldn't believe: one, that Benedict Matherson was seeing her mess of a room, and two, that he sounded jealous.

"Why would he be scared off by our... whatever it is?" she scoffed. "If anything, he'd be scared off by your antagonism. I don't think either of us want him to report back to the Order that a Matherson is rather outspoken about his hatred towards their members."

"I won't be hostile if you don't invite a stranger into your home," Benedict countered, flipping through a botany guide on her desk. She wished he wouldn't look through her things; it felt far too intimate.

"I invited him to dinner to see how he'd hold up against Mum and Grams." Not that she owed him any explanation. "He passed the tests in the vault; any ill intent would have caused him serious harm."

Benedict snapped the book closed. Lucy cringed, wishing she'd kept that part to herself.

"You brought an Order member into the vault?" He acted more hurt than angry. "Why do you trust a man you've only known for a few hours, but treat me like I'm the enemy?"

"I don't treat you like an enemy! And *if* I did, it would be because of all that's happened between us over the years." She put herself between him and her crowded desk so he'd stop prying. It was distracting.

"You played a part in our past. If that Order member learned that my fire flows through you, you can be sure his attitude would change."

"Stop throwing the swap in my face. It wasn't my fault, and he won't find out," she snapped, feeling flames swell in her chest.

"You don't know that, and I'll stop when you stop throwing my family's past in mine," he retorted, closing the gap between them. "That was a low blow at dinner."

Exasperated, Lucy took a minute to breathe.

"I'm sorry for bringing up your family," she said at last. "I wanted to distract you from arguing with him. The thought of you ending up on the Order's list..." She cut herself off, not even knowing how to finish the sentence. "One petty victory isn't worth getting tangled up with the Order."

"Are you sure you weren't just protecting your new friend?" Benedict asked, narrowing his eyes. Testing her.

"Protecting *him?*" His refusal to understand made her want to set the whole damn attic alight.

"You jumped between us, grabbing my hand. You think I'm dangerous." He held out his hand, and she saw the raw pink marks where she'd burned him.

"I didn't mean or want to hurt you. I was protecting you from him." She kept her voice low, needing him to know she hadn't done it on purpose. "You've lost your brother, your dad. I wasn't going to let you get in a fight with him on Foxford soil!"

"I can handle myself, with or without my element."

Lucy sighed, taking his hand so that he'd listen. "You so much as scratch Emerson, do you know what they'd do to the person who hurt someone acting as their representative?"

Benedict stared down at their hands.

"They'd call for you to be handed over for breaking our neutrality clause. Is that what you want? For your mum to hand you over to the Order like she had to do with your father? You can be damn sure I wouldn't be there to watch it happen. Grams has defended you in the past. Even my mum deemed you worthy of claiming her seat – and you wanted to throw all that away because Emerson spoke without thought."

He let the words settle between them in silence, his thumb running over the back of her hand. Lucy decided she preferred it when they were squabbling.

"I'm sorry for mentioning your family," she said again. "No matter how much we fight, I don't want to see you hurt."

Benedict let go of her to run his hand through his hair. She wished they'd kept talking about their elemental problem.

"I shouldn't have antagonised him. I... need you to know that my dad was trying to help those creatures." Her chest tightened at the thick edge of sadness in his voice. "The creatures were infected with a sickness no healer could cure."

She'd heard the story from Grams, but never from Benedict himself. The creatures had come to Foxford several years ago to be healed, but Grams had been unable to help them. Benedict's dad had found a spell that was said to cure all ailments.

"He really believed that spell would be able to help them. I know it seems unlikely, but what you have to believe is that Dad didn't know it would end their lives," Benedict explained.

That had been the cure: death, a merciful end. When the Order had found out, they'd called for his execution. After that, Lucy had become obsessed with translating old grimoires meticulously. She'd wanted to prevent such a mishap from ever occurring again. Maybe if his father had understood it wasn't a *healing* spell, but a *mercy* spell, Benedict would still have a father, and a brother who hadn't died trying to resurrect him after the sentence was carried out.

"You don't need to defend him. Your dad was a good man who wanted to help," she said quietly.

Benedict tilted his head back, as though trying to stop tears from spilling. She'd never seen him so vulnerable. The element spell going wrong must've been triggering for him.

"Peter just wanted him back. It was his grief..." He'd never spoken like this about his family to Lucy before; in spite of herself, her own eyes filled with tears. "He was only sixteen."

Peter's fate haunted her. The penalty for necromancy.

"You try to cheat death, and you become it." He shook his head.

Lucy sat on the edge of the bed. Had he spoken to *anyone* about this before? The pain in his voice added to her guilt. "You don't need to justify their actions to me. I never should've brought them up tonight. I didn't want you to get involved in my work with the Order. My work doesn't involve you, and Emerson's arrival couldn't come at a worse time."

He grimaced. "It does involve me."

"The library and all it contains is my responsibility. How has that got anything to do with you?"

"Because it's *your* responsibility."

The words seemed to surprise him as much as they did her.

"You're worried about me?" she asked, as he suddenly found his feet very interesting.

"Yes! You're...." He cut himself off, standing over her.

"I'm what?" she pressed, seeing a trace of concern in his gaze.

He hesitated. Maybe Grams was right; maybe he did have feelings for her. Her stomach knotted, and she wasn't sure if the sensation was altogether unpleasant.

"You're holding my element and working with a member of the order. If that's exposed, we aren't just going to be judged by the coven for reckless use of magic," he said eventually.

Silence crowded them. Lucy pushed aside any thought of feelings and hoped for a truce. "How about we both agree to react less and think more?"

"Agreed." He nodded, offering her his hand.

She smirked. "Really? We've got to shake on agreeing to be reasonable?"

"Need to make it official," he said. "We've agreed to do much worse."

Lucy rolled her eyes. He clasped her hands, and this time they both stared down at them. The coolness of her water mixed with the heat of his fire made her breath catch.

He released her, and she told herself it was just their magic trying to return to their rightful places.

"Now, what are we going to do about our elements?" Benedict sat unexpectedly close beside her.

"There's no time like the present. Grams and Mum are probably asleep by now," she said, looking at her desk. "We've got the ingredients in the brewing room."

"You want to try to redo the potion tonight?" He sounded nervous.

"Got some other pressing matter to attend?" She picked up the list of qualities and the potion ingredients from her untidy desk.

He shook his head. "You're my number one priority."

"Good. This is the potion Grams used, and here is the one I found in your family's old grimoire." She handed him the notes, only to regret it when he immediately began to read the list of qualities aloud.

"Loyal, kind, capable, passionate... to think your element choose me!" He failed to conceal a smug grin. "How highly you must think of me."

"Don't flatter yourself!" She snatched the list out of his hand before his ego ended their truce.

"I don't have to – your element did it for you."

Lucy headed for the door. "Let's get on with it."

Lucinda

Why is it that whenever you're trying to be quiet, the floorboards and doors decide to greet you extra loudly? Lucinda wondered as she closed the door to the brewing room behind Benedict. Thankfully, her mum and Grams were in bed, so they shouldn't be caught.

"The dimmer is on the wall," she said, pointing to the light switch as she went to gather the ingredients.

"I know. Grams taught me in this room too," he reminded her.

"Only because you were failing potions in the first year." Lucy let out a sigh of relief when she saw there was just enough damiana root for one more spell.

"We all can't be Hawthornes. It's not exactly a fair competition when you've got Grams in your back pocket," Benedict grumbled, looking over the ingredient list she'd placed on the table. Thankfully the base of the potion was only blessed water from the coven temple, and they had plenty bottled.

"Why can't you admit that I'm better than you?" She

took one of the glass bottles from the cupboard while Benedict began to dice the chickweed and chilli.

"Not at all things," he whispered at her back, and Lucy nearly added too much rosewater to the cauldron.

They collected the ingredients from the shelves, this time making sure to grab the bat's blood. Together, they watched the cauldron sizzle and bubble, both too nervous to discuss what they were about to do.

"Almost finished," Lucy finally said, taking the knife he'd used to dice the other ingredients and pressing the point to her finger. Alarmed, he grasped her wrist.

"Relax. It's only a drop of blood," she said, and he reluctantly released his grip on her.

"Is that necessary?" He winced, watching her prick her finger. "We could've used mine."

"Yes – the original potion contained my blood." Lucy wrapped some tissue around her finger. "If this is going to work, we can't change anything except for the wrong ingredient."

Speaking of... She added the bat's blood instead of black pepper. She'd expected something to change, but the glistening water remained identical to the first potion. She tried to conceal her disappointment, hoping that even if the appearance hadn't changed, the meaning had.

"Rose petals?" she requested, and Benedict pulled them free from the flowers on the counter. They floated on the surface until Lucy dropped in the rolled list of qualities she'd written out from memory.

"Is that it?" His brows pulled together, but a sharp bang interrupted her response.

Their eyes snapped to the door, afraid the noise would alert the others. When no one came, they both took an audible breath. Benedict swished away the rising smoke and they peered into the empty cauldron, the piece of paper burnt to ash.

"What now?" he asked as she put away the ingredients and he washed out the cauldron.

"All we can do is wait. It only took a few hours before we felt the effects last time." She opened the door to make sure the way was clear. Luckily, Grams was a heavy sleeper. "I think by tomorrow morning we should have our answer."

"And if it doesn't work?"

"We'll try the curse--stripping potion, but it'll take time for me to find the ingredients," she said, hoping they wouldn't have to use it. He nodded, looking equally uneasy at the prospect. "Or, we wait until after the binding and see what happens."

"I should go before it gets any later," Benedict said, heading for the stairs.

"Are you crazy?" Lucy grabbed him before he stepped on one of the creaky floorboards. "You'll wake the whole house. There's no way you can use the front door. Someone could see you, and what would I tell my family, or worse, the neighbours, if you were seen leaving the house in the middle of the night?" The thought alone made her shudder.

"We *are* engaged. Being alone together is hardly scandalous," he drawled, closing the gap between them.

"Don't try to be cute." The cool glow of her element in his body felt like a balm to the heat emanating from her own.

He opened his mouth in mock outrage. "I'd never! How am I supposed to leave, then, or is this you inviting me to stay?"

Lucy smiled. "You can go the way you came."

He groaned, following her back to the attic without argument.

"What if we're wrong?" he asked eventually.

"About what?" She stilled in the middle of opening the balcony door.

He leaned against the doorframe. "What if the spell worked, and our element swapped to show us that maybe we're meant to be bound?"

"Are you messing with me?" she chuckled. "Do *you* think we're meant to be together?"

"Don't make it sound like a life sentence." There was no trace of humour in his gaze.

"It isn't."

He frowned, straightening his posture.

"Technically, it's a soul sentence. We'd be bound in this life *and* the next."

"Funny," he said flatly.

Lucy followed him out onto the balcony. He was so tense that she felt relaxed in comparison. "You'll get frown lines if you don't lighten up," she teased. "Do you think our elements swapping wasn't a mistake?"

"Don't you think it would be simpler if it wasn't a mistake? If maybe our elements could have seen something we've been missing." He flexed his hands as they rested on the balcony railing.

Lucy didn't know what to say. She tried to speak, but the words caught in her throat.

He shook his head. "I don't know. Ignore me; it's late."

"Tomorrow everything might be back to normal. No one will ever know about our elements, and we can make it to the end of the month in relative peace," she said tentatively.

"About that... Peter came to the manor to congratulate

me on our binding. Your uncle told him about our being bound," he admitted, fidgeting with a splinter of loose wood.

"Oh gods, he knows about our switched elements?" Lucy guessed.

"Unfortunately, yes."

Lucy dropped her head into her hands, feeling a headache coming on.

"I didn't plan to tell him, but he was waiting for me after we had our little storm in the garden. He spotted the matches in my room – something our family has never had any use for. If I wanted to stop him from asking around, I figured it was best to tell him," Benedict reasoned. "You don't need to worry about him telling anyone, and your family don't know it backfired. We just need to make sure the new professor doesn't find out... which might be tricky, considering how he was looking at you."

Lucy glowered. "He wasn't looking at me in any type of way."

"Not your type?" he baited her.

"You don't need to worry about who is and isn't my type."

"So, you wouldn't go on a date with him?"

His question threw her so much so that a nervous laugh escaped. "He works for the Order!"

Benedict glanced sideways at her. "I suppose he's better than the last guy you dated. What was he again?"

"A shapeshifter, and if you're only lingering to discuss my love life, then please see yourself out. I'd like to go to bed."

"Bed is exactly what I want to talk about," he said, eyes going back to her room.

"Get that idea out of your head," she snapped, thinking of the night they'd spent in the Manor.

"I was only going to warn you that sleeping with fire can be tricky." He smiled, clearly enjoying her mistake, as she flushed. He tapped the wooden balcony. "This place would go up like a tinder-box."

"Noted. I'll drink some calming tea," she said, embarrassed. "Off you go."

He followed her back inside before she could close the door.

"If you aren't going to listen to me, listen to them." He nodded to her bookshelf. "'Beware; for I am fearless and therefore powerful.'"

One of the books sat out of place. *He found my favourite.* "Don't go through my things!"

"I had to do something to occupy myself while I waited for you," he protested, "and you need more than calming tea. I set a few fires when I first got my element, and I don't want you to hurt those you love because you don't respect it." He wasn't joking around anymore.

"I picked this up from Myrtle's." He pulled out a silver chain with a crystal from his pocket.

"A carnelian crystal?" Lucy asked as he turned her towards the full-length mirror by her desk.

"Exactly. It'll help draw out the excess fire. Mathersons have been using these amulets for generations to help us with our elements. We wear them while we're maturing so we don't lose control. Fire and hormones have never been a great combination."

He placed the chain around her neck, letting the crystal hang at the base of her throat. The instant it touched her skin, the crawling simmer beneath her skin settled. His fingertips brushed the back of her neck as he clasped it, sending shivers down her spine.

"I've never seen you wear one," she said, trying not to reveal the effect his touch had on her.

Benedict took off his watch and handed it to her. "Flip it over."

The watch face had a crystal base with the same golden-orange hue. Unlike her crystal, which had grown warm against her skin, it was cold without his magic to control.

"When Dad and Peter died, my element grew stronger. Gwendoline had Mulligans' Jewellers fuse the crystal to my dad's old watch to keep it out of sight." He secured the strap. "Keep this to yourself? I don't want people to think I can't control my element."

"We'll add it to the growing number of secrets between us," she promised, understanding how much it must have taken to admit he needed help with his element.

"Just don't let Grams or Wilhelmina see it – they'll know what it's for."

She nodded, clasping the crystal.

"Now that Hawthorne house is safe, I'll be going." He backed up towards the balcony.

Lucy blocked his path, wanting to repay him for his help. "Water can be rather mischievous," she blurted out.

"Any advice?"

"Try watering some plants to help relieve the pressure. It likes to be useful." It was the most harmless thing she could think of.

"I'll water the new hedgerows the gardeners planted in the gardens." He smiled, something she was getting used to seeing. The loss of his brother and father had aged him, along with the weight of his responsibilities, but when he smiled, he looked much younger. "Since someone burnt the others to a crisp."

She masked her wince with a chuckle. "How shocking."

If it hadn't been for their truce, she might have been tempted to shove him as he climbed off her balcony. Instead, she found herself clutching the warm crystal, grateful to him for protecting her family from his element. Hopefully, by the morning it wouldn't be necessary.

"Why are you looking at me like that?" Benedict asked, swinging himself onto the strongest tree branch that hung over the balcony.

"I wasn't looking at you," Lucy said, leaning on the railing. "I was just thinking that maybe you could've used the door after all."

"And have Grams and your mum see me coming out of your room? We'd be bound by dawn." He winked before making his way to the next branch. In his crisp suit and smart shoes, he looked distinctly out of place climbing a tree like a boy, but she guessed his fear of being caught by her family made it worth it. She chewed her blushing smile so he wouldn't think he'd caused it.

"I've got to ask," he said suddenly, hesitating below the balcony.

She huffed, crossing her arms over her chest. "What? I want to go to bed."

"If Hughes asked, would you go out with him?"

She couldn't believe this was what he wanted to discuss. *I thought I'd already been clear.*

"You aren't going to leave until you get an answer?" Maybe she should let him spend the night in the tree.

He shrugged.

"Why do you even think I'd contemplate it?" *What did*

he see at dinner that made him believe there's anything between me and Emerson?

"I overheard Grams talking to you in the kitchen," he confessed, dropping down to another branch. She winced as it crackled under his weight.

"Not helping me trust you," she said dryly.

"At least I admitted it, and that's still not an answer."

She rolled her eyes, needing this conversation to end. "I've no interest in dating Emerson. *You've* complicated my life enough; I don't need to add another man to the mix." A small smile rose to the corner of his lips. "I answered your question. Now go before the branch breaks."

Wait. He must have heard Grams suggest there's something more between us as well.

"Worried about me, pumpkin?" He jumped to another branch. Lucy flinched; the tree was older than the house.

"I want to take over the coven by right, not because you broke your neck," she hissed as he disappeared from sight.

There was a thud, and her heart stilled. She leaned over the railing and found him at the base of the tree, safely on solid ground. He gave a bow and left.

Rubbing her temples, Lucy thought of everything Grams had said. *What if the spell did bring Emerson to me? If so, then why did my element swap with Benedict's?*

"This is why you aren't supposed to mess with love magic," she grumbled in frustration, locking the balcony door.

Placing her glasses on her nightstand, she rubbed the bridge of her nose. Tomorrow, she decided, their elements would be back in their rightful place, and the only thing she'd have to worry about was the binding.

Lucinda

In the early morning, Lucinda found herself sitting at the corner table of Stoker's Café, discussing the importance of stall placement with the rest of the Autumn Festival committee when all she wanted to do was scream.

Instead of waking up to feel the ebb and flow of her own element, she'd woken in a puddle of sweat as the crystal fought to suppress the flames coursing through her veins. Without Benedict's help, she was sure she'd have woken to a house made of ash.

Right now, however, she didn't have time to focus on her disappointment. As much as she wanted to get to the vault and confirm the ingredients for the curse-stripping potion, she couldn't afford to miss another meeting about the committee's biggest event of the year.

Having participated in the festival every year; it would have raised suspicion if she had refused, and she hoped the routine would help her focus. After all, her caramel apples were legend. The secret was that she got Rosie to sniff out perfectly crisp apples in the woods. Their sweet yet tangy flavour couldn't compare to anything found in the supermarket.

Organising the rest of the stalls was a whole different type of pressure. They'd been going over the details for the last three hours, and Mrs Crawford was already on her second coffee, which didn't make her any easier to deal with. Lucy guessed that Benedict's disappointment had got the best of him, since he was a no-show. She'd wanted to stop by the manor, but guilt had stopped her. She justified her cowardice by reminding herself that he could probably do with some space.

"We should set up the food stalls and stage for the puppet show around the gazebo but have the food stalls leading into the alleyway, so no matter what direction the visitors travel in, they'll have food and beverages available to them," she said firmly, looking over the town map.

Mrs Crawford considered Lucy's idea, while Mr Lark waited to see who to side with.

"Certainly a different approach, but I like the idea," Mrs Crawford said finally. "Then we can use the field by the college for the Ferris wheel, and we won't have to worry about keeping everyone in the heart of town. It does get rather crowded until everyone leaves for the fireworks."

Lucy had expected some hostility for missing yesterday's meeting, but it had never come up. Maybe it was because Benedict hadn't made it today.

"Are you sure it won't feel too dispersed?" Mr Lark asked, looking at the new layout Lucy had drawn up hastily.

"Not if we plan it right. And we could give the options

for stores to remain open – then they won't need stalls, *and* people get to experience everything the town has to offer," Lucy suggested.

"We'd reduce costs, as we wouldn't have to rent extra stalls from Willow Valley," Mrs Crawford mused, tapping her long, manicured nail against the map. Willow Valley was the closest sanctuary town, and they often provided each other with whatever they needed as a way of supporting each other.

"There are some who'd prefer not to have to lug their wares through town," Mr Lark agreed. Lucy suspected he was one of those stores; he sold hand-crafted pottery.

"That's settled, then. The stalls will lead from town to the festival grounds in the fields behind the university. People can eat and shop no matter what direction they head in, rather than be clustered in town," she reiterated, hoping to get back to the library soon.

"But are you sure the food vendors won't mind setting up in the side streets and alleys?" Mrs Crawford asked.

Lucy resisted the urge to groan. She was never going to get away! The clock behind the counter told her it was almost eleven. However, it was a valid question – most of the profits they made were from food and drink.

"I think it's a better idea. That way, those who sell vintage clothes, handcrafts and furnishing won't have to worry about their goods smelling like food," Mr Lark said.

"Good point." Mrs Crawford nodded, though her beehive of bright orange hair failed to move.

Lucy raised her eyebrows as they agreed. Oscar Lark and Lidia Crawford had hated each other ever since Lidia had 'accidentally' turned his prize-winning pumpkin patch into lollipops during the annual Glorious Gourds competition. Oscar believed it was intentional, because he was often known as the lollipop man; he ran the sweet shop and had a rather large head compared to his pencil-like body. It wasn't said to offend, but once you heard the nickname, you couldn't unsee it. Lucy was relieved to see them make amends. Then again, he'd already got his revenge by turning her prized rose bushes into oranges. You only needed to look at Lidia's hair to know why – no explanation needed.

Pettiness was rife in Foxford. Add magic to the mix, and the usual small-town drama escalated quickly. Lucy and Benedict were a prime example. However, it was an unwritten agreement that no matter what happened between individuals, they'd always put the town first.

"I can finalise the map, and talk with the vendors to see if they'd like to rent a stall or keep their doors open," Mr Lark offered. As he was on the board of small businesses, there was no one better to handle it.

"Perfect. I'll talk to the dean of the university about the carousel and the ferris wheel being set up on their back fields. I know we usually use the space by the woods, but this way people don't have to walk so far, and we won't have to hire as much security to make sure no visitors wander off." Mrs Crawford loved cutting costs.

"The lights of the carousel and Ferris wheel will highlight the architecture of the university beautifully, and make it more accessible to those with mobility issues," Lucy pointed out, delighted they liked her plan. With everything else feeling so out of control, the small win had her glowing.

"Brilliant! Benedict had a similar plan. Gwendoline was right when she said you'd make an excellent pair for leadership," Mrs Crawford said, ever his champion.

Slightly deflated, Lucy nodded weakly in reply. A lesser

person would've advised an alternative plan to rival Benedict, to show she could stand on her own two feet. However, if she was going to be the leader she needed and wanted to be, picking what worked best for the town was the right option. She rubbed her palms against her thighs, wondering if Gwendoline had been right about the binding after all.

"It's a pity Benedict couldn't join us this morning. He told us how busy you were at the library yesterday, so we understand that you might not both be able to make it to every meeting. It only adds to the positives of your union; if one isn't available, the other can be. The burden won't weigh too heavily on either one of your shoulders," Mrs Crawford pointed out happily.

Lucy's eyes widened. She'd assumed Benedict had taken the opportunity to throw her under the bus; instead, he had defended her. She touched the amulet he'd given her, wondering why he was doing so much to help. It only made her feel worse about the potion not working.

"Thank you for your understanding. Since we've decided on our plan, we should adjourn for now. I'm sure both of us will be able to make the next meeting," she said, trying to conceal her surprise.

After some brief goodbyes, she snuggled her scarf under her chin as she walked out in the brisk air. If she was going to make it through the rest of the day, she was in desperate need of more iced tea.

Benedict

"I shouldn't have let you talk me into this," Benedict said, climbing out of his car. "I didn't miss a meeting about the Autumn Festival to get lost in the woods with you."

"Relax. The crone can smell fear, and we aren't lost," Peter said, leading him down a narrow path between abandoned cottages. "You should be thanking me for making enquiries, since you and Lucy failed to fix your elements."

Benedict locked the car, even though it was pointless. There was no one around for miles. If they wanted to get into his car, something as simple as a lock wouldn't stop them.

He guessed they were about an hour or so from Willow Valley, the closest magical village to Foxford. They didn't abide by the same rules Foxford did. Magic, of all practices, was allowed, and the woods between were lawless and filled with all sorts of creatures. They didn't fear Hunters or the Order, and preferred to run the risk of bloodshed. Benedict didn't know how anyone could live in such fear.

The siblings lingered outside the crone's hovel. She was famous for her lack of morals and the strength of her magic. She had been in the woods longer than anyone could or wanted to remember; not even the Order tried to come after her. It was the last place Benedict wanted to be, but the cool wind brushing the back of his neck reminded him of Lucinda's element stirring in his veins, and he knew he had to do something.

"I always knew Lucinda would be the death of me." He noted the totems made of small animal bones hanging from the overgrown porch: a warning to those who wished harm upon the dweller.

They didn't even need to knock before the door creaked open.

"I never thought I'd see the day when not one, but *two* Mathersons would darken my decrepit door," said the crone. She had a bent back and a long chin.

"I was told you know about elemental magic," Peter said, standing in front of Benedict. Peter couldn't be killed twice, and magic didn't affect Grim Reapers. If the crone decided to add his brother to her collection of bones in the clay pots by her door, she'd have to go through death first.

The crone sniffed the air around them, but settled closer to Benedict with a slick grin. "You've got yourself in quite the pickle. Come inside. I believe I can be of some assistance."

Peter followed her in; Benedict hesitated. He didn't want to go behind Lucinda's back like this, but seeing how much hope she'd had for last night's potion weighed on his heart. The guilt she obviously felt for a mistake she'd had no part in reminded him of the guilt he felt for those he'd lost. If the crone could help, Lucinda never needed to know their attempt to fix the potion hadn't worked. He could merely tell her it had taken some time to kick in.

"I can remove her element from your body and yours from her; however, such harsh magic comes at a price," the crone said suddenly, lighting some black candles in preparation for performing a spell.

Benedict didn't remember walking inside, but he found himself in a sitting room with the crone by his side, her yellowing eyes staring up at him.

"Financial, spiritual or magical?" he asked, eyeing the grandeur within her cottage. The decrepit exterior must be a facade. Inside, it was nothing short of a palace.

"All of the above." She sipped her lilac-coloured tea. Benedict noted the scents of ginseng and liquorice. An aging spell. The crone might appear to be old, but it was a lie, like the house.

He glanced around the room to find no mirrors anywhere in sight. Mirrors weren't just a reflection of people's exterior, but that of their soul, and it was obvious the witch wasn't fond of what could be revealed.

"Cost isn't an issue if you can exchange our elements," he said quickly, caring far more about escaping this place than money.

"You underestimate me. *If* has no place in my hovel." The crone beamed, putting down her chipped tea-cup. "Removing your elements from one another is nothing. However, I said nothing about returning the elements to their rightful place."

"Stripping them of their elements is not what we agreed," Peter snarled. He'd never been particularly patient.

The crone tutted, her smile turning sinister. "You asked if I could remove their elements; you said nothing about returning them."

"Mere wording," Peter growled. Benedict gripped his forearm, trying to ease his temper. He always was quick to react. Death hadn't changed that, nor had it quenched his desire to protect those around him.

"It was *mere wording* that got your brother and Ms Hawthorne in this position." She shuddered, licking her red lips. "Thinking of those goody-goodies messing on our side of the fence is positively tantalising." Peter had told Benedict that the crone had lost her own name long ago. Magic had swallowed her identity, replacing it with only a desire to grow stronger.

The cup clinked against the saucer. "Let me take her water from you. I can smell the goodness radiating from your bones – positively gag-inducing. I can see how much she occupies your mind, how you are at war with your feelings for her. Love and hate are horns on the same beast." She sat on the edge of the couch cushions, prying deeper into Benedict's mind than he cared for.

"If you've no intention of helping, we're leaving." Benedict folded his arms across his chest, refusing to be intimidated, though his heart hammered at the thought of their elemental connection giving the crone insight into Lucinda. He'd come here to help her, not put her in danger.

"I never said I'd help. I said I'd *remove* the element from you!" she repeated. "Collecting elements has long been a hobby of mine, and with the connection you've made I can get two for the price of one."

The smell of rot and decay distracted the siblings from

her words. Benedict felt something move on his hands. Looking down, he was horrified to see that his lap was crawling with maggots.

"Benedict, move!" Peter snapped, flipping the coffee table over as the crone pulled a glass dagger from behind her back.

It hit the table with a thud, and the glamour disintegrated around them. Benedict jumped to his feet, only to hit his head on a rusted cage overcrowded with bats. The crone drew another glass dagger, which barely missed him. He had a feeling she was aiming to maim, not kill him, to siphon Lucinda's element from his body – which would probably be far more painful than being stabbed.

"Kill her!" Benedict growled as he was flung against the far wall, the force taking the wind from his lungs. He took a curtain and its rail down with him. The crone lunged for him, but Peter grabbed her.

"I can't," he panted, trying to hold back the snarling crone. "I'd be stripped of my robes."

The struggle continued as Benedict got to his feet. When his eyes fell on the filthy window behind him, he had an idea. He didn't want to end a witch's life, but they didn't have much choice.

Quickly, he muttered a spell, and the window beneath his hand transformed into a mirror, reflecting his brother struggling behind him. Before he could be relieved the magic had worked, he saw the crone holding a glass dagger centimetres away from his brother's throat. She might not be able to kill Peter, but she could trap his soul in such a blade.

Benedict lunged over the couch, tackling the crone to the ground. She scrambled to her feet, kicking him away as he threw the dagger to the other side of the room. Baring her blackened teeth, she began to chant in a language he didn't recognise. The hovel began to shake, and the floorboards cracked beneath him, sending shards of wood flying.

"We need to get her to the mirror!" Peter shielded his brother, helping him get to his feet.

The brothers took the chance to grab the crone, who was lost in her chant. The movement broke her spell, and the hovel settled. It took all their combined strength to force her before the window-turned-mirror, cursing and screeching.

Her last desperate scream broke all the remaining windows as her reflection warped and twisted until she disappeared from their grasp. Benedict's fist connected with the mirror, shattering the crone's trapped image with a shrill shriek. They both stood panting, trying to catch their breath.

"Fuck," Benedict croaked. "Do you've any idea how lucky we are? If you hadn't spotted the dagger and flipped the table, I'd most likely be dead right now and you'd be trapped as her death-dealing servant."

"Okay, I'll admit this was my bad." Peter picked up a shard of the shattered mirror. As they caught their breath, Benedict eyed all the possessed and cursed objects lining the walls and knew they couldn't leave such items to be discovered. He picked up one of the black candles and tossed it against the potion-lined wall. The wall caught fire in a second, projecting a blue flame towards them.

Peter grinned. "You can take the fire out of the man, but you can't keep the man away from fire."

Benedict kicked open the front door. As soon as they

stepped outside, the hovel collapsed in on itself without the crone's magic to keep it standing.

"We could've been killed!" Benedict ran his hand through his hair as dust and earth settled around them.

"Technically, I'm already dead," Peter reminded him, and Benedict shoved him.

The horrifying smell of the burning, rotting hovel made them grimace. Benedict guessed that by nightfall, all trace of the crone and her sordid deeds would be gone.

"Are you going to tell Lucy about this?" Peter asked, watching the flames.

"Are you kidding? She'd kill me for doing this behind her back."

"Best not, then. Not great to have two women try to kill you in twenty-four hours," Peter advised.

Back at the car, Benedict reached for the door handle when a fierce crack alerted them both to a falling tree. They leapt out of the way just in time. The car windows shattered. Peter winced, his head popping up on the other side of the crushed vehicle.

"I love you, but in the future, help me less," Benedict groaned, lying amongst the leaves. He stared wide eyes at the decaying trunk of the fallen tree.

"I can do that." Peter chuckled, helping him to his feet.

Together, they watched as the other trees, rotten with blackened bark, fell in a perfect circle.

"The crone must have enchanted the trees around the perimeter of her hovel to collapse in case she died," Peter said sheepishly.

Benedict shook his head. "It's going to take us hours to walk back to Foxford. Can't you teleport us home?"

"No can do. My movements are tracked. If I used my magic too close to the hovel, I'd get an earful from the higher-ups," Peter said, slipping his hands into his black coat. "Can't you try?"

"No – I used too much magic in there. I don't have the energy to make the journey safely." Resigned, Benedict began the long walk to the main road.

To their relief, when they got there, headlights appeared in the distance.

"Looks like fate is on our side!" Peter beamed, waving, and thankfully the truck began to slow. The sun was already starting to set, and Benedict didn't fancy being out here all night.

Much to his surprise, Faye Parker rolled down the window. He clenched his jaw, wondering what else could go wrong today. Of all the people to show up, of course it had to be one of Lucy's friends from school.

"Benedict?" she asked, looking like she'd seen a ghost. Then again, he *was* standing on the side of the road covered in mud and blood, hitchhiking with his dead brother.

"Long story. What are you doing out here?"

"I was picking up some ingredients for the bakery from Willow Valley," she said, pointing to the back of the truck. It was loaded with bags of flour and a large box with an industrial mixer.

"Any chance we can get a ride?" Peter asked, already opening the back door.

"Aren't you...?" Faye swallowed, looking at his long black coat.

"Dead? Yes, I thought that was old news by now." Peter enjoyed people's discomfort.

Faye paled, mouth agape as though she didn't know what to say. Most of the town knew Peter was a Grim, but a soul collector was bound to make anyone nervous. It wasn't every day people came face to face with mortality in the flesh.

"Ignore him," Benedict told her, wondering why Peter was looking at her all moony-eyed. He wasn't aware they'd even known each other. He guessed it had less to do with who she was and more how pretty she was. With her cropped auburn hair, dark green eyes and full rose lips, you'd have to be a fool not to acknowledge her beauty – but it was her sad eyes that caused people to keep their distance.

"Get in," she said, leaning across to open the passenger door. Before Benedict could obey, Peter hopped into the front seat. Faye backed up against her door as death got a little too close.

"I love Taylor Swift! This is my song!" Peter turned up the old CD stereo. Faye stifled a laugh, clearly never having seen a Grim dance to the queen of pop. Benedict didn't know her well, but it was the first time he'd seen her smile.

"Forgive him – the dead don't get tired." Benedict wished his brother had an off switch, but oddly, Faye didn't seem to mind.

Getting into the back, Benedict focused his attention on the view outside the window, lost in his thoughts. He'd hoped to bring Lucinda some good news, to have her light up as Faye did when Peter started singing along with her song after song. They were both behaving as though Benedict wasn't there, which suited him just fine. The more she was distracted by Peter, the less likely she was to ask about what they'd been up to in the middle of the woods.

It didn't seem long before Faye dropped them at the Manor. He watched as Peter, obviously reluctant to leave, kissed Faye's hand and thanked her for the ride before disappearing. Benedict doubted his brother knew she was in a relationship.

"Can you do me a favour?" Benedict asked through the open window before she pulled away.

"It's the least I can do," Faye said.

He frowned, not sure what she was talking about.

"For the job at the bakery. I know it was a couple of months ago now, but... thank you." She wouldn't meet his eye, but he could hear in her voice how much it meant to her.

Benedict resisted the urge to curse. He might've got her husband the job at the Clover pub, the only vamp bar in town, but he hadn't had a hand in the bakery hiring her. Peter must have used his likeness again to pull strings. But why would he have helped Faye? They'd seemed like perfect strangers to each other today. It seemed he wasn't the only one with women troubles.

"Don't mention it," was all he said, using his brother's meddling to his advantage for once. "Could you not tell Lucinda about today?"

Her grip tightened on the steering wheel. "We haven't talked in a while. Not much time to hang out, these days," she said sadly. "But if she comes by the bakery, I won't say anything."

"Thank you. Just... I don't want her thinking I was up to anything out there." He'd hate for this little adventure to sow any discord between them.

"You're going to be bound, right?" she asked, concern edging her soft voice.

"Yes, on All Hallows' Eve. I'm sure Lucinda would love for you to be there." He pulled at the back of his neck. It still felt strange to say. "If she'll have me."

"I don't know what's changed between the two of you.

I remember the two of you hating each other in school, but..." Faye took a breath. "Please treat her right. She has the best heart. Don't break it."

He looked her in the eye, having no intention of breaking his word. "I won't."

Lucinda

Waiting by the coffee cart outside the Alchemy & Anarchy bookstore, Lucy couldn't stop thinking about how she had unknowingly agreed with Benedict on how to handle the festival. Glancing across the town square, she decided to bite the bullet. She would stop by the Manor to talk about the potion failing, and find out why he hadn't come to the meeting. She felt oddly at ease once she'd made up her mind, even if she didn't want to see his disappointment.

A tap on the shoulder startled her out of her thoughts.

"We were just talking about you!" Wilhelmina beamed, kissing her daughter's cheek. Emerson followed her out of the bookstore, carrying a full brown paper bag.

"I hope that's not true," Lucy joked, wondering what her mum had revealed to him. Oversharing was in her nature.

"Don't worry, it was all complimentary." Emerson smiled as Wilhelmina ordered for everyone.

"How nice of her to lie for me." She felt far from perfect. "What brought you together?"

"Rosie had to go out and didn't want to leave me in the library alone. Wilhelmina stopped by to return a book and mentioned the bookstore. I couldn't forsake such an opportunity," Emerson said, brightening as Lucy did whenever books were involved.

"Sorry to keep you waiting – the meeting ran on longer than I expected," she explained, hoping he wouldn't hold it against her, though he seemed perfectly happy. It wasn't every day a member of the order got to spend the morning with the most powerful witch this side of the River Lux.

"Mrs Crawford is very particular about the details. I should've known the meeting would run on. Otherwise, we wouldn't have caught you above ground at this hour," Wilhelmina chimed in teasingly, handing Lucy her tea. She wished she'd told her mum to ask for something iced, but she'd been distracted by their arrival.

"Do you not need a sleeve?" Wilhelmina eyed her suspiciously. "It's awfully hot."

Lucy stilled as they all looked at her hands, wrapped around the cup. Thanks to Benedict's element, the heat didn't bother her.

"What? I just used my water to cool it down," she lied, even though there was a steady stream of steam rising from the takeaway cup. Emerson handed her a sleeve anyway, and she placed it on the cup. "Mrs Crawford wasn't all that hard to crack – even Mr Lark agreed to my plan," she added, trying to shift the focus back to the meeting.

"There wasn't any doubt in my mind they'd agree to your proposal," her mum said, the praise making Lucy redden. "Your dedication to your work isn't lost on any of them."

"Even I can vouch for that," Emerson added. "I've seen

the volume of work you've translated. I have to say, I was surprised when I arrived to find you're so young."

"And beautiful – even if some sunlight would help," Mum said, nudging Emerson.

He concealed his reaction with his iced tea. Lucy wanted the bowels of Hell to open beneath her feet and swallow her whole.

"Thank you for making our guest uncomfortable," she hissed, though part of her wondered how a member of the Order could be so bashful.

"Don't be so sensitive," Mum said, claiming her order from the bundled-up barista who'd called out the three-shot latte. Her caffeine addiction was probably how she'd kept going all this time. "You don't drink coffee?" she asked Emerson.

"I find caffeine affects my concentration. I've always been more of a tea drinker," he responded, adding extra slices of candied lemon to his drink.

Lucy winced.

"So is Lucy!" Wilhelmina enthused, sure enough. "Both love tea and academia. You two have—"

"Mum, we've got to get to work, but I need your permission to let him into the archives," Lucy put in, distracting her from her matchmaking.

"Consider it granted." Mum waved a colourfully gloved hand as though it were nothing. *Give him a chance,* she mouthed as Emerson paid for their drinks.

"Stop meddling. You've got me into enough trouble already," Lucy whispered, taking her mum aside.

"Trouble? Has something happened?" Mum's eyes narrowed.

Lucy cursed herself silently. "I meant the binding. I don't need to mess it up right now."

"I'm sorry for pushing; I won't say another word." Mum pretended to zip her lips. Emerson smiled over at them, talking to the barista. "But he does have a dashing smile."

One moment, she was listening to her mum; the next, Lucy's blood sizzled beneath her skin. She tried to get a handle on her breathing, which was coming too fast. Mum reached out, but Lucy flinched away, afraid she'd burn her. Was she having an anxiety attack or losing control of Benedict's element?

"I've got to go. I think I forgot something at Stoker's." She clutched the crystal at her neck, but it didn't seem to be helping. "Take Emerson to lunch, and I'll see him back at the library."

The tea in her hands was only making everything worse. She dropped it in the bin and practically ran away.

"Lucy!" Mum called, but thankfully she didn't follow.

In the alley, Lucy stared at her hands and tried to spark a flame to let the fire breathe. It didn't work; her skin continued to simmer. No element liked to be contained for long. The fire was far more dangerous and temperamental than her water element.

She gripped the crystal around her neck again, but it wasn't doing enough. Starting a bonfire in the middle of town wasn't an option, and there were only so many candles to light. Putting a hand on her chest, Lucy closed her eyes as the world started slipping away around her.

A second later, the sound of running water made her heart leap. *My element! Maybe the potion worked after all!*

Lucy opened her eyes.

She was in a bathroom.

Black tiles surrounded her, and two gold-plated sinks with ornate mirrors reflected her blotchy cheeks. Worse, she wasn't alone. Only a few feet away from her, Benedict Matherson lay in a large bathtub, covered in bubbles, eyes closed and dark hair slicked back away from his face. There was a pile of muddy clothes at Lucy's feet, but she was too distracted by the sight of his naked shoulders to wonder what he'd been up to.

As though he sensed her presence, his eyes snapped open.

"How the hell did you get in here?" he shrieked in a rather unmanly manner.

Water and bubbles sloshed over the edge of the tub. Lucy lifted her feet out of the way.

"I don't know!" She panicked, unsure of where to look. "I didn't come here on purpose. I had this awful feeling, like I was burning alive. Then I was here... in your bathroom." She stared at him, unsure if he was real. "I'm sorry. I don't want to be here as much as you don't want me seeing—" She cut herself off.

Scrubbing his hands over his face, Benedict sat up, revealing smooth, wet skin. Droplets trickled down his abs. Clearly all that running worked well for him. Lucy tried not to look at what was lurking below the diminishing bubbles. Suddenly there wasn't enough air for both of them. Her heart hammered as he grabbed a towel from the rack beside her.

"Can you please leave, or at least turn around?" he asked, raising a sharp eyebrow. Her eyes were immediately drawn to the tension in his hands and forearms as he started to pull himself up, and her heart did a weird flip.

Promising herself it was just the heat of the room and not anything to do with Benedict, Lucy hurried out the door before he caught her lingering gaze.

She hovered at the end of his bed, chewing on her nail. She wanted to apologise again for invading his privacy, but she still didn't understand how she had ended up in his bathroom in the first place.

The door swung open, and she turned to give him some privacy. She heard him walking around the room, but he didn't say anything. When she peeked through her fingers, her gaze trailed down his toned back, one side covered with a long spiralling tattoo of ivy that dipped below the black towel. She chewed her lip to stop herself from smiling. Of course his towels were black.

Benedict cleared his throat. "I'm decent; you can look now. I take it you're here to talk about trying another spell or potion?"

"We can try the curse-stripping potion. It'll just take me a while to order some of the ingredients from Myrtle's," Lucy said quickly. The ingredients were far more complicated than what was usually stocked in town.

"If we don't figure out something between now and then, we can give it a go," he agreed mildly.

Confusion delayed her response. She couldn't believe he wasn't giving her more of a hard time.

"You're not angry?" she asked, lowering her hands from her eyes. He was still in just the towel wrapped around his middle. "I thought you said you were decent."

"What's the point in getting mad? We tried, and we can keep trying. More importantly, I was taking a bath in the privacy of my own home. It'd be rather strange to wear clothes while bathing." Benedict began to dry his hair with another towel.

Lucy tried to focus her attention on the decor and not how good he looked soaking wet. His hair – *just long enough to run your hands through* – was wavy and wet, giving him a far more relaxed appearance than usual. He also had the Matherson sigil tattooed on his chest: the ivy vines from his back wrapped around a Gothic 'M'.

He raised his eyebrows as he caught her staring, then gave her a smug grin. It seemed he was enjoying this, now that the surprise had worn off.

"I thought of you as more of a shower guy. The bubble bath was a surprise," she said, not wanting to admit she'd been staring. She'd seen the tattoo before, when he rolled up his shirt sleeves, but she hadn't known how expansive it was.

"Do you think about me in the shower a lot?" He tossed the hair towel back in the bathroom and closed the door.

Lucy didn't dignify that with a response.

He inhaled deeply. "It helps me relax – something I've struggled with since we got engaged. If I remember correctly, you did tell me to use your element, or it would get too strong."

Her eyes went wide. "My element – it must've pulled me here! Did you use my water to fill the entire tub?"

"You told me to use it!" he repeated.

She waved that away. "I'm not accusing you – you didn't know."

He frowned. "Why are you smiling?"

"Because this means we're still connected to our elements. They must call to us when they're used in volume," she said, getting a little too close in her eagerness to explain. Feeling the warmth emanating from his body, she tried to step back, but he followed her. Heat rose up the sides of her neck, but she didn't try to move away again.

"I suppose that's a good thing. Means we haven't lost them entirely." He sat on the trunk at the end of his poster bed, pushing his wet hair back from his face. "But if your element brought you here..."

"Then... we need to refrain from using each other's element to prevent this from happening again," she finished, and he nodded.

"Luckily, *I* don't need to use fire in any state of undress," she teased, trying to make light of the situation.

He rolled his eyes, but he seemed deep in thought. "What were you doing before you came here?"

"Talking with my mum." She avoided his gaze, studying the expansive poster bed and all the candles of varying lengths. *He has his candles and fire, and I've got my water and flowers,* she thought. His home felt medieval compared to hers, but somehow still cosy.

"About what? If I might ask." He followed her out of his bedroom.

"Emerson. She was showing him the town," Lucy said eventually, leaving out the matchmaking part.

"And then?" he asked, close to her back, as she paused by the couch.

"I don't know. It felt like my insides were burning. My blood started boiling, but I wasn't angry," she explained. Remembering the sensation made her queasy.

"What if my element was defending itself?" he mused.

Frowning, she turned to face him. "You're not thinking your element was jealous of Emerson?" It sounded ridiculous, but there was no hint of humour in his dark eyes.

"My element could've perceived what Wilhelmina was saying as a threat to our binding. If our elements are trying to make sure the binding happens, it'd make sense that you'd be pulled away from him and brought..." He hesitated, his chest rising and falling. "To me." It was so quiet she barely caught the words.

Why was it that whenever he got this close, her heart tried to escape her chest? It didn't feel healthy to be drawn to someone who'd hurt her so much in the past.

"I wasn't pulled away during our dinner," she argued, pulling herself together and moving to the desk to put some space between them.

He rubbed the back of his neck. She wondered if he felt the same as she did. Maybe it was just another side-effect of the spell.

"I was there," he admitted. She stared at him. "Outside. It might've taken me some time to get the courage to face your family after everything that went down with the coven, but when Rosie told me you'd invited him, I couldn't leave."

They fell silent. The thought of him nervously pacing outside her house made her smile.

"It's far more likely that it's the use of our elements. Maybe mine is trying to get back to me," she reasoned.

"If that's true, then why weren't you pulled here when I showered last night? Or when I watered the gardens this morning?" he asked.

"I'm only guessing, but maybe it was the volume of water used. Next time, don't use my water to fill the bath unless you want me to join you." It was silly, but she had to break the tension before it swallowed them both.

"What was that last part?" He stared at her.

"I said don't use my water to fill your bathtub."

He exhaled as though exasperated, but she cocked her head, seeing a small smile trying to fight through. She wondered what he was thinking. Maybe joking about bathing together wasn't the best idea.

"From now on, let's be careful about how much we use." She crossed her arms over her chest. If he was right, that meant she wouldn't be called here every time he bathed – which was a relief, no matter how good he looked in a towel.

"Agreed." He nodded.

"We're getting better at this," she pointed out, picking up a mini gargoyle paperweight from his stack of paperwork. It was the same design as those beneath the library. It made sense, since it was one of his ancestors who'd crafted the stone protectors. In miniature form, the terrifying creature was almost cute.

"At what?"

"Civil conversations." Lucy put down the paperweight, surprised by the amount of paper. For the first time, she noticed he didn't have a laptop. "You wouldn't have to use so much paper with a computer."

"Says the woman who works in a library," he chuckled.

"Touché." She should probably be going, yet somehow she didn't feel the desire to leave.

"To be honest, I don't like having electricity in my quarters; the waves throw off my element. The paper I can burn up with my fire," he told her.

Lucy nodded. Now that she'd experienced his fire firsthand, she realised how difficult it was to manage. "You put a lot of thought into arranging your life around your element. Water is mischievous and always wants to help, but I can't say it affects me like your fire does," she admitted, interested to hear more. Maybe if they understood each other better, they'd stop seeing each other as rivals.

"It's volatile. Fire is the expression of anger, power, and

even lust. If not harnessed correctly, then it's not only dangerous to its bearer, but to those around them," he said, fear settled in his gaze. Fear that his element would hurt her, or the town they both cherished?

"But even if it can be destructive, it brings new life, like my water. We can't survive without it," she said, getting the impression he didn't think about the positives of his element much.

He took a step closer, and a gentle sizzle settled beneath her skin. She didn't know what he was doing, but she wasn't afraid. Benedict took her hand and held it over the candles on his desk. Wordlessly, she let him guide her. The candles lit with ease. Even that small expression of fire eased the boil in her blood, but she still struggled to contain it to a single small flame.

"Better?" he asked at her shoulder. Lucy swallowed as his fingers slipped between hers, sending shivers up her arm. At that moment, she realised she trusted him. She trusted Benedict Matherson.

He stared at her, his gaze moving from her eyes to her lips as though he was seeing her for the first time.

A small crash broke his hold on her. A purple lizard had knocked a candle holder off the side table.

"Greko! How much you've grown!" Lucy exclaimed, picking up the creature and placing him on her shoulder. "I wasn't sure if you still had him."

"Why wouldn't I? Everyone needs a creature of destruction in their home," Benedict quipped, picking up the candle holder.

"Because I gave him to you. I wondered if you might've given him away." Lucy stroked his purple scales. When she'd found the gecko, he'd had an awful accident. She'd managed to cure him, but with the unintended side-effect of turning him a very pretty, yet alarming shade of lilac.

"I'm not entirely heartless," he said, a trace of sadness in his voice.

"I should go. Can't keep the library waiting all day." She didn't want to dwell on their past.

"Duty calls," Benedict said wryly.

Lucy eased Greko's claws from her clothes and placed him on the floor. She was in the doorway when she remembered they hadn't talked about the meeting. She hadn't even asked why he hadn't attended.

"Thank you for covering for me yesterday at the meeting. You could've used my absence to your advantage."

"Don't mention it; I'm sure you'd do the same for me." He shrugged, as though it was nothing.

Lucy left the room, feeling off-balance. She was used to arguing with him, not thanking him. Resting her head on the closed door, she took a deep breath, trying to centre herself. She nearly fell back into Benedict's arms when he surprised her by opening the door.

"You okay?" he asked, reaching for her, but she corrected her balance, trying not to flush in embarrassment. His soft tone made her downright bashful.

Why had he come after her and risk his staff seeing him in a towel? A voice in the back of her mind said she didn't want *anyone* to see him like this. Before she could raise her concern, she looked down at what he was holding out to her.

"It's a ring." She stared, dumbfounded.

Benedict rolled his eyes and took her hand in his. The coolness of his touch was the first relief she'd had in days from the heat. She didn't want to ever pull away. Besides, she was curious to know where this was going... and the ring was beautiful.

"I picked it up this morning. I put in a rush order after we nearly destroyed the gardens. I figured you should have it sooner rather than later," he said, placing the small gold band on her ring finger.

"This is a binding ring?" Lucy breathed as she stared at the glistening crystals held in place by an infinity symbol. It was beautiful, delicate, and fitted perfectly. She'd never expected that he'd be the one to give it to her − or that it would make her stomach flip, in the best way.

"The sunstone and amethyst stones represent both our elements. I know it's tradition for your ring to hold my element and mine yours, but I thought together would be better. The sunstone will help you to control my element; it has the same effect as the carnelian stone in the necklace I gave you," he explained, as if giving her a ring that signified spending the rest of eternity together was completely normal. He rolled his thumb over the stones, her hand still in his.

She wanted to thank him, but the words caught in her throat.

"I'm relieved it fits; I wasn't sure. I took a ring from your room the other night." Maybe her silence was making him nervous. "We didn't go about this thing the traditional way, but you deserve a ring, even if it's just for appearance's sake."

"Benedict," was all she could muster. She didn't care that he'd taken one of her rings, too caught up in the thought he'd put into this. Binding rings had been the last thing on her mind, and she couldn't help but feel guilty. Even if the coven had ordered their engagement, he was still thinking of her feelings.

Before she knew what she was doing, she rose on her tiptoes and brushed her lips against his cheek and the dark shadow of not-quite-yet-stubble. "Thank you."

She drew back an inch, hoping she hadn't gone too far. Benedict's jaw clenched, and she was about to retreat when his head tilted towards her.

Lucy's breath caught. He was about to kiss her. She didn't know if she wanted him to, but the thought of him pulling away troubled her all the more. His hand rose to her face — but he stopped himself, leaving her utterly confused about the disappointment weighing on her heart.

"I-I should go," she stammered.

When Benedict didn't say anything, she followed his hard stare over her shoulder and was horrified to see a maid gaping at them. The shock on her face was probably due to seeing her boss half-naked and only inches away from a woman.

Lucy clenched her fists. This would turn rumours of their political engagement into something far more salacious. It'd be much harder to argue their indifference towards each other now.

"Sorry, sir, there was an issue with one of the guests," the maid said, hurrying back the way she'd come.

"She won't say anything," Benedict started to say, but Lucy cut him off.

"I've to get back to work," she muttered. "Thank you for the ring."

Unable to meet his eyes, she scurried down the hall. The whispers would probably spread throughout town before she even had a chance to reach the library. As she reached the lobby, her heart tightened; the maid was behind the reception desk, whispering to a bag handler. They were doomed.

This was all just thoughtlessness, the ring, their elements, their truce. Out in the air, she pressed her hand over her racing heart.

When she reached the library doors and saw the flowers starting to grow out of the ashes, she realised that if that maid hadn't interrupted, Benedict would have kissed her, and she would've let him.

Lucinda

For the next week, Lucinda kept her head down as rumours of what the maid had witnessed circulated. Some in town congratulated her, and Grams even came home from her tarot reading with some engagement presents from her clients, which felt rather sudden. Others didn't like the idea of a Matherson sitting by her side as head of the coven, as made evident by some not-so-subtle comments when she picked up her groceries, asking if the engagement and rumour were some elaborate prank. In that moment, she'd felt oddly inspired to defend Benedict, but instead of causing a scene beside the organic grapefruits she decided to smile and move along. Benedict might've wanted to try and stop it, but in Foxford nothing stayed secret for long. She was hoping by the next time she saw him, she'd have the ingredients for the curse-stripping potion.

"Another week?" she exclaimed into the phone. "I was hoping to have the ingredients sooner rather than later." She hated to push, but she was starting to panic she'd never get her element back. She'd already accidentally singed two books when a patron yelled at her about being skipped on the waiting list for the book she'd given Suzy. It wouldn't be much longer before Rosie started to get curious as to why she was acting so skittish.

"I'm sorry, but one of the roots you need can only be sourced from the peak of a mountain in Thailand. It's going to take some time," Myrtle said. "However, I've got everything else you ordered ready for collection." Thankfully, Myrtle never asked what she needed such rare ingredients for. Her motto was don't ask, don't tell.

"Thank you for trying – I'm sorry for being impatient." Lucy glanced over at Emerson and Rosie huddled together in the study area of the library, going over some magical cold case. "I'll collect the rest soon."

She hung up, trying not to let the pressure get to her. Emerson was being unbelievably patient about the grimoire, and Lucy suspected it had something to do with wanting to be around Rosie. Given how he looked at her friend, Lucy was sure his arrival had nothing to do with the spell cast to find *her* perfect match. However, it wouldn't be long before the Order demanded he collect what was promised and be on his way. She had the spell and nearly all the ingredients; realistically, she didn't need the grimoire any longer, but she worried that as soon as she handed it over, she'd discover there was something else she needed to check in it. She only hoped Rosie wouldn't be too upset when he left.

Since the day was coming to an end, she decided to sneak off home and leave Rosie and Emerson to their 'work'. She was packing to leave when her phone vibrated with a text. For a moment she thought it might be from Myrtle.

Benedict: Fowler's Bakery. Come now.

Lucy: I'm not a dog you can summon. You said you would handle today's meeting.

I got the map, and the university agreed to the changes with the Ferris wheel. However, Mrs Crawford and Mr Lark have decided that we need a cake for our binding reception. If you don't get here, I'm going to flood the place just so I can escape.

It's cake! I'm sure you can handle such an important decision.

Okay, I'll just tell two coven members that you don't care about our binding banquet. I'm sure that will go over swimmingly.

She glowered at her phone. Since theirs wasn't a traditional binding, she'd hoped they could skip the whole show. It seemed the coven didn't feel the same way. At least there would be cake.

Fine, I'll be right there. There had better be samples.

Just wait and see. He added a cake emoji and a wink.

Outside Fowler's bakery, Lucy felt a little green. She pressed her hand into her cramping stomach. It wasn't just her nerves about seeing Benedict since the incident at the Manor – though she found herself hesitating as she reached for the door handle. The last time they'd been in the same space, he'd almost kissed her and she'd almost let him. She'd put it down to their elements, but the idea of seeing him again used to fill her with dread, and now she didn't know *what* she felt. The worst part was, she'd been awake most of the night thanks to such horrendous cramps. She didn't have the energy to deal with petty squabbles today. But she wasn't about to say, "Sod off, I've got cramps and I want to go home and crawl into bed."

Inhaling deeply, she mustered the courage to face her betrothed. A few cake samples should perk her right up.

The smell of pastries and frosting hit her like a cloud of powdered sugar as soon as she opened the lime green door. She noticed the chairs in the bakery were already up on the tables, except for where Benedict sat looking off into the distance, nursing a coffee.

"Pumpkin, how good of you to come!" he said as she reached the table. Lucy couldn't remember him ever looking so happy to see her. He clearly wasn't suffering from the same emotional turmoil she was. She'd have reasoned it was for the coven members' benefit, but Mr Lark and Mrs Crawford weren't at the table. She'd expected a few others to be joining them, but many were busy with other details, and it wasn't odd for smaller groups to focus on specific tasks for the festival.

"You didn't give me much of a choice," she began, but he kissed her cheek, silencing her.

The warmth of his lips against her skin made her blush; she noticed that he paused and cleared his throat, as though he hadn't intended to do it. To be so close to one other still felt foreign. *Mr Lark and Mrs Crawford must be driving him mad.*

Heavy rain pelting against the bakery windows broke

the tension. They both stared out at the sky, darkened with thick rain clouds; Lucy had missed the downpour by mere seconds.

"I'm sorry to call you away from work," Benedict said. He checked his watch, looking as tired as she felt. "I've got a vamp wedding reception once the sun goes down, and I need to get back to the manor for the final checks. I figured with you here we could get this sorted as soon as possible."

"It's fine, I was hoping to sneak off home anyway. I don't think Rosie and Emerson will even notice I've gone." Lucy wanted to talk about anything but what had just occurred.

Benedict arched an eyebrow, but she decided it wasn't the best time to elaborate on Rosie's brewing feelings for an Order member, considering what had happened the first time he'd met Emerson. There was no point in telling him if it was only a passing flirtation.

"Where are the others?" she asked, slipping off her long coat and hanging it on the back of the white-painted chairs. She recognised Mrs Crawford's orange beehive through the small kitchen window behind the long counter. Her mouth watered at the sight of all the sweet treats. Even if cramps were killing her appetite, she never said no to baked goods.

Benedict pulled at the back of his neck. "There's been a slight mistake. Mr Lark was meant to order the samples in advance to surprise us."

"And he didn't order them?" *Then why did you drag me here?*

"Come and see for yourself." Taking her hand, he led her through the swing doors into the kitchen.

"I thought you said the issue was about the choice," she whispered.

"Did I?"

She stared at their clasped hands. It seemed so natural for him to reach for her. Then again, he probably wanted to appear united in front of the others.

They heard Mrs Crawford talking about festival preparations before they saw her. In the professional chrome kitchen, Ms Fowler, the owner and head baker, stood with the coven members in a green candy-striped apron with matching hair net. It was a rather cheery look for someone wearing such a deep scowl. Then Lucy registered the problem. Cake samples hadn't been prepared, but multi-tiered cakes had. Two, to be precise, ornately decorated. In spite of the queasiness from her teleport here, her cravings – always on the sweeter side during her time of the month – propelled her forward. Red velvet... her favourite...

Mrs Crawford noticed Lucy's arrival and broke away from the others. "Lucy, how good of you to come. We'd hoped to make this a surprise for you both to enjoy, since everything has been going so well with the festival arrangements, but then Benedict said you'd got caught up with work, and now there has been a mix-up," she exclaimed, side-eyeing Mr Lark. Her red cheeks could've equally been caused by a sudden rise in blood pressure or the heat of the kitchen.

"There was no mistake on my part," Mr Lark huffed, folding his arms across his chest. "I ordered two dozen samples, so you could both try each cake. Somehow that has become two cakes, with six tiers each."

"It's such a waste," Mrs Crawford complained. "The coven wanted to arrange the banquet and everything for you both to enjoy."

Lucy guessed that the rumours of their being seen at the Manor together with Benedict in a state of undress had confirmed to the coven that the binding would go ahead without fail. Now wasn't the time to argue the misunderstanding; she'd give Mrs Crawford a heart attack.

"Such beautiful cakes are never a waste! Thank you, Ms Fowler, for preparing these. Regardless of any mistake, this is exceptional work," Lucy said, not caring who'd made the mistake. All that mattered was making sure Ms Fowler wasn't put out with the coven. She catered for many events in town.

"Thank you, Lucy – I'm glad *someone* appreciates the work I put in," Ms Fowler said, softening her harsh gaze.

"I'm surprised you all resisted grabbing a fork!" Lucy tried to lighten the mood, but based on the looks she received from the whole group, their sense of humour had left long before her arrival. Benedict stifled a chuckle with his hand.

"I hardly think now is a time for jokes, Ms Hawthorne. I hope you wouldn't handle coven matters with such a cavalier attitude," said Mr Lark, grimacing.

Chastised, Lucy said, "You're right, forgive me."

"No need to apologise. Benedict told us how swamped you are, and you still came to help us with what was meant to be a *nice* surprise. Must be so unpleasant having someone from the Order breathing down your neck," Mrs Crawford said, wrinkling her nose. The Crawfords would never be happy with an Order member being in Foxford. Emerson might've got a position at the university, but rightly or wrongly, he'd have to win the town over before being accepted here, and who knew how long or what that would take.

"Not at all. Emerson has been very helpful, and if

working together can further our relationship with the Order, then I think that will benefit all of us," Lucy said, trying not to sound too much like a politician.

No one replied, but she felt the rise in tension.

"It just occurred to me." She snapped her fingers. "Benedict mentioned he has a wedding at the hotel today."

Mrs Crawford was looking at their hands, which Lucy suddenly realised were still entwined. She tried to free herself, but Benedict refused to release his grip. With a smirk, he brought her hand to his lips. From Mrs Crawford's amused smile, the display would play in their favour.

"They already have a cake," he told Lucy.

"And I expect to be paid. We put an awful lot of work into these cakes," Ms Fowler put in, rightfully upset. They were covered in ornate designs, one with autumnal scenes and the other themed for the Halloween season with black frosting and gold details of pumpkins, ghosts and gravestones, tastefully done.

"Of course the cost will be covered," Lucy said quickly. Before Mr Lark, who handled the accounts, and Mrs Crawford, who was a stickler for cost-cutting, could argue, she added, "This mix-up won't affect the budget of the festival, and since it was done out of kindness, Benedict and I will be covering the cost." She'd pay for the whole thing herself if it meant she didn't need to add another stress to her life. "Why don't you give the wedding party a call? The red velvet might be a perfect fit for them. Even if they already have some, wedding guests are always eager for more sweet treats. Ms Fowler's cakes are legendary, and wedding cakes book out years in advance."

Ms Fowler beamed, and Benedict nodded.

"I'll ring the wedding planner." He disappeared to the front of the shop.

Lucy forced herself to smile. She wished the coven would stop doing what they thought was best for them, when the interference only made things worse. The sooner this matter was settled, the sooner they could leave, even if they were both out of pocket for cakes they'd never even wanted or asked for in the first place.

"That still leaves us with one," Mrs Crawford sighed.

Benedict rejoined them, putting his phone in his black jacket pocket. "The wedding planner agreed to the red velvet. I've added it to their wedding package, so the Manor will cover the cost."

"And what about the other one?" Mr Lark said, tapping his thin fingers against the table.

"What about freezing it and keeping it for the festival?" Lucy suggested. "We could offer it to viewers as a treat for the midnight movie." It was projected on the side of the town hall every year.

"That's a wonderful idea!" Ms Fowler enthused. "It'd be great advertising for the bakery."

Lucy grinned. "Perfect. Then it's all settled. Crisis averted."

"I'll prepare the invoice," Ms Fowler added.

"We'll join you; we need to talk about the separate arrangements for the movie night," Mrs Crawford said, following Ms Fowler out of the kitchen. Mr Lark followed, leaving Lucy and Benedict alone.

"If I'd known I was going to end up footing the bill, I would've handled it myself," Benedict muttered under his breath.

Lucy scowled. She'd given up her bed to help him. Egged on by her hormones, her annoyance, or both, she picked up a small sample of cake from a tray on the side and shoved it in his mouth to shut him up.

"Hope that'll sweeten your words." She stared up at his startled expression, smile widening. "'Thank you, Lucy, for fixing the problem so I can leave' would be much better." She batted her eyelashes at him.

Rolling his eyes, he chewed and swallowed, then raised his eyebrows. "The red velvet is delicious." He licked the cake from the corners of his mouth. "I hope you enjoyed that."

The traces of icing still on the corner of his lower lip looked rather enticing. Lucy found herself swiping it off with her thumb.

"I did," she agreed, bringing the icing to her lips.

His eyes widened, and she froze. She didn't know what had come over her; the sweet, tangy cream cheese frosting had been too tempting. She wanted to tell him it was the icing and not him, though as he studied her lips part of her was sure he'd be downright delicious.

Just then, a blinding cramp forced her to lean against the counter for support. She needed some painkillers and a water bottle.

"Are you alright?" Benedict rested a hand on her lower back. The pressure was nice; she almost groaned when he removed it. Waiting for the wave of pain to subside so she could reply, she gripped the corner of the table.

Benedict jumped back as the red velvet cake before them burst into flames. He grabbed Lucy, pulling her away from the blazing cake. The icing melted quickly, and the decorations turned black. She was too stunned to speak; she hadn't meant to start it.

"It was the pain," she started to say as Benedict protected her from the rippling flames. As quickly as it had caught fire, he doused it in water. Smoke shrouded them. It was a slightly alarming miracle that the fire alarm didn't go off.

"We can't let them see this!" Lucy panicked, staring at the swing doors as they heard the others returning.

"What the hell are we supposed to do?" Benedict ran his hands through his hair.

Lucy did the only thing she could think of.

"Where the hell is the cake?" Benedict hissed when it disappeared.

"I think I sent it to my house." She wasn't entirely sure.

"You think?!" he barked, checking the door.

"I panicked when I heard them coming. I didn't exactly have time to think it through!"

Benedict shook his head. "So there's a burnt, soggy, six-tier cake around town somewhere?"

Lucy winced, and they both stared at each other for a moment before erupting into laughter. She laughed until her chest hurt, and Benedict braced himself against the counter.

Mrs Crawford and Mr Lark halted at the strange scene. Benedict straightened, fixing his tie as he returned to his stoic self.

"I sent the cake to the Manor," he announced.

"We thought we'd save on time and the courier," Lucy chimed in.

"Good idea. It's late as it is, and we wouldn't want to keep the wedding guests waiting." Mrs Crawford sniffed the air with a small frown.

"I should settle the bill." Benedict distracted Mrs Crawford by leading her out of the kitchen. Lucy wasn't going to argue; she didn't want them to figure out something had gone wrong. She only hoped she'd find the cake in the kitchen when she got home.

Hoping she'd be free to go, Lucy headed out of the kitchen only to find their table covered in small plates of cake. She forced herself to smile, not wanting to offend Ms Fowler since she'd gone to the trouble.

"I pulled some cakes from the counter for you to try, now that everything is settled," the baker said, ushering her to the table. "We should pick the cake for your binding banquet before you leave so I can get started."

Mrs Crawford and Mr Lark took their seats happily. Lucy locked eyes with Benedict, who wanted to leave as much as she did. However, they both bit the bullet and sat down, trying every cake pushed in their direction until they couldn't eat another frosted bite.

"The white chocolate is far too sweet for the season," Benedict said, as though he cared. Lucy knew how much he hated sweet things, except for pumpkin pie.

"We need something rich, but not too sweet," Mr Lark agreed, shoving the giant slice of chocolate fudge over to Lucy.

"Dark chocolate is my favourite," she hedged, so full of sugar she thought she explode if she took another bite.

"Want some pumpkin?" Benedict offered, holding out a fork. The glint in his eye told her he was referencing her and not the cake on it.

"I hate pumpkin, and we want a crowd-pleaser," she said softly.

"Pity; it's my favourite." Benedict winked, popping the piece between his lips.

"The dark chocolate fudge *is* a crowd-pleaser," Mr Lark reiterated.

"What if we do two cakes, since we know the dark chocolate is going to be a success?" Benedict suggested.

"I love that idea," Crawford beamed. "How is it the magless do it? Something old, something new..."

"Maybe we should make it blue."

Lucy gripped her fork as Benedict placed his hand on her thigh in silent warning about her tone. She hadn't meant to sound so mocking. Eyeing the Matherson ring on her thigh, she found it hard to swallow, wishing there was more than just her sheer tights between his hand and her skin.

"Sorry – it's an excellent idea, but I think two cakes would be rather excessive," she said, sliding his distracting hand from her thigh and firmly putting it on the table.

"What a beautiful ring!" exclaimed Mrs Crawford, taking Lucy's hand. "Combining the two stones, how..." She hesitated. "Thoughtful."

"Do you have yours yet?" Mr Lark asked Benedict.

"Not yet – it's in the works," Lucy lied, wishing she hadn't left it so long. She'd been so distracted trying to get the curse-stripping potion organised. "If we're going to have two cakes, then the pumpkin would be a nice choice for the second," she decided. "So we each have our favourite." The ring reminded her of how he had gone against tradition to combine both their elements. The least she could do was let him have his favourite cake flavour.

"The cream cheese frosting is exceptional and would be a great alternative for those with less of a sweet tooth!" Mr Lark put in.

"Then we agree?" Mrs Crawford asked the table.

Lucy took a shallow breath, her cramps growing sharper again. She pressed her palm into her abdomen, willing them to stop.

"Are you okay? You've gone pale," Benedict whispered.

"I'm fine, it's just warm in here," she said, wiping her lips with her napkin. "Could you excuse me for a minute?" Fortunately, only Benedict was paying attention; the other two were still debating the cake issue.

Lucy hurried to the bathroom. Stress made her cramps and flow worse, and with everything going on, this period felt like someone was butchering her insides. Thankfully, she had some pads in her bag, but she let out a little sob when she found her vintage pill box was empty. She'd have to wait to take something for the pain, the last dose having worn off long ago.

Returning to the table, she found the group were ready to leave.

"We decided to go with one cake with different layers. I knew you'd be worried about waste with two cakes," Benedict said, resting a hand on her lower back. Comforted by his touch, she wanted to lean into him.

"Happy with that?" Mrs Crawford asked.

"Perfect," Lucy said, trying to pay attention as the cramps crept into her legs. Mrs Crawford and Mr Lark finalised the details with Fowler while she gathered her things.

"Sorry for making the final decision without you," Benedict whispered, offering her the coat from the back of her chair. "You were so pale when you left, I figured you weren't feeling well and would want to leave."

"I'm just a bit nauseous," she lied, forcing a small smile. "Too much cake, and you're right to split the layers. An excellent compromise."

"We're going to the bar at the Manor to decide on a special cocktail. Benedict said we could design one for the festival guests," Mr Lark announced, meeting them at the door.

"If you're feeling up to it – it was just an idea," Benedict said, concern edging his words as he studied Lucy like she was about to crumble.

"It's a great idea, but I should head home. I'm not feeling too well."

"Sorry to hear that; we'll keep you informed," Mrs Crawford said, resting a reassuring hand on her arm. "Get some rest."

"You go ahead. I'll be along shortly," Benedict told the others as they all left the bakery.

"I wouldn't leave them alone for too long; you know they don't get along," Lucy said, but he kept an arm around her and she was grateful for the support. "I'm fine. You can tell me what you decide. I just need to get home."

"Come back to the Manor. You look like you're about to faint," he said firmly as Ms Fowler locked up behind them.

"I'm not a damsel in distress," she protested, but truthfully she didn't know if she could make the walk back. After setting the cake on fire, she didn't trust herself to use magic to cover the distance.

"Accepting my help doesn't make you a damsel," he pressed, and she hesitated, chewing her lip. "Please don't be stubborn. It's a twenty-minute walk to your house from here, and I'm not letting you walk back alone. It's only five to the hotel."

The fresh air was helping to ease her nausea, and she was too uncomfortable to argue with him. She could rest a bit in the Manor, get some painkillers, and then walk home. "Okay. You win."

He grinned.

"What?" she grumbled.

"Nothing. Just feels good to win."

"Don't get used to it," she muttered, and he squeezed her waist gently.

Lucinda

Making for Benedict's quarters, he and Lucy managed to sneak by the coven members at the bar unnoticed, only to be caught by the vampires' wedding organiser. Lucy told him she could make it the rest of the way herself, but he wouldn't listen, so she waited on the staircase as he handled the situation with ease. A few moments later, he called over some staff to take over and brought her upstairs.

"You've got to be kidding me?" Benedict exclaimed, resting his hands on his head.

A nervous chuckle escaped Lucy when she saw the burnt cake all over his desk. It was a crumbling, charred mess of melted icing and crumbs.

"Sorry – I didn't mean to laugh," she said, though it was nice to have a distraction from the nausea and pain currently competing within her body. "I really didn't mean to send it here. I was trying to think of a safe place; if anything, I thought it might end up in the library."

Benedict stared at her. "You feel safe here?"

"Shouldn't I?" she asked, not wanting to admit what her subconscious had confirmed.

His gaze softened. A question lingered in it, but he didn't say a word.

"We should clean this up," she said, cutting the moment before the tension caused her to set the place on fire. She'd already made a mess of his desk.

"Forget about it for now. I'll worry about it tomorrow," he said, looking over to the desk and the ruined paperwork. The sweet smell of burnt icing lingered in the air.

Lucy took a seat on the black suede couch. It was so soft, she couldn't help slipping off her shoes and snuggling up with one of the matching cushions.

"I'll be right back with some painkillers and tea for your stomach," Benedict fussed. If she hadn't been so uncomfortable, she would've worried he had some alternative agenda. "Don't move; I'll be back in a second."

"I'm not going anywhere," she promised, trying not to be so amused by his worried mother hen impersonation.

He disappeared and she sighed in relief, glad she'd listened to him instead of walking home. She snuggled into the couch to wait.

"I hope this is the right one; we keep a few in stock for the guests." Benedict hurried back, handing her a pink packet of painkillers specifically for menstrual pain. She wondered how he'd known or if he'd guessed as she washed them down with the peppermint tea he'd brought.

Before she could thank him, he disappeared again, only to reappear with a hot water bottle encased in a fluffy unicorn cover. *Why does he have such a thing?*

"Where did you get this?" she asked softly, hugging the white and pink unicorn to her swollen tummy.

"We keep them in the Manor for guests just in case. I

never want anyone to feel uncomfortable," he explained, sitting on the edge of the table across from her. She'd assumed he'd be eager to get some alone time with the coven members downstairs, but he showed no desire to leave.

"A unicorn will certainly cheer up anyone feeling unwell," she joked as the discomfort began to settle thanks to the delicious warmth of the water bottle. Her lack of energy must have weakened his element, because, for the first time since they'd swapped, the chilly night air bothered her.

"We've got plain colours as well," he added, smoothing down his trousers as though he didn't know what to do with his hands. Lucy got the impression he wasn't used to looking after someone, even if it was his job to see to the needs of hundreds daily.

"I got the unicorn? I feel so special!" She wasn't sure she ever wanted to give it back. Her water bottle case at home was so worn that it barely protected her from the scalding temperature she preferred.

"The animals are usually for our younger guests, but I remembered you were obsessed with unicorns," he recalled.

"When I was six!" How had he remembered such a small detail?

"Fine, I'll get you a plain one." He reached for it, but she refused to give it up.

"How did you know it was my period bothering me?"

He looked slightly embarrassed. "During our final exams in school, you were sitting on the ground in the exam hall with your knees under your chin. You looked like you were in pain, and then I heard you talking to a nurse," he told her, while she tried to remember the day in question. "She didn't have any hot water bottles, and there wasn't time for you to go home and get one."

"But she did get me one in the end. Wait... that was you? Did you leave the school to get me one?" Lucy didn't know if it was the gesture or her hormones that were making her eyes water.

"Don't look too much into it! I wanted to place first in the class on merit, not because you were too sick to take the exam," Benedict protested, focusing on twisting his signet ring. She didn't believe his dismissive tone for a second.

"When I didn't see you in the exam hall, I thought you were trying to throw me off, or you'd been caught cheating or something. I never would've guessed that you missed the exam... so I could sit mine?" She couldn't believe he'd done something so kind for her. It wasn't like they'd been friends; if anything, the exact opposite. She'd have expected him to revel in her misery.

"I didn't plan on missing it. When I tried to sneak back in to the hall, I got caught and they wouldn't let me sit the exam. The nurse convinced Principle Pauper to let me sit it the next day because I'd given her the hot water bottle for you," he said lightly, as if it was nothing.

"Why let me think the nurse just found one?"

He shrugged, bringing her a pillow from his bed. "You needed it. Didn't matter who gave it to you."

"If you keep doing kind things for me, I'm going to think you've gone soft," she said, sighing as the painkillers began to ease her cramps.

"We're to be bound, I should keep up appearances."

"No one's watching now – or then," she pointed out, as he adjusted the pillow behind her back.

"Maybe I'm just trying to seduce you and take your

position," he said, his breath a whisper against her neck. She could hear the smile on his lips.

Considerate, empathetic, kind... The spell. Lucy shook away the thought that he might be *the one.* He was only doing this because he wanted her to think he'd be a good leader. Yet he'd risked his final exam to help her even though he had nothing to gain. It could have cost him.

"You should get back to the others before they drink the bar dry. And you have a vamp wedding to see to," she reminded him, trying not to let him see how his kindness had affected her.

He hesitated, worry creasing his brows. "Do you need anything else? Any cravings? I can have room service make you anything you like."

"Thank you, but I'm still full of cake." She was perfectly content, sinking deeper into the pillow behind her head. It smelt like him.

"Me too." He patted his flat stomach. Having seen him in a towel, Lucy couldn't help but think of the smooth skin beneath his shirt. "If you need me, just call down to the bar. Are you sure you're okay alone?" He stepped back slowly, genuinely reluctant to leave her.

"I'm not alone." She stroked the purple lizard resting on the back of the couch. "Greko makes for excellent company." With a click of her fingers, the candles shone brighter, and the fireplace lit up in the corner by his desk.

"Try not to set the room on fire while I'm out," Benedict teased, backing up towards the door.

"I'll do my best," she mused, watching him go.

Once the door closed behind him, she considered leaving. It felt far too intimate being alone in his private space. He apparently trusted her enough to leave her where she could snoop and search for any secrets that might cost him any future election. Yet instead she found herself snuggling deeper into the couch and opening the book he'd left on the coffee table. She couldn't believe it – he was reading a romance.

Maybe Benedict is more soft-hearted than he let on.

"Sorry, I didn't mean to disturb you," Benedict whispered softly, reaching over Lucy to pick up the book. The smell of his aftershave drifting around her was a nice way to be woken up.

His gaze lingered on hers, and there was a hunger there she hadn't seen before. Conflict, desire, anger – she couldn't read him for the first time in years.

She sat up, and he settled, on the coffee table giving her some space.

"I didn't know you were a man of such exquisite taste," she joked, waving the book at him. He reached for it, but she pulled it out of his reach and began to flip through the pages. "Hmm, where was I?"

She hadn't planned on teasing him, but the flush on his cheeks was irresistible. She pretended to clear her throat.

"'Penelope had bound herself to him for life, and their love would live long after they were gone.'" Suddenly awkward, she glanced at Benedict; perhaps this page wasn't the best choice. Refusing to let her nerves get the better of her, she kept reading. "'She braced herself as the viscount, her new husband, came towards her. His unbuttoned shirt exposed his smooth pale skin, and it was the most she'd ever seen of a naked man. He ordered her to face the mirror, and she did as she was told. She wanted him, all of him, but she couldn't stop herself from shaking as he cut through her strings at the back of her wedding dress. He stared at her naked form in the mirror, his dark eyes lingering on every curve, every freckle, until she couldn't take it anymore. She turned around, bringing her lips to his. He gripped her face, deepening the kiss and stealing her breath. Carrying her in his arms, he dropped on the bed and ripped off his clothes, settling between her legs. She didn't care about her inexperience; she trusted him to teach her. His lips travelled to her breasts, her stomach, before settling between her legs, and she gripped the pillow behind her head as he licked and tasted what he had longed for since the moment he'd first laid eyes on her. Heat pooled between her legs, a growing ecstasy—" Lucy flushed under Benedict's gaze, but she wasn't going to break first. "Calling out her beloved's name, he bit—"

"You should stop," he interrupted her, and with a thrill, she noticed his voice was much lower than before. He snatched the book away from her as though it would come alive and, like the viscount, bite her.

"Why?" She stared up at him over the page. Heat flooded her body. He'd never looked at her with such desire.

"Because when I think of fucking someone, it's *you,* in my dreams," he told her, moving into her space.

His gaze fell to her lips as she swallowed, unable to stop thinking about him doing everything she'd just read aloud. He cocked his head, a sly smile dancing on his lips. Lips she suddenly wanted to taste. She was hot all over, but this was different from his element. Sharper, urgent, more consuming.

"You want me, Lucinda. I don't know why you continue to deny what you truly desire."

The next thing she knew, his hand was in her hair, and her head was being twisted to the side as his lips crashed down on hers. She whimpered as the feel and taste of him overwhelmed her. *Oh, shit. I can't. It's Benedict.*

As though reading her mind, he darted away from her. Her eyelids fluttered open; his sudden absence made her dizzy.

"Fuck it." She reached up, grabbing the back of his neck and kissed him greedily. His hand gripped her waist; she shoved aside the blanket, overwhelmed by heat and the desire to remove any barriers between them. His fist tightened in her hair as his lips demanded more. Drunk on the taste of him, she struggled to catch her breath. She loved his mouth, which was surprising, since she spent most of her life wanting him to shut it.

He teased her with his tongue, brushing her lower lip and driving her desperate with need. Slipping his hand up her shirt, he palmed her breast, and she let out a little gasp. Lost in his touch, she struggled to think, to breathe. All she knew was that she needed more, and that she'd never get enough. He trailed his lips along her jaw, his breath hot against her ear.

"If only this were real," he whispered, his lips grazing her sensitive stomach.

The words shocked her out of the dream. "What in the hell type of dream was that?!" She shook the images from her head as they lingered. Period dreams could be rather crazy, so she decided to blame the book and forget it had happened.

Lucy didn't know when she'd fallen asleep, but she was now covered with a blanket, and the book she'd been reading was on the table beside her. It was dark outside, and she guessed she'd slept long into the night.

The water bottle was still warm as she took it from her tummy; she smiled a little. Given the amount of time passed, Benedict must have refilled it when he came back.

Peeling herself off the couch, she tiptoed over the creaky floors until she reached his bedroom to find him sleeping. Leaning against the archway, she couldn't help but admire how peaceful he was. He looked younger, sleep removing all traces of his scowl.

He turned over, clutching a pillow to his chest, and something that resembled butterflies stirred in Lucy's heart. The alarm clock by his bed told her it was already five am. She had to get home and change before work; she didn't want the town to see her walk of shame.

She wanted to repay his kindness, and the only way she knew how was to get his element back to him as soon as possible.

Lucinda

"There you are!"

Lucinda jumped out of her skin as Gwendoline appeared at her back. It wasn't like Mrs Matherson to teleport to see her.

"You frightened me," she exclaimed, dropping a pile of books on the front desk before she scorched them.

"I can see that. Our future High Priestess shouldn't scare so easily," Gwendoline said, eyeing Lucy's unicorn slippers. The woman was practically see-through – an astral projection.

"What can I help you with, Gwendoline?" Lucy asked, switching her shoes beneath the desk. "I'm sure you're busy, since you couldn't come in person."

"I was on my way to get my nails done when I got a text from your mum. I forgot to collect the binding cloaks this morning from Benedict. I thought you might be able to help; your mum wants to get started on tailoring them as soon as possible. What with all that's going on with the changes to the festival – an excellent idea to change the layout, by the way. I knew you and Benedict would make an exquisite team. Though I will try not to take too much credit." Gwendoline winked.

"I can pick them up after we close," Lucy said, fidgeting with her ring behind her back, careful to keep it out of Gwendoline's sight. She wondered why her mum was in a rush to get everything for the binding organised. Maybe she wanted it out of the way so they could focus on the upcoming festival.

"I knew you wouldn't hesitate to help! Wouldn't want you covered in dusty cloaks on your special day." You could only really count on a Matherson to smile when they got their way.

It was customary for the woman to wear the cloak of the male line, though Lucy would have preferred to wear the Hawthorne cloak her mother had worn on the day she was anointed as High Priestess. It'd be more traditional, if not slightly archaic, to wear the Matherson cloak, so it was what the coven would be expecting.

"I would've asked Benedict to drop them off, but he had some mess to clean up, I don't know. I did ask him to dig them out of the attic," Gwendoline went on, speaking a mile a minute. Lucy wondered if the mess was the destroyed cake; she wished she'd cleaned it up for him before she'd left.

"It's no trouble," she said, hoping to move on.

"I can't wait to see you both in Matherson navy. Your mum is magic with the sewing machine. It will be so lovely to see Benedict in the Matherson cloak. He'll be the last to use them in our line, you know. Unless you have any children." Gwendoline's voice turned sad.

Lucy pictured herself in the deep navy cloaks she'd seen in photos, the M over her heart. She'd never thought of giving up her surname if the binding went ahead; she wondered if Benedict would expect it of her. That would mean that even if she became the High Priestess, it would still be two Mathersons at the head of the table. Her mum had kept her name, but that was because Dad was a magless. Lucy wasn't sure which made her palms sweat more – the idea of becoming a Matherson, or the thought of having Benedict's kids. Both made her head spin. They were still learning to cope with each other's company, never mind the pressures of the future being added to their shoulders.

"I think we're getting ahead of ourselves. If we make it to the binding in one piece, that will be enough," she laughed.

Gwendoline offered a sympathetic smile. "One step at a time."

On her way to the manor to pick up the cloaks, Lucy savoured the fresh air. Her conversation with Gwendoline had forced her to think of what being bound would really mean. They would live together, work together. People would expect them to continue the new line of Mathersons. She wasn't sure if she could do it.

She twisted the ring on her finger. If he was willing to try, then she wasn't going to be the first to falter.

A couple of school kids brushed past her as they left Stoker's, and Lucy noticed a pumpkin pie in the window. Benedict's favourite. Maybe she could get some as a small way of saying thank you for last night.

Faye waved through the window from behind the counter. Lucy took it as a sign and went inside, happy to see her old school friend. Faye rarely worked out front, or during the day for that matter.

"Hey – sorry I haven't texted you. I wanted to congratulate you on your binding." Faye beamed, taking Lucy's hands. Lucy noted that she was wearing long sleeves, and that she pulled back quickly.

"No worries at all. You really don't have to be sorry," Lucy said quickly, not wanting Faye to feel like she'd noticed anything. "The situation between me and Benedict is rather complicated."

"When Ian told me, I didn't believe it. I remember when you flooded his locker!"

Faye had cut her hair short, cropped just below her ear. It suited her, and it was a sign that things were going better. The last time they'd hung out, she'd used her hair to cover the bruises.

The memory made Lucy's hands sizzle, and she removed them from the wooden counter just in case. "I forgot about that," she admitted. She couldn't even remember why she'd wanted to flood it.

"In fairness, he did light your hockey stick on fire." There it was.

"I wouldn't have minded so much if the coach hadn't given me detention." Lucy had hated hockey and was terrible at it, but Foxford Prep had a mandatory sports policy for the first three years. Supposedly, it helped the students manage their stress so nobody accidentally used their element and destroyed the school.

"We were so close back then." Faye's smile faded. Lucy wished they hadn't drifted apart. She blamed Ian for isolating her. Faye and Ian had married right after school, and he wasn't the kind of man she wanted for her friend. Or anybody.

"We're still close. You can stop by the house or the library whenever you like," she said cheerfully.

"If I could ever get the time. Now, what can I get for you?" Faye asked, returning to the cheery version of herself she put on for customers.

"Pumpkin pie," Lucy ordered.

"You hate pumpkin!" Faye exclaimed, reaching into the front window to wrap up the freshly prepared pie.

"It's not for me," she admitted. Hopefully Benedict wouldn't think she was being presumptive, just turning up with a pie, but she reminded herself that Gwendoline had given her a mission. She couldn't believe she was looking for excuses to see him.

"I suspected as much." Faye boxed it up with a gold ribbon.

Lucy didn't know what to say. "I saw Luisa and Harriet for the Autumn Equinox. They asked what you were up to, and I said you might join us next time."

Faye stilled. "A pity I missed them, but maybe next time."

It was always next time, and Lucy knew better than to ask why. Working out front in the shop meant Faye was gaining confidence. Lucy didn't want her friend to hide again to escape the questions those who loved her wanted to ask.

"How is Ian?" she asked quietly, afraid of being shut down. "Rosie mentioned he's working in the Clover pub now?"

Ian had had more jobs than most in Foxford. He couldn't keep one to save his life, and if he hadn't been of magical descent, he would've been kicked out of the town long ago. Not that the coven hadn't tried, but when it became clear that he would take Faye with him, they'd all silently agreed that it was best to endure him for her sake.

Avoiding Lucy's gaze, Faye went to the till. "He's the same. Works long hours, which keeps him away from home, and then he's usually asleep during the day, but he loves it," she said.

Lucy tried to conceal her relief. Ian being away from home was great news. "I'm glad things are better."

"They are, at least for now. I don't know what Ian would've done if Benedict hadn't got him that job. I only got to thank him the other day," Faye said gratefully.

"Benedict found him the job?" Lucy struggled to hide her surprise. Benedict had voted for Ian to be banished from the town. She didn't know why he'd go out of his way to help Ian after being so vocal about his banishment. In fact, it'd been one of the few things they'd agreed upon.

"After the last incident, no one would hire him. I don't know what Ian would've done if he hadn't put in a good word for him," Faye said, hope dancing in her eyes.

Lucy wished she cared more for herself than the man who'd hurt her for years. It had started a few months after Faye's wedding; shouts and breaking glass had been heard late at night from their cottage on the edge of town. Lucinda had tried to intervene by telling her mum about the bruises she'd seen, though Faye had brushed it off as nothing. As High Priestess, and a concerned mum, Wilhelmina had tried to counsel Faye, but it hadn't made a difference. Since then, the job at the bakery had at least given her some independence – a job Wilhelmina had convinced Ian to let Faye accept.

"We all would've done anything to keep you in town," Lucy said, grateful to Benedict for helping when no one else could.

"At least I got to pay him back in a small way," Faye said, making an iced tea. Lucy hadn't ordered one, but Faye knew it was her favourite.

"Pay him back?" Lucy frowned.

Faye hesitated as she added a lemon slice to the cup. "Oh – I wasn't supposed to say."

Lucy hated the idea of her friend keeping a secret from her, especially if it was a secret about Benedict. She'd only started to trust him.

"Don't look so worried! It's nothing that concerns you. In fact, it's rather silly. I don't know why he doesn't want me to tell you." Faye shrugged, adding to Lucy's curiosity. "He was probably embarrassed."

"Embarrassed? Now I'm *really* worried," Lucy said, leaning across the counter.

"It was nothing. He was stranded with his brother, Peter, on the side of the road between here and Willow Valley. They were covered in mud, like they'd been wrestling in it."

"When was this?" Lucy asked.

"A week ago, more or less?" Faye shrugged.

Lucy remembered the meeting he'd missed after they'd tried to redo the potion. *Was Peter the reason he hadn't come to the meeting? But what were they doing in the road, and if they were covered in mud, probably in the woods?* She really hoped he hadn't been up to anything dangerous.

Faye distracted her from her thoughts. "I can see your mind spinning."

Lucy shook off her questioning gaze. "Like you said, it was probably nothing. Who are we to question what they get up to?" Still, curiosity ate at her. She couldn't ask Benedict without revealing that Faye had broken her promise to him.

"Could we keep it between us?" her friend asked nervously. "I don't want him to think I was gossiping, after all he's done to help."

"Of course! I won't say a word." If Benedict wanted to tell her about his stroll in the woods with Peter, he would. There was no reason to think the incident had anything to do with her or their element. She hoped. "Stop by Hawthorne House whenever you want. Grams would love some company, and we have too many empty rooms." She kept her voice low, just in case a friend of Ian's was close by.

Faye hesitated. "Ian's going to visit some of his extended family in the mountains next month. No outsiders allowed. I might stop by, for a night or two."

Lucy rested her hand over Faye's. It killed her not to be able to help more. The frustration made her want to light the counter or Ian on fire. But Faye had to decide to leave on her own.

"Stay as long as you want. We're always here when you need us. Grams would love an excuse to cook a feast." Lucy added a tenner to the tip jar and took the wrapped-up pie to the counter.

"Grams does make the best pot roast!" Faye pulled her sleeves over her hands. She was definitely hiding something.

"Rosie and I tend to go to the Dragon's Inn for brunch on Sunday, if you want to join us."

Faye's eyes shifted away. "I might have to work."

Lucy didn't want to push her luck. "We'll be there anyway, and we'll save you a seat in case you can make it. No pressure."

"Maybe next time."

Lucy only made it a few steps down the street when Faye rushed up behind her.

"I hope you and Benedict are happy," she blurted out, then looked over her shoulder, as though afraid she would be heard talking about another man. The fear in her eyes stabbed at Lucy's heart. "He helped me, before. I think we were wrong about him at school." Faye gave her a quick hug before being called back inside by another worker.

Lucy watched her through the window for a moment, but drops of rain fell onto the box, and she hurried along. She didn't want to deliver a soggy pie when she had questions that needed answering.

Benedict

Walking into the quiet of his quarters, Benedict heard a scuffle behind the archway entrance to his room.

"Greko! No climbing the curtains," he warned the lizard automatically, only to spot his scaly best friend sitting on his favourite cushion beneath his desk. A thud stilled him. There was someone in his room. He rounded the corner, quickly trapping the intruder against the bookshelf so they wouldn't be able to escape.

"Ow!" the intruder cried as a book fell from above and hit them on the head.

"Lucinda?" Benedict asked, relaxing his grip on her shoulders. *What the hell is she doing creeping around my bedroom?*

She leaned away from the bookshelf. "Thankfully that wasn't a hardback," she joked, rubbing her head.

"You could've used the door. Or knocked. Or called!" he said, wondering if appearing in his room was becoming a habit for her.

"Nice to see you too," she said, putting the fallen book

back on the shelf. "I thought teleporting would be better, so no one would see me coming and going. I tried to call you when I was on my way over, but you didn't answer."

Benedict recalled that he'd turned his phone off when he'd left the reception desk. His need for some peace had won out.

"Sorry for shoving you, and I don't care about people seeing you come and go," he told her, loving how her big green eyes locked on his. The way she looked at him had changed, softened, though it was still full of questions. "We've nothing to hide or be ashamed of."

"It's fine – you didn't hurt me," she said, looking away. "Gwendoline asked me to pick up the binding cloaks. When I arrived, you weren't here, so I was going to grab them and go."

"I might not have hurt you, but that book did." Benedict ran his fingers through her hair, feeling a bump forming.

"It's nothing, really. A small bump isn't going to kill me."

"I didn't know my books looked like binding cloaks," he said, sitting her down on the edge of his bed.

"Curiosity got the better of me," Lucinda admitted. "I wanted to see what you were reading." Her eyes went to the gaps in the shelves.

"I donated some to the second-hand book stall for the festival," he said, telling a half-truth. He'd already moved the books he suspected she was looking for to the cottage he was renovating, though it wasn't time to tell her about his little passion project yet.

"Speaking of the festival, Mrs Crawford managed to get the fireworks from Willow Valley at a discount, since we're ordering double this year." Lucinda picked at her nails, exposing her lifelong distaste for fireworks. "We discussed the matter at that meeting you missed, after the potion failed. Maybe you should tell me why you missed it, so I don't get our stories mixed up?"

She knows. There was no point in hiding it any longer.

"Peter brought me to see a crone not far from Willow Valley. I should've told you, but there wasn't time." He wouldn't tell her the whole story. She didn't need to know the crone had tried to kill them.

Lucinda rubbed the side of her head, and he took the opportunity to change the subject. "I'll get you some ice for your head," he said gruffly.

"Was the crone able to help? Offer any advice?" she asked as he disappeared into the kitchen. She didn't sound angry or even upset about his meddling, which was a healthy change.

On the small kitchen island, Benedict noticed an ivory pastry box. Faye must have told Lucy about giving him and Peter the lift – not that he blamed her. The woman had enough of her own secrets to keep as it was.

"Sadly, no," he said, untying the ribbon. The smell of pumpkin pie made his mouth water. "Did you bring this?" he called, grabbing an ice pack from the freezer.

"Faye was putting out a fresh one in the window, and I wanted to thank you for the other night," Lucinda said when he returned. "And for this." She held up her ring finger. It was a nice change from the other finger she usually showed him. The thought made him smile almost as much as the pie.

"Faye was working out front?" he asked, surprised. It seemed like a step in the right direction.

Pressing the ice pack to the side of her head, Lucy nodded. "She didn't mean to tell me about you and Peter being stranded on the side of the road, but she got caught up when she mentioned you helped her with Ian."

"I didn't do enough," he disagreed. Lucy didn't say anything, and she wished he could read her mind. "Convincing Marianne to give him a job as the night porter at the bar was surprisingly easy. Figured it would keep him out of trouble at night and asleep during the day." He didn't want anyone to know Peter had been involved.

"That was very sensible of you. I would've expected you to threaten to dismember him and use his decaying carcass to fertilise the gardens," Lucinda said. The look in her eye told him she wished he had.

"I like your imagination, but vampires don't make the best fertiliser." If only he had been so original with his threat. "I told him if he put hands on Faye again, I'd report him to the Order for smuggling dangerous creatures and objects."

"Ian wouldn't be smart enough to pull that off."

"No, he wouldn't. However, I'm smart enough to frame him and make sure he sees sunlight again." Benedict winked.

"If you need some cursed objects, I have plenty," Lucinda offered.

"You've got yourself a deal."

They shook hands.

"I didn't mean to startle you by appearing," Lucinda said. "I wasn't sure if you'd be here."

"No need to apologise. I'm not normally so jumpy. I'm still on edge from visiting that crone."

"What happened exactly?" Lucinda snapped her fingers, lighting the fire in the corner of the room. Seeing her master his element filled him with a possessive pride.

When he didn't respond, not wanting to trouble her

with his near-death experience, she merely sighed. "Well, it hardly matters. Since I still have your element, she wasn't much help. Why do you have all these?" Lucinda pointed to the shelves made up of her favourite books. Judging from her smile, she'd noticed. Benedict cringed at himself for not removing them all fast enough.

"Curiosity. You've always had your nose in a book. Walking to school, coffee shops, in the park, by the town fountain – the world could crumble around you when you're reading, and you wouldn't even notice," he admitted.

"But why buy them?" She walked past him to the shelf.

"I wanted to know what inspired your undivided attention."

"I never knew you paid such close attention. You didn't read all of them, did you?" She blushed a little, the red hue highlighting the freckles he loved.

"Of course. Even the smutty ones," he whispered over her shoulder.

"I wish I could've seen your reactions," she said, running her hand along the spines. The ring he'd given her, gleaming in the candlelight, reminded him that she would be his soon. He swallowed his desire to reach out and take her hand in his own to make sure the moment was real.

"You aren't as innocent as I thought."

"No one ever is," Lucinda muttered, lowering the ice pack. She turned around, staring up at him through her long lashes.

Benedict watched her chew her lower lip and found that he couldn't remember what they'd been talking about. He slipped his fingers into her hair. Thankfully, the bump had gone down. "Better?"

"Much."

He let his fingertips graze the back of her neck, afraid she'd bolt at any moment.

"Don't leave town again without telling me?" Lucinda spoke in a whisper, but the words pierced him more than any insult could have. She placed a hand on his chest, no doubt able to feel his pounding heart. In return, he rested his forehead against hers, as though some force was pulling them together.

"Never," he promised.

She nodded, her eyes focused on his lips. His lips brushed her cheek – a test, a question – and her sharp intake of breath was music to his ears. She closed her eyes; he ran his thumb down the side of her neck, tipping her jaw up towards him. The scent of her strawberry lipgloss held him in a vice grip. He could almost taste her sweetness.

"If it isn't my favourite couple."

The two of them jumped apart to find Peter sitting on the trunk by the bed.

"I'm not interrupting, am I?" he teased, crunching loudly into an apple. "Juicy."

Benedict glared at his brother, who obviously wasn't talking about the apple. *If he wasn't already dead, I'd strangle him.*

"No – I was just collecting the cloaks for our binding ritual," Lucinda babbled.

"Binding cloaks! How official. Have you sent out your invitations yet? I don't exactly have a postage address."

Benedict watched Lucinda roll her eyes. "Don't worry, you're invited to the reception, but the ritual itself is for coven members only."

Hearing her talk about the ritual as though it was something they'd decided for themselves did nothing to settle Benedict's heart rate, nor did her smile at his brother. That she accepted Peter without question meant more to him than he could ever admit.

"Pity – I never made it that far," Peter said, getting up to wrap an arm around her shoulder. "Who could love a Grim such as me?"

Benedict clenched his jaw, noticing how she didn't shy away from his brother's touch.

"I'm sure you'll find someone to annoy for eternity," she said. "I bet there's someone at the Grim office dying for you to make a move."

"Pardon the pun," Peter said, nudging her. Lucy shoved him away playfully. "I'd be lucky to find someone, like you two have found each other." He gave Benedict a knowing look.

Time to put an end to this interaction. Benedict went to the trunk and lifted out suit bags containing the cloaks. They were a little on the dusty side, but he'd done his best to brush off any cobwebs. He could barely hold back a smile as he held them out to Lucinda. During the vampire wedding, he'd been struck with sudden inspiration and texted Lucinda's mum to ask if she would mind him wearing the Hawthorne cloak instead of the traditional Matherson one. Lucinda was more important to him than any archaic tradition, and he wanted the exchange of cloaks to be a sign of their equal partnership. He was joining the Hawthorne family as much as she was joining his. No rule stated he couldn't wear hers – it just hadn't been done before, which tended to make people nervous. But he had the High Priestess's permission, and that was all he needed.

He couldn't wait to see her in the Matherson navy, or her reaction to him in the Hawthorne cloak. Wilhelmina had already dropped by and taken his measurements. He wondered if the High Priestess had told Gwendoline about his plan and that was why she'd sent Lucinda over.

"Great, thank you. I'll get going; I'm sure you two have some catching up to do." Lucinda threw the suit bags over her arm.

"You don't have to go," Peter said, following her to the door. Benedict pulled at his arm to stop him. "Did you tell her about the crone with the pickled fingers in a—?"

"Ignore him," Benedict snapped.

"Already do," Lucinda said as he opened the door for her. She hesitated, and he could see she wanted to say something, but when her eyes darted to Peter, he knew she wouldn't.

He rested his hand on the door, making sure she was gone before he turned on his brother.

"Are you insane?! She might be my wife, but she's a Hawthorne, and you only just got promoted. Let's not tempt fate by confessing what happened in that gods-forsaken hovel!" he hissed.

"Your *wife*? Aren't you getting ahead of yourself?" Peter said smugly.

Benedict ran his hands through his hair. *Was this day ever going to end?* Of course his brother had only heard the least important part of what he'd said.

"You know what I mean. You've got to be more care-ful," he ground out. At least he hadn't called Lucinda his wife to her face. He didn't think he would've survived the ridicule. He hadn't even realised he thought of her as such.

"Seeing you happy so often is quite unnerving," Peter said, amused.

"I'd be happier if you forgot about helping me! Lucinda and I have it all under control. She found a potion in an old Hawthorne grimoire that might help us, and if not then we'll wait it out." As a matter of fact, he was rather proud of how they'd handled each other's elements. So far no one had been drowned or burned alive.

"A powerful crone couldn't help, but a potion in a dusty old Hawthorne grimoire can? I'd love to get a look at that book," Peter mused.

"Don't even think about it. It's going back to the Order, and you don't need to be anywhere near them or it." Benedict wasn't surprised by his desire to see the book. Peter had always been fascinated with power – the more volatile the better.

Peter raised his hands defensively. "Consider it forgotten."

"What happened to the soul you were supposed to collect? I haven't heard of anyone passing recently."

"It's turned out to be a rather complicated case." Peter frowned, which was unusual. He'd never seemed bothered by his job before.

Benedict paled, thinking the worst. "Are you collecting someone we know?"

"I can't reveal my orders. But rest assured it's nobody you know. Well."

Foxford was a small town; Benedict probably knew them in passing. To be honest, there weren't many he wanted to know well. He liked to keep his cards close to his chest.

Trying to veil his concern, he asked, "What makes this case different from any other?"

"I don't want to collect them," Peter admitted, producing a small bottle of vodka from his jacket. Benedict wasn't even sure if Grims could get drunk.

"Nobody close to Lucy?" he panicked, watching his brother wince as he took a swig.

"I can't tell you, but not necessarily," he repeated, clearly frustrated at not being able to name his charge.

"What happens if you refuse?" Benedict asked, not versed in Reaper procedure. Their ways were more secretive than most, because they belonged more to the next world than this.

"They'll send another Grim. You can't mess with fate," Peter said, rubbing his hands over his face.

"Are you going to collect?" If Peter lost his position as a collector, he wouldn't be able to return to the living realm. As much as Peter drove him crazy, the thought of losing him twisted his gut.

"Yes. I don't have a choice."

Benedict rubbed his brow. He hated to think of the death of someone his brother clearly cared about, but at least this meant he wouldn't lose him again. "If you're unable to distance yourself, maybe you should give it over to Gregory. He's your mentor; you should let him help you," he suggested.

"*I* might not be able to change her fate, but she can." Peter sounded like he was talking more to himself. "I can't take this to Gregory – he's already done so much for me. Refusing to collect would be an insult to his recommendation for my promotion. Can you stop looking at me like I'm going to break? It's not Mum, and the Hawthornes are safe."

Benedict let out a sigh of relief. He didn't want Lucinda to have to go through losing a family member. Death was inevitable, but he wanted to spare her that pain for as long as possible.

"I can't imagine how hard it is to do what you do. You should know how proud we are of you."

"It was hard at the beginning, but Gregory reminded me that we get to be there for people at their most vulnerable moment. Help them find closure, and cross over." The contentment in Peter's voice told Benedict he truly believed it.

"What about those who don't cross over, like...?" Benedict had never dared to ask before.

"Like me?" Peter arched an eyebrow. "I'm not ready to go yet, and even if I wanted to, I can't. I still have my debt to pay. One thousand souls for that damned necromantic spell. It's not easily paid off. You'll probably cross over before me, but at least I know you'll be waiting for me."

"Would you warn me if something was to happen to Lucinda?"

"As in would I help you stop it?" Peter asked, getting to the root of his question.

He nodded, taking a seat on the couch in the sitting room. The pillow Lucinda had used the other night was still there.

"You must love her something awful if you want to anger Death." Peter sat on the table across from him, pouring him a drink.

"That's not an answer."

"No matter how much you love someone, you can't change their fate."

"But you said they can," Benedict said, wanting to know what he'd meant earlier.

"Only if a decision, or a series of decisions, alters their course – but it's rare. Death has a habit of catching up." It sounded like Peter had looked into it.

"Being a Grim doesn't sound like such a terrible fate, if it keeps someone alive."

"You've really got it bad," Peter chuckled, leaning his elbows on his knees. "Don't dwell on what ifs! You have her now, so make use of the time you have. Stop thinking about death."

"It's hard not to when a grim reaper is constantly darkening my door," Benedict pointed out, grinning.

"I understand your desire to protect her. You lost Dad and me in a matter of months, but you aren't going to lose her." Peter said quietly.

Benedict lifted the glass of vodka to his lips. The thought of losing her troubled him far more than the thought of being bound to her. An uncomfortable tightness settled in his chest as he thought of never seeing her cycling through the town on her ridiculous pink bike, or hear her lecturing him about something mundane.

He took the pillow and clutched it to his chest, the faint smell of her perfume tugging at his heart. In that moment, Benedict realised that eternity with her might not be enough.

Lucinda

By the second Saturday of October, Lucy hadn't seen Benedict since she'd discovered his fruitless trip to the crone and collected the cloaks. She couldn't believe he'd risked his life to help them get their elements swapped back while she'd waited for the curse-stripping potion ingredients to come in, which they finally had yesterday.

She closed the Hawthorne grimoire with a thud. She couldn't delay handing it over to Emerson any longer, afraid he would start to grow suspicious. There was no reason to hang on to it.

Lucy placed the old grimoire in its protective case and sealed the latch for the last time. Pulling her lilac sleeves over her hands, she couldn't help but feel proud of herself for not having set it alight in the past couple of weeks. It was a waste to see it locked away, probably never to be touched again, but her translations would help provide some insight into past magic practices, and the ingredients and their uses could assist modern medicine. It brought her some relief to focus on the positives, even if she felt like the rest of her life was going up in flames.

"I believe this is for you," she said, handing the case to Emerson up in the library. She hadn't wanted to interrupt his lunch with Rosie, but if she didn't give it back, she feared she'd keep going over every page until she lost her sight or mind.

He stared up at her as though he'd forgotten about his orders.

"Are you sure you're finished?" he asked, placing his hand on the case gently as if it would shatter. "I don't mind waiting any longer. I've already told the Order that your delay was justified."

"Thank you, but I'm afraid there's nothing more to do. Everything they should need to read the pages is within the case," she said, relieved to put it behind her. She suspected his wish to delay had something to do with Rosie. Even though he'd started work at the university last week, he stopped by every day to have lunch with her at the front desk.

Emerson reached for his bag to put away the grimoire, knocking a glass of water over onto the case files Rosie was working on.

"Shoot!" he exclaimed, correcting the glass.

"Just grab the original – the rest are just printouts," Rosie said, jumping up and moving the files to the other end of the table.

"I'm so sorry! I should've been more careful around your work," Emerson exclaimed, using the napkins from their lunch to clean up.

"Lucy, give us a hand," Rosie said, expecting her to protect the documents from the water.

Her request was innocent, but damning. Lucy fidgeted.

"It's just a bit of water, and I have the originals," she said, picking up the sodden papers. "I'll go make new copies in the office."

She hurried off, but Rosie followed. Luckily, Emerson stayed behind to deal with the mess.

"What is going on with you?" Rosie opened the office door and stared at her best friend. "It's not like Emerson doesn't know about your elemental magic."

"Nothing!" Lucy lied, turning on the printer. "It's only water, and you know the coven don't like us to flaunt our elements." She had no idea what to print, but she needed to do something with her hands.

Rosie's eyes narrowed.

"Fill this glass of water," she said, handing Lucy Emerson's empty glass.

A tense silence filled the space between them as she clutched it.

"I can't," she admitted, closing the office door. She didn't want Emerson to hear their conversation.

"Why not?" Rosie demanded, taking the glass and putting it down on the desk. "Tell me what's going on with you lately. You haven't been watering the plants, and you've been avoiding me. Is this because I've been spending time with Emerson? You don't approve?"

Lucy winced. She hadn't meant to hurt her friend. Unable to hide it any longer, she inhaled deeply and explained about the spell, the wrong ingredient, and Benedict's element, which she demonstrated by setting a piece of paper on fire. Rosie squealed at the demonstration and tossed the water from a vase of sunflowers over it.

"How the hell are you going to fix this? How could you keep this from me?! For weeks!" Her claws exposed themselves.

"Please try to calm down," Lucy pleaded, careful to keep her distance just in case. They didn't need a wolf roaming around the library.

Rosie shook out her hands, her manicured nails returning to normal, and waited for the answer.

"I'm sorry for not telling you, for avoiding you, but I promised Benedict I'd keep it a secret. I didn't want you getting wrapped up in my mess," Lucy said, pulling at the ends of her sleeves. "I've got to admit I feel a hell of a lot lighter now that you know."

"Benedict hasn't reported this to the coven?" Rosie asked, taken aback. "Is he blackmailing you? Is that why you've seen him so much recently?"

"No, nothing like that. Since it was the binding agreement that inspired my family's stupidity, he believes he's partially to blame; it was his mum's idea in the first place."

"That's a small mercy. He could've done some serious damage," Rosie said, sitting on the desk beside her.

"You can't tell Emerson about this, as nice as he is," Lucy pleaded. "He's still a member of the Order, and we can only assume his loyalties lie with them first. They would love to hear that two of Foxfords founding families have got themselves into a right mess."

"I'd never say a word – I only wish you'd told me sooner. When did this even happen? The coven meeting was the same night we went to the lake."

Lucy nodded. "I came to find you after Grams and Mum had cast the spell."

"And then later on... I tracked you to Matherson Manor."

There was no point in keeping anything from her at this point. "One of the side effects is that our element draws us together. He found me half-naked, looking for butterflies or fireflies – doesn't matter." Lucy buried her head in her hands. "He made sure no one else saw me so indisposed."

"Oh God, Matherson saw you naked?!" Rosie looked horrified, only to burst into laughter. "I don't mean to laugh, but of all the people you could've run into—"

"Please don't remind me." She wished the tea had erased every moment from her memory. Then again, so much had happened since. She couldn't even begin to explain her evolving feelings for him to Rosie.

"Luisa's tea probably didn't help." Her friend turned her attention to the printer. "I'll make new copies so Emerson doesn't wonder what we're up to. But please, no more secrets."

"Agreed." They shook on it as the printer buzzed.

"Any idea what you're going to do about your elements?" Rosie asked, collecting the printouts.

"That's why I held onto the grimoire. I had to make sure I wasn't missing anything that could help us before I handed it over."

"And did you find something?"

"There's a curse-stripping potion that might help, but if it doesn't work, the effects should wear off once All Hallows' Eve passes, whether we're bound or not." Lucy decided not to go into details about the 'perfect man' clause.

"There's still a couple of weeks to go before then!" Rosie gave her a reassuring hug. "To be without your element must feel like missing a limb."

Lucy sank into her embrace, relieved not to fear burning her.

"It's not easy," she sighed into her friend's shoulder. It felt nice to confide in someone other than Benedict. "I can't believe how much I took it for granted. Fire is a whole different burden to bear. It's true about not judging a person before walking a mile in their shoes."

When she stepped back, Rosie was smirking at her.

"What?" Lucy frowned.

"Sounds like Benedict isn't much of an enemy anymore."

"More like a partner in crime now." Though she still didn't trust him as much as she wanted to, they'd come a long way in a short time. "We should get back to Emerson." Lucy took some of the finished copies from Rosie. She wasn't ready to answer any more questions about Benedict.

They returned to the table to find it already cleaned up, the files stacked in an orderly pile as though nothing had happened.

"Sorry again," Emerson said, pulling out a chair for Rosie.

In her haste to get away, Lucy realised she had left the grimoire out in the open with him. She cursed herself for reacting emotionally and not considering how dangerous such a thoughtless action could be. She trusted Emerson, but with others in the library, it was best not to make careless mistakes.

"No harm done," Rosie promised.

"Not like it was the grimoire," Lucy added, "then we would've had to sacrifice you."

The joke was met with a burst of nervous laughter that made her wish she'd kept her mouth shut.

"She's joking," Rosie said, leaning close to Emerson.

"Ah," he said, before turning to Lucy. "I've got back-to-back lectures this week, but I've got a special warded case in my quarters at the university, if you're comfortable with me keeping it until I can drive to the Order Institute on Saturday, and they'll send it on to Rome."

It was a relief to know his plan. Most of the time, couriers for the Order took her work and disappeared without explaining where they were going. She wondered where one of the institutes of the Order was. Then again, she hoped to never find out. Her kind didn't tend to return from such places.

"My part is done; what you do with it now is up to you," she said, trying not to let her desire to keep it show. "When do you expect to return? Will this affect your position at the university, if you miss a day or two after just taking up your position?" She'd noted Rosie's expression when Emerson talked of leaving.

"I should be able to return Monday evening, if not Tuesday morning. Once the order verifies the authenticity of the grimoire, I'll be allowed to return," Emerson said, glancing at Rosie, who hid her expression behind her pumpkin mug. Lucy could tell she was hanging on to every word. Clearly, she didn't want him to leave.

"Good. I'm glad it won't affect your work too much."

"It would be better if I didn't have to go at all. I feel like I was just starting to get settled," Emerson said sadly.

Rosie concealed a smile behind her cup. Lucy wondered if she was the only one with secrets. *Has something happened between them?*

"Anyway, I should put this in the university vault before my last lecture," Emerson announced, leaving them to get back to work.

"What?" Rosie asked as Lucy caught her watching him go.

"You like him!" Lucy nudged her with a wicked grin.

"He's an Order member. I would have to be insane! And he's a good assistant."

"Sure, an *assistant*," Lucy teased. "When has sanity ever stopped you from doing anything?"

Rosie growled at her in warning, returning her attention to the police file in front of her. "I have work to get to."

"I told you my secret," Lucy whined, leaning over the table.

"I found out about your secret – not the same." Rosie started nervously organising her case files, avoiding eye contact. "Nothing's happened. If it does, then you'll be the first to know."

"You know it's risky. He would have to ask for permission—"

"I know. Our circumstances aren't lost on me. That's why nothing has happened, and it won't happen until I'm sure he is worth the trouble."

"You light up around him," Lucy gently pointed out. She hadn't even taken the time to check in on how her friend was feeling. She knew it wasn't easy to have feelings for someone who was supposed to be your enemy.

"Like a bulb?" Rosie mocked. "Don't you have somewhere to be?"

"Nope. Now that the grimoire is out of my hands, I've actually got some free time!" A weight lifted from her shoulders. If it hadn't been for the curse-stripping potion and her pending nuptials, she really would have nothing left to worry about.

"Well, I do." Rosie grabbed her files. "They found a weird symbol at the site of a disappearance in Willow Valley last week, and I've been asked to consult. Lock up when you leave."

"You'll do anything not to talk about your love life?" Lucy followed her to the door. It was the first time she'd seen Rosie run away from her.

"Nice ring. Wearing it even when you aren't around the coven or Benedict?" Rosie shot back.

Lucy's smile disappeared, and she held her hands behind her back. "Thought you had to get to the train station."

Rosie winked, all bundled up in her coat and pink beret. "I was just leaving."

Lucinda

Lucy finished ordering in the lantern lights they'd discussed at the last coven meeting. Humming to herself, she put away the returns for the day. She wanted to make sure Rosie came back tomorrow to find the library in perfect order.

Suddenly, she clutched her red sweater as her gut twisted. The candle on the desk blew into a giant flame. Terror forced her eyes closed.

Seconds later, she found herself standing in the lobby of Matherson Manor, six inches deep in water.

Releasing her grasp on her crumpled sweater, Lucy watched in bewilderment as disgruntled guests carrying their suitcases headed towards the revolving doors. *Holy Goddess, Benedict flooded the Manor?* She began to sweat. *Maybe leaving each other alone for a few days wasn't the best idea.*

She looked down at her ruined black suede boots. "They were my favourite pair," she said sadly, lifting a foot.

"Lucinda Hawthorne!" Gwendoline barked.

Lucy jumped, sending ripples through the water. This wasn't going to be pretty.

She wanted to flee, but Gwendoline was already hurrying down the grand staircase to yell at her future daughter-in-law. "Why are we five inches deep in water?"

Lucy opened her mouth. She had no idea what to say. Even if she told the truth and said it wasn't her, the circumstances looked extremely damning, and she couldn't tell Gwendoline about the element swap.

"Close your mouth, dear! Are you a trout?" Gwendoline snapped, the ends of her dress soaking up the water. "Speak up."

Lucy didn't want the coven to think she couldn't control her element, but she couldn't let Benedict be reprimanded for her family's mistake.

"I-I'm so sorry, I don't know what happened," she stammered. "I was on my way to see Benedict and I... lost control!" *What the hell happened to him?*

Gwendoline smoothed her hands over her slick bob, taking a slow breath. "I don't know what is going on between the two of you – whether you fought or what – but please keep the Manor out of it. I can't even find Benedict."

"You can't find him? Is he not here?"

"Aren't you listening? He's nowhere to be found. Suzy called me about an issue with some unruly guests. I get here and find *you* standing in my flooded lobby!" Gwendoline pinched the bridge of her nose.

Trouble with guests? That might explain his loss of control... but how bad could the complaint have been, for him to flood the reception – and then leave without cleaning up his mess? Water slipped into the top of Lucy's boots as she walked towards Gwendoline.

"I can't apologise enough. I'll fix this," she assured her, though she had no idea how.

Gwendoline looked to the guests waiting outside, some looking rather impatient. "Hurry, please, we're fully booked. I don't want anyone leaving because of this incident."

Not knowing what else to do, Lucy knelt, ignoring her sodden clothes. Reaching into the cold water, her palm settled on the rough carpet. Sensing her magic emanating around her yet not being able to harness it saddened her, but she could feel the anger that had caused it. Something had happened to infuriate Benedict, and for once she had nothing to do with it.

"Well? Can you undo this or not?" Gwendoline demanded, leaning over her. Lucy hesitated, shaking water off her hand. There was no way to explain herself. Her palms began to sweat as they heated. She had no choice but to tell the truth.

"I can explain," she began, but to her relief, her mum interrupted.

"What on earth?" Wilhelmina said, struggling with the revolving door. She looked to Gwendoline, sloshing through the lobby. "I was on my way to meet you at Stoker's when I heard some guests talking about the flooding!"

"Willa! I'm sorry – in the chaos I completely forgot about our lunch, but I'm so glad you're here." Gwendoline glared at Lucy, who winced.

"Did you do this?" Wilhelmina's eyes went wide as she stared at her daughter.

"It was an accident. I haven't been myself." Lucy hated lying to her.

Her mum's eyes narrowed. Lucy had never made a mistake like this before.

"Gwen, why don't you go outside to your guests?" her mum said, ever the mediator. "I'll help Lucinda clean this up. You'll never know it happened when you return. If anything, you'll get a great carpet clean!"

Lucy saw where Benedict got his sharp stare from. "Fine. I'll overlook this mishap, as I know the pressure you've been under lately. However, this is the only time." Gwendoline tried her best to leave with dignity, but it was hard to do while sloshing through the water.

When she was gone, Lucy took her mum's hand. "Mum, can you please drain the water? I'll explain later, but I *need* to find Benedict."

"This is your mess, darling. I expect you to take some responsibility for your mistake," Mum said, looking at the mess with troubled eyes.

"I do, but please help me just this once? You'll be able to drain the water far faster than I could, and Benedict is missing," Lucy pleaded, fretting about where he could be.

"Okay, but you've to tell me how things went this far. Did you fight with him?"

"Nothing like that. I was dropping off the new map for the Autumn Festival. I... I thought I was doing something nice by watering the new hedgerows, but my element got the better of me. With the stress of everything, I lost control."

The lie was ridiculous, but if her mum asked about the gardens, Gwendoline could confirm they'd had new hedgerows planted. Even if it made Lucy feel ill to lie to her mum, it was better than telling the High Priestess that her element was now in the hands of a Matherson.

"At least you weren't fighting." Wilhelmina gave her a sly look. "I heard you two have been getting on rather well, in fact."

Lucy wanted to cry with relief. The last thing she needed was to tell Gwendoline their fire magic flowed through her veins. She'd take it as a sign that their binding was fated.

"We're making the best of a bad situation, and now isn't the time to discuss this." She needed to leave. The flooding was rather ironic, considering Benedict had been so worried about her burning her house down. She fiddled with the ring on her finger, wishing she'd done more to help him.

Mum sighed. "Go find him, but use the side entrance so Gwendoline doesn't think you left without helping."

"I'll see you at home later. Thank you." Lucy squeezed her hands gently, only to realise her mistake when her mum flinched out of her grasp. In her heightened state, Lucy hadn't realised how hot she was.

"Fire?" Wilhelmina gasped.

"I've got to go!" Lucy hurried out of the lobby, half expecting her mum to come after her. When she glanced over her shoulder, Wilhelmina stood frozen, staring after her.

Out of the Manor and turning down Warlock Avenue, Lucy let her element call her towards the university.

Benedict, where the hell are you? She hurried through crowds of students going from one historic building to the next.

In the shadow of the arched entryway to the practical magic building, she let out a long exhale as she finally spotted Benedict slipping down an alleyway towards the sport fields. Lucy struggled to keep up as he hurried into the woods. *Where the hell is he going when the Manor needs his attention? Maybe he's trying to get away from town in case he loses control again.*

Keeping her distance, Lucy hesitated on the edge of the trees. She clenched her fists, knowing that every moment she wasted in fear of what lay ahead was another step Benedict was taking. All manner of creatures lived in the lawless woods. Many kept to the pathways or to the lake, but he was heading off the safety of the paths.

Does he have a death wish? Or is he looking for a place to expel my element safely? There was no law or order here; only the rules the creatures within created themselves. Those who wished to travel from village to village always kept to the main road. To diverge was to risk their life. *If he gets killed with my element, will it die with him? I can't let him continue without a proper way to defend himself. He doesn't know how to use my water defensively.* She headed in, not letting herself talk herself out of it.

Mist lingered around her ankles as though wishing it could trip her. Her boots were not the right attire for a walk in the thick mud, even if the water in the lobby hadn't already ruined them. Spotting him in the distance, she tripped over a tree root with a grumble. Lucy quietly ducked behind a tree. She doubted he'd be happy about her following him. The coven would have plenty to say if they were caught in the eastern woods.

Tree sap clung to her fingers as she peered around the trunk to make sure she wasn't discovered; he was muttering to himself. Clearly something had upset him. Reluctantly, she wiped the tree sap on her favourite black midi skirt with a long slit that was now getting caught on branches. At least her cropped sweater was nice and thick, so it was keeping her warm. She glanced down and bit her lip to stop herself from cursing when she realised her foot was sinking into a boggy mess. Taking a calming breath, she heaved it out of the mud. However, her relief was short-lived. When she looked back up, Benedict was out of sight.

I hate the woods, I hate the woods, I fucking hate the woods, she chanted to herself. Quickening her pace, she searched the trees for any trace of him, but he was gone. Lucy tried to sense her element again, only to find it was blocked by the energy emanating from the trees. She began to tremble.

A crunch of cracking branches sounded, causing her to freeze. *What if whatever's got Benedict is now hunting me?* She was turning slowly, careful not to startle whatever creature was waiting to pounce, when a figure jumped down from a tree in front of her.

Lucy shrieked, punching the shadow, and cried out again when her knuckles connected with something hard.

"Lucinda! What the fuck?" Benedict held the bridge of his nose.

"Benedict? What is with you and trees?!" She spoke at a pitch she was rather ashamed of. She was surprised she'd managed to land a hit. She'd never been in a fight before.

"I was being followed. How was I to know it was you?" he said, wiping his nose to see if it was bleeding. "Hell of a punch, pumpkin." Looking at her with watery eyes, he sounded proud. "But you didn't have to hit me!"

She'd take any praise she could get to make up for her throbbing hand. Any joy she felt disappeared, however, when she saw three sharp, bloodied lines cutting across his cheekbone. Claw marks, and a black eye developing nicely. Neither injury could have been caused by her.

"I wouldn't have hit you if you hadn't surprised me. Who did this to you?" Lucy asked, instinctively reaching for his cheek.

He flinched, his gaze hardening. "The person I thought

was following me," he said, turning to walk deeper into the wood.

"You flooded the manor. I thought you might need help," Lucy panted, trotting to keep up with him. "I take it that would be the wolves, considering you're headed straight for their territory?" The claw marks were a big hint. *What the hell had caused him to get into a fight with a wolf?*

"How do you know where I'm going?" He stopped, but he didn't look back at her.

"There are maps all over the library. You should study more," she said, trying not to lose her footing as she struggled to keep up with his long strides. "Even if a wolf did that in town, there are no laws out here. They could disembowel you for simply stepping into their territory without permission!" She might want to set the person who'd messed up his face on fire, but she needed him to reconsider.

He spun around, pointing in the opposite direction. "Which is exactly why you should turn around and head back. Your family would never forgive me if I let anything happen to you, and I wouldn't forgive me either."

Lucy squared up to him with a smile, holding up her ringed finger. "Sorry, sweetie, this means your problems are my problems. I'm not going anywhere." She marched ahead of him, stopping him from going any further.

"Go home, pumpkin, this doesn't involve you," Benedict said, though there was no anger in his voice. His hair fell haphazardly, as though he'd been obsessively running his hands through it.

"What about the manor?" she asked, trying to distract him.

He hesitated. "I burst a pipe before I left. I didn't want her to use it against you with the coven members."

"Thank you for protecting me." She meant it, even though the fact that she'd already taken credit for the flood meant she had some explaining to do when they got back. "Now let me protect *you*. Come back with me."

"I will – once I've dealt with the wolves," he said coldly.

"But we've got another issue," Lucy blurted out as he stepped past her.

"What?" he snapped impatiently.

"My mum came by the manor. She felt your element through my skin because I was so upset!"

"So she knows." Benedict shrugged like it was nothing. "Good."

"What?" Lucy gawked as he came back towards her, finally distracted enough to forget his mission.

"Maybe we don't have to hide it. I know you feel what's happening between us as intensely as I do. Otherwise, you wouldn't be here trying to protect me," he said, a hair's breadth between them. "Admit it, you're not here because of the manor."

"Of course I want to protect you. I don't want to see you torn apart by the wolves for stepping into their territory without invitation. I would do the same for anyone!" Now really wasn't the time for romance.

"How long are you going to lie to yourself?" he exclaimed, and she wished they'd go back to talking about the wolves. "What if the switch only showed us what we were too stubborn to see ourselves?"

"Y-you can't mean that," she stammered, nearly tripping over a branch.

He caught her and pulled her close, tipping her chin up to face him. "I do."

"I don't like the idea of others putting their hands on you, of them hurting you," she admitted.

"I'm fine. You don't have to protect me."

"Your face tells a different story." Lucy ran her thumb under his eye, where the skin was darkening. "Grams'll be able to brew up something to help that."

"Some wolves didn't feel like paying their bill. I'm going to settle the issue." Benedict brushed her hand gently from the wound.

"Fine. If you're going, I'm going," she informed him. "If we're going to lead the coven together, then this is a good test for us."

He shoved his hands in his pockets. "There is no way I'm convincing you to return, is there?"

"Not a chance, and I'm not a damsel in need of protection." She crossed her arms over her chest. "If you do this, I do this."

He brushed a fallen leaf from her hair. "Regardless of our binding, you're still in line as the next Priestess by rites, and I can't let anything happen to you." He bit down on his lower lip, as though stopping himself from saying more.

Lucy stepped back into his reach, igniting a spark of uncertainty in his gaze.

"My life's not worth more than yours," she said softly, resting her hand over his heart.

"That's where you're wrong, pumpkin," he murmured, so low she barely heard him. Suddenly, one of his hands was cradling her cheek, and butterflies filled her stomach. His gaze was intense as he brushed a thumb over her lips. "I never expected you to worry about me."

Is it the spell making me feel like this? Lucy found she didn't care.

He gave her a kiss so brief and gentle that it was like a whisper, leaving her craving more.

"Do I..." He rested his forehead against her. "Have permission?"

It was all moving so fast, and in the middle of the eastern woods was hardly the time and place, but there wasn't an ounce of hesitation in her response. Rising on her tiptoes, Lucy boldly pressed her lips against his.

Benedict's eyes went wide in surprise, but any shock was replaced with hunger as he slipped his hand into her hair. Her body melted into his. Magic was thick in the air; it felt like the forest came alive around them. He moved forward until she was flush between his hard body and a tree.

"So much better than the dream," he breathed, and her heartbeat soared as he gripped her thighs.

"You dreamt of me?" Lucy asked, wrapping her legs around his waist and gripping his shoulders.

"Didn't you?"

"Yes." She clung to him, struggling to get out the words. "The dream felt so real." She'd never done anything like this, especially anywhere that wasn't private. "How can we know this is really happening?"

"It is now. I promise you this is real," he said, peppering her face with kisses. She'd never seen this playful side of him. Happy, free, obsessed – and it was because of her.

Their kiss turned desperate, a hasty rush of lips, tongue and teeth, until she was breathless. Lost in the taste, the smell of him and the earthy forest.

His lips moved to her cheek, her neck, and Lucy used

one hand to grip the bark behind her, needing some leverage as he ground his hips against her sensitive core. With so little separating them, she could feel how hard he was. There was something irresistible about him being obsessed with her, as much as she was obsessed with the hard ridges of his body, so perfectly moulded to hers it felt like they'd been doing this forever.

"Fuck, Lucinda!" Panic laced his words, and his grip on her tightened. Startled, Lucy opened her eyes, sure she would have marks on her thighs tomorrow.

A loud crack sounded, and Benedict yanked her away from the tree. They dropped to the soil with a thud. Lying on the ground by his side, she frowned at the loss of contact. However, her disappointment was short-lived when she stared up at the burning tree.

"Shit!" She covered her mouth with her hands, embarrassed and afraid of what she'd done in the heat of the moment. "It was an accident." Her mind, clouded with lust and fear, only fanned the flames.

"How can I stop it?" Benedict asked gently, distracting her.

Taking a steadying breath, she took his hand and placed his palm on the soil between them amongst the falling charred leaves.

"Feel the flow from the earth into you. Don't try to force it," she said calmly, trying not to think of what might happen if the fire spread.

The worry subsided when the first droplets hit her skin. Her hand still rested over his as they watched the rain fall, the flames subside, and the smoke clear.

Benedict

Safely back in his bathroom at Matherson Manor, Benedict let Lucinda sit him on the edge of the tub. She arched a brow at him, daring him to defy her, but he had no interest in doing so. For a moment, it was too quiet. When she licked her lips, studying his injured cheek, it took everything he had not to grab the back of her neck and bring her lips to his.

"Where do you keep your first aid stuff?" Lucinda asked, all business, as though they hadn't almost lost complete control of themselves in the woods. Her hair, loose in big curls and falling over her shoulders, was evidence of that.

"Behind the mirror," Benedict said, trying not to focus on the bare skin exposed by her tiny sweater riding up when she reached the top shelf.

He reminded himself he was supposed to be annoyed at her for stopping him from confronting the wolves. He'd wanted to tear off the furry heads of those who'd hurt the staff, but the thought of endangering Lucinda was unthinkable. He wasn't sure there would be a pack left if they dared to look at her the way they had at him in the lobby. The thought of them laying a claw on her soft skin —

He spotted a few freckles on her back and cleared his throat, trying not to think about wanting to find and taste every single freckle on her body.

"How much aftershave does one man need?" Lucinda muttered, breaking him from his thoughts.

"Is it a crime to smell good?" he asked, trying to hide a smug grin. He was sure traces of his scent were on her. Anyway, it was only a few bottles; he liked to have options, since he kept his wardrobe so limited.

Lucinda muttered something under her breath and grabbed a bottle of disinfectant. The flush travelling from her neck to her cheeks told him she wasn't as unaffected as she pretended by what had happened in the woods.

"I can do it myself. You don't have to burden yourself," Benedict said gruffly, but she shoved him back down.

"You should be honoured to be treated by a healer of my skill." She stepped confidently between his legs and tilted his chin up to get a better look. He usually liked to be in control, but damn, did it turn him on to have her stand over him.

"I don't think the green fox felt the same way," he teased, then winced as she gently wiped a cotton pad over the first scratch. She rested her other hand on his shoulder, distracting him.

"That was years ago. Do you have to remember *every* mistake I've made?" Though her tone was rough, her touch was breathtakingly gentle. "If I turn you green, it won't be an accident." He watched her brow crease with concern. "The scratches are deep, but if we can get some of Grams's balm on it soon, it shouldn't scar." She dipped a new cotton pad in the disinfectant. "You're lucky you don't need stitches. I'm not as neat as Grams with a needle."

"I trust you, but not enough to take a needle and thread to my face." He faked a flinch as she went to touch his cheek again.

Her eyes flashed to his at the word 'trust'. He wished he could hear what she was thinking.

"Stop flinching, I haven't even touched you yet," she grumbled, holding his chin in her hand. "We need to clean it. The more you move, the longer it's going to take."

That was exactly what he was hoping for. His fingertips brushed each side of her thighs, ever so gently, to balance himself. The soft fabric was nothing compared to the warmth of her skin. He cleared his throat, trying to distract himself from such tantalising memories.

Lucinda stared at him, and he realised she was waiting for his permission to proceed.

"Sorry." He nodded.

Watching her, Benedict enjoyed the way she pursed her lips and blew on the wound, drying the disinfectant, how she got so close without any hesitation. His pain was muted as he brushed strands of fallen hair from her face. She didn't flinch, as though it wasn't strange at all for his hands to be on her. He flexed his jaw to stop himself from smiling like an idiot.

"What?" he asked, trying not to fidget as her eyes lingered on every detail of his face. "Do I look hideous?"

"You were lucky they missed your eye," Lucinda told him, her palm against his cheek.

His eye was the last thing he cared about. All he could focus on was the slope of her jaw, the small dimple in her chin and her long, dark lashes. He kept his attention away from her lips, so close to his, even if every fibre of his being was desperate to taste them again.

She removed her hand from his cheek, and he missed the warmth. The smell of disinfectant lingered in the air as she put the lid back on the bottle.

"Not so hard to let someone help you, is it?" she said, putting the bloody cotton in the bin.

"You didn't give me a choice," Benedict retorted. "Following me in the woods was brave, but reckless as hell. You surprised me, Hawthorne; I thought you'd be happy to let the wolves pounce on me."

"I wasn't going to leave you when you were so angry, and injured! They could've done serious damage. I don't think you'd be so charming with half a face."

"I wouldn't need to be charming if I turned into a wild beast," he joked as she pressed a damp cloth to his cheek. "I'd have fear on my side."

"A scratch won't turn you. I doubt you've to worry about sprouting fangs and fur."

"How can you be so sure?" he said, getting up to stand behind her by the sink as she put away the antiseptic. She stared at him in the mirror. "Maybe you should chain me up just in case."

Lucinda rolled her eyes and slipped away from him. Benedict swallowed as she lifted one side of her skirt, revealing black stockings with a delicate lace edge.

"Wh-what are you doing?" he stammered.

She rolled her stocking down to her knee. Her pale skin was dotted with freckles. Then he noticed the four faint silver lines on the side of her thigh.

"A wolf did this?" he snarled, anger renewed. His heart pounded, though he wasn't sure if it was his rage or watching her slip the stocking back over the scar.

"Relax. I only showed you so you'd know you won't change. Mine was an accident, but far deeper than yours, and I'm still 100% witch. You've nothing to worry about," Lucinda promised, and his heartbeat steadied as she rested a hand on his chest. "Don't think you can get out of the binding anyway, even if you did wolf out."

"I wouldn't dream of it," he said, resting his hand over hers. "How did it happen?"

"When Rosie first moved in with us after leaving the woods, I made the mistake of going into her room during a full moon. Without her pack, it was harder for her to control herself." There was no anger or pain in her words, only sadness. "I should've known better; it wasn't her fault. She still feels awful about it."

"How come I never heard of this?" Benedict wondered why the coven hadn't been informed of a wolf-related incident. He hadn't even noticed a bandage on her leg. Then he remembered that she always wore longer skirts and dresses. He'd never thought she might be concealing something.

"I begged Mum and Grams not to report it. Her residency in town hadn't been fully approved yet, and they would've cast her out. She shouldn't be punished because I was careless." She looked down at her leg. "As you saw, the scars are barely noticeable, thanks to Grams's balm. Your pretty face will be back to normal in a few days."

Understanding how far she was willing to go to protect those she cared about made his chest tight. An admirable trait, and one he understood all too well. She might make a good Matherson after all.

"You were kind to take her in. Many in town wouldn't have."

"I wasn't going to let her end up homeless or roaming

the woods alone. She was sleeping in the gazebo in the town square when I found her," Lucinda said.

"Will she ever return to the pack?" he asked, wondering if Rosie had ever considered it. Even though his own family was a mess, he couldn't imagine leaving them and never returning.

"I don't think so. Being cast out cuts a wolf deeper than any harsh words or physical scar. It'd be like someone ripping out our element and only leaving us with traces of it." Lucinda grimaced as she realised what she'd just said.

"It's not the same," he said, not wanting her to beat herself up. Part of him was grateful the switch had happened; otherwise they might never have broken down the walls they'd built up over the years. "She's lucky to have you and your family. Grams is as protective as any alpha."

"I'd be much more afraid of her. Grams won't rip your throat out, but she can do worse," Lucinda agreed with a shiver.

"I thought Hawthornes don't use dark magic?" he joked.

"You forget that my great-great-grandfather married the last Douglas," she admitted, reminding him of the only blot in their pristine magical ledger.

"Necromancers. How could I forget?" He tutted.

She chuckled. "My great-great-great-grandmother nearly had an aneurysm about the match, given his lineage, but Aurora didn't practice herself. She was the last of their name, and this was all before they even came to Foxford. Though we have got the last Douglas grimoire in our private vault − it was brought with us to Foxford. There are more dangerous and forbidden spells in it than I dare to mention, and it was the one grimoire Grams swore never to hand over to the Order."

Curious to know if she was ever tempted, he asked, "Can you read it?"

"Yes, but I don't dare to translate it. Nothing good can come from those pages. Grams showed me once, and the drawings alone haunt me." She shuddered. "And the blood connection is weak, so I'm not sure if my translations would even be accurate."

"So there is a bit of darkness in you," Benedict said, inching closer to brush her hair over her shoulder. "I don't have to worry about corrupting you."

"I'm not a complete goody-goody." Lucinda scowled, folding her arms across her chest.

"Ha! Oh, I know. I remember the piranhas." He was only teasing her. Even if there were traces of darkness in her lineage, she wouldn't harm a fly.

"You're not as bad as you think you are," she said, stabbing his chest with her finger.

He closed the gap between them, pressing her up against the sink. Her eyes went wide, but she didn't try to push him away.

"You've no idea." He rested his hand on her waist, running his thumbs over the inches of bare skin as her sweater rose. "I've been on my best behaviour. What happened in the woods is only a taste."

Watching her swallow, he brushed his lips against hers. She leaned in for more, but he pulled away. The annoyance in her eyes nearly broke his composure.

"What's spinning around that mind of yours?" He ran his thumb over his lower lip, begging her to confide in him.

"What if this isn't real?" she whispered.

He shook his head. "It feels real."

"What about the spell? How can we know for sure? What if it wears off after the binding and we hate each other again?"

"Pumpkin. I've never hated you." It took every inch of his self-control not to kiss her again. Since the woods, he felt like he was starving and she was his favourite meal.

As he leant down, she pressed her lips against his furrowed brow, bringing him back to reality. "We should wait until we do the curse-stripping potion. I need to know what you feel for me is real and not because of some stupid switch."

"Lucinda," he breathed, tightening his grip on her hips. She was a fool to believe that any spell or potion could have caused his feelings for her.

"Please," she pleaded against his lips. "Anything you say is only going to hurt more."

"Okay; we'll wait." He released her, but she didn't move away from him. "I promise you, with or without this spell, I'll still want you."

Her chest rose and fell, as though she was trying to remind herself to breathe. He didn't want to push her. Even if he could feel her desire for him, he wanted them to be together without fear or doubt.

"You should go."

"Why?" He hated how hurt she sounded; he didn't want her to take it as a rejection.

"Because I don't want to hear you say no if I ask you to stay."

"What if I want to stay?" she started, only to stop herself. They both knew it was the right decision; she needed time to trust him fully. To give herself to him fully without any hesitation.

"I want you to stay because of me, not because you don't want to go home and face your mum," he told her, bringing her hand to his lips.

"That's not the reason."

"Okay, but I think you should talk to Wilhelmina. I don't want her to think I'm keeping you captive." He winked, cupping her cheek. "Even if I want to lock the door and throw away the key."

He kissed the small smile at the corner of her mouth, and the soft sigh that escaped her nearly brought him to his knees.

"This'll all be over soon. We have everything we need to try the potion." She sounded as though she was trying to reassure herself as much as him.

He wondered why she was pushing the potion so much. The binding should fix them anyhow, and he couldn't help wondering if she didn't want to go through with the ritual. Or perhaps she did and wanted to be sure of his feelings for her.

If this was what she needed, then he'd give it to her. He'd give her everything.

Lucinda

After work on Friday evening, Lucy hesitated outside the door to Mulligan's jewellers.

Nervously, twisting the ring on her finger, she considered that if she couldn't reverse what her family had done to their elements, then the least she could do was help Benedict remain in control. She also didn't want him to attend another coven meeting without a ring and have them think she wasn't putting in the same amount of effort as he was. Had that been his reasoning for giving it to her? She hoped not, but the doubt was enough to taint the gesture.

Inhaling deeply, Lucy forced herself inside. Mr Mulligan sat behind the glass counter, polishing some rings.

"I was wondering when the young Ms Hawthorne would darken my door," he said, eyeing her hand.

"With the festival and everything else, I haven't had a chance," she said, wishing she'd come sooner.

"No worries, dear; I don't think Benedict even thought about his own. I told him I could make a pair, but he wanted yours as soon as possible. Even had me rush-order the stones!" Mr Mulligan said, wheeling himself out from behind the counter.

"I'm ashamed to admit it, but the thought of binding rings had slipped my mind until he sprang it on me. I wanted to place an order for Benedict. I don't have his ring size, but since he gets most of his stuff here, I figured you would." *Why am I prattling on like this? It's only a ring.*

A ring signifying your spending eternity together, her subconscious taunted.

"Gwendoline mentioned you made the Matherson signet ring he wears from a fallen meteorite?" she asked, ignoring her thoughts.

Mr Mulligan moved around the workshop, putting the polished rings back in their cases. "I think I've got some fragments left. He'll love it," he said, adjusting the magnified glass under the lamp on his workbench. "Would you like to add the same stones as your own?"

"Yes! If you could engrave the infinity detail from mine but with stones set into the band rather than on top? If it's possible." Benedict wouldn't want anything to stand out too much, and the stones would help with his element.

"The meteorite is hard to manipulate, but I can use a spell to make it work." He looked through the small drawers fixed to a unit of the wall filled with all the materials he could need. "I should have just enough fragment left to make the band – must be fate." Tipping a tiny meteorite stone into his rough palm, he wheeled his way back to the counter. "How's this?"

"Perfect! It should match the others he wears perfectly." She didn't want anything to detract from the signet ring he never took off.

"When would you like to pick it up? I guess this is

another rush order, since there isn't long before the big day."

"I don't want to put you under any pressure; it's my fault for leaving it so long. How much time do you need?"

"Shouldn't take too long. I'll give you a call when it's ready for collection... and I might have already formed a band for him, just in case you stopped by." Mr Mulligan winked.

"I can pick it up whenever. I might be delayed if I'm working at my stall for the festival, but I'll sneak away when I get a chance," she said, trying to contain her elation.

"Toffee apples again?" He beamed, putting the pieces for her order on the work bench behind him.

"Wouldn't be a festival without them!" She was looking forward to them herself. The best part about making them was being able to eat as many as possible.

"My favourite," he said, patting his stomach.

"I'll save an extra one for you. The least I can do for the rush orders we've put you through."

"I'll look forward to it, but it's no trouble. Benedict ordered extra stones just in case, so I don't have to wait for them," he said, writing up a receipt.

"I insist – as many apples as you like, free of charge."

"Thank you," he chuckled, handing her the carbon copy of the receipt. She didn't even want to look at the price, but since it would be the only binding ring she'd ever buy, it was worth it.

The air felt thin as the thought settled in. They were going through with it.

"Good thinking with the dark stone. He'll be pleased to see how well you know him. Certainly makes my job a lot easier," Mr Mulligan said.

"It's easy when you've known each other forever."

"Pardon me for saying, but I was only saying to my granddaughter how you both make a fine match," he told her. "She was here when Benedict came in to collect your ring. She's only eight, but any mention or rumour of bindings and she's obsessed with the idea of loving someone forever."

Lucy smiled. She wished it was so easy, to find someone and just love them. Yet in a way, she wondered if she'd always loved Benedict; they'd spent most of their lives together, and she had never truly wanted any harm to come to him. As troublesome as he was, she couldn't imagine her life without him, whether they were bound or not. He was a constant in her life that she was sure she'd miss if he was gone.

"Sorry for rambling on – it was my roundabout way of saying congratulations," Mr Mulligan said, waving a hand as she moved to pay him. "No rush on that, you can pay on collection." He placed the order request under a magnet on his workbench behind the counter. "Need to make sure you're happy with the work first."

"I'm sure it'll be perfect." Lucy tried not to chortle. She was putting more care and thought into the ring than she had about agreeing to be bound to Benedict in the first place! "Thank you again for the rush order. I'll let you lock up." She hadn't realised how late it was until she'd noticed the clock on the back wall.

"Get home safe!"

She stilled by the door. "If Benedict comes in, please don't mention the ring?"

"My lips are sealed."

Lucy found herself still smiling as she headed home. She kept picturing Benedict's face when she gave it to him.

He'd smile, hopefully, which always felt like a big win. She almost got more joy out of making him smile than his usual scowl.

Outside the gate to Hawthorne House, she stopped, reminding herself they weren't actually engaged. But Benedict was right when he'd said that just because they'd agreed to be bound for political reasons, it didn't mean they shouldn't take part in what everyone else got to experience. Like others before them, they were deciding to spend this life and the next with each other. Maybe it was okay to be excited about that.

"I think we have some things to discuss."

Lucy winced, stalling on the porch steps when she saw her mum sitting in Grams's rocking chair. They'd managed to avoid each other since the incident at the manor, mostly because Lucy had been kept busy with the arranging of the festival and the library. Getting up before her and getting home late also helped. Thankfully, her mum had also been distracted arranging her retirement adventures with Lucy's dad.

"Everything's fine. Thank you for helping at the manor the other day," Lucy babbled. Rain was pouring off the roof; she just wanted to get inside and get dry.

"Not so fast. You can't avoid me forever," Mum said, patting the seat on the porch swing.

"I'm tired. Between the library and the festival, I'm desperate for a cup of tea and my bed. I promise I've got everything under control," Lucy pleaded, wanting to be left alone.

She'd done enough talking at the festival meeting earlier in the day about last-minute details for the festival's opening night dance tomorrow – a special way of welcoming everyone to the town, and also of getting them drunk on pumpkin punch, so they didn't care how much they spent at the market stalls. Her ears were still ringing from Mrs Crawford's demands for more chaperones. More often than not, some of the underage magic folk managed to get hold of a few cups of pumpkin punch. Last year they'd turned the town hall into a giant jack-in-the-box. Terrifying and hilarious, but illegal, and there had been more than a few complaints from the magless. Thankfully no one had been hurt. Benedict had agreed to double the number of chaperones and bottle the punch just to get out of the vamp bar before night fell. She'd expected him to ask her why she hadn't got started with the curse-stripping potion, but it had never come up. Then again, he'd been busy with the Manor, sorting out the mess created by the wolves and the burst pipe. A lot of guests had wanted to check out, but after some damage control and a massive amount of charm, he'd managed to make everyone forget about all the drama.

Anyway, she couldn't use the brewing room at home because she was trying to avoid her family. It wasn't like she was delaying intentionally.

"You're under a lot of pressure, but I want – *need* to know that everything is fine," Mum said, closing the book on her lap. "I want you to drain the water from that flower-pot."

"I forgot to water them this morning. They could use a good soak." Lucy reached for the door handle.

"Lucinda, don't make me ask twice." It wasn't a request.

Lucy clenched her teeth, doing her best not to argue. Instead, she glared at the flowers glistening with raindrops and let her anger pour out. Her mum leaned forward and narrowed her eyes; it only took a few seconds for the rainwater to steam until the soil was bone dry and the flowers scorched.

"Sit and explain," Mum ordered.

There was no way she was escaping now that she'd confirmed she didn't have her element. Lucy sat, gripping the edge of the porch swing and trying to bite her tongue, but she couldn't hold it in any longer. If she did, she was afraid they'd wake up tomorrow in a pile of ash.

"What do you think happened?" she barked. "Your hybrid love potion backfired, like I warned you and Grams it would!"

Mum studied the scorched flowers.

After a shaky breath, Lucy elaborated. "The spell switched my element with Benedict's. He flooded the manor because he lost control of his temper after some guests caused trouble. He broke the pipe to make it look non-element-related." She did feel much lighter, not having to hide the truth any longer, though she wouldn't mention the wolves.

"How could this have happened?" Mum said, almost to herself. "I made sure there was no way anything could go wrong."

"You might have, but Grams added the wrong ingredient. It changed the spell from a drawing spell," Lucinda explained.

Mum paled. "I can fix this," she said, guilt softening her tone.

"We already tried to reverse it by correcting the spell, but it didn't work," Lucy told her.

"It'll probably fix itself after the binding."

"You can't know that. We're going to try a curse-stripping potion."

"I know."

Lucy stared at her. "How?"

Mum moved the colourful blanket from her lap, revealing the spell Lucy had copied from the Hawthorne grimoire. Her mum held it in her hands like it was poisonous.

"Using such a potion from that book is taking things too far. The old magic is far more dangerous than what we harness now. It could strip you both of your elements," she hissed.

"It's a Hawthorne potion! We should be fine," Lucy argued, reaching for the paper, but Mum snatched it out of reach.

"Why is it so urgent? Perhaps our spell is trying to tell you something!" she urged.

"That's the problem," Lucy snapped, letting her anger get the better of her. "How are Benedict and I to know if anything that happens between us is real and not because of our elements, because of a spell, a potion? This is why you don't mess with love magic!"

"You care for him?" Mum asked, surprise quietening her voice. "Something has happened between you? A rumour is one thing, but I want to hear it from you."

Lucy wished she could believe with absolute certainty that what had happened was because she cared for him and not because of some magical draw between their elements. The doubt made her heart ache, and the thought of his feelings being manipulated by her own family tainted the memory with guilt. *What if the magic wears off and he no longer wants me? What if he despises me for bewitching him?*

"Does it matter? There's no way to know whether it's genuine or not." She wished she could go back to the night of the coven meeting and just let them vote then and there. Yet, as she fidgeted with the ring on her finger, it hurt to think they'd never have become so close.

"Lucy, I think you're overthinking this. The spell was never intended to make you do anything; if anything, it was meant to show you. Perhaps there has always been something lingering between you, and this has given you the opportunity to walk a mile in each other's shoes."

"Easy for you to say. It's not your life, your heart, your future."

"I'm sorry. I thought we were helping," Mum said, reaching for her.

Lucy didn't want to hear it, and in her anger, she didn't want to burn her. Her mum's face fell as she pulled away.

"Let me help. I might be able to find a way that doesn't involve a curse-stripping potion."

"I don't want your help." Lucy had had enough for one day. "Benedict and I can figure this out ourselves. You've done enough – and please don't tell Grams, I don't want her meddling either."

Mum's lips firmed into a line. She got to her feet. "We only wanted the best for you," she said. "And this puts you both in too much danger." As Lucy watched in horror, the paper disintegrated in her hand.

"How could you take that from us? You've no right! It's our life, our elements!" There was no way of getting hold of the original again now that Emerson had returned it to the Order. Lucy lifted her hands from the swing, exposing the scorch marks her anger had left behind.

"I'm still the High Priestess of this town, and you will respect my decision," Mum declared, standing over her.

"Fine, you're my High Priestess. But it was *your* decision to retire early. *Your* decision to allow the coven to bind your daughter to another, *your* decision to then cast a Frankenstein spell! Forgive me for cleaning up your mess!"

"I won't be talked to this way," Mum snapped, heading for the door.

"How can you expect and trust me to lead the coven in a matter of days when you don't trust my judgement or listen to anything I have to say?" Lucy yelled after her.

"I've only ever done what I thought was best for you," Mum said, the fight leaving her. Tears swelled in her eyes, magnified by her thick glasses.

"Maybe the best thing for me is for you to do nothing at all."

Silence had never been so deafening.

Afraid of what else could be said in the heat of the moment, Lucy pushed past her mum and left her on the porch. Fighting with her couldn't have happened at a worse time; tomorrow was the opening night dance for the festival. Now, not only was she angry at her mum, but feeling guilty about having to hide what Wilhelmina had done to Benedict. *Is a moment, an hour, a day of peace too much to ask for?*

It was only when she reached her room and slammed the door closed that she realised she couldn't even remember the last time they had argued.

Lucinda

With the library closed on Saturday, Lucy deserved a lie-in. She'd spent the morning reading in bed and was desperate for a snuggle, but Chaos was still avoiding her. It was clear there was a six-foot-something man she wanted to snuggle more.

Speaking of whom... Lucy winced as she eyed Benedict's missed call. She covered her head with her bedcovers and was about to turn off her phone when a text arrived from Rosie.

> Rosie: I've got a giant favour to ask. Emerson asked me out!!! Finally! But I promised I would chaperone the dance tonight from seven to nine. We are going for dinner after we finish looking at some cottages around the village, so please please please can you cover for me? I'll buy that super expensive yucky tea you love. PLEASE, and remember I have sharp teeth ;)

She couldn't say no; she and Emerson were looking at

cottages to rent so he wouldn't have to stay in his university accommodation. Most of the professors had their own places, and Emerson getting a place in town might establish that he was here to stay.

Lucy groaned. There was no way she'd be able to avoid Benedict if she went to the festival's opening night costume party. It wasn't that she didn't want to see Benedict, but if she did, she'd have to tell him about her mum destroying the curse-stripping potion.

Staring at the message, she pulled herself from her sheets. She shouldn't let her friend's love-life suffer because hers was a mess.

> Lucy: Are you threatening to bite me if I say no?!

> Don't say no then. Pretty please! I thought I'd have to be the one to ask him and then this morning he just blurted it out while I was working. Xxx

Great, now she had to find a costume by seven. The calendar with the 31st circled in red mocked her. The town square had transformed into what could only be compared to the towns from *The Nightmare Before Christmas* or *Hocus Pocus*, two of her favourite Halloween movies, to mark the ten-day countdown to the festival.

> Fine, I'll do it. It'll get me away from my mum. Are you still able to cover the toffee apple stall? We only need to have it open for the fireworks.

> I could kiss you! Thank you! Yes, I'll be there for nine and stay until midnight so you don't have to be around the fireworks. You should talk to Willa, ignoring each other isn't going to help matters. She was wrong to destroy the potion, but she probably didn't want to risk both of your elements.

Rosie had offered for Lucy to stay at hers for a few days, but so close to the binding, all eyes would be on her. Rumours of a rift amongst the Hawthorne women would mean everything that had happened over the last four weeks would've been for naught.

> She's avoiding me as much as I'm avoiding her, and I think I'd prefer your teeth. ;)

> Was that text meant for Benedict? Speaking of, have you spoken to him about what you're going to do? Emerson still has the grimoire, I could ask him?

> Never mind, I think I have plans tonight.

> No, don't say a word to Emerson. I don't want the order to know we're using the grimoire. They'd never send me another one.

Her stomach dropped at the thought of Emerson discovering she was going to use a forbidden potion. No matter how much Rosie trusted him, he was the last person she wanted to know about their plan.

My lips are sealed. We're going to the haunted manor in Willow Valley. The one where the girl killed her whole family because she was possessed. I promised Emerson I'd bring him, so I thought dinner in Willow Valley would be a good idea since I don't want him going there alone.

How romantic, a crime scene for a first date.

Don't yuck our yum, and you might have fun tonight! The best part of being the chaperone is that no one is watching you.

Do you know who else signed up?

Mrs Crawford didn't tell me. But this might win you some points from the Matherson supporters. Going the extra mile.

Good point. But you still owe me.

GIANT WOLF HUG. I'm going to call Emerson! Also, don't forget your costume! We can debrief at the apple stall later tonight! x

Later that night, Lucy's black patent stilettos clicked against the porch. It was already a little past six, so she had plenty of time to get to the town square for seven. She'd enchanted her heels so they wouldn't hurt her feet – there hadn't been time to shorten the floor-length dress.

She found her mum and Gwendoline sitting on the porch with a pitcher of wine between them. The crimson liquid was topped with herbs, probably to prevent them from getting a hangover.

"Lucinda, darling! You look fabulous, although I'm not sure why you're dressed as your Great-Aunt Belinda?" Gwendoline said, eying Lucy's harshly straightened hair.

"I'm not. I'm meant to be Morticia Adams," she said, waving the long black mesh sleeves. "I only had the old crates in the basement to find something, and this dress from Belinda's chest was the only thing in black that didn't need altering."

She wasn't good at using the sewing machine, and since she wasn't really on speaking terms with her mum, she hadn't wanted to ask for help. Any extra inches around the waist she had cinched in with a black corset from her great-grandmother, even if it was digging into her ribs and she felt like her boobs were pressed up under her chin.

"Sorry – it was the hair that threw me off, but they do say the character for the show was based on your great-aunt. The original, that is. Belinda had a thing for showbiz – all the lies and deceit. Loved it." Gwendoline sipped her wine.

Lucy had never heard such a thing, but her great-aunt had lingered on the fringes of good and bad. Never having married or had kids, she'd been a free spirit. Lucy was jealous of her nomadic, glamourous lifestyle.

"I didn't have time to get a black wig." She didn't want to use her magic, fire and hairspray never went well together.

"Regardless, you look beautiful – truly wicked," Mum said, beaming. Removing the blanket from her lap, she stood and reached up to run her fingers through Lucy's hair. The colour changed to raven black. "Now you're perfect."

"Thank you," Lucy said, adding her black lipstick to her clutch. It was their first exchange in days. She swallowed her relief; she hated not talking to her mum, who had always been her best friend. "Are you sure neither of you want to pop by? I'm sure those visiting our humble town would love to meet such highly esteemed witches."

"If we showed up, everyone would have to be on their best behaviour – and anyway, this is our time off." Gwendoline clinked her glass against Wilhelmina's.

"You've got a fun night ahead of you; I remember the years of trying to stop people spiking the pumpkin punch. I've got to the point where I want to spike it just to throw the little devils off," Lucy's mum added.

"Hopefully they'll only be spiking the drinks instead of using magic as they please," Lucy prayed. The opening night of the festival coincided with the end of potion exams for the senior school. Magless schools hold their exams at Christmas, but since Samhain was the magic world's biggest festival, potions and spell exams finished in October so they would be able to enjoy the festival.

"Unfortunately, I doubt it. Alcohol and magic are not a good combination for those so young. Even if they're seventeen, eighteen, it takes until they're twenty-five for their elements to truly settle," Wilhelmina said. "But since it's the end of the seniors' final exams, show them some leniency unless they endanger anyone."

Lucy nodded.

"Surely you got up to some mischief when you finished your final exams?" Gwendoline teased her, though Wilhelmina nudged her friend.

"I didn't go to the opening dance that year," Lucy said quickly, not wanting to discuss it.

Gwendoline frowned, pouring herself another glass. "Why? I was sure Benedict asked you. Peter teased him mercilessly for weeks until he finally plucked up the courage!"

Lucy gripped her clutch bag, trying not to reveal her annoyance. "Benedict asked, but he only did it to embarrass me." Her tone wasn't as polite as it should have been. Even if they'd come a long way in a short time, it didn't erase the past.

"To embarrass you?" Gwendoline gawked. "No. He wouldn't have done such a thing."

"He asked me when everyone was gathered to get their spell assignments. No one would ever believe a Matherson was asking out a Hawthorne and meant it."

The mortification of that moment still stung. She had been unable to bring herself to go to the opening night in the end, with or without a date. Now, she wished she hadn't let him get to her.

"There must've been some misunderstanding. Peter told him you were upset about not being asked out because of Wilhelmina being High Priestess."

"That's true – they were afraid I wouldn't be any fun or would tattle on them for drinking or using magic."

"I thought you just didn't want to go because you were stressed and tired after your exams," Wilhelmina said, taking her daughter's hand.

"Benedict wouldn't have lied to Peter when he said he wanted to ask you. Are you sure there wasn't a mix-up?"

Lucy thought back. It wouldn't be the first time they had misunderstood each other. The school theatre had been so crowded and loud when she'd seen him in the audience, during the monthly assembly. His smile made her suspect he was up to something. When she'd made it to her seat in front of him, he'd leaned forward and asked her about the festival opening out of the blue. His delivery had been so blunt, she'd immediately assumed he was mocking her. She wanted to go so badly that she'd almost accepted anyway, but before she could even think about her answer, his friends had started laughing, confirming it was a set-up.

"I'm sure there was no misunderstanding, but we were young. It wouldn't have been the first prank," she said. They'd both driven each other crazy. Not that they didn't now – it was just a different type of crazy.

Gwendoline shook her head, sinking back into the rocking chair. "I'm so disappointed to hear that. I was sure he'd been looking forward to it; he even turned down going on a camping trip with Peter and his friends because the opening was the night before. When he didn't go, I thought neither of you wanted to," she admitted, looking truly dismayed.

Lucy didn't want to dwell on the past; whether Benedict had intended to humiliate her or not, it didn't matter now. Still, after she'd said her goodbyes and closed the gate behind her, she fought the urge to text him. She wasn't sure he'd even give an honest answer.

The lanterns lighting the town highlighted the orange and red leaves that littered the streets, getting Lucy into the festival spirit. Walking through an alley narrowed by food stalls that smelled mouth-wateringly delicious, Lucy vowed that next year, whether she was High Priestess or not, she would leave the festival to Benedict. Every detail of the planning had stressed her out, and listening to Mrs Crawford and Mr Lark argue over the placement of every stall had nearly sent her over the edge. How she hadn't set the whole town on fire was a mystery.

The only positive outcome was how well she and Benedict had worked together. Wherever she'd expected to clash with him, they'd seemed to fall into step. He'd listened to her opinion, and where they differed, they'd compromised. It was almost too easy, and others were starting to notice the change. Before, most of the townspeople had been hesitant to congratulate them; now, they acted like it was an event to be celebrated.

Lucy's phone buzzed.

> Benedict: Crawford put us together for the night. I'm waiting by the gargoyles at the town hall.

> Lucy: How'd you know I was coming tonight?

> Rosie told me you were filling in for her. She didn't tell you I volunteered?

> Nope. I'm almost there.

Rosie had probably wanted it to be a fun surprise. So much for avoiding him.

> Hurry up, if I stand here alone any longer people are going to think I've been stood up.

> You've waited a decade, you can wait five more minutes.

> ???

Lucy reached the town square, already crowded with

people enjoying the music from the gazebo converted into a stage. The smell of popcorn and burgers filled the air. When she saw Benedict resting his arm against the gargoyle, she brought her clutch to her lips to stop herself from laughing. The past no longer mattered; Frankenstein's monster was waiting for her.

Benedict

Benedict's eyes widened, taking in every inch of Lucinda's costume. She was dressed from head to toe in his favourite colour. Even her hair flowed in sleek raven lengths. She looked every bit the Matherson, and it took every ounce of his will to be a gentleman to stop himself from throwing her over his shoulder and dragging her to the manor like a damn caveman.

"If you keep staring at me like that, you're going to make me think I've got something on my face," Lucinda said, smiling nervously.

"Your hair, the dress — I almost didn't—" Benedict stammered, running his hands through his hair. "You look..." Without her glasses, her emerald eyes shone out against the dark hair and pale skin, highlighted by smoky makeup and a black lip.

"Who knew Frankenstein's monster had such a way with words?" she teased as his gaze settled on her waist. The corset highlighted her luscious curves. "Can you guess who I am?"

He arched a brow. "Mine." She rolled her eyes. "I don't

know how I feel about others seeing you look this good," he added, stepping closer. Her breath caught as his words brushed her ear.

"Very funny." She pushed him away gently.

"Mrs Addams." He gave her a mock bow. "I must say, evil looks good on you."

"You don't look so bad yourself," she said, nodding to his patched-up suit. His hair was slicked back with gel, and he'd added some bolts to the sides of his neck and some false stitches on the joins of his suit. "My very own monster." She took his arm and kissed his cheek.

He cleared his throat, trying to remember they were here to work. "Shall we go in?"

True to its theme of Phantom of the Opera, the room was decorated with long, gold-rimmed mirrors and lit chandeliers on loan from the hotel.

"It might look good, but this corset doesn't like my ribs," Lucinda confessed. "I shouldn't have asked Grams to tie the strings."

"Do you want me to loosen them?" Benedict asked as they came to stand by the banquet table, surveying the room to make sure no one was up to no good.

She blushed. "Hardly appropriate, given our current environment."

"I meant it as a non-sexual, purely kind gesture." He kept scanning their surroundings, trying not to let her distract him, which was awfully hard when her perfume coiled around him like a serpent trying to seduce him.

"Are you going to share what's in that flask, or will we have to suffer through this night sober?" Lucinda asked, slipping her hand into his jacket pocket − she must have seen its outline. He loved how comfortable she was touching him now. She put the flask to her lips and took a swig, only to cough at the strong liquorice taste of the liquor.

Benedict smirked, taking it from her. "I was going to dilute it, but I figured we have a long night ahead of us." It was a little after seven, and they'd still have to check out the festival grounds after the dance to make sure what they'd spent weeks planning went off without a hitch.

"Thanks for telling me after the fact."

"Who was I to get in the way of your rebellious act?" He poured some of the liquor into two cups and topped his off with alarmingly fluorescent pumpkin punch. For hers, he added the spiced apple punch instead.

"I'm sorry," Lucinda said suddenly.

"For what?"

"For thinking you were making fun of me when you invited me to the dance during the assembly in our final year." Her apology caught him off guard; he hadn't thought about the incident in years. "I assumed it was a prank, especially when all your friends laughed."

"I got that impression when you stormed off and left me in the crowd looking like an asshole. You didn't even get to see me telling them to shut the hell up." He drank to drown out his own embarrassment at the memory.

"I didn't think you'd ever ask me. That was the same week that I gave you——"

"You gave me Greko. And in my teenage, grief-riddled brain I told you to piss off and leave me alone when I should have thanked you." He smiled sadly.

They went quiet, both thinking of the tiny lizard she'd gifted him when his dad passed away.

"I wanted to say thank you. I thought about writing to you, since we couldn't manage to get through one conversation without arguing. I also couldn't muster the courage to call in case Grams or your mum picked up the house phone." Remembering how much thought he'd put into it, Benedict couldn't believe it had taken him so many years to figure out his feelings for her. "Anyway, Peter mentioned you were upset about no one asking you to the festival dance, and I wanted to make up for how I spoke to you and to thank you for Greko."

Lucinda nodded solemnly. "I wanted to have fun just as much as everyone else. I wouldn't have ratted on anyone." He hated that she knew many believed she was a goody-goody who'd run back to tell her High Priestess mummy if anyone used their magic recklessly. "I'm sorry I assumed the worst of you," she added.

"Me too. I thought when you stormed off you were mortified to be asked by a Matherson to the dance."

"Look at us, acting all adult." Lucinda nudged him, breaking the tension. "Why couldn't we have done this before?"

"Because we were too busy competing. We should do a round of the room, so at least it looks like we're doing our job," he said, his hand grazing hers as they walked around the hall, enjoying the atmosphere of the spooky classics.

"I wouldn't say it was much of a competition," Lucinda teased.

His hand settled on her back, playing with her corset strings. "I don't know how you can breathe in this thing," he said, eyeing her cleavage without a shred of discretion.

"Stop flirting with me. People will talk." He felt her shiver against his touch.

"I can't resist," he teased, inching closer.

"I should've taken that flask from you. I'll have to add that you flirt when tipsy to my list of new discoveries about you." She took his hand, before he started pawing at her again. "It has nothing to do with the flask, and everything to do with the dress." He leaned in, and her eyes widened. Clearly, she thought he was going to kiss her in front of everyone. But he stopped short. "And the woman in it."

Lucinda swallowed, and he loved watching her struggle to string a response together.

Before she could say anything, his eye was drawn to a group of kids by the back door, laughing. They couldn't be older than twelve, but there was something sinister in the laughter that caused both Benedict and Lucinda to approach the group.

"Give it back," one of the boys pleaded, but another boy in a Peter Pan costume pushed him back.

Benedict put a hand on Lucinda's arm, stopping her from interceding. She glared at him, but he didn't want to make it worse for the kid.

"Why? It's a fake pin. You think your scales prove anything?" one of the bigger boys snarled, pointing at the scarred skin on the side of the boy's neck.

"It's a birthmark, not scales! This birthmark and my family pin means we used to fight dragons!"

The group laughed again. Benedict admired the kid's guts; he was smaller and outnumbered, but he didn't cower or run away.

"That's just a myth! Dragons are long gone – there's no proof of anyone fighting them," a younger girl said, her words whistling through a missing tooth. "You could've got the pin anywhere."

Lucinda slipped her hand into Benedict's, and he realised he'd clenched his fists. He hated seeing anyone bullied or accused of lying. He would've been a social outcast himself, if he hadn't excelled in every way he could.

"You don't have to be so mean." The boy's jaw wobbled. "Just give me back my pin. It was my grandad's! I'm telling the truth."

"This?" The older boy tossed the small pin into the air and caught it. "Why? You haven't earned it. You haven't slain a dragon! I bet your grandad lied and found the pin somewhere." He threw the pin out the back door and into a puddle on the steps.

The other kids laughed, leaving the crying boy behind. Benedict clenched his jaw at such cruel behaviour. Family pins and signet rings were a way for magical folk to identify themselves to each other, and a symbol of how their ancestors had survived.

Lucinda left his side and crouched down by the young boy.

"Did you drop this?" she asked, picking up the pin from the puddle from the back steps. Her kindness dissolved his anger.

"Yeah. It fell off my cloak," he lied, wiping his nose with the back of his sleeve and smudging his ghostly make up.

Benedict wanted to go after the kids, drag them in front of their parents and ask them what the hell they were doing, filling their kids with such prejudice. They had the privilege of living in a sanctuary; he didn't know how they could dare to raise the next generation with the same prejudice they'd suffered. *No one is born hateful – it's bred into them.* It was one of the sad truths shared by magical folk and magless alike.

"You must be Thomas. Your mum volunteers at the library on Sundays, right?" Lucinda said gently.

Thomas nodded, a small smile replacing his sad expression. "She's always reading me stories."

"You've only been in town a year; give yourself some time to settle in. Friends will come in time. Sometimes others can be jealous," Lucinda assured him.

His smile wobbled. "Mum said that about the last town, but they said we were lying about our lineage and kicked us out."

"I'm sorry that happened to you. But I promise Foxford will be your home now, and I think in time you'll come to love it. If you have any trouble, please don't hesitate to come to Hawthorne House, or tell your mum."

"I don't want to upset her," Thomas said quietly.

Benedict knelt down to his level. "You shouldn't believe what they tell you. This pin is all the proof you need. Same way my Matherson ring tells me who I am, and so long as we know, we don't have to prove a thing to anyone."

"But I only have my grandfather's stories and this pin. Even Mum doesn't like to talk about it," he said, wiping his nose with his sleeve.

"I think Lucinda can help with that. In the town library there are many books about how dragon slayers saved an ancient kingdom!" Benedict said. Lucinda looked at him with gratitude.

"He's right. If you want to come with your mum to the library on Sunday, I have plenty of books to show you." Lucinda attached the pin, in the shape of a dragon's tail wrapped around a sword, to Thomas's cloak.

Thomas nodded.

"And she's going to be the High Priestess," Benedict told him. "So if *she* says she believes in your family, you can trust her."

"Okay," Thomas whispered, adjusting the pin so it sat straight.

"In the future, please don't take what they say to heart," Lucinda said, taking a tissue from her bag and wiping his tears.

"I just wanted to be their friend," he mumbled sadly.

Benedict took his hand to bring him back inside. "If they can't see how lucky they are to have you as a friend, then that's their loss."

"My mum is over by the punch bowl! Can I go?" Thomas asked, letting go of Benedict.

"Of course, and please come by the library," Lucinda said, reminding him to stop by.

Thomas ran to his mum. Benedict watched him cling to her waist, remembering the first time he'd been sent home crying because some kids had found out that his great-great-uncle liked to torture animals using curses. What had been lost in the history books was that his uncle only tortured the beasts the Order had sent to sniff out those of magical descent. He wished Gwendoline had embraced him and told him it was going to be okay; instead, she'd told him not to waste his tears on people who were beneath them.

When Lucinda took his hand again, he realised that was probably the last time he'd cried in front of her.

"I wish I could do more," she said. "I hate to think of anyone being treated that way just because of their name, their family. Being treated that way will surely only drive him to the dark."

"Not necessarily. It's up to that kid to choose the light or dark. How he deals with it will be his test."

"Have you always been this wise?"

Benedict kissed the side of her head, wanting to put her at ease. When she took Wilhelmina's position, the whole village would become her children. He only hoped she would let him help her lessen the burden.

"His little red cheeks broke my heart. How can they be so awful?" Lucinda said, anger edging her words. "They'll grow out of it... they're young." She sounded like she was trying to convince herself.

"What worries me is where they learned it from," Benedict said, looking around the room at all the smiling faces, wondering who would want to spread such venom.

Lucinda gripped his hand a little tighter. "The kids probably heard some stories and are acting out."

"Pumpkin, you see the good in everyone and everything. There are those in Foxford who don't see things that way." He lifted her hand to kiss it, the heat of his element warming his lips.

"You weren't treated that way! You had more friends than me in school," she protested.

"Actually, I was, once or twice. But when you have perfect grades, play the right sports and make allies of those who want to find fault in you, life is rather smooth. The only trouble I got in was thanks to you," he admitted.

"I never knew you felt the need to be so perfect."

"I've done everything I can for this town," he reminded her. "I even opened the door to Matherson Manor to strangers to help Foxford."

"You didn't have to," she said, but even she didn't sound like she believed it.

The music slowed. Benedict led her to the dance floor, wanting – *needing* any excuse to take her in his arms, even if only for one song. Everyone around them was too busy enjoying their night to pay much attention.

"After what happened with my dad, and then my brother, my mum stopped being summoned to coven meetings," he told her. "Invitations to parties, lunches and dinners from people she'd known her whole life suddenly went missing. If Wilhelmina hadn't intervened, we wouldn't have lasted in this town."

"Then why did you risk your perfect image tormenting me?" Lucinda asked, only concern in her words as they lingered on the edge of the dance floor.

"You were so good at everything. Everyone trusted you merely for your name alone. You could do no wrong – it was infuriating, and I couldn't resist. I wanted to know if you were truly so perfect or if there was darkness in you, if you were acting as much as I was to become what others wanted of you." His adolescent jealousy felt ridiculous now. "I didn't expect you to give as good as you got."

She rolled her eyes, and he pulled her closer.

"I never understood why you were so determined to hate me, but I suppose that makes sense. Whenever I tried to be nice to you, the meaner you got," she murmured.

"Because if you were really so good, then you would never agree to be mine," Benedict admitted.

He could see it clearly now. He'd spent so many hours, days, years obsessed with Lucinda Hawthorne. She was the one thing he'd always wanted, but no matter how perfect he tried to be, she saw through him to the depths of his soul. One look from her, and he couldn't pretend anymore.

Lucinda's eyes, full of questions, lingered on his, but nothing needed to be said. She wrapped her arms around his neck, and they swayed to the remainder of the song in silence.

Lucinda

L ucy waited by the entrance for Benedict to return from scolding a few students. They'd bewitched the buffet to make it look like the food was riddled with maggots. Disgusting to look at, but take a bite and they turned into delicious jellies. Lucy had once pulled the same prank on Benedict's lunchbox when they were in school.

Thankfully, their time was almost up; more of the senior students were starting to arrive, and the buffet would just be the start. Lucy and Benedict would get to enjoy the rest of the night while the next round of chaperones dealt with the chaos.

"Lucinda Hawthorne! We didn't realise you were chaperoning. Nothing could possibly happen with you here," said Cynthia Berkley, head of the parent-teacher association, appearing next to her. The PTA was the closest she could get to power in Foxford, and the way she wielded such power gave them all the more reason to make sure she never joined their table.

"We were just finishing up our shift. Are you taking over?" Lucy asked.

"Oh no, I'm merely here to pay the caterers so they can head off."

"Shouldn't they have been paid beforehand?"

"And risk them doing a mediocre job? Not a chance. You'd be amazed how much service improves when you keep the envelope close." Cynthia pressed her hand against her breast pocket. Given that she was the mother of the child who'd been tormenting Thomas, it was clear the apple hadn't fallen far from the tree.

"Aren't they staff from the Matherson Manor? I doubt they'd have done any less of a good job. Benedict was kind enough to share his staff for the festival opening, even though the Manor is packed to the brim," Lucy said, trying to hide her dislike behind a bright smile.

"And it was a kind offer, but you can never be too sure. He's always hiring people with questionable backgrounds." Cynthia shivered.

Lucy resisted the urge to roll her eyes. "I'll go and find Benedict so you can ask him yourself about his staff. We wouldn't want anything to go wrong and spoil all the work you've done."

"Maybe I should stay and help you chaperone. I do worry..." Cynthia trailed off, but her gaze drew Lucinda's attention to Benedict laughing with one of the teachers across the room. He'd softened over the last few weeks, and she loved that he didn't hide his kindness as much. If she'd lost her Grams and mum, the two people closest to her, she didn't think she would even be able to get out of bed, but he never complained.

"And why would you be worried?" she demanded.

Cynthia leaned in. "Despite all that he's done for

Foxford, he *is* a Matherson. You can never be too careful, especially not when you see how him and that mother of his schemed to take your seat. You have to know that you have the PTA behind you," she whispered.

"I appreciate the support, but I don't think we should judge anyone because of their past or their familial name." Lucy folded her arms. "Wasn't it the Berkley family who sacrificed their firstborns back in the day? Maybe it's you we should be keeping an eye on."

Cynthia's glare could have cut glass. "You do waste your time reading about ancient history."

"Oh, there's plenty to know about your family, and some isn't so ancient. How is Mr Kepner, the history teacher? I heard you both organised this event very closely," Lucy hissed, placing her hand on a nearby ice sculpture and letting the heat from her touch swell.

Cynthia swept her curls over her shoulder. "You two are as bad as each other. You should be glad my family doesn't have a vote, because neither of you is fit to guide us."

The ice sculpture liquified, and water cascaded over a squealing Cynthia.

"Oh my goodness! It must have been the heat of all the candles and the lights." Lucy reached for her, but Cynthia shrugged out of her grasp.

"Don't think I didn't know this was you," she hissed, wiping the mascara smudged down her face.

"Please do be reasonable – I'd never use my element to pull such a stunt."

"Everything okay?" Benedict asked, hurrying to Lucy's side.

"Perfect! Cynthia and I were just catching up. She was telling me she sadly can't attend our binding ceremony, and then the ice sculpture melted," she said sweetly. She'd had enough of the Berkley family for one evening.

"I wouldn't be caught dead supporting either of you!" Cynthia turned, her anger catching the attention of a few nearby guests.

"I'm sorry you feel that way," Benedict said, clearly confused. Fortunately, when Cynthia stalked off the guests lost interest and drifted away.

Benedict gathered up the water coating the dance floor. Within seconds the ice sculpture stood once again as though nothing had happened.

"Hardly subtle," he admonished her.

"The kids must have pulled another prank," she said with a grin. From his eye roll, he didn't believe her for a second.

"What was eating her, anyway?"

"Nothing that wouldn't spit her back out again."

Benedict laced his fingers through hers. Lucy realised her fingers were tipped with flames, the anger in her veins still not satisfied.

"When I saw you grip the table, I thought you were going to set it alight," he joked.

"I would have, but I figured melting the sculpture wouldn't expose our elements. Her stupid comments got under my skin and I couldn't resist. Thought she could use some cooling down," she said, still irritated. No wonder Cynthia's kid had been tormenting Thomas; it was horrible to think there were more like her in town.

The next round of chaperones appeared to relieve them, but as they left she couldn't stop thinking about the discrimination she'd witnessed. Spotting Thomas leaving with his mum, she stopped in her tracks. Benedict jerked back as she held his hand.

"I can't believe I didn't catch it before. Essence of dragon," she said, staring at his confused face. "There was an old spell in the grimoire I was translating for the Order. In one of the final spells, I couldn't figure out the translation. It was too vague to decipher, but it was because I mistranslated. It read essence of dragon. In the old myths, 'essence' referred to their venom!"

"You've lost me. Surely the Order aren't going to look too closely at one small error?" Benedict said as Lucy started towards the festival grounds. Rosie and Emerson must be there by now.

"It's not about the Order, it's about our elements! Dragon venom stripped anyone or anything of its magic or element."

"So it's another element-stripping option?" he asked. "We haven't even tried the last one you found yet."

"That was a curse-stripping potion; there was no guarantee we'd get ours back." She didn't want to admit her mum had destroyed the spell. "Dragon venom works directly on our elements. Those who hunted dragons made a potion to restore their elements if they were exposed to venom!"

"But how does it restore our elements?" Benedict frowned, clearly not following.

"I don't know! We're talking about an ancient spell. But it's written in the grimoire I just spent the past few months translating! All we need to do is use the venom to strip our current elements, and then use the restoring potion to restore our water and fire to their rightful places."

His eyes widened as he grasped the weight of her words, but he shook his head. "We need the venom of a creature that's been extinct for over 500 years?"

"I know where we can find some!" Lucy couldn't believe she hadn't realised sooner. She owed Thomas and his family one hell of a debt. "The university has some – it's powdered in their restricted relics section. Maybe we could get in somehow." Listening to herself talk about breaking into the university and stealing something gave her pause, but she'd only take a tiny amount of venom. "I just need a key to the restricted relics section."

Lucy bit her lip, unsure how she was going to come up with a good enough excuse to convince someone at the university to hand over a key without raising alarm bells.

"I do know a way we might be able to get in," Benedict said thoughtfully. "Emerson is only new to the university, but from what I've heard—"

"I should have known you'd have people watching him."

"—the students enjoy his lectures, and the other professors are pleased with his work. They gave him a key to the ancient relic section, even if such privileges are usually reserved for those who have tenure." Benedict had been on the university board since he'd paid for its new wing with the money his father had left him.

"I might've had something to do with his getting the key," Lucy confessed.

"How?"

"I... might have spoken to the dean on his behalf. He needed access for his lectures. It's one thing to read about rare artefacts, but seeing them is a different story."

"Are you out of your mind? You hardly know him!"

"If he can be trusted with our rarest and most powerful grimoires, he can be trusted around some dusty old relics. Anything of value or that is dangerous is stored in the vault, anyway." She didn't mention her own doubts about letting him into the restricted ancient relic section. When Rosie had asked for her help, she'd felt it would be a way to make up for lying about the whole elemental switch debacle. "Emerson asked Rosie on a date tonight. It's why she had me fill in for her. They should be at the toffee apple stall by now."

Benedict followed her through the winding alleys of delicious foods and baked goods. "A member of the Order is dating a werewolf?"

She'd expected him to be angry. Instead, he looked amused.

"I don't think that matters right now. Let's just find Emerson." Lucy started walking, forcing him to keep up with her. She had never understood how anyone would want to eat before going on the rides, but then again, the food stalls smelt so good it was almost impossible to resist.

"Breaking into the university is a terrible idea, but it seems we're out of options," he mused.

"Like going into the woods and visiting a blood-thirsty – sorry, element-thirsty – crone was so genius?" she asked over her shoulder as they moved through the crowd.

Benedict opened his mouth to defend himself, but she wasn't surprised when he couldn't come up with a reasonable excuse for his stupidity. He shook his head, and she waited for him to continue. "I suppose we aren't technically breaking in, if we have a key. Though I'm not sure if my element is having a bad effect on you; I never thought I'd see the day when I'd have to talk a Hawthorne out of breaking and entering."

"We won't be breaking anything, merely entering. You can't talk me out of anything. I'm doing this with or without you, though I'd prefer if we did it together. This is our chance to set things right – we only have ten days before the ritual!" She gave him her biggest puppy eyes.

"Enough with the eyes! I'm in. But we can't just run off and get the venom now. We need as many people as possible to see us so it doesn't look like we are neglecting our duties." He offered her his hand. "If you take my hand, they'll be too busy gossiping about our PDA to notice we've disappeared."

"Broken into places before, have you? You seem to have mastered the art of disappearing," she teased, threading her fingers between his.

"Only when my wife-to-be decides to break the law. We can only afford one questionable reputation in our union." He kissed the back of her hand. She rolled her eyes.

Calmly, they walked hand in hand through the festival grounds. Just before they reached the toffee apple stand, where Emerson and Rosie were handing out delicious treats, Benedict was pulled away by Mrs Crawford, who was complaining about the clowns scaring the kids. Lucy groaned at the interruption, but Benedict motioned for her to go ahead.

"Refurbishing the carousel was a good idea. I think we'll make back the cost of the decorations on that alone," Rosie said, handing Lucy a wicker basket of apples before she even had a chance to say hello.

"Hopefully the ticket sales will be enough to cover the refurbishment itself," Lucy agreed. "The festival is getting bigger. With more magless arriving every year to attend, we have to go big or they'll go home and never come back." She checked the thermometer in the caramel, making sure it was hot enough to stay melted without burning. It felt good to be back on familiar ground. Her mind was whirling at the new idea of using the venom, but she tried to put that aside and focus on helping Rosie for now. "How was your date?"

"A-mazing! I thought it might be a dud, since all we ever talk about is work, but we actually have more in common than I thought," Rosie enthused, placing each skewered apple in a small bowl of their own. "We almost lost track of time when we couldn't find a free cottage for him to rent, or at least one that didn't need a bundle of money to be spent on repairs." Lucy could hear both nerves and an unfamiliar giddiness in her voice. "I figured he could move in with me. I have a spare room, and I don't even know if anything more will happen between us... we're only dating, and I know he's a member of the Order, which I'm not taking lightheartedly—"

Lucy cut her off, afraid she might pass out if she didn't take a breath. "You don't need to explain. As long as you're happy, then I am too."

"He had to get more paper bowls – we ran out of the ones I ordered with the pumpkins, but thankfully I got a few of the ghost ones as well," Rosie explained, handing a customer their change. Lucy focused on getting more apples ready for the growing queue, having no choice but to wait until Emerson returned.

To her surprise and delight, she was offered a hot dog smothered in relish and mustard, candy floss, two white chocolate cookies shaped as ghosts, and a hot chocolate by various people congratulating her on her engagement. If she'd known it was going to lead to free food, she would've got engaged a lot sooner – even if her corset was about to give up.

Benedict

B enedict checked his watch, wondering what was keeping Lucinda. She'd texted him to meet up outside the community theatre, though he wasn't sure why; they had more important things to focus on, such as breaking into the university. He'd barely got away from Mrs Crawford to meet her.

The door to the theatre opened as the Punch and Judy show wrapped up, and Benedict politely held it for those leaving before the next show started.

"Thank you," a woman said, looking back at him.

Benedict's stomach dropped. It was Mrs Ladbrooke, the woman who'd written the bad review of the Manor. She was with her son, who was trying to pull her towards the rest of the festival.

"I was hoping I would run into you. I was going to stop by the Manor tomorrow, but we've been so busy," she said, clearly embarrassed.

"Mrs Ladbrooke, I'm delighted and surprised to see you decided to give our town a second chance," Benedict said smoothly. Part of him was still stinging from her review, wishing she'd listened to reason. Then again, without it, he and Lucinda might never have got so close. Still, he hoped she wasn't back for another one.

"I hope you aren't put out by the magazine. In fact, that was the very thing I wanted to talk to you about," she said, her smile creasing the corner of her eyes.

"There is no need; your review was quite something, and given the fright you and your family suffered, I can understand your upset."

"Yes, I was rather upset. However, I must tell you that the incident is all in the past. Ms Hawthorne wrote to me, which I have to say was a surprise. Most people who receive such reviews don't write an apology to me. Anyway, she informed me of what happened – that it was a prank gone wrong on her part and you were merely a victim. At her behest, I thought I would return to Foxford with my family and start fresh."

Benedict tried to conceal his smile. Only Lucinda could've convinced her to return when an actual siren hadn't been able to. He couldn't believe she had gone so far to help him and the Manor.

"Ms Hawthorne set us up at the Pumpkin Patch Inn on the edge of town," Mrs Ladbrooke was going on. "She gave us passes for the festival, and unlimited food tokens to make up for the misunderstanding. I have to say that once again I've been charmed by this town. I can't count how many times my son has taken a turn on the Ferris wheel; the last time made my husband positively green."

"I'm relieved to hear that you and your family are enjoying your stay, and once again, I apologise for prior events. We wish for anyone who visits us to have a great time," Benedict said, glancing down at the little boy currently stuffing his face with orange candy floss decorated with jelly spiders. "I hated the thought of anyone leaving with a sour taste in their mouth. Thank you for giving us a second chance."

"All water under the bridge, and I look forward to writing a retraction once I get home. You've won us over wholeheartedly." Mrs Ladbrooke beamed, shaking his hand.

"I look forward to reading it, as I'm sure will many others in town," Benedict told her.

"Must be going – have to get back to the inn and make sure my husband has turned back to a normal shade," she said, clearly delighting in her husband's misery. With a quick goodbye, she and her son disappeared into the crowd.

Letting out a long exhalation, Benedict barely got a chance to register what had happened before he saw Lucinda walking towards him. Her smile and frenzied wave made him chuckle. He'd never thought he'd see the day where she was happy to see him. Maybe *he* should have written Mrs Ladbrooke a thank you letter.

She didn't get a chance to speak before he threw his arms around her. Lost in her perfume, he didn't want to ever let her go. He wanted to swallow her whole in his embrace and protect her from anything and anyone who would dare to threaten her loving heart.

"Benedict!" His name muffled was against his chest. "I'm suffocating."

"Sorry," he said, releasing her, but only a little.

"What was that for?" Lucinda demanded, staring up at him with those green eyes he could never get enough of.

"I ran into Mrs Ladbrooke," he told her, enjoying how her cheeks turned pink. "She was leaving the theatre with her son."

Lucinda was suddenly fascinated with the buttons on his shirt. "How lovely that she decided to come back."

"I think it might've had something to do with the letter you wrote, or maybe paying for her and her family to stay at the Pumpkin Patch, or the—"

She placed a hand over his mouth, and he kissed her palm.

"Fine, I get it. And technically I didn't pay. I just promised Michel that Grams would help his husband with his back pain free of charge," she admitted.

"Thank you," he said, kissing her hair. It smelled of strawberries.

"You're welcome." She sank into his embrace, wrapping her arms around his waist. "Sorry I was late," she added, leaning back. "I ran into Faye on the way out. She was with Peter."

Benedict wondered what the hell his brother was up to. It wasn't like him to fraternise with the living. He didn't want Lucinda reporting this back to her uncle. Grim Reapers weren't forbidden from speaking to the living, but there was something in the way Peter had talked to Faye that made him nervous. He decided to distract her instead.

"Surprised you noticed – thought you were too busy hugging Order members."

She swatted his arm. He didn't want to be jealous, but when he'd looked over mid-conversation with Mrs Crawford and seen Emerson with his arms around Lucinda, he'd wished he could set him on fire.

"If I hadn't hugged him, then I wouldn't have this, now would I?" She produced a small brass key from her cleavage.

"What else are you hiding in there?" he asked, reaching

for it. She snatched it away from him. "I can't believe you stole from an Order member. Who are you and what have you done with Lucinda?" His shock was tinged with pride.

"Anyway, you have nothing to be jealous about. He's moving in with Rosie. I was merely congratulating them – and borrowing this at the same time."

"Moving in together?" he whispered, following her into the staff entrance of the theatre. No one asked for their tickets. *Where the hell is she taking me?*

"I don't think we're in any position to talk about moving too fast in a relationship." She threw her words over her shoulder, leading him past the tiered seats in front of the stage.

"We've known each other since forever – it's different!" Benedict barely got the words out before he was shushed by a family.

She held her fingers to her lips as she slipped behind the red curtain concealing the stairs to the back of the stage. In the flurry of activity backstage, they went unnoticed. Benedict watched in bewilderment as Lucinda led him to an empty prop room and pushed on a wooden statue carved into the wall. He thought she'd lost her mind for a second, but then she disappeared into a secret stone passage. He followed.

"How'd you even know there was a tunnel here?" Benedict asked, brushing a cobweb from her shoulder. The passage smelt like damp and clothing left in the wardrobe for too long, which made sense, considering that most of it was filled with old costumes and stage sets long forgotten about. He estimated they'd been walking for about fifteen minutes, but it looked like they'd reached the end now.

"I found it by accident when I was forced into compulsory theatre class in my first year at uni. I didn't have to take part if they couldn't find me," Lucinda explained, pressing on a stone.

"Aren't you just full of secrets? I've got to admit, I didn't think you'd be skipping class, creeping around secret passages and stealing keys," he marvelled as the door opened out into the university library. Light filtered in through the long, arched windows, revealing rows of old books.

"You said you didn't want to break in. Since no locks were involved, I don't think this counts, and I didn't steal the key, I merely borrowed it," Lucinda said proudly.

Benedict shook his head, torn between amusement and concern. She might technically be correct, but he didn't want to think about what would happen if they were caught in the ancient relic section after hours with a stolen key.

Lucinda

Lucy unlocked the steel door to the restricted relics section at the back of the library. The loud creak as she pulled it open made her cringe. Hopefully the security guard wandering around the various floors of the university would be too far away to notice the disturbance.

"Let's get this over with," Benedict said at her back.

Lucy nodded, closing the door behind them before he changed his mind. She understood his hesitation; he'd be blamed if they were caught. No one would suspect *she* was the mastermind behind a plot to steal from an Order member and break into the university during one of the most important events of the year.

They searched glass case after case until they found the Dragon bestiary. A vial of chalk-like dust was suspended above the open book illustrating the vicious slaying of the winged beast. Lucinda didn't hesitate to use Emerson's key to unlock the case. She reached for the vial, but Benedict's hand clamped around her wrist.

"We'll have to break the wax seal," he whispered,

looking at the red wax sealing the powdered venom within the vial. "When they do their routine checks, there's no way they won't notice a seal that's been tampered with, and that key will lead them back to Emerson. All keys are charmed to reveal their owner, remember?"

"Not if I can reseal it with your fire," Lucy said confidently.

"Too much heat and you could smash it altogether."

"I'll just melt the wax seal." She reached for the suspended vial and disconnected it from the glass hook.

"Are you sure you can maintain control?"

"I can only try." Lucy used the side of the key to break the wax seal, going past the point of return. "We need something to hold the powdered venom."

"I have this," Benedict said, removing a small pill box in his pocket. She looked at the small box, wondering if it closed tight enough to keep the fine powder safe, but they didn't have a choice.

"It'll have to do," she said, tipping out the gum it contained into his hand. He popped them in his pocket.

Uncorking the vial, she tapped out about half a teaspoon's worth. The venom in powdered form would be concentrated, and she didn't want to kill them by accident. She needed just enough to strip their element, and then the reset of the potion should restore it. Death by dragon venom in Foxford in the twenty-first century would certainly raise a few eyebrows.

"Pumpkin, hurry up!"

Lucy nearly dropped the vial at his sudden urging. She wanted to snap back at him, but they needed to keep quiet.

"I'm going as fast as I can," she hissed, corking it again

and handing Benedict the pill box. He popped it in his jacket pocket as she summoned his element.

"Careful," he breathed, so close she could barely concentrate on the melting wax. Her skin blazed, but she managed to contain the flow of heat as she resealed the vial. "That's enough. Any more and the vial will warp," Benedict instructed, his voice gentle and cautious rather than commanding.

Lucy admired her work. The red wax was a little too shiny for an old relic, but it would dull once it cooled. Benedict hissed as she handed him the heated vial; it was petty, but he deserved it for spooking her.

"Why do you have to call me pumpkin just to annoy me?" she asked, locking the case once he'd put it back in its rightful place.

"I never intended to annoy you. It's just my favourite. The food that makes me feel like I'm home," he admitted, like it wasn't supposed to turn her into a puddle of mush.

She swallowed, unsure of what to say, of what it meant. Was he messing with her? But the way his eyes narrowed, waiting for her to respond, forced her to acknowledge the confession as true.

His thumb brushed over her wrist, causing her to shiver in his grasp. Her lips parted and he tilted his head, leaning in with a silent question in his eyes.

"We should get out of here," she said, as their lips brushed. He nodded, following close behind her. With the door secured, a floorboard creaked as they reached the main door to the university library. He pulled her back towards the shelves, and she gasped.

"Shhh," Benedict whispered, pressing a finger to his lips.

"Don't shush me," she snapped.

"The security guard is at the door." He pointed to the shadow under the door at the end of the room.

"What if they come in?" Lucy mouthed. Even with the door to the relic section secured, they'd be in trouble for entering the library after dark. And if the guard checked the restricted relics section, he might see that the wax seal hadn't fully solidified.

"Can I kiss you?" Benedict asked, pulling her away from the restricted section into the stacks.

"Now is not the time!" she protested, but did nothing to stop him. Her breath caught as his fingertips brushed the sensitive skin at the nape of her neck.

"We have to distract the guard," he breathed, brushing the hair from her shoulder. He brought his lips daringly close to her neck but refused to make contact. Her heartbeat quickened, and she clutched his jacket.

"Yes," she sighed, tipping her head to the side as his hand slipped into her hair.

Benedict backed her up against a bookshelf, their breath mingling as his lips teased her without quite kissing her.

The door opened, and footsteps marched in.

"You two! What do you think you are doing in here at this hour?" Arthur, the security guard, blinded them with his torch. Benedict shielded his eyes.

"Sorry, Arthur, we just wanted to look at the binding cup we'd be drinking from during our ceremony," he lied as easily as breathing. "Got a bit carried away..."

"Mr Matherson? Is that Lucinda with you?" Arthur's frown was barely visible in the dark, but his gruff voice made it clear he wasn't happy with them.

"Guilty," she said, hiding her shame in Benedict's chest.

"You'll see it soon enough." Arthur sighed, lowering the torch. "Congratulations, by the way."

"Thank you. Sorry about the intrusion." Benedict took Lucy's hand, and she tried not to break his fingers.

"I was young once, but rules are rules. No one's to be in the library after dark."

"We're very sorry," Lucy said meekly. "We really just wanted to stand before the cup, to get a sense of what it would be like on the day."

"All right then. Enjoy the rest of your night," Arthur said, letting them go with a grin he couldn't quite hide.

Outside, the fresh air settled Lucy's nerves. She cursed herself for putting them both at risk, again, but a triumphant grin spread across Benedict's face.

"Piece of cake," he said, patting his breast pocket.

"Let's never do that again," she breathed.

"Kissing?" he asked with a frown.

"Breaking and entering," she said, swatting his arm playfully to hide her embarrassment.

"Let's hope that venom was worth the risk," was all he said as they walked through the archway and back to the festivities. Lucy eyed his breast pocket, where the venom rested, and hoped she wasn't about to add fuel to the fire with another Hawthorne scheme.

Benedict

At Matherson Manor, Benedict watched Lucinda remove two paper bags, a panel of vials and a notebook packed with spells and potions from the kitchenette in his quarters.

"How long have you been hiding this stuff in my kitchen?" She'd been coming and going for the last few weeks; she must have done it when he wasn't paying attention.

"Since my mum ruined the first lot I gathered, and I figured keeping my translation notes here was a safe bet in case she found the research I'd been doing on the Hawthorne grimoire and wanted to stop us from using anything I found in there," Lucinda explained, slipping off her heels while she arranged the ingredients on the counter. "Not that it matters now, because we've got the dragon venom. We can mix the powder with the restoring potion, and it should switch us back in no time."

Benedict didn't like how she shrugged when she said 'should'; he wanted a bit more certainty before he consumed poison. Then again, with magic nothing was certain. Watching her scan her notes on the restoring potion from the grimoire, all he could do was put his trust in her.

"Your mum did what? Why didn't you tell me?" He handed her a pot from beneath the kitchen sink, since he didn't have a cauldron.

"I didn't want you to think poorly of her. She was trying to protect both of us," Lucinda said, taking out a glass jar containing blessed water from the coven temple.

"Is that why you wanted to do this here and not in the brewing room at yours? Because you're avoiding Wilhelmina?" he pried, watching her simmer the water on the stove. Going against the High Priestess's orders in her own home would only cause a bigger rift between mother and daughter. He hadn't even thought the Hawthorne women could argue, and he didn't like that he was partly the cause of it.

Watching Lucinda work, pride swelled in his chest as he saw how easily it came to her. Sure, he knew what he was doing with potions, but there was a dance in the way she sliced, chopped and measured out the ingredients that he'd never been able to master. The potion came together faster than he'd expected with a final puff of smoke. Once the boiling liquid had cooled, she filled two shot glasses from the cupboard with the finished potion.

"This should do the trick," she told him, covering the remainder of the potion in the pot with a glass lid. "For you." She offered him a shot glass.

"I suppose a Hawthorne potion got us into this mess, so it's only right a Hawthorne potion will undo it," Benedict said hesitantly, taking it. The liquid glowed midnight blue.

"We drink on three."

He admired her courage. "Is it supposed to be that colour?"

"It's just the powdered venom. Trust me."

"One last question. We aren't about to have a *Romeo and Juliet* moment, are we?" He winced, smelling the potion. It was sharp and pungent.

"Even if it kills us, I'm sure fate would find some way to bring us back together." Lucinda winked, sitting on the kitchen island beside where he sat on the black barstool.

"Leaving our future up to fate doesn't reassure me much." He got up and stood between her legs; if he was going to be poisoned to death, then he wanted her eyes to be the last thing he saw. If there was one person he was willing to bet his life on, it was her.

"You drink this, and hopefully tomorrow when we wake up, you'll have your fire back and I'll be back to watering my flowers instead of scorching them."

"And that's all you're worried about? Our elements?" Benedict asked, resting his free hand on her thigh. Her shoulders relaxed, and she settled her hand over his.

"We'll also know if what's happening between us is caused by the call in the potion or if our feelings for each other are real..." Lucinda stared up at him, confessing her insecurities.

"If this is what you need to be sure of my feelings for you, then I'm in." He didn't want her to doubt how much he had fallen for her for even a second longer.

"To us, then." She clinked her glass against his, but her tightening grip on his hand revealed her nerves.

"To us."

He tried not to laugh when Lucinda grimaced at the taste of the foul liquid, only to almost gag himself. A tense moment settled between them as they waited to turn green or stop breathing.

"Still alive," Lucinda pointed out eventually. "Do you feel anything?"

"Try not to sound so surprised at the lack of our demise." Benedict made a show of patting himself down and checked his pulse mockingly. "I don't feel a thing."

Lucinda took the empty glasses and dropped them into the empty sink along with the pot and remaining potion. She made the shattered glass and the pot disappear with a simple spell to erase what they'd done.

"Neat trick," Benedict said, standing behind her to find his sink spotless.

"I hated doing the dishes when I was younger," she admitted, turning to face him. "Pleased to see that you're still gorgeous, and you haven't sprouted wings or dropped dead."

"I think there was a time when you'd have loved to see me drop dead."

"Me? Never," she said innocently.

"But I do think I need something to sweeten the after-taste." He took her in his arms, and she chuckled as he dipped her low and kissed her. Bringing her back up to standing, he smacked his lips. "Much better."

She squirmed. "You're intolerable."

"Potion worked – you're back to loathing me!" Even though he wanted his element back, he couldn't imagine not being able to feel her presence every moment.

"You're not getting rid of me that quickly. It'll probably take some time to kick in." Lucinda wrapped her arms around his neck as he lifted her back onto the counter.

"Good. Then we should use up what time we have left before we start despising each other," he joked, sweeping her hair over her shoulder and watching as it switched back to its natural colour. "Pity; Matherson black looked good on you."

"Sorry to disappoint you, but the magic had to wear off at some point." She searched his eyes for any hesitation, as if he was going to cast her aside. Potion or not, that was never going to happen. At least on his part. He could only hope the same was true for her.

"I wouldn't change a thing about you," Benedict said, squeezing her thighs, wrapped around him. He tucked a strand of chocolate-brown hair behind her ear. "You've always been perfect."

Lucinda rolled her eyes. "We'll both be back to perfect once our elements are back in their rightful places."

Rightful places? He knew *he* was right where he was meant to be – with her, and he was tired of trying to separate himself from her.

"Be serious for a minute?" she asked, resting his hands on the back of his neck.

"Fine." He put on his best grimace.

"Hand," she ordered, and he set his between hers.

"I don't think it's going to work that fast."

"Just try to summon your fire."

Benedict closed his eyes and pictured a flame blooming in his palm. Nothing happened. He opened his eyes, and his heart stilled as he saw the sadness in her face.

"Let's be patient. We don't know what tomorrow will bring." He tipped her chin up, wanting to absorb her anxiety.

"You're right. I shouldn't have pushed. They have to come back eventually. Or the coven will—" She cut herself off, smoothing her hands over his chest. He wasn't sure if she was trying to comfort him or herself.

"Whether our elements swap back or disappear entirely, I don't care. I don't want you because of your element, or some find your perfect man spell your family cast, or because you'll make an excellent High Priestess. I want you for *you*, now and forever, with or without the binding," Benedict said, needing her to understand.

"That sounds awfully like a proposal." Lucinda stared up at him, eyes wide with alarm.

"It is."

She buried her face in her hands.

"You don't need to hide from me." Holding her hands, he wanted to kiss away the furrow in her brow.

"I want you to be sure," she whispered. "What if we wake up tomorrow and it's only the potion, and you regret saying all this?"

"My only regret is not realising how I felt sooner, not telling you how much I wanted to take you to that damn dance, not kissing you by the lake when you gave me Greko. If you agree to be my wife, then I won't have any other. You bewitched me, body and soul, long before any spell or potion," he said, searching her wide eyes for the answer he so desperately wanted. *Needed*. If she didn't answer soon, his heart would surely stop, and it'd have nothing to do with dragon venom.

She hesitated. "Maybe we should wait until the morning? If your feelings—"

"Fuck the spell. I don't care if you stole my teddy when you were three or beat me up when I was six or flooded my locker just to piss me off. That just makes you cuter, my little force of destruction. It's always been you. If you weren't so sure of the potion affecting me... what would you say?" Benedict closed the gap between them, his gaze pleading with hers.

Lucinda took a deep breath and rested her hands on his chest. He was sure she could feel his hammering heart.

"It could never have been anyone other than you, even if the potion had worked as intended. It still would've been you. I'd rather spend the rest of my life bickering with you than at peace with anyone else. I've never had to be perfect with you. I don't have to be a Hawthorne – with you I'm just Lucinda," she confessed, placing her hand on his cheek. The love in her touch overwhelmed his senses.

His lips crashed onto hers.

He growled as she sank into the kiss, and his grip on her tightened. His hand travelled into her hair, pulling her closer. She let out a small moan, which broke the intense spell.

Benedict eased his grip on her, a question in his gaze. "We don't have to do anything until you're sure. If you want to see what happens when we wake up tomorrow, if the potion changes anything for you...?"

Lucy leaned forward, kissing one cheek and then the other. "Let's not think about tomorrow. I just want to be in the moment with you. I don't need any potion or ritual to convince me that you're *my* person, just as I'm yours."

He pushed her further back on the counter, pressing his body close to hers so that there wasn't an inch to spare between them.

"Are you sure?" He loved the hunger in her eyes.

"I'm tired of waiting," she admitted. He wasn't sure if it was his hands on her or the corset that was making her breathless.

"Thank fuck for that."

His entire body hummed with need. For her. All the pent-up tension, fear, desperation and desire had led to this moment.

He needed her like he needed air, and her fevered kiss told him she felt the same way. Her soft moans were music to his ears. He was going to give her a night that would keep her coming back for more, make her body so high on his touch that she'd be ruined for anyone else.

She seems rushed. Like she thinks this might end. Like there's a time limit on this. He pulled back slightly, needing to slow down. Her eyes travelled to his lips, full of pleading. Hearing her groan at the loss of contact made him regret pulling away.

"We don't need to rush this. We have all night, and I want to savour every second." His words were interspersed with kisses trailed along her neck.

Lucinda sucked in a breath as he nipped at her shoulder. "Fuck, Benedict."

"I think you left out the 'me' in that sentence," he murmured, licking the sore spot. Not giving her a moment of reprieve, not one moment to overthink. He only wanted her to feel.

"Yes please."

Her words were nearly his undoing. It took every ounce of his self-control not to rip off her dress and bend her over the counter. He kissed her like his life depended on it, like there was no oxygen left and he was only sustained by the sweet taste of her mouth. Her arms curled around his neck as he yanked at the strings of her corset. He felt the smile on her lips when he had to turn her around thanks to a stubborn knot.

"You're forbidden from wearing this damn thing again," he rasped when it finally dropped to the floor.

"I promise." She crossed her heart, but he took her hand and pinned it above her head, swallowing her moans as he brushed her dress from her shoulders and it pooled at their feet.

His breath caught when he saw her lingerie, black lace hugging her skin. She peered up at him through her dark lashes as if she'd planned this. *Fuck, she never fails to surprise me.* His kiss turned desperate as he lifted her into his arms, legs around his waist, and she gasped at the sudden movement. The giggle she gave as he dropped her onto his bed nearly killed him.

To have Lucinda Hawthorne laid out in front of him was the best gift he ever could have received. She watched him hungrily as he stripped off his shirt, then made fast work of his belt. He kissed her like it had been the only thing on his mind for years – because it had.

Sitting up, she dragged him down on top of her. Benedict nearly lost his balance. He caught himself on his elbows before crushing her, but from the look of disappointment in those gorgeous green eyes, that was exactly what she'd wanted. He kissed over her breasts, slipping off the lacy straps and releasing the clasp as her nipples hardened beneath his tongue. Lucy shivered.

"Benedict!" she cried out when he took her nipple between his teeth.

"I love hearing my name on your lips," he whispered, smiling as she arched her back into his touch.

"Good, because you'll be hearing it often," she rasped, bucking her hips as he moved to the other. Her skin was so hot and smooth, he didn't think he'd ever get enough of her.

"Good. You don't know how long I've waited to hear you call out my name as I fuck you." He kissed down her stomach and hip bones, pulling her underwear down her legs. Softly, he ran the pads of his fingers over her. When she bit her lip to stop crom crying out, he knew he'd found her sensitive spot. His smile widened as he brushed over it and felt her muscles tighten, her hips rolling.

"Please." She reached for his boxers and wrapped her fist around him.

The noise he made was downright primal. Nothing else mattered – no potion, no element, no binding ritual. Only the sensation and her mischievous smile. Desperate as he was, he refused to give in to his own release. He needed her first, all of her.

"Keep talking like that and I won't be able to control myself much longer," he groaned, pinning her hands to her side. He pressed his mouth back to hers, feeling her body tremble as he slid his fingers inside her.

"Then don't." He loved watching the tremors of pleasure taking took over her body, her thoughts, until all that existed for her was his touch. His heart pounded as her lips crashed back into his and he replaced his touch with the part of him she craved most. Her hands slid up over the back of his neck and into his hair, gripping tight as she moaned. A growl rolled from deep in his chest as he filled every inch of her. Lucinda arched her back, panting with need. The sheer ecstasy of her quivering around him made him lightheaded.

There was nothing gentle in their kisses. Teeth clashed, tongues twisted, and her hands gripped his hair, his shoulders, her nails dragging so ferociously down his back that he was sure he'd have marks tomorrow. She moaned and sighed against his lips, and with every thrust he felt her tightening around him. He was so damn close. He wanted to drag it out forever, but neither could wait that long. He thrust wildly as she dug her nails into his hips, pleading for more.

Her body took all he had to give, ruining him. Arms around each other, they rode wave after wave of sheer pleasure, not sure where one began and where the other ended.

It was impossible to say how many breathless moments passed before they found the ability to speak. Needing to know she was okay, that she didn't regret it, forced Benedict out of the thought-shattering-sex trance. He rested on his elbow, tracing the tattoo between her shoulder blades.

"I don't think I can survive another orgasm," Lucinda murmured, moving closer to him. Her hair fanned across the pillow; he loved how at ease she was with him.

"I promise to give you all the time you need to regain your strength," he said, kissing her shoulder. She smiled, but didn't open her eyes.

"When did you get this?" His finger followed the lines of the tattoo over skin spattered with freckles.

He never wanted her to leave his bed. Fuck the coven. Fuck the town. He'd block up the door and keep them away from anything that could shatter this perfect moment.

"Twenty-first birthday. Me and Rosie went to Willow Valley to celebrate our graduation and her permanent residence being granted," Lucinda explained, half-asleep.

"Why a new moon?"

"Start of a new phase. We graduated and started at the library. Making it our own."

He kissed a freckle on her neck, unable to resist. "Rosie has one?"

This got a small chuckle out of her; clearly giving up on the idea of sleep – not that he was planning on letting her get any – she rested her forearms under her chin. "Hers only lasted until the next full moon. Once she shifted, her healing took over, and when she changed back to human form it was gone. She was so upset because it had been her idea in the first place. It meant more to her, since she'd come so far alone. I wanted to do it with her."

Benedict pressed his lips against the crease between her brows.

"Doesn't matter now. For her birthday, I managed to find another pack that made jewellery for wolves. I had a new moon chain designed. It's enchanted to change shape as they do. It doesn't break or strangle her when she shifts —"

She bolted upright, nearly knocking him off the side of the bed.

"What the—?" Benedict stammered as she pulled the blanket out from beneath him and scuffled out of the bedroom. "Lucinda!" He found her half-hearted attempt to conceal her modesty amusing. It wasn't like he hadn't seen every inch of her already.

He followed her into the sitting area, jealous of whatever had stolen her attention.

"What was that?" he asked, playfully wrapping his arms round her as she rooted through her purse like a mad woman.

"I can't give it to you if you don't let go!"

"Maybe I don't want it, then," he said, trailing kisses along her neck. "There's something I want much more." Fuck, he didn't think he'd ever not want her. He had always believed she'd be the death of him. Being in bed with her wrapped around him might not be the worst way to go.

"Benedict!"

Her stern voice caused him to surrender. She turned, struggling to keep the sheet from getting tangled around her legs, and he frowned, looking at the arm she held behind her back.

"I'm sorry I didn't do this sooner," she began.

"You're not about to stab me with a letter opener, are you?" He arched a brow, but made no attempt to protect himself.

Lucinda sat on the couch, dragging him along with her. "Close your eyes," she ordered.

"If you're going to kill me, I want you to be the last thing I see."

"I'm not going to kill you. Now close your eyes."

Benedict huffed and closed his eyes, blinking once or twice until a glare made him settle. Lucinda took his hand. When he didn't resist, she rewarded him with a kiss – he smiled – and placed a small box in his hand. He frowned, studying it before opening the lid.

"This is—" Benedict choked on his words as he stared at the ring she'd put her heart into. He lifted it out of the suede cushion, admiring the stones in the meteorite band.

"Do you like it? I had Mr Mulligan match the stones. I know it's tradition, but the sunstone and amethyst stones match mine – except they aren't raised like mine, so your signet ring will fit over it nicely," she rambled.

Without any hesitation, Benedict slid on the binding ring. Lucinda let out a sigh of relief as it slotted perfectly with the Matherson signet ring.

"There are no words to express how much I love you. If only I could be worthy of you." Benedict found himself welling up, suddenly terrified of losing her as he'd lost so many. To see the ring his father had given him matched so perfectly with the other half of his heart – his family, and the love of his life... He'd never known he could feel so much love.

Lucinda settled onto his lap, distracting him from his tears.

"Is that a yes?" she asked, wiping a stray tear from his cheek.

"I thought I was the one proposing," he sniffled through his laughter.

"I think it's only fair. Equality and all that." She smiled, clearly waiting for an answer.

"Our elements may never return, our ancestors may reject our desire to be together, but Lucinda Hawthorne, I swear in this life and the next. I am yours." With each word he dotted her body with kisses while she squirmed to free herself.

"I think we should stay here forever," she decided.

"In the Manor, or this moment?"

"Both, but I think we should stay close. These old manors can be awfully draughty."

Benedict pressed his lips to the side of her head in agreement, silently vowing that they would never be parted.

Lucinda

orty-eight hours later, their elements had failed to switch back – and to make matters worse, Lucy woke with a start to find Grams standing over her.

She had a finger to her lips, probably so that she wouldn't alarm a half-naked Benedict in bed beside Lucy. Thankfully neither of them were completely naked, or she never would have recovered from being discovered like this – though Grams didn't look surprised in the least.

The fright should have caused her to set her beloved grandmother on fire, but to her surprise, there was no rush of heat coursing through her. Yesterday she and Benedict had simply assumed that the potion hadn't worked, but as she tried to light the candle on her bedside table with the tip of her finger, her eyes widened in alarm. *Maybe this potion just takes longer to work than the first.* She wanted to wake Benedict and tell him, but startling a mostly unclothed Benedict in front of Grams probably wasn't a good idea. Nor was revealing they'd both consumed a potion containing dragon venom.

"How did you get in?" she snapped, keeping her voice low.

Benedict was still fast asleep, snoring with an arm thrown over her waist. True to his word, he hadn't really left her side since they'd drunk the potion, but they'd been so busy with the festival that neither had talked about their pending nuptials. Their mothers had taken over all the planning, which gave them some reprieve; Lucy had never seen him so exhausted. She wondered if he was keeping an eye on her until the binding in case the potion kicked in and she suddenly hated his guts again – that, or he couldn't get enough of her. Not that she was complaining; she liked having a man-sized water bottle to snuggle into.

She tied her dressing gown around her waist and climbed out of bed slowly so she wouldn't disturb him, though he was clearly dead to the world. They'd been up late trying to figure out how to divide their duties as joint leaders of the coven and how such duties would impact their current responsibilities. The stress had worn them both out, but at least they had each other to help work out the tension. She wasn't so sure being joint leaders was a bad idea after all.

"Such a simple lock wouldn't keep me out – although I'll admit I wasn't aware you had company," Grams whispered, smirking at Benedict's muffled groan. Instead of waking to pull Lucy close, he grabbed her pillow and cuddled it to his chest. Lucy stifled a laugh as a small smile formed in the corner of his mouth.

"What's so urgent? You never come up here," she said, trying to take the attention away from him.

Grams rooted in her wardrobe and threw her a pair of jeans and a thick, oversized jumper. She caught them, glad

Grams hadn't said anything about the clothing discarded on the cream carpet like a roadmap of the previous night's activities. *Why didn't I take Benedict up on his offer to stay at his?*

She stopped following Grams down the stairs when she realised all over again that she really didn't feel the sizzling simmer beneath her skin. She resisted the urge to go back to Benedict and wake him. *His element is gone.*

A small squeal escaped her as she covered her mouth, only for a nervous chuckle to follow. The elation was so overwhelming that she didn't even notice Grams had stopped talking and was staring at her.

"What's wrong with you?" Grams frowned.

Lucy resisted the urge to groan; she couldn't have the whole element celebration with Grams here. It'd have to wait, and she couldn't get too excited anyway, not until her water returned. She didn't feel a hint of its coolness yet.

"Nothing," she lied.

Gram's eyes narrowed, but her curiosity was short-lived. "Get dressed – I need you to cover for me at the tarot shop. I've had a call from Alpha Beline. One of their youngest wolves is sick. Fever won't break after their first change, poor thing."

Lucy paused. "You're going to go into wolf territory alone?" Grams had gone out on healing calls before, but lately Lucy got nervous when she visited the wolves. Getting lost in the woods, especially with her memory failing, wasn't a fate Grams should suffer.

"There's nothing to worry about; I'm more than capable," Grams said, resting a reassuring hand on her forearm. "I've long been given permission to enter their lands, so there shouldn't be any trouble."

Lucy glanced over her shoulder, wondering if she

should suggest Benedict accompany her. Then again, given his recent run-in with the wolves at the Manor, she quickly thought better of it.

"Without my help, they've little hope of the child surviving," Grams said urgently. "If I need an extra set of hands, I'll send someone from the pack to get you."

Lucy reluctantly agreed, though she couldn't help feeling guilty – if she ended up going and Benedict found out, he'd be furious to know she'd put herself in a dangerous situation without an element to protect herself. At least Grams was going there to help, and the Hawthorne name was well respected. The wolves wouldn't have reached out if the situation wasn't desperate.

It was extra chilly out today, so Lucy was relieved that Grams had opted to keep her shop open instead of hiring a stall; it meant she could keep her back to the toasty radiator and serve customers instead of standing out in the cold. Thankfully most of the customers were just coming in for crystals and some potion jars. Lucy could read tarot, but it didn't come as naturally as potion-making or translating.

"Lucy, can we talk for a moment?" Emerson asked, appearing in the doorway. "There's something delicate I want to talk to you about."

Lucy smiled, speaking in her best physic voice. "You've come to the right place for delicate questions. A card reading can help you find the answers you seek."

"I'm not here for a reading," he said as she shuffled the deck on the table.

She frowned.

"I need the key for my afternoon lecture," he explained. He wasn't asking like someone who had discovered he'd been stolen from; Lucy was beginning to wonder if anything could disturb this man's peace.

She went to the till and removed the key from beneath the cash tray.

"You knew?" she asked, offering it to him. There was no point in lying about it. She'd planned on dropping it in the library to make it look like it might have slipped out of his pocket while he was working with Rosie.

"Rosie wanted to have a look at one of the objects in the restricted relics section to compare the symbol she found in the case she's been working on. It was only when we got there that I noticed it wasn't in my pocket. I checked everywhere. and then one of the professors said that he saw you and Benedict leaving the university library quite late the night of the festival opening."

"I'm sorry – I should've asked. I didn't want to get you involved or put you in an awkward position."

"I would've given it to you without question. You are the reason I was even able to get a key in the first place," Emerson reminded her.

"I know, but that didn't give me the right to take it." Lucy hesitated. "You don't want to know why?"

"It's none of my business. And by the way, I didn't tell Rosie about this."

Lucy wanted to thank him, though she couldn't help wondering if he was keeping it from her friend to use it against her in the future. "How about you let me give you a reading to say thank you? I'm not as talented as my Grams, but Rosie said you've been trying to figure out what your future looks like now that you've decided to settle in Foxford."

Emerson shrugged. "Sure, maybe a quick reading. I don't have a lecture for another hour or so." He took a seat at the round table encrusted with crystals.

"A four-card draw shouldn't take too long. And anything we discuss or that comes up will be kept between us. A witch never discusses her readings," Lucy said, always respecting the privacy of others. Readings could bring up past emotional issues, or personal concerns and troubles, so it could become emotionally charged. She hung a busy sign on the door so that no one would interrupt, knocked on the deck of cards three times to remove any energy lingering from past readings, and handed the deck to him.

"Close your eyes and let your mind quieten. Don't try to hold any thought or concern; let whatever thoughts come to the front of your mind settle," she instructed, lighting a candle at the heart of the table.

Emerson eyed the cards laid out with an aura of unease. Then again, Lucy didn't doubt that he was the first Order member to have his cards read. Her ancestors wouldn't believe their eyes if they could see this.

She flipped the first card.

"Death Reversed." She would have said it was the most positive card in the deck, despite its reputation. "Don't panic, this isn't a death sentence."

"I'm relieved. I still have some things to tick off my bucket list before I kick it." He smiled, but there was wariness in his gaze.

"It can mean the death of your old habits, or a way of life. The closing of one and moving on to the next. You've just moved to a new town, so I'm not surprised this is your first draw."

"But it's upside down?"

"That can mean there is some resistance. Perhaps there is a part of you clinging to old habits, or a reluctance to leave the past behind."

He didn't verify or deny her reasoning. It wasn't her job to pry; she only read the cards. She reached for the next.

"Seven of Wands, and it's upright, which is interesting. Romance could be on the horizon. A love you are fighting for and defending. A love that will face some challenges, but if you are true in heart and intention, you could have long term success," Lucy explained, thinking how delighted Rosie would be. Her best friend was never one to shy away from a challenge; she only hoped he was up to it.

Emerson fidgeted with the collar on his coat. Concealing her smile, she turned over another card.

"Three of Swords, upright." She hesitated, staring at the crossed swords.

"You look concerned. Should I be worried?" He leaned forward.

Lucy forced a smile and ran her hand over the card for a clearer reading. *Lies, deception, scheming...* the messages flashing through her mind were unclear, so she opted for a less serious explanation so as not to spook him. "A little suspicion, either from you or directed towards you."

"That makes sense. Not everyone has been accepting of my arrival."

"Some conflict at work?" she asked, and for the first time since she had grown to trust him, she felt a flash of irritation. He wouldn't meet her gaze, and he kept glancing at the door.

"I got the new job at the university, which I'm sure others weren't happy about," he hedged.

Wanting to end the reading, she wished she hadn't proposed, given his unsettled reaction and her renewed suspicion, Lucy reached for the next card.

Emerson visibly swallowed before she turned it over. Suddenly, he reached into his tweed jacket for his phone. "The dean is calling me! I still have to get to the relics section before my lecture. We can finish this some other time," he said, getting up with such haste that the chair nearly fell back.

"Are you sure you can't stay for another minute? We're almost done." She wondered if he was lying to get out of the rest of the reading; she hadn't heard the phone ring or vibrate. "Have I said something to upset you?"

"No." He shook his head, his floppy curls exaggerating his denial. "Just a busy day, and I don't want to take up any more of your time." He couldn't get out of the shop fast enough.

"Don't forget you and Rosie are helping me with the toffee apple stall tomorrow!" Lucy called out after him, unsure whether he heard her. If he'd been a cartoon, a puff of smoke would have been left in his place as the door closed behind him.

In his absence, she turned over the last card.

"The Hanged Man." The words escaped her in a sigh. "A sacrifice of the heart? His or another's?"

As she picked it up, she felt a forced separation: a harsh change that had changed his outlook, changed a deep-seated belief. That made sense, considering he'd drawn the death card first. The draw was coming up full circle.

Tossing it back on the table, she worried she was reading into the cards too much. There were many ways they could be interpreted, but clearly there was more to his story than Emerson was letting on. She considered taking the cards to Grams to get her insight, but maybe she was just being paranoid, wanting to protect her friend. Even if Lucy had the best intentions, Rosie wouldn't be too happy if she knew she was using cards to get a better insight into their new resident Order member.

The cards stared up at her. *If there's nothing wrong, then why did he run?*

Lucy shook away the thought and went to the pantry. She'd feel better once she removed the energy from the deck. Finding a sage stick and standing over the cards, she tried to light it without thinking, but nothing happened. She almost missed the heat stirring in her veins. To distract herself, she tried to summon her water, but it still hadn't returned. Her breath caught. *What if I've stripped us of our elements for good?* If her water returned, she vowed never to take it for granted, for even a second.

"Pumpkin!" Benedict called from the front of the small shop. Lucy put down the sage stick, gathering up the incriminating cards. "Why does the sign on the door say you're closed?"

"I was giving Emerson a private reading."

His eyes narrowed. "How was that? Learn anything new about the perfect professor?"

"Did you come here to ask me about card readings?" Benedict had only just started not to hate Emerson entirely; now wasn't the time to bring up her suspicions.

"No – I like to be surprised by what fate has in store." He winked, kissing her cheek. "Speaking of, I went to the library, but Rosie said you were here, and I couldn't wait to show you." Like an excited kid, he walked over to the table of half-melted candle samples. Grams let customers light them to make sure they loved the scent before purchasing.

"Want to see a magic trick?" he asked, rubbing his hands together like some cheesy magician.

Lucy stared wide-eyed, watching him run his hand over the table. Tall flames sparked upon each wick. Her hands flew to her mouth.

"Your element is back!" she exclaimed, wrapping her arms around his neck excitedly.

"It's a bit twitchy," he said into her hair. "This is the most I can do for now, but it'll probably take some time. The potion worked. Fuck, it feels good to have it back." He sighed, and she released him.

"When did – how did—?" she stammered, her mind spinning with a mix of relief and excitement. Benedict couldn't stop beaming. She didn't think she'd ever seen him smile so big.

"I went back to the Manor, and one of the porters was trying to light the fireplace in the lobby. I felt this rush of heat, thought I was going to pass out, and the next thing I knew the fire was lit. I always thought you might poison me one day, but with that poison you cured me. You gave me back my fire!" He picked her up and twirled her around, unable to contain his joy. Lucinda thanked the gods for letting the magic work and giving him back what her family had taken. His happiness was infectious.

"What about your water? Anything?" he asked, looking her over as though she was about to spring a leak.

"No sign of it yet, but like yours, I'm sure it'll just surprise me when I least expect it." Lucy tried to hide her disappointment so he wouldn't feel guilty about his excitement.

"Why not give it a try? It's not been long since my return, and you could just need a little push like I did with the fireplace," he suggested, picking up one of the small cactus pots and placing it on the reading table.

"I don't want to force it. I'm sure it'll find its way back to me in time," she started to reason, but seeing how eager he was, she figured it couldn't hurt to try.

Hesitantly, she studied the soil. Benedict's gaze on her back didn't help her anxiety. Letting out a slow exhale, she called to her element, but nothing happened. Her shoulders slumped.

He came up behind her and wrapped his arms around her waist. The love she felt in his touch was as much of a relief as it would have been if her element was back.

"You're right, I shouldn't have pushed. Let's be patient." He kissed the side of her head as she shook off her worries.

"We should call today a win anyway, since we're halfway there," she said, turning around in his arms.

"Still want to marry me?" He lifted her onto the counter.

"A customer might come in!" she squealed.

"Let them," he said, pulling her closer. She tried to nudge him away, but he gripped her waist, refusing to budge. "I'm still waiting for my answer," he said, tilting his head towards her so their noses were barely touching.

Lucy studied his lips, feeling a tumble of excitement in her tummy at the thought of kissing him. She slipped her hands to the back of his neck and let them drift into his hair. "No."

His face fell and he tried to pull back, but she held him close. His confusion was so adorable she nearly broke her composure.

"I want a binding," she clarified, and he shook his head, trying to conceal his bashful smile. "I need to make sure no one else gets a taste of these magnificent lips in this life or the next."

Benedict lifted her off the counter and hauled her over his shoulder. "You're going to pay for that!" He carried her into the back as she stifled a laugh and pleas to be let down.

The bell tinkled. They both looked up to see a customer standing in the door, eyebrows raised.

"Sorry, we're closed for the rest of the afternoon. My wife and I need to have a talk," Benedict said firmly before Lucy could do anything.

The customer gaped before nodding and backing out of the shop. Benedict let Lucy down, and she stood mortified as he quickly closed the door and pulled down the blind.

"I can't believe you did that!" Though her stomach had done a little flip as he called her his wife...

He grinned. "Then what I'm going to do next is going to be an even bigger shock."

Lucinda

"**M**ore apples are coming! Sorry for the wait!" Lucy promised those waiting in the long queue as she manned the toffee apple stall. Rosie and Emerson had left to get the extras stored in the Manor's kitchen but were taking a little longer than she'd hoped. Those in the queue were grumbling a little, and she hated to disappoint the kids waiting most of all. Staving off a yawn, she noticed the moon was almost full overhead. The day of the binding would soon be upon them. She only hoped her element would return by then.

"Please feel free to pop over to another stall while you wait," she added. "The hot dog with relish or the vegan burgers at the end of the lane will knock your socks off!"

A few petered off, while others loitered close by. Lucy couldn't believe how quickly they were running out of stock; clearly the new layout of the festival was working. Mrs Lark had also reported that the carousel had already made back the money they'd spent on the renovations.

"Lucinda! Please come quick," Mr Rodriguez bellowed, making his way through the crowd.

"Take a breath. What's wrong?" Lucy asked as he rested his hand on the rather rickety candy-striped stall and dabbed his forehead with a handkerchief. The queue, waiting for their overwhelmingly sweet apples, eyed him in bewilderment.

"Rosie and P-Professor Hughes..." he stammered, motioning for her to follow. "Come now!"

Before she could ask any questions, he was already down the lane. Lucy followed close behind, trying not to bump into anyone on the way.

"If you'd tell me what has happened—" She was interrupted by a shout and a loud growl. There was a crowd gathered in the square; something had clearly drawn their attention other than the festival antics. Lucy shoved her way through to see Rosie and Emerson standing by the white gazebo surrounded by a group of four visitors she didn't recognise. It wasn't unusual for new people to come to town for the festival, but the way they were standing made it look like someone was about to start chanting "Fight!".

"Filthy traitor. He's a member of the Order. We had to come and see it with our own eyes," spat one of the men, in a rather worn shirt and jeans. The two other males nodded along. Behind them, a woman in a grey dress looked like she'd rather be anywhere but there.

Wolves, Lucy realised, missing Rosie's reply. She stood protectively in front of Emerson, who spoke up next.

"There are families around. We should go our separate ways and enjoy the festival," he said.

The smallest male's eyes flashed amber. "Are you giving us orders? I should rip your throat out for even speaking to us!" Stepping forward, he knocked the tray of apples from Emerson's arms. Thankfully, he didn't react other than to take Rosie's arm. Hopefully she wouldn't go feral; her claws were extended.

Lucy couldn't believe no one had intervened yet; thank goodness Mr Rodriguez had informed her before the confrontation got out of hand. Even the band performing on the gazebo were peering down and over at the crowd.

A glimmer of silver shone in Emerson's waistband. *Is that a gun?* Lucy's eyes must be playing tricks on her – there were enough fairy lights littered around town to make her head spin. It could have just been a reflection.

The way he removed his hand from the inside of his jacket when she stepped forward had her thinking otherwise. She clapped her hands, and all eyes fell on her.

"Everyone, please return to what you were doing! There is so much to experience, and only two hours left before the stalls and shops close up for the night." She kept her voice calm and level, but with an edge of authority that told them to move the hell on and there was nothing to see here. While the crowd dispersed and the group of troublemakers turned to each other, clearly trying to figure out who was ruining their show, Lucy stepped up beside Rosie.

"Retract the claws," she ordered, not wanting her friend to get in trouble. Committing violence at the festival in front of magless and visitors would carry a harsh punishment.

Rosie, lost in her wolf rage, growled at her before realising who she was.

"What's going on?" Lucy asked, calmly and clearly. The group of wolves glared at her, but she kept her attention on Rosie and Emerson.

"We were coming back to the stall when this lot came out of the house of horrors and wouldn't let us pass,"

Emerson explained while Rosie kept her attention on the group.

"Emerson, take Rosie back to the manor and get the remaining trays for the stall. Our customers are waiting," Lucy commanded, refusing to give the group of wolves any attention.

"Lucy, I'm not leaving—"

"Now, Rosie." She was speaking not as her friend, but as the future leader of Foxford.

Emerson took Rosie's hand. Touching a wolf on the brink of changing was dangerous, but Rosie visibly relaxed. The crowd parted to let them through.

"They aren't going anywhere," the head of the group growled.

"Yes, they are," Lucy replied coolly. "As are you. I suggest you return to the woods or enjoy the rest of the night. I highly recommend the Punch and Judy show at the theatre."

"Are you giving us orders now? Are you protecting this traitor and *him?*" The werewolf squared up to her, but she couldn't imagine he'd do anything. There was no way Alpha Beline would allow them to cause trouble in town.

Lucy let out a long sigh. "Yes, I am. Allow me to introduce myself: Lucinda Hawthorne." She extended her hand and the wolf sneered at her. "Does your alpha know that you've come here to cause such a disturbance? Mr Hughes is a guest of this sanctuary, and thus under the coven's protection. Rosie is a resident who has long cut ties with your pack. You are welcome here, just as they are. However, I won't allow any threat of violence during the festival that many in this town have worked so hard on."

"A Hawthorne? Do you think a name is going to intimidate us?"

A crowd was gathering again, and she didn't want any human casualties if tempers got out of hand. "No, I wouldn't want to intimidate anyone. The Hawthornes have been serving the pack as healers for generations. I only hope that the respect goes both ways," she said, refusing to raise her voice. She wanted to diffuse the situation, not make it worse, and she didn't like the odds of four against one.

"This isn't about the pack or your family. How can you stomach the sight of an Order member in your town – and with one of our kind? We can't accept it," the wolf said, standing a little too close for her liking. "What has Foxford come to? Why should we respect you or your rules when you don't even respect yourself?"

Lucy noted his claws, extended at his sides. She took a step back, getting out from his reach. To her outrage, he tried to follow, and the other members of the group started to circle her. *How fucking dare they challenge me?* She remembered what they had done to Benedict and the manor a few weeks back, and wondered if Alpha Beline was losing her grip on her pack.

"Why don't we all just cool down?" she snarled, and before she could stop herself, the water from the dunk tank opposite them leapt out of the tank and onto the confronting group.

Lucy froze, completely overtaken by her element. Her body shivered as she felt the cool stream of magic rush through her veins. Benedict had been right when he'd said it would reappear... but that wasn't exactly how she'd wanted to manage the situation. She winced as the drenched troublemakers growled at her, but the remaining onlookers dissolved into laughter. *Well, that's one way to break the tension.*

The wolf tried to take a swipe at her, but to Lucy's surprise the woman in the grey dress got between them and blocked the blow.

"Enough. We should go. You've had too much to drink, and Hawthorne is right. Beline won't be happy about this. The eldest Hawthorne just helped little Maisie – you've no right to draw your claws on her!"

Lucy wondered if she was the true leader of the group, as they fell in behind her, huffing and muttering to each other, egos bruised and metaphorical tails tucked.

"Excuse my brother; we were merely shocked to see Rosie after so many years, and we weren't expecting her to keep – such company," the woman said, tipping her head respectfully to Lucy.

"No harm done. Sorry about giving your brothers a bath. We can all get a bit carried away," Lucy said, relieved.

"Don't worry, they could use one." They had a small laugh, much to the irritation of the other wolves. "We'll leave now, but I hope you can be discreet about what has happened."

She doesn't want the story to get back to Beline. "We all make mistakes. A lot of people saw what just happened, so I can't promise word won't get back to her. However, it won't come from me," Lucy promised impulsively. She hoped that a bit of mercy and forgiveness would help ensure such events wouldn't happen again. "I understand you live by your own laws in the woods, but when your kin ventures into town, I hope they abide by *our* laws. For everyone's safety."

"You have my word."

"That's all I can ask for."

"We will leave you now. Please send our regards to

Grams, and let her know that Maisie is doing much better."

"I will." Lucy watched them leave. There was still a trace of aggression or rebellion in the first wolf's eyes, but she was glad that his sister had been able to bring them to their senses. So close to the full moon, it was amazing that everyone had managed to get through the altercation without a scratch.

She smiled politely at the people staring at her as she turned to head back to the toffee apple stall. She was sure the coven would learn about the altercation before the night was out, but given that no one had been injured and their relationship with the pack remained intact, there wasn't much else she could have done.

Benedict

B enedict was in the Matherson kitchen, discussing menus with the chef, when Rosie and Emerson came in. Rosie was clearly upset, and he asked what was going on, half hoping it was Emerson himself. Rosie explained what was going on with the wolves.

Afraid Lucinda needed him, he rushed to the town square just in time to see the wolves leaving. Judging from the festival-goer sitting in an empty dunk tank and the soaking wet wolves, she'd got her element back. Maybe not under control, but back.

He waited until the wolves disappeared into the crowds in the direction of the woods. Lucinda ran her hands through her hair and turned in his direction. He offered her a small wave and a smile, and her tired, flat expression lifted. Benedict chuckled to himself; it wasn't too long ago that his appearance had had the opposite effect on her.

Lucinda crossed the road to where he stood in front of the bakery and wrapped her arms around his waist, resting her head on his chest.

"I needed a hug," she groaned, and he kissed the top of her head.

"Want to go home?"

"I've got to get back to the stall and make sure Rosie and Emerson are okay."

On the way back to the toffee apple stall, Benedict listened intently as she explained what had happened. He felt so proud to call her his. The town had seen how she'd diffused the situation, and how she was going to make an excellent High Priestess. She led with her heart, which was the very thing Foxford needed in a leader to thrive. Like his heart, the town belonged to her.

"You shouldn't have revealed your identity to them!" Rosie was snapping at Emerson when they reached the stand.

"I thought they would back off. I didn't like the way they were looking at you," Emerson said, taking cash from the next customer. There were only a few waiting, so hopefully they could all call it a night soon.

Benedict awkwardly cleared his throat as he and Lucinda walked right into the argument.

"I grew up with them, and of course they were suspicious of you. They're suspicious of everyone who isn't part of the pack. They wouldn't have hurt me, but by opening your mouth you only escalated the situation!" Rosie hissed.

"You thought a group of wolves would respect your position with the Order? You're lucky you kept that pretty face," Benedict muttered, and Lucinda elbowed him the side. He hadn't necessarily meant to speak aloud.

To his surprise, Emerson turned on him and shoved him, though Rosie quickly got between them.

Lucinda took Benedict's hand, but he had no intention

of striking the man. Lucinda had already diffused one situation tonight – he didn't want to make it two.

"Don't get upset. Exposing your position was ballsy. But our ancestors would roll over in their graves if they thought a werewolf needed protection from a human!" he quipped.

Emerson squared up to him, his jaw clenched tightly. *So there is a fighter in him after all,* Benedict thought.

"If they'd so much as touched me – her – this place would be swarming with Hunters in the morning," the professor ground out, defending his stupid decision.

"How reassuring. I'm sure your girlfriend loves that you can click your fingers and bring Hunters down on the pack," Benedict said, looking to Rosie, who didn't look too comfortable with the thought.

"Don't be an arsehole! I'd never call for Hunters. It was just a threat. We all know Alpha Beline wouldn't want me reporting to the Order that her wolves were intimidating residents of Foxford or one of their members." Emerson kept his voice level, but he couldn't hide his frustration. Rosie, her anger fading, took Emerson's hand. "I'm sorry, Benedict, but you aren't in a position to judge my actions when you weren't there."

Both men continued to glare at each other, but Benedict conceded that he had a point. He knew Lucinda was able to handle herself, but if someone had threatened his wife – oops, he meant fiancée – in front of him, he'd probably burn them alive. Or at least singed them slightly.

Lucinda ♥

B enedict walked away first. Lucy looked to Emerson while Rosie caught up to Benedict, probably trying to talk him down.

"I know I shouldn't have threatened the pack with hunters," Emerson confessed, looking after her. "I couldn't help it. She'd put herself in harm's way for anyone, and I've seen the cases she works on. When I learnt about how her mum died, and with the rumours of our dating floating around town... I was terrified the wolves would hurt her for just walking down the street with me."

"Rosie's heart is her best asset and biggest weakness. Thank you for looking out for her, but in future, be careful with Beline's wolves. They could've ripped your throat out," Lucy warned him. Emerson didn't look dissuaded. "You can't mention a word of this to the Order, or it won't be Rosie you'll have to worry about." She looked him in the eye, making sure he wouldn't put any of them at risk.

"Not a word. It was never my intention to get them involved." Emerson held up his hands defensively. "Rosie is safe with me. I would never let anyone hurt her."

Distracted by the laughter ahead, they watched Benedict shove Rosie into a pile of leaves gathered in a heap, breaking the tension. Emerson looked warily at the pair. Lucy placed her hand on his arm.

"They've always been like that. Best not to intervene," she explained, not wanting to break up another fight.

"Do you think he'll stop looking at me like I'm the enemy any time soon?"

"Wanting to protect Rosie earned you some points, even if the way you went about it was foolish. Give it time – you might even become friends," she said. Hopefully time would be enough.

Emerson arched his eyebrow.

"Friendlier," she conceded. Magic might be real, but she wasn't so sure about miracles.

"I'll take it," he sighed.

"Are you going to pick up the pace, or do I need to throw you over my shoulder?" Benedict interrupted, thankfully in a better mood. Emerson slung his arm around Rosie's shoulder, falling behind. Staring at her best friend, Lucy wondered if Emerson would leave the Order for her. If he didn't, would Rosie have to give up Foxford?

"Leave them be. We should know better than to get involved with matters of the heart," Benedict said, breaking her out of her thoughts. Lucy felt the warmth of his hand in hers. She just wanted Rosie to find her person, as she'd found hers. If that was Emerson, she'd respect her choice.

Rosie and Emerson left them once they reached the university entrance. Lucinda watched them walk away, hand in hand. She looked to Benedict, but he seemed far away in thought. She wanted to talk more about what had happened, but she didn't even know where to begin, and she was too overwhelmed and tired to figure out where to start. Perhaps it was best to just savour that they were both safe and sound.

He walked so quietly by her side for the next twenty minutes that her relief slowly turned to unease. She'd never been so desperate to know what he was thinking. She opened her mouth to speak several times but struggled to find the right thing to say.

"Are you okay?" she finally dared to say as he opened the gate to the Manor for her.

"I was just thinking something," he started, but she could see how much he struggled to get the words out, and something in his eyes troubled her.

"Mind-reading isn't a skill of mine," she pressed. She couldn't let him leave without knowing what was weighing on his heart.

"The wolves. If you were hurt... I know you're able to fight your own battles, but the thought of you getting hurt —being high priestess will also come with an element of danger, and the thought of something happening to you makes me—" He scrubbed his hands over his face.

Lucy took them away from his face and held them to her chest. "I'm here. I'm safe. Not a hair out of place."

He let out a long exhale, but there was a fear she hadn't seen in him since he'd lost his dad and brother.

"My head knows that, but even the possibility..." Tears lined his eyes, and she hated the pain she'd caused him. "I can't lose someone else. Especially not you."

"I'm not going anywhere," she promised, eyes pleading with him to listen.

"Neither were they." The grief in his words threatened to cripple her heart.

Lucy finally understood that there was nothing else she

could say that would make him feel better. All she could do was be here with him, and wait for this moment of loss to pass.

She wrapped her arm around his waist, and they walked back to the Manor together.

Lucinda

After spending her morning organising the sacrificial goblets in the vault, Lucy found three missed calls on her phone from Gwendoline, which were followed up with a message telling her to be at Margot & Murphy tailors at 4pm. She hoped she'd get a chance to see Benedict this evening; this would be their last night together before the binding tomorrow night. This urgent visit to the dress makers was presumably because she'd failed to choose a gown for her binding.

She'd found two in the basement of Hawthorne House, one a champagne shade and the other a blush pink that would go nicely with the navy of the Matherson cloak, but she loved both too much to pick. The cloak would cover most of the dress for the binding ritual, but for walking to the altar and for the rest of the evening, she wanted something special. She'd meant to find a spell to somehow combine elements of each dress into one gown, but with the stress of the festival, getting her element back under control, and the drama with the wolves, it had completely slipped her mind.

She couldn't blame her mum for not reminding her, either; Wilhelmina had been rather upset with Lucy's dad, since he'd called to say he couldn't get away from the dig for the ritual. Lucy understood that the dig came first, but she still wanted him there. Even if she'd tried to explain her understanding, her mum was still pissed, and Lucy had figured giving her some space would help ease her mind. She had plenty to deal with, anyway, considering she was retiring in a matter of days.

"I have an idea in mind, but it hasn't been finalised," Lucy told Gwendoline when she called back, not going into the detail about the wolf ordeal.

"You don't have it altered yet? I was sure your mum would have finished altering it by now."

"It's not her fault... she can't alter a dress I haven't picked yet." Lucy winced, waiting for a scolding – for Gwendoline to tell her how irresponsible it was, and how the ritual must mean so little to her if she'd forgotten such an important element.

Instead there was a moment of silence, before a small sigh. "Bring the two gowns to Margot and Murph's, and we'll come up with something. We need to match your chosen outfit to Benedict's suit today, and he has a final fitting at five," Gwendoline said, her tone softer than Lucy had ever heard. Gwendoline had always been guarded, as though protected by thick stone walls cemented with iron. Then again, Lucy couldn't even imagine the sorrow and heartbreak she'd experienced throughout her life. She'd caught a glimpse of it through what Benedict had told her, but to be a mother and lose your husband and son in so short a time – to have to give up your home, to sustain your family alone... She couldn't help respecting Gwendoline, even if her methods of fortifying the Matherson name could be rather morally grey.

She realised she hadn't replied, but Gwendoline went on anyway. "I'll see you at four. We'll just have to try and not let Benedict see you!"

The excitement in her voice was contagious. *I never thought the day would come when I'd be talking about binding outfits with Gwendoline Matherson, let alone be looking forward to it!* She'd have to close up the library early so she'd have time to get home and grab the gowns.

"Thank you, I really appreciate your help. I'm sorry again for leaving it to the last minute," she said, wondering whether to include Grams and Mum in the final decision. She decided to go alone. She felt she owed it to Gwendoline to get to know her: not just as the Matherson matriarch or the stern right hand of the High Priestess, but as the woman welcoming her into her family.

"Don't be late. Margot and Murph have closed their boutique just for us."

The dresses Lucy had brought with her were quickly discarded on the back of an antique chair in the corner of her dressing room. She hadn't expected Gwendoline to bring other options. To touch the gowns of the Matherson ancestors was terrifying, let alone to be trusted to wear them. They were a piece of history, but Gwendoline refused her refusals, and it was clear she was never going to get out without trying on every dress. In fact, it meant a lot to her to see how excited Gwendoline was by the whole process.

"Are you going to come out of there or am I going to have to pull you out?" Gwendoline asked, waiting on the other side of the curtain.

"I'm struggling with the buttons. There are dozens of them, and the bodice is on the tighter side," Lucy panted, stretching and reaching, but the boned bodice refused to allow much movement.

"I've got a spell for that – just step out. No one is going to see you, and Margot needs to see what work needs to be done," Gwendoline called.

"I'm sorry to be taking up so much of your time. I'm going as fast as possible." Lucy couldn't stop staring at the floor-length gown in rich navy that complemented her pale skin. The off-the-shoulder sleeves attached at her bust line made her feel like royalty. Like a high priestess. She could barely believe it was her own reflection.

"Don't be ridiculous. Your mum has some matters to deal with before she steps down, and Margot is the best tailor in town. Aside from your mum, that is. We should be glad they were willing to close the shop. Now stop stalling! I want to see how the dress sits on you." Gwendoline rustled the dressing room curtain as a final warning.

Benedict would be arriving soon as well. Taking a deep breath, Lucy pulled back the curtain to see Gwendoline sitting on the velvet maroon couch with gold trim. Margot, the seamstress, coming through with her measuring tape, stopped still and gawked at Lucy like she was an angel appearing from the heavens. She resisted the urge to fidget. A high priestess did not fidget.

"That navy is divine on you! Thank goodness for your dark hair and pale skin – you look positively glowing. The Matherson cloak will work beautifully with it; the shades are identical. The lighter colours wash you out, and a high priestess on the day of her binding should stand out above everyone else," Gwendoline announced, adjusting the skirts so they weren't caught under Lucy's feet. "We'll have to take it up a few inches – Matherson woman are on the taller side." Her command was directed to Margot, who quickly got to pinning without a word. Gwendoline circled them like a shark circling its prey. "We can let out the bodice an inch or two by adding another panel. We don't want you passing out from lack of oxygen at the altar. Hawthorne woman have always been curvier."

Gently, Gwendoline turned Lucy towards the mirror, and together they looked at the sheer navy sleeves that glittered and shimmered in the low light.

"It really is a beautiful gown," Lucy breathed. "Are you sure you don't mind me wearing it?" The satin skirts, over-laid with the same shimmering fabric, swished and glittered effortlessly as she moved, and she loved the little satin buttons that ran down her back before disappearing into the skirts.

"Do you love it?" Gwendoline asked, arching an eyebrow.

Lucinda smiled and nodded, playing with the ends of the sleeves.

"Then that's all that matters." Her future-mother-in-law's tone was curt, but in the long mirror, Lucy could see a small smile in the corner of her mouth. Clearly the moment meant as much to her as it did to Lucy.

They drifted into silence while Margot and Gwendoline discussed the changes to be made.

"Do you mind if I have a moment alone with Lucy?" Gwendoline asked at last.

"Of course. I'll make a start on the new panel," Margot said, getting up with ease as if she wasn't in her eighties.

"This is overdue, but I wanted to thank you for allowing me to do this for you. Given how this binding came about, I'd have understood if you didn't think kindly of me. However, I wanted to show you this," Gwendoline said, taking out an envelope from her bag on the couch. "This is this week's *Travel Digest*."

Lucy scanned the short retraction and saw nothing but glowing praise for their small town.

"Benedict told me you wrote to them, and I know I overreacted." Gwendoline sounded ashamed. "I want you to understand that the Manor is one of the last things I have to remember my late husband. I can still hear his laughter in the hallways, and the chaos he used to create in the kitchen."

Lucy took a seat next to her on the couch.

"I didn't want anyone to think poorly of what we'd created here, but seeing how you reached out to the woman and her family out of the kindness of your heart made me regret my hostility, misplaced as it was. I think it was the thought of your mum stepping down – I felt like everything was slipping away. I wanted Benedict's future to be secure for the day when I no longer held my position in the coven."

"You were worried about your son. After all that's happened to your family, I can't blame you for being protective, but you'll always have a place in the coven. The other members value your opinion – not only because of what the Manor has done for the town. You and Benedict are our most fierce protectors, and never afraid to make the hard decisions," Lucy said, resting her hand over Gwendoline's. "I promise you, this town *and* Benedict mean everything to me."

"Despite your quarrels, you've always been there for

him when I should've been," Gwendoline murmured. "He shouldered too much responsibility, and I'm ashamed to admit my part in it. I hope we can move on from the past. I see how much Benedict loves you; Peter always used to tease him about following you around, pulling your pigtails. He's been so afraid to be close to anyone after losing his brother, but you've lit up his world. I wish you both never-ending happiness, and I want to promise you that whatever happens, I will support you both. All I ask is that you don't swap elements again. I don't think the old foundations can handle another flooding."

Lucy froze. "You know about our elements? We've swapped back, it was all a big mistake—"

Gwendoline shook her head. "It's okay; Benedict explained everything to me after what happened with the wolves in the town square. Not that I didn't already know." She winked. "Nothing happens in the Manor or Foxford without my knowledge."

"You aren't angry that they tried to stop the binding?" Lucy asked, worried about causing a rift between her mum and her oldest friend.

Gwendoline laughed. "Are you kidding? Your grams is the best potion master from here to who knows where. Willa is the most powerful witch in the country. You think they'd make an error? I think everything went exactly to plan."

"I think it was everything *not* going to plan that brought us together." Lucy didn't have the mental or emotional energy left to decipher exactly what the hell the matriarchs of Foxford had been up to.

"Fate can be rather amusing in that sense; sometimes a wrong turn can lead us to where we're meant to be," Gwendoline said, smoothing down her sleek black suit trousers as she got up. She towered over Lucy in her stilettos, even when Lucy got to her feet too.

Without any hesitation, and much to Lucy's surprise, Gwendoline embraced her like a daughter. Lucy let out a long sigh of relief. She couldn't believe she'd been so fearful about their elements being discovered. In the future, she vowed to trust those around her and not let fear guide her decisions.

"Sorry I'm late," said Benedict from the front of the shop, and both women froze. Gwendoline released Lucy. "There was a argument between a vampire and a shifter at the early bird buffet," Benedict continued obliviously as he walked through to the back of the boutique.

Gwendoline jumped in front of Lucy.

"Turn around!" both women screamed in unison.

Benedict jumped, then covered his eyes and turned his back. "Okay, I'm deaf," he said over his shoulder. "Why can't I look?"

"Because we don't want you to see Lucinda's gown before the binding!" Gwendoline fussed, helping her back into the changing room.

"It's not like a magless wedding – it's not bad luck to see the bride and all that nonsense," Benedict protested, turning round as Gwendoline quickly shut the curtain.

Safely inside, Lucy couldn't stop herself from blushing with embarrassment. She glared at herself in the full-length mirror. How in the hell had she gone from feeling like a powerful high priestess to a blushing bride in a matter of minutes?

Once she'd handed off the gown and got dressed, she found Gwendoline chatting to Margot about the binding preparations. She could've sworn Margot say something about a reception, but she was distracted by Benedict's muffled voice echoing in the other room with Murph, and she was dying to sneak a peek. She'd seen him in a suit more times that she could count, but this felt different – special. She couldn't help the giddiness swelling up inside her at the thought of tomorrow.

"Are you listening to me?" Gwendoline asked as she settled up at the counter with Margot. Lucy hadn't wanted to let her pay, since she was already allowing her to wear such a precious heirloom, but of course Gwendoline wouldn't hear of anything else.

"Sorry. I was thinking about—" She couldn't come up with a lie fast enough.

"About the groom?" Margot teased, handing her the receipt slip to pick up the dress in the morning. "Don't worry, we're going to take good care of him."

Lucy blushed again and followed Gwendoline outside, determined to pay attention.

"As I was saying, I know how you Hawthornes like to dilly-dally. However, I expect you to be at the Manor by nine pm sharp, so there is plenty of time to get ready. And you don't have to worry about running into Benedict. He's getting ready elsewhere."

And there's the Gwendoline I know. Lucy wondered where Benedict was getting ready. Probably a guest room – or maybe Grams had convinced him to get ready at Hawthorne House, since they wouldn't be there.

"I'll be there at 8:59 and not a minute over," she promised, crossing her heart. The ritual wasn't taking place until midnight, so between Gwendoline and the Hawthorne women, they should have plenty of time to pull off a Cinderella moment.

Gwendoline disappeared down the street, but Lucy waited for Benedict. She missed the warmth of his element, but it felt good to have her own back. It wasn't too long before he came out to join her.

"If it isn't my blushing bride," he said, kissing her hand tenderly.

"I wasn't blushing," she scoffed.

"Pity. If we weren't getting hitched tomorrow, I could spend the night finding ways to make you blush." He winked.

"I'm sure you can survive one night without me," Lucy said, rolling her eyes as they crossed the street busy with evening traffic.

"I know tonight is your last night of freedom, but try and get some rest," Benedict said when they got back to her house.

"Do you want to come up? I'll let you use the front door," Lucy offered, suddenly changing her mind about spending the night apart.

Benedict stepped into her space, and she thought he was going to follow her in. Instead, he placed his hand over hers on her gate and pressed his lips against her cheek. She knew it meant goodbye.

"As much as it hurts me, I must resist. I've got some matters to sort out before our big day, and we're not to see each other before we reach the altar. We wouldn't want to break tradition."

She didn't know how long they stayed there; all she knew was that her nose and fingers were turning red and she couldn't feel her toes, even though she was hugging a life-sized heat blanket.

"You should get inside. I can hear your teeth chattering, and if you don't go I'll be tempted to warm you up." A small laugh escaped Benedict, and the sound meant she could breathe again.

She knew how sad she was that her dad couldn't be there, but knowing neither his brother nor father would be present had to be playing on his mind, even if he hadn't said it. She'd considered asking him if Peter would like to attend, but she doubted Grim Reapers got vacation days. She'd never really understood before that loving someone meant taking on their pain and their past, but she'd take it all if it meant lessening the sorrow in his soul.

"Are you okay? You went all quiet," Benedict said, tipping her chin up to meet his eye.

"I'm fine – tired." She gave him one last squeeze.

"You're a terrible liar, Lucy."

She gasped in surprise. "You called me Lucy?!" He'd always called her Lucinda, or pumpkin – which, unfortunately, was growing on her as a nickname. The actual food itself never would. At least they'd never have to argue over the last slice of pie.

He rolled his eyes. "Get inside. I'll see you at the altar, pumpkin."

"If you're lucky." Lucy kissed him chastely before hurrying up the garden path before he could grab her.

When she glanced over her shoulder, he was already walking down the road, head down and hands in his pockets. She didn't know how she'd never noticed how much weighed on him, never able to see past the perfect wall he'd built around himself. But even if he wanted to keep the wall around his heart, she understood. He'd let her in, and what was a wall without a garden to protect?

Lucinda

"I've got the champagne ready." Grams fussed with the champagne flutes in the corner of the room. "Don't look at me like that, Willa. I haven't smoked my pipe all week. A little tipple won't kill me, and my grand-daughter deserves a toast."

Gwendoline smoothed out Lucy's skirts. They'd spent the last few hours getting every last detail on the navy gown altered to perfection in Gwendoline's quarters. Lucy spun around to see the small train of shimmering golden starlight. Her family stood around her in the long, gold-trimmed mirror; with teary eyes and quivering lips, she couldn't help but be proud to stand amongst them.

"A _small_ glass. We don't want to be tipsy for the ritual," Mum said, sitting down on the chaise. Lucy couldn't remember the last time she'd seen her mum so at ease.

"I think I need it for my nerves," she admitted.

"You look every bit the high priestess," Mum beamed.

"You deserve the best after all we've put you through the past month. It's my small way of welcoming you to the family," Gwendoline said as Lucy brushed the glimmering, feather-light navy dress. She couldn't help fidgeting.

"You do look every bit the Matherson," Grams said, handing her granddaughter a glass of champagne, but Lucinda was too awestruck to drink it. Grams was right – with her dark hair pinned up and eyes darkened with liner, she could practically see Benedict by her side in the mirror. They fitted together perfectly; they'd just been the last ones to see it. In an hour she'd be standing with Benedict under the Blood Moon, reciting vows that would bind them in this life and the next.

"I wish your dad could see you. He's so proud of you and Benedict," Willa said, trying to blot away her tears so she wouldn't ruin her make-up. "I'm sorry he can't be here to support you."

"It's fine, Mum. He's half-way across the world on a classified dig. It's not like he can just slip away." As much as she wanted her dad there, she'd accepted his responsibilities. In spite of her decision not to have a big reception, she did feel a little guilty that the town wouldn't have a chance to celebrate with them, after they'd done so much to support her with gifts and congratulations.

"Thank you for letting me borrow this," she said again to Gwendoline, taking a sip of champagne to steady her hands. Although she worried about spilling anything on the gown, she needed the liquid courage.

"Tsk, tsk. Like I said when you picked it, it's yours. it's been sitting in that dusty trunk for far too long," Gwendoline said, wiping a stray tear from her eye. Lucy wanted to hug her again, but they weren't quite there yet.

"I can't thank you enough for giving her such a gift. It's so precious." Wilhelmina didn't give her friend a choice before wrapping her in an embrace. Lucy hid a smile as Gwendoline froze a little.

"A dress is nothing to cry about," she said tartly.

"Nonsense! I remember the day your mother wore the gown to her own binding. Beautiful woman. A real siren; could've had any man in town. I swear she could've taken your grandfather and I would've let him go," Grams teased, placing a gold hair chain with dangling delicate stars around her low messy bun.

"She'd have wanted to see it passed on," Gwendoline said, helping Lucy step into the matching shoes they'd enchanted to fit, since Lucy was a size bigger. The skirt was floor-length, and she wasn't going to sit down and struggle with the velvet navy straps. "At one time, I didn't think we'd have another generation to pass these things down to. Seeing you in it, seeing how happy you've made Benedict—" Gwendoline cleared her throat, struggling on her words. Lucy couldn't find the words to reply, too choked up on the moment.

"Seems we were right to force them together," Wilhelmina interrupted, taking Gwen's hand. Her hooded silver cloak, the symbol of her position that would soon be Lucy's, covered their joined hands.

"They weren't going to get there on their own without destroying the town in the process," Grams said, putting in her own pearl earrings before giving her granddaughter a quick squeeze.

"We wouldn't have destroyed the town," Lucy protested. "Not completely, anyway."

Grams threw her hands up in dismay and followed her daughter out of the room, but not without taking another glass of champagne.

Gwendoline left her with a reassuring nod, and Lucy

took a moment to herself. Taking a deep breath, she stared back at herself in the mirror. The day had come so fast, but the prospect of seeing Benedict waiting at the altar settled any remaining nerves. Following the women who'd watched over the town for the last thirty and more years, supporting one another, she smiled contently to herself as they climbed into the back of the black SUV. No matter what happened in the future, support and love would always surround her. Power and titles didn't matter when she had everything she needed in her growing family.

Benedict

Silvery moonlight bathed Benedict and Lucinda as High Priestess Wilhelmina recited the binding vows. Benedict's gaze remained fixed on Lucinda, never straying from her mesmerising eyes. Despite the heat from the temple's blazing candles, he felt a shiver run down her spine as he carefully draped the Matherson cloak over her bare shoulders.

Wrapped in the darkness of the cloak, Lucinda had never looked more exquisite. With the M crest over her heart, the drama about who would become the next coven leader seemed pointless. He wanted to sweep her off her feet and start the honeymoon early.

Grams stepped up onto the altar and handed Lucinda the cloak she was to place on his shoulders. He loved the small gasp that escaped her lips, painted red, as she let the cloak unfold. The Hawthorne crest turned her wide-eyed. Benedict could tell how much she wanted to *ask, who, what, when?!,* but she was forced to keep silent and continue with the ritual.

"With this cloak, I invite you into my family, my life

and my heart. May my ancestors protect and keep you," she recited, making him as much a Hawthorne as she was a Matherson. There were a few audible whispers from the coven members as they broke tradition, but it wasn't the first time, and he knew it wouldn't be their last.

In the hushed ambiance of the temple, Lucinda pricked Benedict's finger, and he, in turn, contributed a few drops of his blood to the jewelled cup between them. He didn't want to cause her pain, but they had agreed to follow the ritual to the letter as much as they could. Mist began to seep over the rim of the cup as their blood mingled with the potion, casting an enchanted veil over the vessel.

The temple was consumed by an anticipatory tension as everyone present held their breath, waiting for the mist to clear. The outcome of the ritual depended on the potion's hue. If it turned a vibrant purple, it would signify that their binding had been sanctified by their ancestors. Lucinda chewed on her lips, and Benedict flexed his hands by his side impatiently. He focused all his attention on her, attempting to put aside the magnitude of what they were about to undertake.

"Ancestors, we stand before you, humble and true, and ask that you give your blessing to Lucinda Hawthorne and Benedict Matherson so that they may be bound in mind, body and spirit, in front of witnesses who sanctify this union with love and acceptance." Wilhelmina recited the passage with utmost solemnity, holding the glowing cup beneath the moonlight before lowering it once more.

As the mist gradually dissipated, all that remained was the potion with their answer. The entire coven audibly exhaled in unison as their high priestess tipped her head in gratitude.

Benedict couldn't stand the anticipation.

"The ancestors of the Matherson and Hawthorne families have given their blessing. Let us proceed with gratitude and humility," the high priestess said.

Benedict smiled softly as relief blossomed in his heart, and Lucinda winked cheekily. However, getting their ancestors' approval was only step one.

"Blessed be," the coven said as one.

The words echoed around the temple, and Benedict clenched his jaw. It was time.

Wilhelmina extended the binding cup to him, and he accepted it. However, instead of drinking from the cup to complete the binding of their families, he placed it on the candlelit altar around which they all stood. He gave the high priestess a reassuring smile as he watched her mind racing.

"I'm sorry to interrupt, and I know that personal vows aren't traditional. However, there is something I wish to share with the woman I love and those who brought us here today." He cleared his throat. He and Lucinda had agreed that they wanted to do something to make the ritual feel a little more personal, especially since it had changed from something they'd felt trapped by, to their dearest wish, so they'd each written their own personal vows.

"Lucinda, I never had to wait for the love of my life to walk through the door, because you were already in my corner. You were never a dream, because you have been my reality. Our love may have been a surprise to us, but your kindness, love, fierce passion and understanding never fails to amaze me. With this cup, I ask you to be mine, today, tomorrow, and forever." He lifted the cup from the altar and drank without any hesitation.

Lucinda was welling up as he handed it back to her mother. They smiled at each other while the other coven members watched in awe.

Lucinda glanced at the crowd. Benedict admired how she took hold of his hand, a symbol of their united front. With pride swelling in his chest, he watched as Lucinda picked up the cup with the other.

"Benedict, our love might not have come easy, and over the years we have brought out the best and worst in each other. But in that struggle to find our love for one another I know that we will always find our way back to each other, no matter what's thrown at us. Even when we're lost, we find peace in each other. There is no tear, no laugh, no grief or moment that I don't want to share with you. So, with this cup, I ask you to be mine, today, tomorrow, and forever."

Benedict suddenly didn't care about the ancestors' acceptance of their love; she was his, and he was hers. Nothing was going to change that.

She was about to take a sip, but he placed his hand over the cup. She frowned at him. He knew he'd pay for surprising her later, but there was one more thing he had to do before they continued the ritual.

To the surprise of everyone in the room, he fell to one knee before Lucinda. Staring up at her with sheer admiration, he declared, "Lucinda Hawthorne is the High Priestess we need." He rose to stand by her side. "I withdraw my candidacy," he added, looking between her and the coven.

"You don't have to do this," Lucinda started, but he shook his head.

"This is the right thing for Foxford."

Mrs Crawford stepped forward from the crowd and

attempted to question his decision, but a sharp stare from Benedict silenced her.

"Lucinda's right to leadership never should have been questioned. I'm honoured to stand by her side now and for the rest of our lives," he told them all. "There is no one else who'll love and protect Foxford as she will."

Lucinda stood tall at his side, and he couldn't help but feel a sense of anticipation for what lay ahead.

"I'm in awe of the faith Benedict has in me," she began, the moonlight radiating off her beautiful dress. "I love this town and desire to lead this coven as my ancestors have. I know I'll struggle, stumble, and no doubt fall, but such things don't phase me any longer, because I will have every person in this temple to guide me."

Looking at Benedict, she placed her hand over her heart, and he knew it was her way of silently thanking him.

"When you decided to bind me and Benedict, you were right in saying we both have qualities the other is lacking, but you neglected to include yourselves in that equation. This coven is not ruled by one or two people, but by all founding families. This coven, our town, our home, hasn't become a sanctuary for so many because of my mother or grandmother but because we all put aside our self-interest for the town."

There was a mutter of agreement. Lucinda's words rang true. Their unity had always been the secret to their strength, even with differing opinions among the families.

"My mother has no fear in stepping down, because she is leaving it to all of us. I can only ask for you to accept me as I am. Not because of any binding or the approval of our ancestors, but because each of you wishes for me to be your leader."

The anticipation in the room was palpable. As the

silence grew, Lucinda's expression began to falter, but Benedict knew her heart, her spirit, was the answer to all their concerns. Suddenly, applause erupted, and he watched as Lucinda blinked away tears.

"Lucinda, whenever you are ready," Wilhelmina said, looking to the cup still in her hand.

"If you have no other surprises for me, can we get hitched now?" Lucinda teased Benedict, who nodded with a grin. The coven clapped and cheered as she drank from the cup and completed the ritual.

With one final kiss, their souls were joined as one in front of those they loved.

Lucinda

B enedict and Lucy walked leisurely, hand in hand, under the stars into the town. It was long past midnight, and the All Hallows' Eve festival had closed, but she'd wanted to walk with him and let all they'd overcome in the last month wash over them. They had each other, and she was sure that no matter what life threw at them, they'd be able to handle it together. So long as they didn't kill each other first.

At the end of Lover's Lane, Lucy paused when she saw everyone gathered on the green surrounding the gazebo in the town square.

"What's all this?" she asked, stepping forward to get a better look at the long tables decorated with food platters and wildflower centrepieces.

"Surprise," Benedict whispered in Lucy's ear, kissing her cheek. She stared at him in complete shock as the whole town came forward to greet the newly-weds.

Not wanting to smudge her mascara, she dabbed at her tears. "When did you have to the time to do all this?" She looked to her mum, walking down behind them, for answers, but Wilhelmina only shrugged.

"It was all Rosie! And many of the coven members helped," Benedict said. Her hands flew to her mouth; Rosie was waiting at the head of the group, looking stunning in a plum gown with her hair all pinned up with flowers. "When did you start? How could you keep this from me? You're terrible at surprises!"

"I had to bite my tongue! We sourced a lot from Willow Valley so you wouldn't find out," Rosie admitted, glancing to a grey-suited Emerson, who was offering Benedict curt congratulations. "Emerson and I picked up the tables and the centrepieces on opening night so you wouldn't find out."

"I should've known something was up when you said you were bringing him there!" Lucy squished her friend in her arms, counting her blessings to have a friend like this. "I can't believe you all went to so much trouble for us," she added, addressing all the townspeople and coven members sitting at the tables. This explained why so many members had been absent from this year's festival planning meetings. They'd been too busy planning her reception.

As music played around the square, the couple made the rounds thanking everyone for celebrating with them.

"I know you said you didn't want a big reception, with everything going on with the festival, but we couldn't congratulate our new High Priestess and her partner without a grand celebration," Mrs Crawford said, shaking her hand – which was as close to a hug as the woman ever gave.

"Now we don't have to worry about either of you destroying the town during one of your petty squabbles," Mr Emery chuckled, eating a tiny quiche. His wife elbowed him, nearly causing him to choke. Lucy tried not to laugh, but Benedict did nothing to hide his amusement.

"I don't know, marriage isn't always so rosy," Mrs Emery said slyly. Benedict's face fell, but once he wasn't looking, Mrs Emery winked at Lucy behind her glass of wine.

The festival was the perfect background. Seeing all the food on the tables, she wasn't sure where to begin. All that mattered right now was seeing everyone having a good time celebrating their union with Benedict by her side. Lucy couldn't believe she'd wanted to forgo the tradition.

"I can't believe this is all for us!"

"It wasn't *all* their idea."

Lucy spun around as she recognised the familiar voice. Her dad, with a shaggy grey beard and tanned skin fresh from the dessert, greeted her with open arms.

"I can't believe you're here!" she squealed, and looked to her mum, who could barely contain her tears.

"I wasn't going to miss this night, or I think your mum would have turned me into a frog," he whispered as he embraced her tightly. He'd lost weight since she'd last seen him, and he smelt like sun cream, but she didn't want to ever let him go.

"Did you know about this?" she asked Benedict.

"I swear I didn't have a clue." He shrugged innocently.

"It was a last-minute decision," her dad said, patting his son-in-law on the shoulder. "I surprised him at the Manor this morning, and he was kind enough to hide me in one of the guest rooms. I thought about coming to the ritual, but I didn't want to overwhelm you before your big moment."

"All I care about is that you are here to celebrate with us." Lucinda hugged the most important men in her life, lost for words.

"I had just enough time to ask for his blessing," Benedict said once she gave them some room to breathe.

"It was never a question. Your grams has been telling me you'd find each other one day since you were in school." Lucy's dad rested a hand on his shoulder, and she found herself hoping that he might fill some of the space in Benedict's heart where he was missing his own dad. Her family was his now, and his was hers.

"We've one more surprise," Benedict said gently, resting his hand on her lower back and guiding her away from the table. Lucy wasn't sure if she could take much more.

Benedict lifted his glass, and the lights in the town went out. Lucy frowned, barely able to make out what was going on. However, one by one, lights flared around the courtyard, and she realised everyone was holding a floating lantern, which they released into the sky.

"I know they aren't fireflies, but it was the best I could do," he whispered, reminding her of their first night together. It was like the stars had come down from the heavens to celebrate with them. She swatted his chest playfully. He moved behind her, and wrapped his arms around her waist.

"You've given me the moon and stars – I couldn't ask for anything more," she murmured over her shoulder. Warmth poured from those dark eyes she loved so much, and she reached up on her toes to kiss him.

The band on the gazebo started up again, and in his arms, surrounded by their loved ones, Lucy danced the night away with the town until the sun started to rise.

She couldn't imagine a better way to spend All Hallows' Eve. It was the perfect start to their story.

Lucinda

One Month Later

"Why are you waking me up?" Lucy groaned, stretching her arms above her head. "And you have to start using the front door!"

"Using the front door means running into Grams, and we don't have a moment to spare, since we're going on a little adventure." Benedict sat on the edge of her bed; Chaos was hissing at him for daring to wake them. "I kept it hot for you." He handed her a warm cup, ignoring the cat, who tried to nudge him off the bed.

"Coffee?" Lucy asked, sitting up on her pillows. She tried to hide her amusement as Chaos covered him in cat hair before hopping off the bed.

He winked. "Tea, of course!"

She smiled as she tasted the sweetness. "You remembered honey!"

"I'm not sure if honey suits me as a nickname," he said, kissing her hair.

She wanted to wake up every morning like this; she was

impatient for them to move in together. They had been going back and forth between her house and the Manor, but with their schedules, sometimes they didn't see each other for days. Her family wanted them to move into Hawthorne house, and Gwendoline argued they had all the room in the world — their own floor — in the Manor. Neither wanted to upset the other set of in-laws, and there were no houses for sale in town with the library Lucy wanted or the office space and grounds for archery that Benedict desired, so they had reached a standstill.

"Very funny. I don't think pumpkin suits me, but we'll both have to deal with it."

"Fair enough, but you need to get dressed." He eyed her cupcake-covered crop top and matching shorts as he pulled back the covers. "As delicious as you look, bed will have to wait. You can bring the tea with you."

"I've got to go to work."

"No, you don't. I cleared today with Rosie. It's payment for you covering for her date with Emerson. Don't worry we aren't going far."

"Let's stay in bed." She snuggled a pillow to her chest.

"As much as I love to hear you inviting me into your bed, I want to make use of the good weather today," Benedict pressed, and Lucy glanced at the sunlight coming in through the balcony. It *would* be nice to see the sun after so many grey days.

"Can't you tell me where we're going?" she asked, slowly easing off the bed. She tried to conceal a small smile as his eyes lingered on her bare legs. She slept in tiny shorts, something she'd got used to with his element keeping her warm the past few weeks. This morning, with only her cool water, goosebumps rose on her skin.

"It's a surprise."

"Don't you think we've had enough surprises for one year?" Lucy asked, trying to tempt him as she stripped off her clothes.

He shook his head and averted his gaze. "This is one you'll enjoy." Whatever they were doing had to be important.

"That's all I'm getting?" She tied her robe shut, giving up on her half-hearted seduction.

He zipped his lips, and she hurried off to the bathroom, wondering what it could be. *A bookstore? A museum? Some artifacts? The Matherson vault* – she had always wanted to see what dark secrets lay within it, what they had kept hidden from the Order. Full of excitement at the possibilities, she showered and tossed her hair up in an ornate butterfly claw clip, settling for some mascara and lip gloss. She didn't want to leave him alone in her room for too long, as he had a habit of rooting through her things.

When she returned, she found Benedict lying on her bed with his arm tucked behind his head, eyes closed. His long black coat was tossed over the end of her bed, leaving him in a grey jumper that had risen just high enough over his belt to expose the pale skin above it. She didn't know how seeing such a small fraction of skin could make her flush.

It was exhilarating to know that she felt this way even without the potion. The thought of going back to the old days made her chest tight, but they still bickered now and then. She tiptoed over, wanting to surprise him, but he looked so peaceful that she leaned over him, bringing her lips to his gently.

"What was that for?" Benedict asked, opening his eyes and smiling at her.

"For wanting to surprise me."

"You don't know what it is yet."

"I know, but it's the thought that counts." Lucy slipped a pair of straight-leg jeans over her hips. It wasn't often that she wore them, as she didn't like feeling constricted, but she wanted to be prepared for anything. "Are jeans okay?"

"Perfect," he said, patting her butt while she put on a chunky pastel pink cardigan. "You should wear these more often."

"Okay — if you start wearing colours," Lucy challenged, sitting on the edge of the bed while she pulled on her boots.

He laughed as he pulled on his black jacket. "Nice try."

"I think you'd look great in blue — really bring out those eyes," she teased, leading him by the hand out of her room. She didn't care if he was seen by her family. There was nothing to hide anymore, and it was so early they probably weren't awake yet.

"Maybe one day," he conceded, closing the front door behind them. Lucy had a feeling he meant 'never'. Then again, here they were, walking hand in hand to his car — something that had once been impossible. Just as he opened the door for her, Chaos hopped into the passenger seat before settling in the back.

"Out," Benedict ordered, but the two only proceeded to have a staring match that Lucy figured would go on until the sun set.

"Just let her come with us." Lucy slid into the seat. Benedict rolled his eyes. She figured he was still upset by Chaos's rejection after their elements had returned to their rightful places. She hoped in time they'd learn to get along.

Rolling down the car window, Lucy snuggled her scarf

up under her chin as they drove. The smell of the damp woods and the crisp morning air was worth the chill.

"You're going to catch a cold."

"I missed the cold. You burn way too hot," she said.

"A nickname and a compliment in one morning; you didn't brew another love potion, did you?" he asked, resting a hand on her thigh as he pulled into a side street that wasn't far from the temple.

"Is this where you kill me and take my place?" Lucy joked as they walked down a rickety cobbled path covered in overgrown weeds and moss. Hardly anyone lived this far from town or this close to the woods. Those that did lived few and far apart.

"Damn it, you discovered my diabolical plan!" Benedict squeezed her hand. The trees had blocked out any trace of sunlight, so it was rather creepy with only the sound of rustling leaves and waking birds surrounding them.

"I can rule out the wolves, since they live in the opposite direction."

"You won't be able to guess, and you don't need to look so frightened," he said. "Trust me."

Lucy glanced around, spotting an old torch on a tree that looked like it had been cleaned up recently. Benedict rested his hand on the bark, and their path was lit by torches attached to more trees, highlighting the way ahead and revealing a house.

Her jaw dropped.

"Welcome to the original Matherson Manor," he announced, chuckling at her reaction.

"How did I never know this place existed? How long have you been working on this?" It was far smaller than the current Manor, but it had the same Victorian architecture and looked like it needed some repairs. From the scaffolding on the far side of the wraparound porch, such work was already underway.

"I've been working on it since it was left to me – a little passion project." Benedict opened the front door with an old key while she admired the stained-glass window in the door, and they were welcomed by a host of lit candles laid out on the wooden floorboards.

"Come through here," he said, guiding her past a staircase. Lucy nearly tripped over a piece of uneven floorboard. There was a workstation in the centre of a high-ceilinged room lined with new shelves and a large circular window that looked out to the back of the house. Some shelves lay on the floor by an old fireplace.

"What's this?" she asked, astonished by the work he'd done. The smell of freshly cut wood and varnish smelled like the library. All it needed was the musty smell of books to complete it.

"I figured you'd want a home library; the books in your room are piled so high on the floor and shelves that I'm surprised you haven't drowned in them."

Lucy blushed, feeling her packrat-self exposed. "I could've converted one of the rooms at home, but I like my books close. However, this library is so beautiful I could part with them so they can sit on such pretty shelves." The fact that he had done this for her melted her heart. She had done so much to push him away, but he had never been anything but certain.

"There's something else I want to show you." He took her hand and led her through a long hallway to the kitchen.

"I don't think I could love anything more than a library," she argued, stopping in the middle of the kitchen by the cobweb-covered sink.

"This didn't require any effort on my part." He stood by an old stove and pressed on a daisy-engraved tile beside it. With a puff of dust, the stove retreated into the tiled wall and exposed a stone stairwell beneath.

"I do love a hidden staircase," she said gleefully. She wondered what other secrets their new home held. "Unless it's a dungeon."

"I promise there's nothing to fear." Benedict picked up one of the candles and led the way.

"I'm not afraid," she promised. "I trust you." She meant it, though if someone had told her just eight weeks ago that she'd not only trust Benedict but enough to let him lead her down a secret staircase in a derelict home, she would've questioned her sanity.

At the bottom of the stairs, the silver cobwebs were highlighted by emerging torches, exposing a circular door at the end of a short corridor. An M sat at its centre, and she gripped Benedict's arm, stopping him in his tracks.

"Is – is that what I think it is?" she stammered.

He smiled, clearly pleased. "I knew you'd like it."

"Are you sure you want to do this? This is sacred to your family, even if we're bound!" As much as she wanted to see what the dark steel vault contained, it was as intimate a gesture as seeing one naked, if not more so. He was willing to show her his past, his ancestors' history.

He kissed the back of her hand. "I trust you."

He placed his free hand on the M, and the steel vines twisted around the letter started to unravel themselves. With a loud clunk and a cough-inducing scattering of dust, the vault opened.

Lucy hurried inside, a squeal escaping her. She probably should've waited for permission in case of traps, but excitement got the better of her. Benedict chuckled as she left him behind, exploring the vast shelves of varying arte-facts and leather-bound texts. He said nothing to hurry her, merely answering whatever questions she had without hesitation. From the farthest shelf, she pulled out a book. She could barely read the incantations within; the excite-ment of learning all the Matherson vault contained nearly caused her to drop the book.

"There's so much to learn and explore. Have you read all of these? How far do they go back? Does Gwendoline know you're showing me this? This is as exciting as the library!" Her thoughts came out in a flurry before she turned around and threw herself at him.

"I'm going to need a bigger budget for books if this is the reward every time." Benedict laughed as she buried her face in his chest, wrapping his arms around her waist. "And yes. Gwendoline knows you're down here, and she'll help you if you have any questions. I want you to make yourself at home."

It was the first time she'd felt at home anywhere other than at Hawthorne House – and it had nothing to do with the house, but the infuriating man in her arms.

"You want me to move in?" She rested her hands on the back of his neck and stared into eyes. She needed to know, to feel this moment was real.

"I want *us* to move in." His soft lips brushed hers, silencing her cry of excitement. "Once I fix it up a bit more."

"I've got a few spells that might be able to speed things up." She beamed, desperate to make the house their home. "Can we get started today?"

"I thought you wanted to spend the day in bed?" he asked slyly, tightening his hold around her. His devilish grin nearly stopped her heart.

"I think you should show me the bedrooms next." She peppered him with teasing kisses.

A loud clatter as a few dusty relics were knocked off the shelves ruined the moment. Lucy cringed as her grey cat popped her head out from behind an old book.

"How did she even get in here? That cat is going to destroy the place," Benedict grumbled, shaking his head. Lucy would have sworn Chaos winked at him.

She grinned, picking up her purring pet. "Don't be such a grouch. What's life without a little Chaos?"

Did You Pre-Order Potions & Proposals?

Scan the QR code below and fill in the form to claim your bonus content.

Thank you so much for pre-ordering Lucinda & Benedict's story. I hope you love the exclusive chapter.

Acknowledgements

Thank you so much for making it this far! I have to start by saying that I don't think Lucinda and Benedict would have found their ending without my dear friend and fabulous editor, Emma. Writing and publishing wouldn't be half as fun without her. To my mum, whom I have to credit with the original idea for this story. This story never would've existed without her wonderfully creative brain. To Pru, who created the most beautiful cover that brings together all the magical elements in the best way. Readers, you have my heart and soul and always will. Thank you so much for all the love and encouragement you've shown Lucy and Benedict from the first moment I mentioned their existence. I wouldn't be able to do what I love without the love you give my stories. Every share, comment, review, fabulous video or photo brightens my world. I'm so excited to share that this is my most pre-ordered book to date, and this is all because YOU took a chance on an indie author with an obsession for books. Thank you for letting me live my dream, and I don't take a single one of you for granted.

This is only the start of our Foxford journey, and I can't wait to continue the adventure with all of you.

Join The Mailing List

Sign Up To Be The First To Hear About:
- Advanced Release Copies
- Cover Reveals
- Teasers & More

Scan Me

2025

Don't Go Baking My Heart

VILLAGE OF FOXFORD #2

KATE CALLAGHAN

About The Author

Kate Callaghan released her debut YA dark fantasy trilogy, *Crowned A Traitor: A Hellish Fairytale* in 2020. She loves dark tales, villains and happily-ever-afters—something you will find in all of her books. Chatting with readers and getting to share many different stories is her favourite part of being an indie author. Currently she lives in Dublin. She loves dramas with subtitles (to silence the characters), coffee, and reading too many mysteries and romances. If missing, please check your local coffee shop. You will find her with her computer and an iced beverage.

Follow the links below if you want to know to learn more about future stories! Signed copies are also available on the author's website.

www.callaghanwriter.com

9 781916 684362